The Women's Press Ltd
124 Shoreditch High Street, London E1

From

Fox

Kate Chopin

Kate Chopin was born Katherine O'Flaherty in 1850, in St Louis, Missouri. A member of a comfortable middle-class family, she grew up fêted as a society belle, admired for her wit, gaiety and powers of mimicry. She read widely, both at home and later at her covent school, from which she graduated in 1868. The following year she met Oscar Chopin whom she married in 1870. They lived in Louisiana, his home state, for nine years. There Oscar worked as a cotton factor and their six children were born. New Orleans and Grand Isle, the holiday resort where the family spent their summers, provided the setting for many of Kate Chopin's stories and her second and last published novel, *The Awakening*. When Oscar's business failed they moved to Cloutierville, in the north-western Cane River area of Louisiana, where his family owned land. He died four years later of swamp fever and Kate took over the family plantation and village store. She came to know the local people well and later made them the subject of most of her short stories as well as her first novel, *At Fault*. She returned to St Louis in 1884 and after her mother's death began to write. She became an established short story writer, until her second published novel outraged and alienated critics and readers because of its frank, amoral treatment of a woman's adultery and suicide. In 1904 she died of a brain haemorrhage.

Helen Taylor

Helen Taylor lectures in English at Bristol Polytechnic and teaches courses on women writers at the Polytechnic and Bristol University Extra-Mural Department. She introduced The Women's Press edition of Kate Chopin's *The Awakening,* published in 1978, and is a member of the Bristol Women's Studies group which produced *Half the Sky: An Introduction to Women's Studies,* Virago, 1979. She has published articles on Charlotte Brontë and is currently working on a study of late nineteenth-century American women writers.

KATE CHOPIN
PORTRAITS

Short Stories Selected and Introduced by
HELEN TAYLOR

The Women's Press

Contents

Introduction   vii
Further Reading   xxi
A Note on the Stories   xxiii

Wiser Than A God   1
Miss Witherwell's Mistake   10
A Shameful Affair   18
Doctor Chevalier's Lie   24
Boulôt and Boulotte   26
Old Aunt Peggy   28
Miss McEnders   29
A Visit to Avoyelles   37
Ma'ame Pélagie   41
Désirée's Baby   49
Madame Célestin's Divorce   55
A Lady of Bayou St. John   59
La Belle Zoraïde   64
In Sabine   70
A Respectable Woman   78
The Story of an Hour   82
Lilacs   85
Regret   96
The Kiss   100
Athénaïse   103
Two Summers and Two Souls   132
Two Portraits   135
Fedora   140

A Pair of Silk Stockings   143
Aunt Lympy's Interference   148
A Family Affair   155
At the 'Cadian Ball   167
The Storm: A Sequel to "At the 'Cadian Ball"   176
Charlie   181

Introduction

Like many women writers of the nineteenth century, Kate Chopin began to write late in life, and after her husband's death. In 1888, when she was 38, she wrote her first poem, partly to supplement a meagre income after the deaths of her husband and mother, partly also because she was encouraged by her family doctor and close friend, Dr Kolbenheyer, who had admired her descriptions of Louisiana life in the letters she had written to St Louis during the 14 years she lived in the Deep South. Her first published work was a poem, "If it might be", which appeared in a Chicago magazine, *America*, in 1889. The following year, two of her stories, "Wiser than a God" and "A Point at Issue" were published in local papers, and after that many of her stories and sketches were to appear in St Louis literary and general periodicals.

But Kate Chopin was never content with a local readership, and after her early successes she aspired to publication in the major national magazines, published in the East. Before she had any success with her stories for adults her children's stories, including "Boulôt and Boulotte", were accepted for national magazines such as *Harper's Young People*. In 1892 however, "At the 'Cadian Ball" was published in *Two Tales*, and the following year *Vogue* accepted "A Visit to Avoyelles" and "Désirée's Baby". This story, now her best known, was so successful that between 1893 and 1900, *Vogue* accepted 18 more stories, even though they considered her choice of themes "daring". Her greatest year was 1894 when two prestigious national magazines published three of her stories, and her first collection of tales and sketches, *Bayou Folk*, was accepted by the publishing house Houghton Mifflin. For the next five years Kate Chopin enjoyed considerable fame as a Louisiana regionalist short story writer.

The short story was the obvious form for her to use. Because of nineteenth-century laxity over international copyright rules, English and European novels were imported and reissued by American publishers, who made more profit than would have been possible if they had commissioned indigenous writers. But the mid to late nineteenth century in America was the great age of the annual, "lady's book" and literary magazine, and the writers whose *novels* we now read – Poe, Hawthorne, Melville, Harriet Beecher Stowe and Mark Twain – wrote a great deal for these publications. As in Europe, the short story was seen as ideally suited for the portrayal of rural subjects, regional life, simple peoples, and romantic outsider figures. Chopin used many of the same devices as her earlier counterparts: folk humour, condensation and understatement, an interest in dialect; a predilection for the rural and uneducated; focus on one or two individuals who are separated from their fellows because of some eccentricity, unorthodoxy or rebellion.

Despite her local and national publishing triumphs, and her formal and thematic similarities with other American short-story writers, Kate Chopin's publication history is neither straightforward, nor a catalogue of successes. She had considerable difficulty getting certain stories published at all: "Mrs Mobry's Reason", a story about hereditary insanity, in tone and theme somewhat reminiscent of Ibsen's *Ghosts*, was refused by many journals until a liberal New Orleans newspaper accepted it; "Miss McEnders", "Lilacs" and "A Vocation and a Voice" proved very difficult to place and "Two Portraits" was rejected by every magazine she approached. R. W. Gilder, the influential editor of the national magazine *Century,* refused to publish "The Story of an Hour", "A Night in Acadie" and "Athénaïse" because he felt they were unethical, and she rewrote her story "A No-Account Creole" to suit his request that she tone down her women characters. Sending him the revised story, Kate Chopin wrote of her new improved heroine Euphrasie, surely with tongue in cheek: "I have tried to convey the impression of sweetness and strength, keen sense of right, and physical charm beside."

She paid for the publication of her first novel about divorce and alcoholism, *At Fault;* her second novel *Young Doctor Gosse,* referred to by William Schuyler in 1894 as "her very strongest work" found no publisher, so was destroyed by its author. Her second and last published novel *The Awakening,* about a woman's discontent with marriage and motherhood, and subsequent adultery and suicide, was so heavily condemned by critics and the reading public that her considerable reputation as a short-story writer was severely damaged and led to critical neglect of all her work until the 1960s. In 1899, the same year *The Awakening* was published, Kate Chopin wrote a story which she didn't even attempt to get published – "The Storm", a tale about joyous uncomplicated adultery, now regarded as one of her finest achievements. When she put together stories for her third collection, *A Vocation and a Voice*, she excluded those she had learned from experience would run into difficulties with censorious editors.

The reason Chopin had so many troubles with editors and critics was that she would insist on dealing with dangerous themes – the lives of assertive, unorthodox women characters, unsatisfactory marriages, the frisson of illicit love and the lurking spectres of adultery, incest and prostitution.

Publishing houses and magazine editors of the 1890s were particularly sensitive about any subject matter or tone which smacked of the new realism and naturalism which American writers were increasingly borrowing from Europe. Realism, "the poison of Europe" as W. D. Howells called it, was seen as a pernicious disease, a blight on that precious native American innocence. European literature was condemned for its representations of the worlds of poverty and crime; for morally lax and unregenerate characters; for dissolute men and women, and their involvement with seduction, illegitimate births, prostitution and adultery – along with an absence of Christian morality or saving grace. Howells defended his moral stand on the nature of the American novel on the grounds that in his country the reading public comprised young girls, not the men and married women he assumed to be the consumers of pernicious *European* fiction.

In 1894 *Harper's* serialised Thomas Hardy's novel *Jude the Obscure*, but made several cuts. The editor wrote to Hardy explaining his objections on the grounds of "purism . . . which is undoubtedly more rigid here than in England" and explained his rule that "the magazine must contain nothing which could not be read aloud in any family circle". Kate Chopin satirised the horror of contemporary critics at the bleak view of life adopted by the realists in "Miss Witherwell's Mistake". When Miss Witherwell's niece asks her whether, to conclude a love story she's writing, she should marry the hero and heroine, Miss Witherwell exclaims: "The poison of the realistic school has certainly tainted and withered your fancy in the bud . . . Marry them, most certainly, or let them die."

Kate Chopin was by no means the first writer of her generation to be excited and influenced by European realists, nor was she the only writer in the 1890s to suffer from censorship and condemnation for emulating them. She read many of the new scientific works which came from Europe – Darwin, Huxley, Spencer and so on – and had clearly read widely in the works of Tolstoy, Flaubert, Hardy and Zola, since echoes of, and direct references to them appear in her own writings. To give one specific example, "Two Portraits", Chopin's story about the sexual sublimation inherent in the forms and rituals of Catholicism, makes a connection between sexual and spiritual fervour identical in tone to Flaubert's in his novel *Madame Bovary*. A quotation from each will demonstrate the similarity. Of Emma Bovary's last rites, Flaubert writes: "The priest rose to take the crucifix. Reaching forward like one in thirst, she glued her lips to the body of the Man-God and laid upon it with all her failing strength the most mighty kiss of love she had ever given." This was one of the passages which led to Flaubert's trial for obscenity. Kate Chopin's story was refused for publication probably because of its similar insinuations: "She pressed her lips upon the bleeding wounds and the Divine Blood transfigured her . . . She could not describe in words the ecstacy; that taste of the Divine love which only the souls of the transplanted could endure in its awful and complete intensity . . .For an hour she had swooned in rapture; she had lived in Christ. Oh, the beautiful visions! The visions come often to Alberta now, refreshing and strengthening her soul; it is being talked about a little in whispers."

The sensuality of Catholicism is a theme many mid-nineteenth-century European writers made central to their work and Kate Chopin—Catholic in name but in practice a sceptic—shared this preoccupation, certainly a European rather than an American Protestant, Puritan theme. "Lilacs", "Two Portraits", "Madame Célestin's Divorce" and the novels *At Fault* and *The Awakening* all share a European flavour in terms of their implied criticism of the Catholic Church and its ministers.

Kate Chopin's main European influence was Guy de Maupassant, whose works she read exhaustively, translated into English, and studied in order to perfect her own technique. She learned from him how to write concisely, clearly, and economically. His preoccupation with love, sexuality, marriage and adultery undoubtedly emboldened her to take on such themes, and his ironic, morally relativistic tone is one she mastered expertly. He was probably responsible for her detached, objective handling of subjects like suicide, madness and despair though she is by no means a pale imitation of her master. She avoids his sometimes heavy-handed bitterness of tone, and his profound disgust with life, especially with the notions of romantic love, fidelity and loyalty. She had a capacity too for symbolic and explicit erotic writing which Maupassant lacked and she was able to capture a sense of the mystery of sexual attraction and expression which Maupassant rarely attempted. Finally, her insight into the complexity of her women characters' needs and motivation goes beyond Maupassant's considerable range.

America also provided Kate Chopin with an established literary tradition, though one into which she fitted rather uneasily, and against which she certainly struggled. In particular she was, and still is to some extent, seen as a prominent member of the "Local Colour" school, at the height of its popularity when she began to write.

"Local colour" had featured in the work of ante-bellum writers such as Rose Terry Cooke, but it became a recognisable literary movement only in the late 1860s, after the Civil War. It reflected a new sense of regionalisation and fragmentation in post-war America, as well as a reaction against the political and cultural domination of the East, especially Boston and New York. Its practitioners were mainly short story writers who focused on one region of the country, chronicling dying communities, celebrating folklore, dialect, customs and other picturesque details of the lives of small-town, rural Americans. "Local colourists" have been both dismissed as purveyors of trivia and a kind of literary gossip and celebrated as the harbingers of a truly national American literature, an American literature in which, as Hamlin Garland said in *Crumbling Idols*, 1894, "the common American rises spontaneously to the expression of his concept of life . . . a statement of life as indigenous as the plant-growth".

Kate Chopin wrote a riposte to Garland's *Crumbling Idols*, revealing her own prejudice against what she felt to be a narrow definition of a national literature. As she was eager for national recognition, not surprisingly she disliked the trend in the 1890s for middle America to reject the cultural hegemony of Boston and New York, and to prefer a literature which focused on detail, region, *difference*, instead of attempting to contribute to a world literature – what she calls "true art", an art of the feelings – "such primitive passions as love, hate etc." She argued that Garland overstressed the present and undervalued the past: "Social problems, social environments, local colour and the rest of it are not *of themselves* motives to insure the survival of a writer who employs them." She deplored any movement which seemed to encourage regionalism in literature, and because she was eager to be compared with established writers such as William Dean Howells and Henry James, hated the way in which critics referred to her as a "local colourist". This label implied that she was adept at the miniature, the quaint and the sentimental, rather than the ambitious, subtle, and complex.

Although, as Chopin predicted, "Local Colour" has come to be regarded as minor literature, of historical interest only, nevertheless it was an important post-war movement of considerable significance to Chopin herself. It provided her with many models for her own work: from New England, Sarah Orne Jewett (1849–1909) and Mary Wilkins Freeman (1852–1930); from the mid-West, Hamlin Garland (1860–1940); from her adopted state Louisiana, George Washington Cable (1844–1925), Ruth McEnery Stuart (1849–1917) and Grace King (1851–1932). Its existence also meant that there was a ready market for her earliest writings which tend towards the quaintness she despised, but from which she built up her more powerful, psychologically subtle later portraits. The success of *Bayou Folk* in 1894, partially dependent as it was on the popularity of regional writing at that time, gave Chopin the necessary apprenticeship and boost to her confidence which led her to explore bolder, more sensitive themes, culminating in the rich mixture, in *The Awakening*, of psychological realism, incisive characterisation, and local colour in its most sophisticated form.

Kate Chopin's "local colour" setting was the South – that part of America which has been made into myth and symbol by many other writers before and since – from *Uncle Tom's Cabin* and Longfellow's *Evangeline* to Faulkner's creation, Yoknapatawpha County. It is a South of which, as Wilbur Cash describes it in *The Mind of the South*, "the dominant mood is one of well-nigh drunken reverie . . . of such sweet and inexorable opiates as the rich odours of hot earth and pinewood and the perfume of the magnolia in bloom – of soft languor creeping through the blood and mounting surely to the brain" – a mood the sequel to which, he argues, is invariably a thunderstorm (see Chopin's "The Storm"). Extravagant though this description is, it captures the sensuousness which Chopin's stories suggest in their portrayal of Louisiana.

In an article called "Aspects of the Southern Philosophy", Richard Weaver relates climate and landscape to temper and mood: he says of Southerners that "through a kind of vision, in which the dominant features are a land and sky of high colour, a lush climate, a spiritual community, [they are] a people inclined to be good humoured even in the face of their eternal 'problems' and to adapt themselves to the broad rhythms of nature" and he speaks of their non-analytical bias, and a piety which is "an acceptance of the inscrutability of nature". Dangerous though such generalisation can be without reservations, I think it contains strong elements of truth both for the people and the literature of the South and helps clarify the contradictions which strike an Anglo-Saxon mind between what the characters in Chopin's stories say, and the ways in which they act, especially someone like Athénaïse, in her apparent retreat into the biological trap of motherhood in an unsatisfactory marriage, or Madame Célestin's decision to abandon her divorce plans. The comfort which Chopin's characters seem to feel with their bodies, and their certainty about physical realities, seem to me a reflection of the South and Southerners which Chopin handles with considerable success.

Almost all Kate Chopin's stories are concerned with three groups of people: the Creoles, the French Acadians and the Negroes of Louisiana. American Creoles are mainly white descendants of early French and Spanish settlers in Louisiana, a wealthy, aristocratic group who inhabit and dominate the commercial and social life of New Orleans and district. This is the race into which Kate Chopin married; they provided the subject matter for many of the stories and *The Awakening*.

The Acadians, or Cajuns, were of French origin and lived in Acadia (now Nova Scotia) until 1755 when they left, refusing to swear allegiance to the victorious British after the war with France in America. Though many settled in other states, a large number made their way to Louisiana where they settled among French Catholic groups in the north-western part of the state, in Natchitotes Parish on the Cane River, the setting for the majority of Chopin's stories, as well as her first novel *At Fault*. Daniel Rankin described the Cajuns in this way: "They speak an ancient French of the seventeenth century and an amalgamated English, the literally translated phrases of which are, to the stranger, full of enchanting surprises . . .They slightly chant their phrases in agreeable Southern voices. Their Christian names are Evariste, Placide, Numa, Alcée, Artemise, Calixta, Fronie, Ozème, Pélagie, Euphrasie; their best-known family names are quite like Santien, St Denis Godolph, Laballière, Benitou, Bonamour." (Many of these names feature in the stories in this collection.) Rankin says that Chopin's reproduction of Cajun speech avoids excessive elaboration. According to him, she gives "suggestions of the soft, harmonious tongue, a curious clipping and shortening, to which the Bayou Folk have reduced English speech . . .The dialect is not prominent . . . It is the actual speech of a people intelligently and intelligibly rendered in all its softness and charm."

The Negroes of the Cane River area are predominantly newly emancipated share-cropping farmers, co-existing fairly peaceably with the other groups. They feature less than the other groups and Chopin tends to simplify and idealise them, though in a sketch like "Old Aunt Peggy" there is a subtlety and lack of condescension rare among writers in the self-conscious post-Civil War decades. In "Athénaïse" an important parallel is implicitly drawn between the situation of black slaves and white married women, in this story, a French Acadian. Cazeau, Athénaïse's husband, a kind and thoughtful man, goes to fetch her from her parents' home to which she has fled two months after their wedding. As they ride home a certain live-oak tree reminds Cazeau of a trip he and his father had made many years earlier to catch a runaway slave. Chopin showe Cazeau as uncomfortably aware of this "hideous" *déjà vu:* "They had halted beneath this big oak to enable the negro to take breath; for Cazeau's father was a kind and considerate master, and everyone had agreed at the time that Black Gabe was a fool, a great idiot indeed, for wanting to run away from him."

In all Kate Chopin's stories, the three racial groups share many qualities; all three are seen as easy-going, hedonistic and high spirited; all are superstitious, passionate and volatile. The contrasts and relationships between the three cultures provide much of the humour, as well as the dramatic and ironic tension throughout her work.

In her best short stories, Chopin surpasses the other notable Southern "local colourists", notably George Washington Cable, Grace King, Mary Noailles Murfree and Ruth McEnery Stuart. Her range of characters and locations is wider; furthermore, her interest in them is not an antiquarian one. Since she did not grow up in Louisiana, her preoccupations were those of an outside observer; she had the strengths of someone not infatuated with the people of whom she wrote. In an article on women local colourists in America between 1865 and 1914, Ann Douglas Wood has argued that the "Local Colour" movement has been dominated by *women* writers and – although I am begging many questions here about what exactly constitutes "local colour" – I believe Kate Chopin belongs to a strong female line of writers which continues into the twentieth century with Willa Cather, Eudora Welty, Carson McCullers and Flannery O'Connor. Although there have been male local colourists in both centuries, the most prolific and popular have been women. Furthermore they constituted the first artistically respectable group of women writers, since only in the 1880s was writing fully acknowledged as a respectable profession for middle-class women. Ann Douglas Wood calls these women "corpse watchers", writing from nostalgia and despair about people who have lost status and power, and who live lives of impoverishment, claustrophobia, and paranoia. She argues it is a literature of retreat, barrenness and death, with little engagement in any public sphere or commitment to change. Interestingly, she makes Kate Chopin the exception to all these generalisations.

Women local colourists were reacting against a long, well-established tradition of sentimental women writers, who wrote of – in Sarah Jewett's words – "Breathings, Sighs, Cameos, Silhouettes", and these post-war writers were attempting to examine in the sober, precise detail of a characteristically American realism exactly what was happening to small-town rural America. Debunking the sentimental tradition, these writers refused to mythologise women's lives and to pretend that all women had kindly husbands or lovers to provide them with all their needs.

They depicted in their writing those women in small towns and villages who were in dire financial straits, left alone – after a war which had killed their husbands or lovers, and led to mass male migration to the cities – to run farms, earn their bread and somehow make meaning out of a meagre existence.

Kate Chopin's work is free of the bleakness and sterility of the lives of Sarah Jewett's and Mary Wilkins Freeman's women characters, because the Cajun and Creole communities were relatively free of the worst effects of the war and of massive centralised industrialisation. Although the period between 1880 and 1900 saw the development of the "New South" with large-scale industrialisation and commercialisation – cotton mills built amid cotton fields, the growth of new towns, factories and schools – nevertheless in rural Louisiana, by the early 1880s, life had reverted somewhat to the flavour of ante-bellum days. Plantations were being rebuilt, albeit with Negroes as sharecroppers rather than slaves. The carefree atmosphere of the Cane River area which pervades many of these stories is partly a reflection of the easier life which Chopin knew intimately from her life in Louisiana – though the tensions of industrialisation, the emancipation of slaves and the intrusion of city values into rural life are all suggested and are never sentimentalised in her fiction.

Since its inception, the short story has tended to concentrate on a significant moment, an instant of perception, a sudden intuition or insight, what James Joyce called an "epiphany" – a moment of spiritual or emotional revelation rather than a progressive development of character. The critic Myra Stark has argued that these moments of insight and intuition which occur in most short stories by *men* are remarkably absent from *women's* stories. She says that while male authors' characters are given insight into the human condition which frees and transforms them in some way, insights within women's writing invariably overwhelm and defeat them, filling protagonists with rage or despair about what it means to be a woman. Most women's stories contain, in her words: "shock, rage, despair, defeat. These are notes from underground, letters from the prison house." The title of a recent collection of women's short stories – *Bitches and Sad Ladies* (ed. Pat Rotter, Dell, 1975) – underlines Stark's view of women writers' sense of the choices open to their sex.

Yet, although Stark makes no reference to her, Kate Chopin is clearly an exception to this overriding pessimism. Chopin's work resounds with metaphors of epiphany – awakening, discovery, the breaking of light, the delight of a spontaneous laugh, the finding of self after a long period of sleep or darkness. Many of her short stories conclude hopefully, joyfully, triumphantly. Rage, despair, and the prison house are alien to her predominant tone of voice. True, she is aware of woman's circumscribed destiny, and with women like Mentine in "A Visit to Avoyelles", Athénaïse, and Aurélie in "Regret", as well as Edna Pontellier in *The Awakening,* she demonstrates a biological determinism, albeit equivocal, about woman's role as child-bearer. Yet in many of the stories the final moment of truth gives a woman the last laugh, and a real sense of power or exultation – however momentary: Mildred Orme in "A Shameful Affair", with her frank admission of sexual desire which leaves the man blushing; 'Tite Reine in "In Sabine" who escapes with another man from her oppressive drunken husband, on the husband's horse; Mrs Baroda, in "A Respectable Woman" with its final enigmatic hint of her future adultery; and the triumphant Calixta of "The Storm", who gives full vent to her sensuality with another woman's husband and then welcomes home her husband and son with an uncharacteristic carefree gaiety. In many ways then, Chopin is the exception to the trends defined by feminist critics as shaping women's short-story writing. Her optimism, cheerfulness about sex and love, and defiant, unconventional heroines are rare in the canon of women's fictional writing.

Kate Chopin left few personal documents, and those statements she made in her extant writings are usually self-conscious or deliberately humorous and self-effacing. We don't know how she reacted to critical neglect, editorial censorship and overt hostility after the publication of *The Awakening*. She made few direct comments on her problems as a woman writer, though we can deduce much from her essays, diary and the works themselves. In an essay "On Certain, Brisk, Bright Days" published in the St Louis *Post-Dispatch* on 26 November 1899, the year in which *The Awakening* appeared, she commented on the strange questions which newspaper editors put "to a defenceless woman under the guise of flattery". Speaking of that woman (clearly herself) as a "victim" of the editor, she cites the questions how many children does she have, and whether she smokes cigarettes. In the same essay she exclaims: "How hard it is for one's acquaintances and friends to realise that one's books are to be taken seriously, and that they are subject to the same laws which govern the existence of others' books!" It's interesting to note that these are precisely the sorts of complaints many women writers, from the late eighteenth century on, have made about the double standard of critical attention. Chopin is by no means the first or last woman writer to find critics and friends more concerned about her husband and housework arrangements than about the nature of her work.

Kate Chopin began to write when she was widowed, and indeed left without a beloved mother. In her most successful publishing year, 1894, she commented in her diary on the difficulty women have in growing as artists within close marriage and family relationships, as well as the sacrifices involved in not being able to have both: "If it were possible for my husband and my mother to come back to earth, I feel that I would unhesitatingly give up everything that has come into my life since they left it and join my existence again with theirs. To do that, I would have to forget the past ten years of my growth – my real growth." For many modern readers this will instantly recall Virginia Woolf's comment, also in her diary, on 28 November 1928, the anniversary of her father's birth: "Father's birthday. He would have been 96, 96, yes, today; . . . but mercifully was not. His life would have entirely ended mine. What would have happened? No writing, no books; – inconceivable."

Along with other women writers in the nineteenth century, Chopin made many of her female characters *artists*, possibly as a way of discussing her own situation obliquely and coming to terms with the nature of woman's creativity. Like Madame de Staël in *Corinne*, Elizabeth Barrett Browning in *Aurora Leigh*, Sarah Jewett in *The Country of the Pointed Firs* and Charlotte Perkins Gilman in *The Yellow Wallpaper*, Kate Chopin used as characters in her stories women painters, musicians, journalists, dancers and singers, as well as writers. Her satirical portrait of a woman poet, in "Charlie" (whose poetry is dreadful and best forgotten, Chopin implies), seems to bear out humorously what many nineteenth century women writers had to learn bitterly: that writing was a *masculine* activity, one which for much of the century women were allowed to do on sufferance, so that women who wrote were in a sense, as Ann Douglas puts it, "tomboys poaching on male preserves". (Jo, in Louisa May Alcott's *Little Women*, is a similar tomboy-writer figure.)

The choice of becoming an artist was seen by Chopin, like many of her predecessors, as one which was dangerously exclusive of other kinds of life – particularly love. Yet in her work the artists frequently get their own way: Edna, in *The Awakening*, discovers herself through her painting and also chooses freely where to give her love; Paula, in "Wiser than a God" becomes an internationally famous concert pianist and though she loses the man she loves, is pursued by a second-best suitor who will accept her on *her* terms; the fact that Charlie writes poetry is seen as integral to her rejection of conventional lady-like behaviour. Although the rather insipid hero marries her sister, clearly finding Charlie rather difficult to come to terms with, nevertheless a more tolerant and thus worthy suitor accepts her totality, and is prepared to wait for her.

Kate Chopin is unusual too in avoiding tragic endings for women who want love *and* a life of their own, not by emasculating her universe, as Rebecca West suggests Sarah Jewett does in order to remove the threat of male power and violence, nor by oversimplifying the possibilities for women—even if some of the stories have rather false endings which reek of uneasy compromise. In her best stories she confronts the problems women face in the seemingly irreconcilable struggle between a liberating autonomy and their obligations to family and community. Some of her stories do contain female victims ("Désirée's Baby", "Ma'ame Pélagie", "Doctor Chevalier's Lie", "Lilacs" etc), but women aren't the only victims – partly perhaps because Chopin is not centrally concerned with all-female communities in which women must cling together just to survive. She demonstrates the ways in which racial and class inequality, and fixed notions of sex roles and conduct within marriage, place obstacles in the way of spontaneous creative behaviour, by men as well as women. This was a style of behaviour in which the Creoles and Cajuns excelled, and which Chopin prized in them and in her own life. She had a strong belief in the sustaining power of community; her homes are rarely the prisons of Mary Wilkins Freeman's stories, nor can her villages and towns be described as bitterly repressive, as in Sarah Jewett's work, however limited Chopin's people may be.

Kate Chopin thoroughly disliked didacticism, reformism and institutionalisation of people and ideas. She avoided groups and societies, and wrote in her diary that what she valued in literature was "originality, spontaneity, or originality of perception". Her own stories were written quickly, usually within a day, without notes and with little revision. She trusted, as her most sympathetic characters do, to her instinct: "I am completely at the mercy of unconscious selection." In one of her essays she quotes her words to a young friend who has come to her for advice: "Illusions . . . belong to youth, and they are poetry and philosophy, and vagabondage, and everything delightful. And they last till men and the world, life and the institutions, come along with – but gracious! I forgot whom I was talking to. Run on and get your skates."

Near the end of her novel *At Fault,* Kate Chopin's male protagonist tells his wife-to-be that people must learn "to know the living spirit from the dead letter". The "dead letters" in these stories are the frightened, cautious and conventional – usually those who are unhappily obeying the letter of the law or a stultified moral code. In contrast, she gives us the "living spirits" of Charlie, who, riding off to supervise the plantation, tells Aunt Maryllis to throw away the handcream she has been compelled to use as a "lady"; of Mrs Sommers, who spends her precious windfall *not* sensibly and self-sacrificially on her children but for once, deliciously, on herself and her silk stockings; and of Calixta and Alcée, who satisfy each other's profoundest sensual yearnings then return happily to their respective spouses. Drab sobriety and correctness are challenged with sympathetic humour and critical shrewdness which make these portraits of living spirits both an inspiration and a delight.

Further Reading

Primary Texts

Mary E Wilkins Freeman, *The Revolt of Mother and Other Stories*, The Feminist Press, 1974

Sarah Orne Jewett, *The Best Stories of Sarah Orne Jewett*, Houghton Mifflin, 1925

Guy de Maupassant, *Selected Short Stories*, Penguin, 1971

Secondary Texts

Louisiana Studies, Vol. xiv, No. 1, Spring 1975, "Special Kate Chopin Issue"

Daniel Rankin, *Kate Chopin and Her Creole Stories*, University of Pennsylvania Press, 1932

Regionalism and the Female Imagination (formerly *The Kate Chopin Newsletter*) ed. Emily Toth, Pennsylvania State University, 1975–79

Per Seyersted, *The Complete Works of Kate Chopin*
> *Kate Chopin: A Critical Biography*, Louisiana State University Press, 1969
> *Kate Chopin Miscellany*, Northwestern State University Press (forthcoming)

Marlene Springer, *Edith Wharton and Kate Chopin: A Reference Guide*, G. K. Hall, 1976

Ann Douglas Wood, "The Literature of Impoverishment: The Women Local Colorists in America 1865–1914", *Women's Studies* Vol. 1, No. 1 (1972), pp. 3–45

Larzer Ziff, *The American 1890s: Life and Times of a Lost Generation*, Chatto and Windus, 1967

A Note on the Stories

Kate Chopin wrote about 100 short stories, including several for children; a handful of essays for newspaper publication, and poems; a few translations of stories by Maupassant; a piece of music; and two novels – on the second of which, *The Awakening* (published 1899), her reputation largely rests. Of the stories in this selection, the majority were published in her lifetime, and most in one of the two published collections, *Bayou Folk* (1894) and *A Night in Acadie* (1897). Her third collection of stories, *A Vocation and a Voice,* though initially accepted for publication, was never brought out. Of that collection, the stories included here – "The Story of an Hour", "Lilacs", "The Kiss", "Two Summers and Two Souls", "Two Portraits", and "Fedora" – originally appeared either in Daniel Rankin's biography, *Kate Chopin,* University of Pennsylvania Press, 1932, or in Per Seyersted's edition of *The Complete Works of Kate Chopin*, Louisiana State University Press, 1969.

Wiser Than A God

"You might at least show some distaste for the task, Paula," said Mrs. Von Stoltz, in her querulous invalid voice, to her daughter who stood before the glass bestowing a few final touches of embellishment upon an otherwise plain toilet.

"And to what purpose, Mutterchen? The task is not entirely to my liking, I'll admit; but there can be no question as to its results, which you even must concede are gratifying."

"Well, it's not the career your poor father had in view for you. How often he has told me when I complained that you were kept too closely at work, 'I want that Paula shall be at the head,' " with appealing look through the window and up into the gray, November sky into that far "somewhere," which might be the abode of her departed husband.

"It isn't a career at all, mamma; it's only a make-shift," answered the girl, noting the happy effect of an amber pin that she had thrust through the coils of her lustrous yellow hair. "The pot must be kept boiling at all hazards, pending the appearance of that hoped for career. And you forget that an occasion like this gives me the very opportunities I want."

"I can't see the advantages of bringing your talent down to such banale servitude. Who are those people, anyway?"

The mother's question ended in a cough which shook her into speechless exhaustion.

"Ah! I have let you sit too long by the window, mother," said Paula, hastening to wheel the invalid's chair nearer the grate fire that was throwing genial light and warmth into the room, turning its plainness to beauty as by a touch of enchantment. "By the way," she added, having arranged her mother as comfortably as might be, "I haven't yet qualified for that 'banale servitude,' as you call it." And approaching the piano which stood in a distant alcove of the room, she took up a roll of music that lay curled up on the instrument, straightened it out before her. Then, seeming to remember the question which her mother had asked, turned on the stool to answer it. "Don't you know? The Brainards, very swell people, and awfully rich. The daughter is that girl whom I once told you about, having gone to the Conservatory to cultivate her voice and old Engfelder told her in his brusque way to go back home, that his system was not equal to overcoming impossibilities."

"Oh, those people."

"Yes; this little party is given in honor of the son's return from Yale or Harvard, or some place or other." And turning to the piano she softly ran over the dances, whilst the mother gazed into the fire with unresigned sadness, which the bright music seemed to deepen.

"Well, there'll be no trouble about *that*," said Paula, with comfortable assurance, having ended the last waltz. "There's nothing here to tempt me into flights of originality; there'll be no difficulty in keeping to the hand-organ effect."

"Don't leave me with those dreadful impressions, Paula; my poor nerves are on edge."

"You are too hard on the dances, mamma. There are certain strains here and there that I thought not bad."

"It's your youth that finds it so; I have outlived such illusions."

"What an inconsistent little mother it is!" the girl exclaimed, laughing. "You told me only yesterday it was my youth that was so impatient with the commonplace happenings of everyday life. That age, needing to seek its delights, finds them often in unsuspected places, wasn't that it?"

"Don't chatter, Paula; some music, some music!"

"What shall it be?" asked Paula, touching a succession of harmonious chords. "It must be short."

"The 'Berceuse,' then; Chopin's. But soft, soft and a little slowly as your dear father used to play it."

Mrs. Von Stoltz leaned her head back amongst the cushions, and with eyes closed, drank in the wonderful strains that came like an ethereal voice out of the past, lulling her spirit into the quiet of sweet memories.

When the last soft notes had melted into silence, Paula approached her mother and looking into the pale face saw that tears stood beneath the closed eyelids. "Ah! mamma, I have made you unhappy," she cried, in distress.

"No, my child; you have given me a joy that you don't dream of. I have no more pain. Your music has done for me what Faranelli's singing did for poor King Philip of Spain; it has cured me."

There was a glow of pleasure on the warm face and the eyes with almost the brightness of health. "Whilst I listened to you, Paula, my soul went out from me and lived again through an evening long ago. We were in our pretty room at Leipsic. The soft air and the moonlight came through the open-curtained window, making a quivering fret-work along the gleaming waxed floor. You lay in my arms and I felt again the pressure of your warm, plump little body against me. Your father was at the piano playing the 'Berceuse,' and all at once you drew my head down and whispered, 'Ist es nicht wonderschen, mama?' When it ended, you were sleeping and your father took you from my arms and laid you gently in bed."

Paula knelt beside her mother, holding the frail hands which she kissed tenderly.

"Now you must go, liebchen. Ring for Berta, she will do all that is needed. I feel very strong to-night. But do not come back too late."

"I shall be home as early as possible; likely in the last car, I couldn't stay longer or I should have to walk. You know the house in case there should be need to send for me?"

"Yes, yes; but there will be no need."

Paula kissed her mother lovingly and went out into the drear November night with the roll of dances under her arm.

II

The door of the stately mansion at which Paula rang, was opened by a footman, who invited her to "kindly walk upstairs."

"Show the young lady into the music room, James," called from some upper region a voice, doubtless the same whose impossibilities had been so summarily dealt with by Herr Engfelder, and Paula was led through a suite of handsome apartments, the warmth and mellow light of which were very grateful, after the chill out-door air.

Once in the music room, she removed her wraps and seated herself comfortably to await developments. Before her stood the magnificent "Steinway," on which her eyes rested with greedy admiration, and her fingers twitched with a desire to awaken its inviting possibilities. The odor of flowers impregnated the air like a subtle intoxicant and over everything hung a quiet smile of expectancy, disturbed by an occasional feminine flutter above stairs, or muffled suggestions of distant household sounds.

Presently, a young man entered the drawing-room,—no doubt, the college student, for he looked critically and with an air of proprietorship at the festive arrangements, venturing the bestowal of a few improving touches. Then, gazing with pardonable complacency at his own handsome, athletic figure in the mirror, he saw reflected Paula looking at him, with a demure smile lighting her blue eyes.

"By Jove!" was his startled exclamation. Then, approaching, "I beg pardon, Miss—Miss—"

"Von Stoltz."

"Miss Von Stoltz," drawing the right conclusion from her simple toilet and the roll of music. "I hadn't seen you when I came in. Have you been here long? and sitting all alone, too? That's certainly rough."

"Oh, I've been here but a few moments, and was very well entertained."

"I dare say," with a glance full of prognostic complimentary utterances, which a further acquaintance might develop.

As he was lighting the gas of a side bracket that she might better see to read her music, Mrs. Brainard and her daughter came into the room, radiantly attired and both approached Paula with sweet and polite greeting.

"George, in mercy!" exclaimed his mother, "put out that gas, you are killing the effect of the candle light."

"But Miss Von Stoltz can't read her music without it, mother."

"I've no doubt Miss Von Stoltz knows her pieces by heart," Mrs. Brainard replied, seeking corroboration from Paula's glance.

"No, madam; I'm not accustomed to playing dance music, and this is quite new to me," the girl rejoined, touching the loose sheets that George had conveniently straightened out and placed on the rack.

"Oh, dear! 'not accustomed'?" said Miss Brainard. "And Mr. Sohmeir told us he knew you would give satisfaction."

Paula hastened to re-assure the thoroughly alarmed young lady on the point of her ability to give perfect satisfaction.

The door bell now began to ring incessantly. Up the stairs, tripped fleeting opera-cloaked figures, followed by their black robed attendants. The rooms commenced to fill with the pretty hub-bub that a bevy of girls can make when inspired by a close masculine proximity; and

4

Paula, not waiting to be asked, struck the opening bars of an inspiring waltz.

Some hours later, during a lull in the dancing, when the men were making vigorous applications of fans and handkerchiefs; and the girls beginning to throw themselves into attitudes of picturesque exhaustion— save for the always indefatigable few— a proposition was ventured, backed by clamorous entreaties, which induced George to bring forth his banjo. And an agreeable moment followed, in which that young man's skill met with a truly deserving applause. Never had his audience beheld such proficiency as he displayed in the handling of his instrument, which was now behind him, now over-head, and again swinging in mid-air like the pendulum of a clock and sending forth the sounds of stirring melody. Sounds so inspiring that a pretty little black-eyed fairy, an acknowledged votary of Terpsichore, and George's particular admiration, was moved to contribute a few passes of a Virginia break-down, as she had studied it from life on a Southern plantation. The act closing amid a spontaneous babel of hand clapping and admiring bravos.

It must be admitted that this little episode, however graceful, was hardly a fitting prelude to the magnificent "Jewel Song from 'Faust,' " with which Miss Brainard next consented to regale the company. That Miss Brainard possessed a voice, was a fact that had existed as matter of tradition in the family as far back almost as the days of that young lady's baby utterances, in which loving ears had already detected the promise which time had so recklessly fulfilled.

True genius is not to be held in abeyance, though a host of Engfelders would rise to quell it with their mundane protests!

Miss Brainard's rendition was a triumphant achievement of sound, and with the proud flush of success moving her to kind condescension, she asked Miss Von Stoltz to "please play something."

Paula amiably consented, choosing a selection from the Modern Classic. How little did her auditors appreciate in the performance the results of a life study, of a drilling that had made her amongst the knowing an acknowledged mistress of technique. But to her skill she added the touch and interpretation of the artist; and in hearing her, even Ignorance paid to her genius the tribute of a silent emotion.

When she arose there was a moment of quiet, which was broken by the black-eyed fairy, always ready to cast herself into a breach, observing, flippantly, "How pretty!" "Just lovely!" from another; and "What wouldn't I give to play like that." Each inane compliment falling like a dash of cold water on Paula's ardor.

She then became solicitous about the hour, with reference to her car, and George who stood near looked at his watch and informed her that the last car had gone by a full half hour before.

"But," he added, "if you are not expecting any one to call for you, I will gladly see you home."

"I expect no one, for the car that passes here would have set me down at my door," and in this avowal of difficulties, she tacitly accepted George's offer.

The situation was new. It gave her a feeling of elation to be walking through the quiet night with this handsome young fellow. He talked so freely and so pleasantly. She felt such a comfort in his strong protective nearness. In clinging to him against the buffets of the staggering wind she could feel the muscles of his arms, like steel.

He was so unlike any man of her acquaintance. Strictly unlike Poldorf, the pianist, the short rotundity of whose person could have been less objectionable, if she had not known its cause to lie in an inordinate consumption of beer. Old Engfelder, with his long hair, his spectacles and his loose, disjointed figure, was hors de combat in comparison. And of Max Kuntzler, the talented composer, her teacher of harmony, she could at the moment think of no positive point of objection against him, save the vague, general, serious one of his unlikeness to George.

Her new-awakened admiration, though, was not deaf to a little inexplicable wish that he had not been so proficient with the banjo.

On they went chatting gaily, until turning the corner of the street in which she lived, Paula saw that before the door stood Dr. Sinn's buggy.

Brainard could feel the quiver of surprised distress that shook her frame, as she said, hurrying along, "Oh! mamma must be ill—worse; they have called the doctor."

Reaching the house, she threw open wide the door that was unlocked, and he stood hesitatingly back. The gas in the small hall burned at its full, and showed Berta at the top of the stairs, speechless, with terrified eyes, looking down at her. And coming to meet her, was a neighbor, who strove with well-meaning solicitude to keep her back, to hold her yet a moment in ignorance of the cruel blow that fate had dealt her whilst she had in happy unconsciousness played her music for the dance.

Several months had passed since the dreadful night when death had deprived Paula for the second time of a loved parent.

After the first shock of grief was over, the girl had thrown all her energies into work, with the view of attaining that position in the musical world which her father and mother had dreamed might be hers.

She had remained in the small home occupying now but the half of it; and here she kept house with the faithful Berta's aid.

Friends were both kind and attentive to the stricken girl. But there had been two, whose constant devotion spoke of an interest deeper than mere friendly solicitude.

Max Kuntzler's love for Paula was something that had taken hold of his sober middle age with an enduring strength which was not to be lessened or shaken, by her rejection of it. He had asked leave to remain her friend, and while holding the tender, watchful privileges which that comprehensive title may imply, had refrained from further thrusting a warmer feeling on her acceptance.

Paula one evening was seated in her small sitting-room, working over some musical transpositions, when a ring at the bell was followed by a footstep in the hall which made her hand and heart tremble.

George Brainard entered the room, and before she could rise to greet him, had seated himself in the vacant chair beside her.

"What an untiring worker you are," he said, glancing down at the scores before her. "I always feel that my presence interrupts you; and yet I don't know that a judicious interruption isn't the wholesomest thing for you sometimes."

"You forget," she said, smiling into his face, "that I was trained to it. I must keep myself fitted to my calling. Rest would mean deterioration."

"Would you not be willing to follow some other calling?" he asked, looking at her with unusual earnestness in his dark, handsome eyes.

"Oh, never!"

"Not if it were a calling that asked only for the labor of loving?"

She made no answer, but kept her eyes fixed on the idle traceries that she drew with her pencil on the sheets before her.

He arose and made a few impatient turns about the room, then coming again to her side, said abruptly:

"Paula, I love you. It isn't telling you something that you don't know,

7

unless you have been without bodily perceptions. To-day there is something driving me to speak it out in words. Since I have known you," he continued, striving to look into her face that bent low over the work before her, "I have been mounting into higher and always higher circles of Paradise, under a blessed illusion that you—cared for me. But to-day, a feeling of dread has been forcing itself upon me—dread that with a word you might throw me back into a gulf that would now be one of everlasting misery. Say if you love me, Paula. I believe you do, and yet I wait with indefinable doubts for your answer."

He took her hand which she did not withdraw from his.

"Why are you speechless? Why don't you say something to me!" he asked desperately.

"I am speechless with joy and misery," she answered. "To know that you love me, gives me happiness enough to brighten a lifetime. And I am miserable, feeling that you have spoken the signal that must part us."

"You love me, and speak of parting. Never! You will be my wife. From this moment we belong to each other. Oh, my Paula," he said, drawing her to his side, "my whole existence will be devoted to your happiness."

"I can't marry you," she said shortly, disengaging his hand from her waist.

"Why?" he asked abruptly. They stood looking into each other's eyes.

"Because it doesn't enter into the purpose of my life."

"I don't ask you to give up anything in your life. I only beg you to let me share it with you."

George had known Paula only as the daughter of the undemonstrative American woman. He had never before seen her with the father's emotional nature aroused in her. The color mounted into her cheeks, and her blue eyes were almost black with intensity of feeling.

"Hush," she said; "don't tempt me further." And she cast herself on her knees before the table near which they stood, gathering the music that lay upon it into an armful, and resting her hot cheek upon it.

"What do you know of my life," she exclaimed passionately. "What can you guess of it? Is music anything more to you than the pleasing distraction of an idle moment? Can't you feel that with me, it courses with the blood through my veins? That it's something dearer than life, than riches, even than love?" with a quiver of pain.

"Paula listen to me; don't speak like a mad woman."

She sprang up and held out an arm to ward away his nearer approach.

"Would you go into a convent, and ask to be your wife a nun who has vowed herself to the service of God?"

"Yes, if that nun loved me; she would owe to herself, to me and to God to be my wife."

Paula seated herself on the sofa, all emotion seeming suddenly to have left her; and he came and sat beside her.

"Say only that you love me, Paula," he urged persistently.

"I love you," she answered low and with pale lips.

He took her in his arms, holding her in silent rapture against his heart and kissing the white lips back into red life.

"You will be my wife?"

"You must wait. Come back in a week and I will answer you." He was forced to be content with the delay.

The days of probation being over, George went for his answer, which was given him by the old lady who occupied the upper story.

"Ach Gott! Fräulein Von Stoltz ist schon im Leipsic gegangen!"— All that has not been many years ago. George Brainard is as handsome as ever, though growing a little stout in the quiet routine of domestic life. He has quite lost a pretty taste for music that formerly distinguished him as a skilful banjoist. This loss his little black-eyed wife deplores; though she has herself made concessions to the advancing years, and abandoned Virginia break-downs as incompatible with the serious offices of wifehood and matrimony.

You may have seen in the morning paper, that the renowned pianist, Fräulein Paula Von Stoltz, is resting in Leipsic, after an extended and remunerative concert tour.

Professor Max Kuntzler is also in Leipsic—with the ever persistent will—the dogged patience that so often wins in the end.

Miss Witherwell's Mistake

It was seldom that the Saturday edition, of the Boredomville *Battery* appeared with its pages ungraced by a contribution from Miss Frances Witherwell's lively and prolific pen. If it were not a tale of passion, acted beneath those blue and southern skies—traditionally supposed to foster the growth of soft desire, and whither she loved to cast her lines—it might be an able treatise on "The Wintering of Canaries," or "Security Against the Moth." I recall at the moment, a paper for which the matrons of Boredomville were themselves much beholden to the spinster, Miss Witherwell, entitled, "A Word to Mothers."

Her neat and pretty home standing on the outskirts of the town, proved that she held nothing in common with that oft-cited Mrs. Jelleby, who has served not a little to bring the female litterateur into disrepute. Indeed, many of her most pungent conceptions are known to have come to her, whilst engaged in some such domestic occupation as sprinkling camphor in the folds of the winter curtains, or lining trunks with tar-paper, to prevent moths. And she herself tells of that poetic, enigmatic inspiration "Trust Not!" having flashed upon her, whilst she stood at the pantry-shelf washing with her own safe hands, her cut-glass goblets in warm soap-suds.

Being exact and punctilious in her working methods, and moreover, holding a moneyed interest in the *Battery*, she stood well with the staff of that journal. With promptness and precision that seldom miscarried, her article was handed in on Wednesday; the following Friday found her in the editorial rooms, proof before her. Then, with eagle eye to detect, and bold hand to eliminate, she removed the possibility of those demoniac vagaries, in which the type-setter proverbially delights.

One crisp November morning, a letter came to Miss Witherwell. It was from her brother Hiram, a St. Louis merchant, who had removed from Boredomville with his modest capital, when he sagaciously detected signs of commercial paralysis falling upon that otherwise attractive town. The letter threw Miss Witherwell into a singular flutter of contending sensations; announcing as it did, a visit from her niece, Mildred. Naturally to a maiden lady of fixed and lofty intellectual and other habits, there could only be a foretaste of disturbance in such an announcement. That the girl had had a love affair, made the situation none the more inviting to Miss Witherwell, for whom two such divergent cupids, as love in real life, and love in fiction, held themselves at widely distant points of view. It was hoped that a visit to her aunt, would help to turn the fair Mildred's thoughts from a lover, to whom her parents strongly objected. Not on any ground touching his personality, as Hiram Witherwell informed his sister; for the young man possessed the desirable qualifications of gentle birth, exceptional education, and no pronounced bad habits. Yet, was he so ineligible, from the well understood, worldly standpoint, that not for a moment, could he be thought a fitting mate for Mildred. Mr. Witherwell went on to say that his daughter had behaved well, in the somewhat painful matter of submitting to her parents' wishes. The young man had been no less tractable; indeed, he had lately quitted St Louis; and Mr. Witherwell felt hopeful, that time and change of scene would bring Mildred back to them completely reconciled, poor child, to the wordly wisdom of those who know the world so much better than she.

Miss Witherwell's agitation upon the receipt of this letter, resolved itself into a kind of folded and practical resignation, which moved her to the inspection of the cakebox. She remembered her niece as a girl of twelve, afflicted with a morbid craving for sweets, which might have survived her young ladyhood; possibly, too, she had retained the habits of teasing Mouchette, and bothering the cook out of her seven senses. Her astonishment partook therefore of the nature of a shock, at beholding the tall, handsome girl who kissed her effusively, and greeted her with an impressive, "dear aunt Frances" and brought into the quiet household a whiff of ozone that actually waked the slumbering songsters.

So little of the hoyden of twelve remained in this well mannered young lady of nineteen, that it was, with hesitancy, that Miss Witherwell passed her the large cake at tea, and was well pleased to find one recognizable trait enduring in spite of years and thwarted love.

"I very much fear, my dear, that such attractions as Boredomville can offer will prove inadequate in reconciling you to this temporary separation from the more varied enjoyments of your St. Louis life," said Miss Witherwell to her niece, with a dignity vastly impressive, but quite ordinary, with the august spinster.

"You mistake my purpose in coming to you, dear aunt, if you fancy I am seeking vain enjoyment," answered the girl, spreading a generous layer of delicious peach jam on her third slice of buttered bread. "The joys of life, with much of its sorrows, I hope, lie behind me. If I could feel sure that the future held some field of usefulness! Let me trouble you for half a cup of that exquisite tea—thanks, aunt Frances—as I was saying—another lump of sugar, please—some field of usefulness; don't you know, that would serve to draw me out of myself; that would let me forget my own troubles in lightening the misery of others."

"Ah! to have tasted the bitter cup so young," thought Miss Witherwell; "poor girl! poor heart!" But being an undemonstrative woman she said nothing; only coughed behind her hand, and then looked gloomily down whilst she rolled a very large napkin and forced it into the compass of a very small ring.

A few eventful days went by, in which Mildred gathered mild solace from the sympathetic hearing which her aunt lent to the unfolding of her pessimistic views of life. At last there came some very ugly weather, and with it, what Miss Witherwell called one of her "staying colds."

"Mildred, my dear," she said to her niece on a Friday morning, when icy honors held possession of out-doors, "I shall ask you to do me a service to-day. I have observed that however inclement the weather may be, it does not deter you from your daily walk. And you are right. Therein, lies the secret of the canker at your heart, having left the bloom in your cheek untouched." Then laying a finger lightly on the girl's glowing cheek, "You will stop at the office of the *Battery*, will you not, my dear? and say that I sent you. There will be no impropriety, else I should not want you to go. Ask to see the proof of my article which will appear to-morrow, and look it carefully over, correcting all errors. If you should encounter difficulties, Mr. Wilson will gladly assist you in meeting them."

"Mr. Wilson?" "Yes, the new assistant editor; a charming young man whom I find much more amenable than Hudson Jones."

The wind and an open umbrella helped to hurry her over the glassy street, and as the driving sleet pricked her glowing face like sharp needles, Mildred clutched tragically at her ulster, muttering, "Wilson, Wilson;

heaven and earth, what memories!" Her heart sank as she realized how common the name was. Had she ever looked into a newspaper that it had not confronted her with its prefixes of Johns, Toms or Harrys, and usually, heaven save the mark, in the police record. In yielding to her parents' wishes, and shutting Roland Wilson out of her life, Mildred meant and hoped to put him as effectually from out of her heart. Much help that promised to count, was at hand, in her happy and healthful youth with its unbounded resources, but!—

After bewildering the small Cerberus, who mounted guard at the head of the editorial stairs, with the glaringly unbelievable announcement that she was "Miss Witherwell," and then, making known her errand to a person whose province in life seemed the acceptance of any and everything with impartial resignation, she was politely seated at a desk and left to her own devices, and Miss Witherwell's proof.

The situation was certainly new, and she thought extremely interesting, as she flutteringly settled herself and qualified for her unaccustomed task by a generous moistening of her Faber No. 2 between the prettiest of red lips. She was quick enough to detect errors, and at the same time to feel her ignorance of what she knew must be technical methods of correction. She looked about her for the outside assistance which her aunt suggested, but she was quite alone in the small room that was separated from an adjoining one by a light partition. Through the door that stood ajar she could hear that some one was at work. By leaning and peering forward she saw the angle of a shirt-sleeved arm. A further craning of the neck and she caught sight of a shoulder, a leg, and a section of a blonde head that made her heart leap and beat in a most undisciplined manner. Another and more comprehensive look into the adjoining room revealed to her Roland Wilson standing behind a high desk. She trembled lest he should see her; then grew faint at the possibility of his *not* seeing her. When the latter contingency seemed likely to become a certainty, she coughed, an aggressive little cough, and so probably unreal and unlike anything which had ever afflicted her before, that it failed to bring the hoped-for recognition from Roland Wilson. A second and third repetition of that exasperating little cough, finally moved the young man to the consciousness that some female, with a trouble of the larynx, was somewhere in his *too* close vicinity, and turning to close the door and shut out the interruption, he saw Mildred, pale and red—almost crying, but most certainly laughing, looking up at him.

There was a rapturous meeting of outstretched hands, followed by a moment of hesitancy. Uncertainty on his part—indecision on hers. Then a spontaneous pressure of the yet clasped hands, warm and full of assurance from each. If little Cerberus had not been so near, and if there had not been the likelihood of sudden interruption, there is every reason to believe the cordiality of this unlooked-for meeting would have waxed much more emphatic; for surely, youth and red lips are temptations.

"Mildred, child! this passes my understanding," said Miss Witherwell on the following morning to her niece, as she looked over her article in the *Battery*, "The Use and Abuse of the Corset," an unusually strong thing, Hudson Jones had pronounced it—handled in that free, fearless, almost heroic style, permitted to so well established a veteran in journalism as Miss Witherwell. Never before had anything from her pen appeared in so slovenly garb. Instinctively she sent her pencil dashing through it in cabalistic correction. The defects were grievous; the errata appalling!

"Can it be possible you saw Mr. Wilson?" she asked. "A tall, light young man?"

"Oh! yes, aunt, quite certain. Tall as you say, and fair; with dark-blue eyes like two deep wells of thought; a man to remind one of celestial music, and a silky moustache. Oh! I'm quite sure!"

"Humph! that will do; I dare say it was he; but not in his proper mind."

"Well, aunt Frances, I admit that I don't believe he saw it."

"What?" turning upon her in blank surprise.

"Yes; you see, I tried to correct the thing—I mean the article—myself, and didn't know how. Mr. Wilson was willing enough to help me, but I bundled it up and told him it was all right. You know, yourself, aunt Frances, it isn't a theme any girl would like to dwell upon with a young man—highly indelicate. I couldn't have done it."

"False modesty, indeed; perniciously false! This confession implies a serious error in your bringing up, and I wonder at your father for it."

Mildred begged permission to vindicate herself on the following week, and so skilfully did she perform her task; in such trim and pleasing shape did "Some Errors in Modern Elocution" appear, on the following Saturday, that Miss Witherwell was ready to forgive. Thereafter, as the winter was very inclement and Miss Witherwell's cold clung to her with more than the persistency of a lover, besides the lady thought it was well to give her niece something to keep her out of mischief, Mildred was entrusted with the proud task of correcting Miss Witherwell's proof-sheets, once a week, at the *Battery* office.

The days crept into midwinter, and Mildred had yet shown no disposition to return home. This was considered a good omen by all, and no interference was offered to what seemed a whimsical idea of hers, to linger so long in Boredomville.

Mildred sat one day, deep in a comfortable arm-chair on one side the pleasant grate-fire, that was throwing dim and fitful lights into the cosy room. Miss Witherwell occupied the other side, but not in the same lounging attitude as her niece. Miss Witherwell, the elder, sat prim and upright. The canaries were dead asleep under the dark cover that she had thrown over their cage; and Mouchette lay curled on the rug, insensible to any world but that which haunts feline dreams.

"Aunt," said Mildred, moved by a sudden impulse to be communicative, "do you know, I have a little story in my mind: a little love story."

"Ah!" exclaimed Miss Witherwell in pleased surprise; and seizing the poker she drove it into the soft yielding coal with an emphasis that started a burst of joyous, dancing lights. What she *thought* was, that a happy deliverance from love-sickness and a colorless future had come to her niece in the form of this pleasing vocation. What she *said* was: "Have you thought it out fully? I shall be pleased to hear the synopsis."

"No," returned Mildred, dubiously fixing her gaze far in the fire and clasping her hands over her knee. "That's where I want your help, don't you know, to complete it. You see, it's about two lovers—"

"Yes, certainly. It is a very proper number."

"They, poor things, have been separated by a cruel, unjust fate or by a sordid parent. What do you think of the situation?"

"An excellent one," said Miss Witherwell, approvingly. "Not altogether new, yet with capabilities of development. Well?"

"Well, he's just the noblest, the truest of men, with every honorable instinct that a human being could possess."

"Be careful not to overdraw, Mildred."

"Yes, to be sure. That is an important point I had forgotten. In short, however, he has everything in his favor, save wealth. And they love each other—oh, devotedly! But they submit to what seems an inevitable decree and part, thinking never to meet again; then this same capricious fate brings them once more together, under peculiar circumstances."

"That might be made extremely effective," interrupted Miss Witherwell, her bold imagination crowded with situations which offered only the difficulty of a choice.

"This is the point where I need your advice, aunt. Bear in mind that being brought—almost forced together—through outside influences, they grow to love each other to desperation."

"Your hero must now perform some act to ingratiate himself with the obdurate parent," spoke Miss Witherwell, didactically, but warmly. "Let him save the father from some imminent peril—a railroad accident— a shipwreck. Let him, by some clever combination, avert a business catastrophe—let him—"

"No, no, aunt! I can't force situations. You'll find I'm extremely realistic. The only point for consideration is, to marry or not to marry; that is the question."

Miss Witherwell looked at her niece, aghast. "The poison of the realistic school has certainly tainted and withered your fancy in the bud, my dear, if you hesitate a moment. Marry them, most certainly, or let them die."

"Thanks, aunt Frances; I believe your suggestion is worth consideration."

This ended the conversation; but, needless to say, Miss Witherwell took a keen, though unobtrusive interest in the course of her niece's love story, and she could not so far do violence to her journalistic habit that had become second nature, as to withhold points that were always gratefully received.

"I think I shall end it to-day, aunt; you shall know the dénouement this evening," said Mildred, as she started for her accustomed Friday afternoon visit to the *Battery* office.

It was later than her usual hour for returning. The lamps had long been lighted, and Miss Witherwell had grown first a little impatient at her niece's prolonged absence, then disturbed; and was finally becoming alarmed, when she heard the garden gate slam. This was the signal with her to pour boiling water on the tea, which having done, she reseated herself with regained composure.

Mildred entered the room, followed by a tall young man whose handsome, open countenance beamed with happiness.

"Mr. Wilson," said Miss Witherwell, advancing toward him with dignity and extending her hand, "I am pleased to see you, and glad that you should have accompanied my niece home. An unseemly hour for her to have been on the streets alone," with a reproving glance at Mildred. "Pray be seated, and permit me to offer you a cup of tea."

The young man stood erect and unbending before her, not offering to take the hand which she held out to him.

"Miss Witherwell," he said, "before accepting your hospitality, I must make a disclosure!"

Miss Witherwell sank into a chair under pressure of a premonitory suspicion.

"He only wants to tell you the end of my story, aunt Frances," said Mildred, kneeling upon the low cushion which stood beside her aunt's chair, and at the same time taking that lady's hand in both hers. Then she turned toward Roland Wilson, saying : "Come, Roland, I know that aunt Frances will forgive us; for I have only followed her advice in closing my little love story with the happiest of marriages!"

Roland Wilson is now editor in chief of the Boredomville *Battery*, and is in a fair way to realize a handsome competence, if not a large fortune. Hiram Witherwell has grown reconciled to the match, and is secretly very proud of his son-in-law. Miss Witherwell still writes her brilliant articles for the *Battery;* she has grown older in years, but not in reality; indeed, the company and proximity of her niece and nephew has so brightened and cheered her, that she seems to grow younger every day; and is often heard to say, in her decided manner, that no mistake was ever more lucky.

A Shameful Affair

Mildred Orme, seated in the snuggest corner of the big front porch of the Kraummer farmhouse, was as content as a girl need hope to be.

This was no such farm as one reads about in humorous fiction. Here were swelling acres where the undulating wheat gleamed in the sun like a golden sea. For silver there was the Meramec—or, better, it was pure crystal, for here and there one might look clean through it down to where the pebbles lay like green and yellow gems. Along the river's edge trees were growing to the very water, and in it, sweeping it when they were willows.

The house itself was big and broad, as country houses should be. The master was big and broad, too. The mistress was small and thin, and it was always she who went out at noon to pull the great clanging bell that called the farmhands in to dinner.

From her agreeable corner where she lounged with her Browning or her Ibsen, Mildred watched the woman do this every day. Yet when the clumsy farmhands all came tramping up the steps and crossed the porch in going to their meal that was served within, she never looked at them. Why should she? Farmhands are not so very nice to look at, and she was nothing of an anthropologist. But once when the half dozen men came along, a paper which she had laid carelessly upon the railing was blown across their path. One of them picked it up, and when he had mounted the steps restored it to her. He was young, and brown, of course, as the sun had made him. He had nice blue eyes. His fair hair was dishevelled. His shoulders were broad and square and his limbs strong and clean. A not unpicturesque figure in the rough attire that bared his throat to view and gave perfect freedom to his every motion.

Mildred did not make these several observations in the half second that she looked at him in courteous acknowledgment. It took her as many days to note them all. For she signaled him out each time that he passed her, meaning to give him a condescending little smile, as she knew how. But he never looked at her. To be sure, clever young women of twenty, who are handsome, besides, who have refused their half dozen offers and are settling down to the conviction that life is a tedious affair, are not going to care a straw whether farmhands look at them or not. And Mildred did not care, and the thing would not have occupied her a moment if Satan had not intervened, in offering the employment which natural conditions had failed to supply. It was summer time; she was idle; she was piqued, and that was the beginning of the shameful affair.

"Who are these men, Mrs. Kraummer, that work for you? Where do you pick them up?"

"Oh, ve picks 'em up everyvere. Some is neighbors, some is tramps, and so."

"And that broad-shouldered young fellow—is he a neighbor? The one who handed me my paper the other day—you remember?"

"Gott, no! You might yust as well say he vas a tramp. Aber he vorks like a steam ingine."

"Well, he's an extremely disagreeable-looking man. I should think you'd be afraid to have him about, not knowing him."

"Vat you vant to be 'fraid for?" laughed the little woman. "He don't talk no more un ven he vas deef und dumb. I didn't t'ought you vas sooch a baby."

"But, Mrs. Kraummer, I don't want you to think I'm a baby, as you say—a coward, as you mean. Ask the man if he will drive me to church to-morrow. You see, I'm not so very much afraid of him," she added with a smile.

The answer which this unmannerly farmhand returned to Mildred's request was simply a refusal. He could not drive her to church because he was going fishing.

"Aber," offered good Mrs. Kraummer, "Hans Platzfeldt will drive you to church, oder vereever you vants. He vas a goot boy vat you can trust, dat Hans."

"Oh, thank him very much. But I find I have so many letters to write to-morrow, and it promises to be hot, too. I shan't care to go to church after all."

She could have cried for vexation. Snubbed by a farmhand! a tramp, perhaps. She, Mildred Orme, who ought really to have been with the rest of the family at Narragansett—who had come to seek in this retired spot the repose that would enable her to follow exalted lines of thought. She marvelled at the problematic nature of farmhands.

After sending her the uncivil message already recorded, and as he passed beneath the porch where she sat, he did look at her finally, in a way to make her positively gasp at the sudden effrontery of the man.

But the inexplicable look stayed with her. She could not banish it.

II

It was not so very hot after all, the next day, when Mildred walked down the long narrow footpath that led through the bending wheat to the river. High above her waist reached the yellow grain. Mildred's brown eyes filled with a reflected golden light as they caught the glint of it, as she heard the trill that it answered to the gentle breeze. Anyone who has walked through the wheat in midsummer-time knows that sound.

In the woods it was sweet and solemn and cool. And there beside the river was the wretch who had annoyed her, first, with his indifference, then with the sudden boldness of his glance.

"Are you fishing?" she asked politely and with kindly dignity, which she supposed would define her position toward him. The inquiry lacked not pertinence, seeing that he sat motionless, with a pole in his hand and his eyes fixed on a cork that bobbed aimlessly on the water.

"Yes, madam," was his brief reply.

"It won't disturb you if I stand here a moment, to see what success you will have?"

"No, madam."

She stood very still, holding tight to the book she had brought with her. Her straw hat had slipped disreputably to one side, over the wavy bronze-brown bang that half covered her forehead. Her cheeks were ripe with color that the sun had coaxed there; so were her lips.

All the other farmhands had gone forth in Sunday attire. Perhaps this one had none better than these working clothes that he wore. A feminine commiseration swept her at the thought. He spoke never a word. She wondered how many hours he could sit there, so patiently waiting for fish to come to his hook. For her part, the situation began to pall, and she wanted to change it at last.

"Let me try a moment, please? I have an idea—"

"Yes, madam."

"The man is surely an idiot, with his monosyllables," she commented inwardly. But she remembered that monosyllables belong to a boor's equipment.

She laid her book carefully down and took the pole gingerly that he came to place in her hands. Then it was his turn to stand back and look respectfully and silently on at the absorbing performance.

"Oh!" cried the girl, suddenly, seized with excitement upon seeing the line dragged deep in the water.

"Wait, wait! Not yet."

He sprang to her side. With his eyes eagerly fastened on the tense line, he grasped the pole to prevent her drawing it, as her intention seemed to be. That is, he meant to grasp the pole, but instead, his brown hand came down upon Mildred's white one.

He started violently at finding himself so close to a bronze-brown tangle that almost swept his chin—to a hot cheek only a few inches away from his shoulder, to a pair of young, dark eyes that gleamed for an instant unconscious things into his own.

Then, why ever it happened, or how ever it happened, his arms were holding Mildred and he kissed her lips. She did not know if it was ten times or only once.

She looked around—her face milk-white—to see him disappear with rapid strides through the path that had brought her there. Then she was alone.

Only the birds had seen, and she could count on their discretion. She was not wildly indignant, as many would have been. Shame stunned her. But through it she gropingly wondered if she should tell the Kraummers that her chaste lips had been rifled of their innocence. Publish her own confusion? No! Once in her room she would give calm thought to the situation, and determine then how to act. The secret must remain her own: a hateful burden to bear alone until she could forget it.

III

And because she feared not to forget it, Mildred wept that night. All day long a hideous truth had been thrusting itself upon her that made her ask herself if she could be mad. She feared it. Else why was that kiss the

21

most delicious thing she had known in her twenty years of life? The sting of it had never left her lips since it was pressed into them. The sweet trouble of it banished sleep from her pillow.

But Mildred would not bend the outward conditions of her life to serve any shameful whim that chanced to visit her soul, like an ugly dream. She would avoid nothing. She would go and come as always.

In the morning she found in her chair upon the porch the book she had left by the river. A fresh indignity! But she came and went as she intended to, and sat as usual upon the porch amid her familiar surroundings. When the Offender passed her by she knew it, though her eyes were never lifted. Are there only sight and sound to tell such things? She discerned it by a wave that swept her with confusion and she knew not what besides.

She watched him furtively, one day, when he talked with Farmer Kraummer out in the open. When he walked away she remained like one who has drunk much wine. Then unhesitatingly she turned and began her preparations to leave the Kraummer farmhouse.

When the afternoon was far spent they brought letters to her. One of them read like this:

"My Mildred, deary! I am only now at Narragansett, and so broke up not to find you. So you are down at that Kraummer farm, on the Iron Mountain. Well! What do you think of that delicious crank, Fred Evelyn? For a man must be a crank who does such things. Only fancy! Last year he chose to drive an engine back and forth across the plains. This year he tills the soil with laborers. Next year it will be something else as insane— because he likes to live more lives than one kind, and other Quixotic reasons. We are great chums. He writes me he's grown as strong as an ox. But he hasn't mentioned that you are there. I know you don't get on with him, for he isn't a bit intellectual—detests Ibsen and abuses Tolstoi. He doesn't read 'in books'—says they are spectacles for the short-sighted to look at life through. Don't snub him, dear, or be too hard on him; he has a heart of gold, if he is the first crank in America."

Mildred tried to think—to feel that the intelligence which this letter brought to her would take somewhat of the sting from the shame that tortured her. But it did not. She knew that it could not.

In the gathering twilight she walked again through the wheat that was heavy and fragrant with dew. The path was very long and very narrow. When she was midway she saw the Offender coming toward her. What could she do? Turn and run, as a little child might? Spring into the wheat, as some frightened four-footed creature would? There was nothing but to pass him with the dignity which the occasion clearly demanded.

But he did not let her pass. He stood squarely in the pathway before her, hat in hand, a perturbed look upon his face.

"Miss Orme," he said, "I have wanted to say to you, every hour of the past week, that I am the most consummate hound that walks the earth."

She made no protest. Her whole bearing seemed to indicate that her opinion coincided with his own.

"If you have a father, or brother, or any one, in short, to whom you may say such things—"

"I think you aggravate the offense, sir, by speaking of it. I shall ask you never to mention it again. I want to forget that it ever happened. Will you kindly let me by."

"Oh," he ventured eagerly, "you want to forget it! Then, maybe, since you are willing to forget, you will be generous enough to forgive the offender some day?"

"Some day," she repeated, almost inaudibly, looking seemingly through him, but not at him—"some day—perhaps; when I shall have forgiven myself."

He stood motionless, watching her slim, straight figure lessening by degrees as she walked slowly away from him. He was wondering what she meant. Then a sudden, quick wave came beating into his brown throat and staining it crimson, when he guessed what it might be.

Doctor Chevalier's Lie

The quick report of a pistol rang through the quiet autumn night. It was no unusual sound in the unsavory quarter where Dr. Chevalier had his office. Screams commonly went with it. This time there had been none.

Midnight had already rung in the old cathedral tower.

The doctor closed the book over which he had lingered so late, and awaited the summons that was almost sure to come.

As he entered the house to which he had been called he could not but note the ghastly sameness of detail that accompanied these oft-recurring events. The same scurrying; the same groups of tawdry, frightened women bending over banisters—hysterical, some of them; morbidly curious, others; and not a few shedding womanly tears; with a dead girl stretched somewhere, as this one was.

And yet it was not the same. Certainly she was dead: there was the hole in the temple where she had sent the bullet through. Yet it was different. Other such faces had been unfamiliar to him, except so far as they bore the common stamp of death. This one was not.

Like a flash he saw it again amid other surroundings. The time was little more than a year ago. The place, a homely cabin down in Arkansas, in which he and a friend had found shelter and hospitality during a hunting expedition.

There were others beside. A little sister or two; a father and mother—coarse, and bent with toil, but proud as archangels of their handsome girl, who was too clever to stay in an Arkansas cabin, and who was going away to seek her fortune in the big city.

"The girl is dead," said Doctor Chevalier. "I knew her well, and charge myself with her remains and decent burial."

The following day he wrote a letter. One, doubtless, to carry sorrow, but no shame to the cabin down there in the forest.

It told that the girl had sickened and died. A lock of hair was sent and other trifles with it. Tender last words were even invented.

Of course it was noised about that Doctor Chevalier had cared for the remains of a woman of doubtful repute.

Shoulders were shrugged. Society thought of cutting him. Society did not, for some reason or other, so the affair blew over.

Boulôt and Boulotte

When Boulôt and Boulotte, the little piny-wood twins, had reached the dignified age of twelve, it was decided in family council that the time had come for them to put their little naked feet into shoes. They were two brown-skinned, black-eyed 'Cadian roly-polies, who lived with father and mother and a troop of brothers and sisters halfway up the hill, in a neat log cabin that had a substantial mud chimney at one end. They could well afford shoes now, for they had saved many a picayune through their industry of selling wild grapes, blackberries, and "socoes" to ladies in the village who "put up" such things.

Boulôt and Boulotte were to buy the shoes themselves, and they selected a Saturday afternoon for the important transaction, for that is the great shopping time in Natchitoches Parish. So upon a bright Saturday afternoon Boulôt and Boulotte, hand in hand, with their quarters, their dimes, and their picayunes tied carefully in a Sunday handkerchief, descended the hill, and disappeared from the gaze of the eager group that had assembled to see them go.

Long before it was time for their return, this same small band, with ten year old Seraphine at their head, holding a tiny Seraphin in her arms, had stationed themselves in a row before the cabin at a convenient point from which to make quick and careful observation.

Even before the two could be caught sight of, their chattering voices were heard down by the spring, where they had doubtless stopped to drink. The voices grew more and more audible. Then, through the branches of the young pines, Boulotte's blue sun-bonnet appeared, and Boulôt's straw hat. Finally the twins, hand in hand, stepped into the clearing in full view.

Consternation seized the band.

"You bof crazy *donc*, Boulôt an' Boulotte," screamed Seraphine. "You go buy shoes, an' come home barefeet like you was go!"

Boulôt flushed crimson. He silently hung his head, and looked sheepishly down at his bare feet, then at the fine stout brogans that he carried in his hand. He had not thought of it.

Boulotte also carried shoes, but of the glossiest, with the highest of heels and brightest of buttons. But she was not one to be disconcerted or to look sheepish; far from it.

"You 'spec' Boulôt an' me we got money fur was'e—us?" she retorted, with withering condescension. "You think we go buy shoes fur ruin it in de dus'? *Comment!*"

And they all walked into the house crestfallen; all but Boulotte, who was mistress of the situation, and Seraphin, who did not care one way or the other.

Old Aunt Peggy

When the war was over, old Aunt Peggy went to Monsieur, and said:—

"Massa, I ain't never gwine to quit yer. I'm gittin' ole an' feeble, an' my days is few in dis heah lan' o' sorrow an' sin. All I axes is a li'le co'ner whar I kin set down an' wait peaceful fu de en'."

Monsieur and Madame were very much touched at this mark of affection and fidelity from Aunt Peggy. So, in the general reconstruction of the plantation which immediately followed the surrender, a nice cabin, pleasantly appointed, was set apart for the old woman. Madame did not even forget the very comfortable rocking-chair in which Aunt Peggy might "set down," as she herself feelingly expressed it, "an' wait fu de en'."

She has been rocking ever since.

At intervals of about two years Aunt Peggy hobbles up to the house, and delivers the stereotyped address which has become more than familiar:—

"Mist'ess, I 's come to take a las' look at you all. Le' me look at you good. Le' me look at de chillun,—de big chillun an' de li'le chillun. Le' me look at de picters an' de photygraphts an' de pianny, an' eve'ything 'fo' it 's too late. One eye is done gone, an' de udder 's a-gwine fas'. Any mo'nin' yo' po' ole Aunt Peggy gwine wake up an' fin' herse'f stone-bline."

After such a visit Aunt Peggy invariably returns to her cabin with a generously filled apron.

The scruple which Monsieur one time felt in supporting a woman for so many years in idleness has entirely disappeared. Of late his attitude towards Aunt Peggy is simply one of profound astonishment,—wonder at the surprising age which an old black woman may attain when she sets her mind to it, for Aunt Peggy is a hundred and twenty-five, so she says.

It may not be true, however. Possibly she is older.

Miss McEnders

I

When Miss Georgie McEnders had finished an elaborately simple toilet of gray and black, she divested herself completely of rings, bangles, brooches—everything to suggest that she stood in friendly relations with fortune. For Georgie was going to read a paper upon "The Dignity of Labor" before the Woman's Reform Club; and if she was blessed with an abundance of wealth, she possessed a no less amount of good taste.

Before entering the neat victoria that stood at her father's too-sumptuous door—and that was her special property—she turned to give certain directions to the coachman. First upon the list from which she read was inscribed: "Look up Mademoiselle Salambre."

"James," said Georgie, flushing a pretty pink, as she always did with the slightest effort of speech, "we want to look up a person named Mademoiselle Salambre, in the southern part of town, on Arsenal street," indicating a certain number and locality. Then she seated herself in the carriage, and as it drove away proceeded to study her engagement list further and to knit her pretty brows in deep and complex thought.

"Two o'clock—look up M. Salambre," said the list. "Three-thirty—read paper before Woman's Ref. Club. Four-thirty—" and here followed cabalistic abbreviations which meant: "Join committee of ladies to investigate moral condition of St. Louis factory-girls. Six o'clock—dine with papa. Eight o'clock—hear Henry George's lecture on Single Tax."

So far, Mademoiselle Salambre was only a name to Georgie McEnders, one of several submitted to her at her own request by her furnishers, Push and Prodem, an enterprising firm charged with the construction of Miss McEnder's very elaborate trousseau. Georgie liked to know the people who worked for her, as far as she could.

She was a charming young woman of twenty-five, though almost too white-souled for a creature of flesh and blood. She possessed ample wealth and time to squander, and a burning desire to do good—to elevate the human race, and start the world over again on a comfortable footing for everybody.

When Georgie had pushed open the very high gate of a very small yard she stood confronting a robust German woman, who, with dress tucked carefully between her knees, was in the act of noisily "redding" the bricks.

"Does M'selle Salambre live here?" Georgie's tall, slim figure was very erect. Her face suggested a sweet peach blossom, and she held a severely simple lorgnon up to her short-sighted blue eyes.

"Ya! ya! aber oop stairs!" cried the woman brusquely and impatiently. But Georgie did not mind. She was used to greetings that lacked the ring of cordiality.

When she had ascended the stairs that led to an upper porch she knocked at the first door that presented itself, and was told to enter by Mlle. Salambre herself.

The woman sat at an opposite window, bending over a bundle of misty white goods that lay in a fluffy heap in her lap. She was not young. She might have been thirty, or she might have been forty. There were lines about her round, piquante face that denoted close acquaintance with struggles, hardships and all manner of unkind experiences.

Georgie had heard a whisper here and there touching the private character of Mlle. Salambre which had determined her to go in person and make the acquaintance of the woman and her surroundings; which latter were poor and simple enough, and not too neat. There was a little child at play upon the floor.

Mlle. Salambre had not expected so unlooked-for an apparition as Miss McEnders, and seeing the girl standing there in the door she removed the eye-glasses that had assisted her in the delicate work, and stood up also.

"Mlle. Salambre, I suppose?" said Georgie, with a courteous inclination.

"Ah! Mees McEndairs! What an agree'ble surprise! Will you be so kind to take a chair." Mademoiselle had lived many years in the city, in various capacities, which brought her in touch with the fashionable set. There were few people in polite society whom Mademoiselle did not know —by sight, at least; and their private histories were as familiar to her as her own.

"You 'ave come to see your the work?" the woman went on with a smile that quite brightened her face. "It is a pleasure to handle such fine, such delicate quality of goods, Mees," and she went and laid several pieces of her handiwork upon the table beside Georgie, at the same time indicating such details as she hoped would call forth her visitor's approval.

There was something about the woman and her surroundings, and the atmosphere of the place, that affected the girl unpleasantly. She shrank instinctively, drawing her invisible mantle of chastity closely about her. Mademoiselle saw that her visitor's attention was divided between the lingerie and the child upon the floor, who was engaged in battering a doll's unyielding head against the unyielding floor.

"The child of my neighbor down-stairs," said Mademoiselle, with a wave of the hand which expressed volumes of unutterable ennui. But at that instant the little one, with instinctive mistrust, and in seeming defiance of the repudiation, climbed to her feet and went rolling and toddling towards her mother, clasping the woman about the knees, and calling her by the endearing title which was her own small right.

A spasm of annoyance passed over Mademoiselle's face, but still she called the child "*Chene*," as she grasped its arm to keep it from falling. Miss McEnders turned every shade of carmine.

"Why did you tell me an untruth?" she asked, looking indignantly into the woman's lowered face. "Why do you call yourself 'Mademoiselle' if this child is yours?"

"For the reason that it is more easy to obtain employment. For reasons that you would not understand," she continued, with a shrug of the shoulders that expressed some defiance and a sudden disregard for consequences. "Life is not all *couleur de rose*, Mees McEndairs; you do not know what life is, you!" And drawing a handkerchief from an apron pocket she mopped an imaginary tear from the corner of her eye, and blew her nose till it glowed again.

Georgie could hardly recall the words or actions with which she quitted Mademoiselle's presence. As much as she wanted to, it had been impossible to stand and read the woman a moral lecture. She had simply thrown what disapproval she could into her hasty leave-taking, and that was all for the moment. But as she drove away, a more practical form of rebuke suggested itself to her not too nimble intelligence—one that she promised herself to act upon as soon as her home was reached.

When she was alone in her room, during an interval between her many engagements, she then attended to the affair of Mlle. Salambre.

31

Georgie believed in discipline. She hated unrighteousness. When it pleased God to place the lash in her hand she did not hesitate to apply it. Here was this Mlle. Salambre living in her sin. Not as one who is young and blinded by the glamour of pleasure, but with cool and deliberate intention. Since she chose to transgress, she ought to suffer, and be made to feel that her ways were iniquitous and invited rebuke. It lay in Georgie's power to mete out a small dose of that chastisement which the woman deserved, and she was glad that the opportunity was hers.

She seated herself forthwith at her writing table, and penned the following note to her furnishers:

"Messrs. Push & Prodem.

"*Gentlemen*—Please withdraw from Mademoiselle Salambre all work of mine, and return same to me at once—finished or unfinished.

Yours truly,

Georgie McEnders."

II

On the second day following this summary proceeding, Georgie sat at her writing-table, looking prettier and pinker than ever, in a luxurious and soft-toned robe de chambre that suited her own delicate coloring, and fitted the pale amber tints of her room decorations.

There were books, pamphlets, and writing material set neatly upon the table before her. In the midst of them were two framed photographs, which she polished one after another with a silken scarf that was near.

One of these was a picture of her father, who looked like an Englishman, with his clean-shaved mouth and chin, and closely-cropped side-whiskers, just turning gray. A good-humored shrewdness shone in his eyes. From the set of his thin, firm lips one might guess that he was in the foremost rank in the interesting game of "push" that occupies mankind. One might further guess that his cleverness in using opportunities had brought him there, and that a dexterous management of elbows had served him no less. The other picture was that of Georgie's fiancé, Mr. Meredith Holt, approaching more closely than he liked to his forty-fifth year and an unbecoming corpulence. Only one who knew beforehand that he was a *viveur* could have detected evidence of such in his face, which told little more than that he was a good-looking and amiable man of the world, who might be counted on to do the gentlemanly thing always. Georgie was going to marry him because his personality pleased her; because his easy knowledge of life—such as she apprehended it—commended itself to her approval; because he was likely to interfere in no way with her "work." Yet she might not have given any of these reasons if asked for one. Mr. Meredith Holt was simply an eligible man, whom almost any girl in her set would have accepted for a husband.

Georgie had just discovered that she had yet an hour to spare before starting out with the committee of four to further investigate the moral condition of the factory-girl, when a maid appeared with the announcement that a person was below who wished to see her.

"A person? Surely not a visitor at this hour?"

"I left her in the hall, miss, and she says her name is Mademoiselle Sal-Sal—"

"Oh, yes! Ask her to kindly walk up to my room, and show her the way, please, Hannah."

Mademoiselle Salambre came in with a sweep of skirts that bristled defiance, and a poise of the head that was aggressive in its backward tilt. She seated herself, and with an air of challenge waited to be questioned or addressed.

Georgie felt at ease amid her own familiar surroundings. While she made some idle tracings with a pencil upon a discarded envelope, she half turned to say:

"This visit of yours is very surprising, madam, and wholly useless. I suppose you guess my motive in recalling my work, as I have done."

"Maybe I do, and maybe I do not, Mees McEndairs," replied the woman, with an impertinent uplifting of the eyebrows.

Georgie felt the same shrinking which had overtaken her before in the woman's presence. But she knew her duty, and from that there was no shrinking.

"You must be made to understand, madam, that there is a right way to live, and that there is a wrong way," said Georgie with more condescension than she knew. "We cannot defy God's laws with impunity, and without incurring His displeasure. But in His infinite justice and mercy He offers forgiveness, love and protection to those who turn away from evil and repent. It is for each of us to follow the divine way as well as may be. And I am only humbly striving to do His will."

"A most charming sermon, Mees McEndairs!" mademoiselle interrupted with a nervous laugh; "it seems a great pity to waste it upon so small an audience. And it grieves me, I cannot express, that I have not the time to remain and listen to its close."

She arose and began to talk volubly, swiftly, in a jumble of French and English, and with a wealth of expression and gesture which Georgie could hardly believe was natural, and not something acquired and rehearsed.

She had come to inform Miss McEnders that she did not want her work; that she would not touch it with the tips of her fingers. And her little, gloved hands recoiled from an imaginary pile of lingerie with unspeakable disgust. Her eyes had traveled nimbly over the room, and had been arrested by the two photographs on the table. Very small, indeed, were her worldly possessions, she informed the young lady; but as Heaven was her witness—not a mouthful of bread that she had not earned. And her parents over yonder in France! As honest as the sunlight! Poor, ah! for that—poor as rats. God only knew how poor; and God only knew how honest. Her eyes remained fixed upon the picture of Horace McEnders. Some people might like fine houses, and servants, and horses, and all the luxury which dishonest wealth brings. Some people might enjoy such surroundings. As for her!—and she drew up her skirts ever so carefully and daintily, as though she feared contamination to her petticoats from the touch of the rich rug upon which she stood.

Georgie's blue eyes were filled with astonishment as they followed the woman's gestures. Her face showed aversion and perplexity.

"Please let this interview come to an end at once," spoke the girl. She would not deign to ask an explanation of the mysterious allusions to ill-gotten wealth. But mademoiselle had not yet said all that she had come there to say.

"If it was only me to say so," she went on, still looking at the likeness, "but, *cher maître!* Go, yourself, Mees McEndairs, and stand for a while on the street and ask the people passing by how your dear papa has made his money, and see what they will say."

Then shifting her glance to the photograph of Meredith Holt, she stood in an attitude of amused contemplation, with a smile of commiseration playing about her lips.

"Mr. Meredith Holt!" she pronounced with quiet, surpressed emphasis —"ah! *c'est un propre, celui la!* You know him very well, no doubt, Mees McEndairs. You would not care to have my opinion of Mr. Meredith Holt. It would make no difference to you, Mees McEndairs, to know that he is not fit to be the husband of a self-respecting bar-maid. Oh! you know a good deal, my dear young lady. You can preach sermons in *merveille!*"

When Georgie was finally alone, there came to her, through all her disgust and indignation, an indefinable uneasiness. There was no misunderstanding the intention of the woman's utterances in regard to the girl's fiancé and her father. A sudden, wild, defiant desire came to her to test the suggestion which Mademoiselle Salambre had let fall.

Yes, she would go stand there on the corner and ask the passers-by how Horace McEnders made his money. She could not yet collect her thoughts for calm reflection; and the house stifled her. It was fully time for her to join her committee of four, but she would meddle no further with morals till her own were adjusted, she thought. Then she quitted the house, very pale, even to her lips that were tightly set.

Georgie stationed herself on the opposite side of the street, on the corner, and waited there as though she had appointed to meet some one.

The first to approach her was a kind-looking old gentleman, very much muffled for the pleasant spring day. Georgie did not hesitate an instant to accost him:

"I beg pardon, sir. Will you kindly tell me whose house that is?" pointing to her own domicile across the way.

"That is Mr. Horace McEnder's residence, Madame," replied the old gentleman, lifting his hat politely.

"Could you tell me how he made the money with which to build so magnificent a home?"

"You should not ask indiscreet questions, my dear young lady," answered the mystified old gentleman, as he bowed and walked away.

The girl let one or two persons pass her. Then she stopped a plumber, who was going cheerily along with his bag of tools on his shoulder.

"I beg pardon," began Georgie again; "but may I ask whose residence that is across the street?"

"Yes'um. That's the McEnderses."

"Thank you; and can you tell me how Mr. McEnders made such an immense fortune?"

"Oh, that ain't my business; but they say he made the biggest pile of it in the Whisky Ring."

So the truth would come to her somehow! These were the people from whom to seek it—who had not learned to veil their thoughts and opinions in polite subterfuge.

When a careless little news-boy came strolling along, she stopped him with the apparent intention of buying a paper from him.

"Do you know whose house that is?" she asked him, handing him a piece of money and nodding over the way.

"W'y, dats ole MicAndrus' house."

"I wonder where he got the money to build such a fine house."

"He stole it; dats w'ere he got it. Thank you," pocketing the change which Georgie declined to take, and he whistled a popular air as he disappeared around the corner.

Georgie had heard enough. Her heart was beating violently now, and her cheeks were flaming. So everybody knew it; even to the street gamins! The men and women who visited her and broke bread at her father's table, knew it. Her co-workers, who strove with her in Christian endeavor, knew. The very servants who waited upon her doubtless knew this, and had their jests about it.

She shrank within herself as she climbed the stairway to her room.

Upon the table there she found a box of exquisite white spring blossoms that a messenger had brought from Meredith Holt, during her absence. Without an instant's hesitation, Georgie cast the spotless things into the wide, sooty, fire-place. Then she sank into a chair and wept bitterly.

A Visit to Avoyelles

Every one who came up from Avoyelles had the same story to tell of Mentine. *Cher Maître!* but she was changed. And there were babies, more than she could well manage; as good as four already. Jules was not kind except to himself. They seldom went to church, and never anywhere upon a visit. They lived as poorly as pine-woods people. Doudouce had heard the story often, the last time no later than that morning.

"Ho-a!" he shouted to his mule plumb in the middle of the cotton row. He had staggered along behind the plow since early morning, and of a sudden he felt he had had enough of it. He mounted the mule and rode away to the stable, leaving the plow with its polished blade thrust deep in the red Cane River soil. His head felt like a windmill with the recollections and sudden intentions that had crowded it and were whirling through his brain since he had heard the last story about Mentine.

He knew well enough Mentine would have married him seven years ago had not Jules Trodon come up from Avoyelles and captivated her with his handsome eyes and pleasant speech. Doudouce was resigned then, for he held Mentine's happiness above his own. But now she was suffering in a hopeless, common, exasperating way for the small comforts of life. People had told him so. And somehow, to-day, he could not stand the knowledge passively. He felt he must see those things they spoke of with his own eyes. He must strive to help her and her children if it were possible.

Doudouce could not sleep that night. He lay with wakeful eyes watching the moonlight creep across the bare floor of his room; listening to sounds that seemed unfamiliar and weird down among the rushes along the bayou. But towards morning he saw Mentine as he had seen her last in

37

her white wedding gown and veil. She looked at him with appealing eyes and held out her arms for protection,—for rescue, it seemed to him. That dream determined him. The following day Doudouce started for Avoyelles.

Jules Trodon's home lay a mile or two from Marksville. It consisted of three rooms strung in a row and opening upon a narrow gallery. The whole wore an aspect of poverty and dilapidation that summer day, towards noon, when Doudouce approached it. His presence outside the gate aroused the frantic barking of dogs that dashed down the steps as if to attack him. Two little brown barefooted children, a boy and girl, stood upon the gallery staring stupidly at him. "Call off you' dogs," he requested; but they only continued to stare.

"Down, Pluto! down, Achille!" cried the shrill voice of a woman who emerged from the house, holding upon her arm a delicate baby of a year or two. There was only an instant of unrecognition.

"*Mais* Doudouce, that ent you, *comment!* Well, if any one would tole me this mornin'! Git a chair, 'Tit Jules. That 's Mista Doudouce, f'om 'way yonda Natchitoches w'ere yo' maman use' to live. *Mais*, you ent change'; you' lookin' well, Doudouce."

He shook hands in a slow, undemonstrative way, and seated himself clumsily upon the hide-bottomed chair, laying his broad-rimmed felt hat upon the floor beside him. He was very uncomfortable in the cloth Sunday coat which he wore.

"I had business that call' me to Marksville," he began, "an' I say to myse'f, '*Tiens*, you can't pass by without tell' 'em all howdy.' "

"*Par exemple!* w'at Jules would said to that! *Mais*, you' lookin' well; you ent change', Doudouce."

"An' you' lookin' well, Mentine. Jis' the same Mentine." He regretted that he lacked talent to make the lie bolder.

She moved a little uneasily, and felt upon her shoulder for a pin with which to fasten the front of her old gown where it lacked a button. She had kept the baby in her lap. Doudouce was wondering miserably if he would have known her outside her home. He would have known her sweet, cheerful brown eyes, that were not changed; but her figure, that had looked so trim in the wedding gown, was sadly misshapen. She was brown, with skin like parchment, and piteously thin. There were lines, some deep as if old age had cut them, about the eyes and mouth.

"An' how you lef' 'em all, yonda?" she asked, in a high voice that had grown shrill from screaming at children and dogs.

"They all well. It 's mighty li'le sickness in the country this yea'. But they been lookin' fo' you up yonda, straight along, Mentine."

"Don't talk, Doudouce, it 's no chance; with that po' wo' out piece o' lan' w'at Jules got. He say, anotha yea' like that, he 's goin' sell out, him."

The children were clutching her on either side, their persistent gaze always fastened upon Doudouce. He tried without avail to make friends with them. Then Jules came home from the field, riding the mule with which he had worked, and which he fastened outside the gate.

"Yere 's Doudouce f'om Natchitoches, Jules," called out Mentine, "he stop' to tell us howdy, *en passant*." The husband mounted to the gallery and the two men shook hands; Doudouce listlessly, as he had done with Mentine; Jules with some bluster and show of cordiality.

"Well, you' a lucky man, you," he exclaimed with his swagger air, "able to broad like that, *encore!* You could n't do that if you had half a dozen mouth' to feed, *allez!*"

"Non, j'te garantis!" agreed Mentine, with a loud laugh. Doudouce winced, as he had done the instant before at Jules's heartless implication. This husband of Mentine surely had not changed during the seven years, except to grow broader, stronger, handsomer. But Doudouce did not tell him so.

After the mid-day dinner of boiled salt pork, corn bread and molasses, there was nothing for Doudouce but to take his leave when Jules did.

At the gate, the little boy was discovered in dangerous proximity to the mule's heels, and was properly screamed at and rebuked.

"I reckon he likes hosses," Doudouce remarked. "He take' afta you, Mentine. I got a li'le pony yonda home," he said, addressing the child, "w'at ent no use to me. I 'm goin' sen' 'im down to you. He 's a good, tough li'le mustang. You jis' can let 'im eat grass an' feed 'im a han'ful o' co'n, once a w'ile. An' he 's gentle, yes. You an' yo' ma can ride 'im to church, Sundays. *Hein!* you want?"

"W'at you say, Jules?" demanded the father. "W'at you say?" echoed Mentine, who was balancing the baby across the gate. " 'Tit sauvage, va!"

Doudouce shook hands all around, even with the baby, and walked off in the opposite direction to Jules, who had mounted the mule. He was bewildered. He stumbled over the rough ground because of tears that were blinding him, and that he had held in check for the past hour.

He had loved Mentine long ago, when she was young and attractive, and he found that he loved her still. He had tried to put all disturbing thought of her away, on that wedding-day, and he supposed he had succeeded. But he loved her now as he never had. Because she was no longer beautiful, he loved her. Because the delicate bloom of her existence had been rudely brushed away; because she was in a manner fallen; because she was Mentine, he loved her; fiercely, as a mother loves an afflicted child. He would have liked to thrust that man aside, and gather up her and her children, and hold them and keep them as long as life lasted.

After a moment or two Doudouce looked back at Mentine, standing at the gate with her baby. But her face was turned away from him. She was gazing after her husband, who went in the direction of the field.

Ma'ame Pélagie

When the war began, there stood on Côte Joyeuse an imposing mansion of red brick, shaped like the Pantheon. A grove of majestic live-oaks surrounded it.

Thirty years later, only the thick walls were standing, with the dull red brick showing here and there through a matted growth of clinging vines. The huge round pillars were intact; so to some extent was the stone flagging of hall and portico. There had been no home so stately along the whole stretch of Côte Joyeuse. Every one knew that, as they knew it had cost Philippe Valmêt sixty thousand dollars to build, away back in 1840. No one was in danger of forgetting that fact, so long as his daughter Pélagie survived. She was a queenly, white-haired woman of fifty. "Ma'ame Pélagie," they called her, though she was unmarried, as was her sister Pauline, a child in Ma'ame Pélagie's eyes; a child of thirty-five.

The two lived alone in a three-roomed cabin, almost within the shadow of the ruin. They lived for a dream, for Ma'ame Pélagie's dream, which was to rebuild the old home.

It would be pitiful to tell how their days were spent to accomplish this end; how the dollars had been saved for thirty years and the picayunes hoarded; and yet, not half enough gathered! But Ma'ame Pélagie felt sure of twenty years of life before her, and counted upon as many more for her sister. And what could not come to pass in twenty—in forty—years?

Often, of pleasant afternoons, the two would drink their black coffee, seated upon the stone-flagged portico whose canopy was the blue sky of Louisiana. They loved to sit there in the silence, with only each other and the sheeny, prying lizards for company, talking of the old times and planning for the new; while light breezes stirred the tattered vines high up among the columns, where owls nested.

"We can never hope to have all just as it was, Pauline," Ma'ame Pélagie would say; "perhaps the marble pillars of the salon will have to be replaced by wooden ones, and the crystal candelabra left out. Should you be willing, Pauline?"

"Oh, yes Sesoeur, I shall be willing." It was always, "Yes, Sesoeur," or "No, Sesoeur," "Just as you please, Sesoeur," with poor little Mam'selle Pauline. For what did she remember of that old life and that old splendor? Only a faint gleam here and there; the half-consciousness of a young, un-eventful existence; and then a great crash. That meant the nearness of war; the revolt of slaves; confusion ending in fire and flame through which she was borne safely in the strong arms of Pélagie, and carried to the log cabin which was still their home. Their brother, Léandre, had known more of it all than Pauline, and not so much as Pélagie. He had left the management of the big plantation with all its memories and traditions to his older sister, and had gone away to dwell in cities. That was many years ago. Now, Léandre's business called him frequently and upon long jour-neys from home, and his motherless daughter was coming to stay with her aunts at Côte Joyeuse.

They talked about it, sipping their coffee on the ruined portico. Mam'selle Pauline was terribly excited; the flush that throbbed into her pale, nervous face showed it; and she locked her thin fingers in and out incessantly.

"But what shall we do with La Petite, Sesoeur? Where shall we put her? How shall we amuse her? Ah, Seigneur!"

"She will sleep upon a cot in the room next to ours," responded Ma'ame Pélagie, "and live as we do. She knows how we live, and why we live; her father has told her. She knows we have money and could squander it if we chose. Do not fret, Pauline; let us hope La Petite is a true Valmêt."

Then Ma'ame Pélagie rose with stately deliberation and went to saddle her horse, for she had yet to make her last daily round through the fields; and Mam'selle Pauline threaded her way slowly among the tangled grasses toward the cabin.

The coming of La Petite, bringing with her as she did the pungent atmosphere of an outside and dimly known world, was a shock to these two, living their dream-life. The girl was quite as tall as her aunt Pélagie, with dark eyes that reflected joy as a still pool reflects the light of stars; and her rounded cheek was tinged like the pink crèpe myrtle. Mam'selle

Pauline kissed her and trembled. Ma'ame Pélagie looked into her eyes with a searching gaze, which seemed to seek a likeness of the past in the living present.

And they made room between them for this young life.

II

La Petite had determined upon trying to fit herself to the strange, narrow existence which she knew awaited her at Côte Joyeuse. It went well enough at first. Sometimes she followed Ma'ame Pélagie into the fields to note how the cotton was opening, ripe and white; or to count the ears of corn upon the hardy stalks. But oftener she was with her aunt Pauline, assisting in household offices, chattering of her brief past, or walking with the older woman arm-in-arm under the trailing moss of the giant oaks.

Mam'selle Pauline's steps grew very buoyant that summer, and her eyes were sometimes as bright as a bird's, unless La Petite were away from her side, when they would lose all other light but one of uneasy expectancy. The girl seemed to love her well in return, and called her endearingly Tan'tante. But as the time went by, La Petite became very quiet,—not listless, but thoughtful, and slow in her movements. Then her cheeks began to pale, till they were tinged like the creamy plumes of the white crêpe myrtle that grew in the ruin.

One day when she sat within its shadow, between her aunts, holding a hand of each, she said: "Tante Pélagie, I must tell you something, you and Tan'tante." She spoke low, but clearly and firmly. "I love you both, —please remember that I love you both. But I must go away from you. I can't live any longer here at Côte Joyeuse."

A spasm passed through Mam'selle Pauline's delicate frame. La Petite could feel the twitch of it in the wiry fingers that were intertwined with her own. Ma'ame Pélagie remained unchanged and motionless. No human eye could penetrate so deep as to see the satisfaction which her soul felt. She said: "What do you mean, Petite? Your father has sent you to us, and I am sure it is his wish that you remain."

"My father loves me, tante Pélagie, and such will not be his wish when he knows. Oh!" she continued with a restless movement, "it is as though a weight were pressing me backward here. I must live another life; the life I lived before. I want to know things that are happening from day to day over the world, and hear them talked about. I want my music, my books, my companions. If I had known no other life but this one of privation, I suppose it would be different. If I had to live this life, I should make the best of it. But I do not have to; and you know, tante Pélagie, you do not need to. It seems to me," she added in a whisper, "that it is a sin against myself. Ah, Tan'tante!—what is the matter with Tan'tante?"

It was nothing; only a slight feeling of faintness, that would soon pass. She entreated them to take no notice; but they brought her some water and fanned her with a palmetto leaf.

But that night, in the stillness of the room, Mam'selle Pauline sobbed and would not be comforted. Ma'ame Pélagie took her in her arms.

"Pauline, my little sister Pauline," she entreated, "I never have seen you like this before. Do you no longer love me? Have we not been happy together, you and I?"

"Oh, yes, Sesoeur."

"Is it because La Petite is going away?"

"Yes, Sesoeur."

"Then she is dearer to you than I!" spoke Ma'ame Pélagie with sharp resentment. "Than I, who held you and warmed you in my arms the day you were born; than I, your mother, father, sister, everything that could cherish you. Pauline, don't tell me that."

Mam'selle Pauline tried to talk through her sobs.

"I can't explain it to you, Sesoeur. I don't understand it myself. I love you as I have always loved you; next to God. But if La Petite goes away I shall die. I can't understand,—help me, Sesoeur. She seems—she seems like a saviour; like one who had come and taken me by the hand and was leading me somewhere—somewhere I want to go."

Ma'ame Pélagie had been sitting beside the bed in her peignoir and slippers. She held the hand of her sister who lay there, and smoothed down the woman's soft brown hair. She said not a word, and the silence was broken only by Mam'selle Pauline's continued sobs. Once Ma'ame Pélagie arose to mix a drink of orange-flower water, which she gave to her sister, as she would have offered it to a nervous, fretful child. Almost an hour passed before Ma'ame Pélagie spoke again. Then she said:—

"Pauline, you must cease that sobbing, now, and sleep. You will make yourself ill. La Petite will not go away. Do you hear me? Do you understand? She will stay, I promise you."

Mam'selle Pauline could not clearly comprehend, but she had great faith in the word of her sister, and soothed by the promise and the touch of Ma'ame Pélagie's strong, gentle hand, she fell asleep.

III

Ma'ame Pélagie, when she saw that her sister slept, arose noiselessly and stepped outside upon the low-roofed narrow gallery. She did not linger there, but with a step that was hurried and agitated, she crossed the distance that divided her cabin from the ruin.

The night was not a dark one, for the sky was clear and the moon resplendent. But light or dark would have made no difference to Ma'ame Pélagie. It was not the first time she had stolen away to the ruin at nighttime, when the whole plantation slept; but she never before had been there with a heart so nearly broken. She was going there for the last time to dream her dreams; to see the visions that hitherto had crowded her days and nights, and to bid them farewell.

There was the first of them, awaiting her upon the very portal; a robust old whitehaired man, chiding her for returning home so late. There are guests to be entertained. Does she not know it? Guests from the city and from the near plantations. Yes, she knows it is late. She had been abroad with Félix, and they did not notice how the time was speeding. Félix is there; he will explain it all. He is there beside her, but she does not want to hear what he will tell her father.

Ma'ame Pélagie had sunk upon the bench where she and her sister so often came to sit. Turning, she gazed in through the gaping chasm of the window at her side. The interior of the ruin is ablaze. Not with the moonlight, for that is faint beside the other one—the sparkle from the crystal candelabra, which negroes, moving noiselessly and respectfully about, are lighting, one after the other. How the gleam of them reflects and glances from the polished marble pillars!

The room holds a number of guests. There is old Monsieur Lucien Santien, leaning against one of the pillars, and laughing at something which Monsieur Lafirme is telling him, till his fat shoulders shake. His son Jules is with him—Jules, who wants to marry her. She laughs. She wonders if Félix has told her father yet. There is young Jérôme Lafirme playing at checkers upon the sofa with Léandre. Little Pauline stands annoying them and disturbing the game. Léandre reproves her. She begins to cry, and old black Clémentine, her nurse, who is not far off, limps across the room to pick her up and carry her away. How sensitive the little one is! But she trots about and takes care of herself better than she did a year or two ago, when she fell upon the stone hall floor and raised a great "bo-bo" on her forehead. Pélagie was hurt and angry enough about it; and she ordered rugs and buffalo robes to be brought and laid thick upon the tiles, till the little one's steps were surer.

"Il ne faut pas faire mal à Pauline." She was saying it aloud—"faire mal à Pauline."

But she gazes beyond the salon, back into the big dining hall, where the white crèpe myrtle grows. Ha! how low that bat has circled. It has struck Ma'ame Pélagie full on the breast. She does not know it. She is beyond there in the dining hall, where her father sits with a group of friends over their wine. As usual they are talking politics. How tiresome! She has heard them say "la guerre" oftener than once. La guerre. Bah! She and Félix have something pleasanter to talk about, out under the oaks, or back in the shadow of the oleanders.

But they were right! The sound of a cannon, shot at Sumter, has rolled across the Southern States, and its echo is heard along the whole stretch of Côte Joyeuse.

Yet Pélagie does not believe it. Not till La Ricaneuse stands before her with bare, black arms akimbo, uttering a volley of vile abuse and of brazen impudence. Pélagie wants to kill her. But yet she will not believe. Not till Félix comes to her in the chamber above the dining hall—there where that trumpet vine hangs—comes to say good-by to her. The hurt which the big brass buttons of his new gray uniform pressed into the tender flesh of her bosom has never left it. She sits upon the sofa, and he beside her, both speechless with pain. That room would not have been altered. Even the sofa would have been there in the same spot, and Ma'ame Pélagie had meant all along, for thirty years, all along, to lie there upon it some day when the time came to die.

But there is no time to weep, with the enemy at the door. The door has been no barrier. They are clattering through the halls now, drinking the wines, shattering the crystal and glass, slashing the portraits.

One of them stands before her and tells her to leave the house. She slaps his face. How the stigma stands out red as blood upon his blanched cheek!

Now there is a roar of fire and the flames are bearing down upon her motionless figure. She wants to show them how a daughter of Louisiana can perish before her conquerors. But little Pauline clings to her knees in an agony of terror. Little Pauline must be saved.

"Il ne faut pas faire mal à Pauline." Again she is saying it aloud—
"faire mal à Pauline."

The night was nearly spent; Ma'ame Pélagie had glided from the
bench upon which she had rested, and for hours lay prone upon the stone
flagging, motionless. When she dragged herself to her feet it was to walk
like one in a dream. About the great, solemn pillars, one after the other,
she reached her arms, and pressed her cheek and her lips upon the
senseless brick.

"Adieu, adieu!" whispered Ma'ame Pélagie.

There was no longer the moon to guide her steps across the familiar
pathway to the cabin. The brightest light in the sky was Venus, that
swung low in the east. The bats had ceased to beat their wings about the
ruin Even the mocking-bird that had warbled for hours in the old
mulberry-tree had sung himself asleep. That darkest hour before the day
was mantling the earth. Ma'ame Pélagie hurried through the wet, clinging
grass, beating aside the heavy moss that swept across her face, walking
on toward the cabin—toward Pauline. Not once did she look back upon
the ruin that brooded like a huge monster—a black spot in the darkness
that enveloped it.

IV

Little more than a year later the transformation which the old Valmêt
place had undergone was the talk and wonder of Côte Joyeuse. One
would have looked in vain for the ruin; it was no longer there; neither
was the log cabin. But out in the open, where the sun shone upon it, and
the breezes blew about it, was a shapely structure fashioned from woods
that the forests of the State had furnished. It rested upon a solid foundation
of brick.

Upon a corner of the pleasant gallery sat Léandre smoking his afternoon
cigar, and chatting with neighbors who had called. This was to be his
pied à terre now; the home where his sisters and his daughter dwelt. The
laughter of young people was heard out under the trees, and within the
house where La Petite was playing upon the piano. With the enthusiasm
of a young artist she drew from the keys strains that seemed marvelously
beautiful to Mam'selle Pauline, who stood enraptured near her. Mam'selle
Pauline had been touched by the re-creation of Valmêt. Her cheek was as

47

full and almost as flushed as La Petite's. The years were falling away from her.

Ma'ame Pélagie had been conversing with her brother and his friends. Then she turned and walked away; stopping to listen awhile to the music which La Petite was making. But it was only for a moment. She went on around the curve of the veranda, where she found herself alone. She stayed there, erect, holding to the banister rail and looking out calmly in the distance across the fields.

She was dressed in black, with the white kerchief she always wore folded across her bosom. Her thick, glossy hair rose like a silver diadem from her brow. In her deep, dark eyes smouldered the light of fires that would never flame. She had grown very old. Years instead of months seemed to have passed over her since the night she bade farewell to her visions.

Poor Ma'ame Pélagie! How could it be different! While the outward pressure of a young and joyous existence had forced her footsteps into the light, her soul had stayed in the shadow of the ruin.

Désirée's Baby

As the day was pleasant, Madame Valmondé drove over to L'Abri to see Désirée and the baby.

It made her laugh to think of Désirée with a baby. Why, it seemed but yesterday that Désirée was little more than a baby herself; when Monsieur in riding through the gateway of Valmondé had found her lying asleep in the shadow of the big stone pillar.

The little one awoke in his arms and began to cry for "Dada." That was as much as she could do or say. Some people thought she might have strayed there of her own accord, for she was of the toddling age. The prevailing belief was that she had been purposely left by a party of Texans, whose canvas-covered wagon, late in the day, had crossed the ferry that Coton Maïs kept, just below the plantation. In time Madame Valmondé abandoned every speculation but the one that Désirée had been sent to her by a beneficent Providence to be the child of her affection, seeing that she was without child of the flesh. For the girl grew to be beautiful and gentle, affectionate and sincere,—the idol of Valmondé.

It was no wonder, when she stood one day against the stone pillar in whose shadow she had lain asleep, eighteen years before, that Armand Aubigny riding by and seeing her there, had fallen in love with her. That was the way all the Aubignys fell in love, as if struck by a pistol shot. The wonder was that he had not loved her before; for he had known her since his father brought him home from Paris, a boy of eight, after his mother died there. The passion that awoke in him that day, when he saw her at the gate, swept along like an avalanche, or like a prairie fire, or like anything that drives headlong over all obstacles.

Monsieur Valmondé grew practical and wanted things well considered:

that is, the girl's obscure origin. Armand looked into her eyes and did not care. He was reminded that she was nameless. What did it matter about a name when he could give her one of the oldest and proudest in Louisiana? He ordered the *corbeille* from Paris, and contained himself with what patience he could until it arrived; then they were married.

Madame Valmondé had not seen Désirée and the baby for four weeks. When she reached L'Abri she shuddered at the first sight of it, as she always did. It was a sad looking place, which for many years had not known the gentle presence of a mistress, old Monsieur Aubigny having married and buried his wife in France, and she having loved her own land too well ever to leave it. The roof came down steep and black like a cowl, reaching out beyond the wide galleries that encircled the yellow stuccoed house. Big, solemn oaks grew close to it, and their thick-leaved, far-reaching branches shadowed it like a pall. Young Aubigny's rule was a strict one, too, and under it his negroes had forgotten how to be gay, as they had been during the old master's easy-going and indulgent lifetime.

The young mother was recovering slowly, and lay full length, in her soft white muslins and laces, upon a couch. The baby was beside her, upon her arm, where he had fallen asleep, at her breast. The yellow nurse woman sat beside a window fanning herself.

Madame Valmondé bent her portly figure over Désirée and kissed her, holding her an instant tenderly in her arms. Then she turned to the child.

"This is not the baby!" she exclaimed, in startled tones. French was the language spoken at Valmondé in those days.

"I knew you would be astonished," laughed Désirée, "at the way he has grown. The little *cochon de lait!* Look at his legs, mamma, and his hands and fingernails,—real finger-nails. Zandrine had to cut them this morning. Is n't it true, Zandrine?"

The woman bowed her turbaned head majestically, "Mais si, Madame."

"And the way he cries," went on Désirée, "is deafening. Armand heard him the other day as far away as La Blanche's cabin."

Madame Valmondé had never removed her eyes from the child. She lifted it and walked with it over to the window that was lightest. She scanned the baby narrowly, then looked as searchingly at Zandrine, whose face was turned to gaze across the fields.

"Yes, the child has grown, has changed," said Madame Valmondé, slowly, as she replaced it beside its mother. "What does Armand say?"

Désirée's face became suffused with a glow that was happiness itself.

"Oh, Armand is the proudest father in the parish, I believe, chiefly because it is a boy, to bear his name; though he says not,—that he would have loved a girl as well. But I know it is n't true. I know he says that to please me. And mamma," she added, drawing Madame Valmondé's head down to her, and speaking in a whisper, "he has n't punished one of them —not one of them—since baby is born. Even Négrillon, who pretended to have burnt his leg that he might rest from work—he only laughed, and said Négrillon was a great scamp. Oh, mamma, I 'm so happy; it frightens me."

What Désirée said was true. Marriage, and later the birth of his son had softened Armand Aubigny's imperious and exacting nature greatly. This was what made the gentle Désirée so happy, for she loved him desperately. When he frowned she trembled, but loved him. When he smiled, she asked no greater blessing of God. But Armand's dark, handsome face had not often been disfigured by frowns since the day he fell in love with her.

When the baby was about three months old, Désirée awoke one day to the conviction that there was something in the air menacing her peace. It was at first too subtle to grasp. It had only been a disquieting suggestion; an air of mystery among the blacks; unexpected visits from far-off neighbors who could hardly account for their coming. Then a strange, an awful change in her husband's manner, which she dared not ask him to explain. When he spoke to her, it was with averted eyes, from which the old love-light seemed to have gone out. He absented himself from home; and when there, avoided her presence and that of her child, without excuse. And the very spirit of Satan seemed suddenly to take hold of him in his dealings with the slaves. Désirée was miserable enough to die.

She sat in her room, one hot afternoon, in her *peignoir*, listlessly drawing through her fingers the strands of her long, silky brown hair that hung about her shoulders. The baby, half naked, lay asleep upon her own great mahogany bed, that was like a sumptuous throne, with its satin-lined half-canopy. One of La Blanche's little quadroon boys—half naked too— stood fanning the child slowly with a fan of peacock feathers. Désirée's eyes had been fixed absently and sadly upon the baby, while she was striving to penetrate the threatening mist that she felt closing about her. She looked from her child to the boy who stood beside him, and back again; over and over. "Ah!" It was a cry that she could not help; which she was not conscious of having uttered. The blood turned like ice in her veins, and a clammy moisture gathered upon her face.

She tried to speak to the little quadroon boy; but no sound would come, at first. When he heard his name uttered, he looked up, and his mistress was pointing to the door. He laid aside the great, soft fan, and obediently stole away, over the polished floor, on his bare tiptoes.

She stayed motionless, with gaze riveted upon her child, and her face the picture of fright.

Presently her husband entered the room, and without noticing her, went to a table and began to search among some papers which covered it.

"Armand," she called to him, in a voice which must have stabbed him, if he was human. But he did not notice. "Armand," she said again. Then she rose and tottered towards him. "Armand," she panted once more, clutching his arm, "look at our child. What does it mean? tell me."

He coldly but gently loosened her fingers from about his arm and thrust the hand away from him. "Tell me what it means!" she cried despairingly.

"It means," he answered lightly, "that the child is not white; it means that you are not white."

A quick conception of all that this accusation meant for her nerved her with unwonted courage to deny it. "It is a lie; it is not true, I am white! Look at my hair, it is brown; and my eyes are gray, Armand, you know they are gray. And my skin is fair," seizing his wrist. "Look at my hand; whiter than yours, Armand," she laughed hysterically.

"As white as La Blanche's," he returned cruelly; and went away leaving her alone with their child.

When she could hold a pen in her hand, she sent a despairing letter to Madame Valmondé.

"My mother, they tell me I am not white. Armand has told me I am not white. For God's sake tell them it is not true. You must know it is not true. I shall die. I must die. I cannot be so unhappy, and live."

The answer that came was as brief:

"My own Désirée: Come home to Valmondé; back to your mother who loves you. Come with your child."

When the letter reached Désirée she went with it to her husband's study, and laid it open upon the desk before which he sat. She was like a stone image: silent, white, motionless after she placed it there.

In silence he ran his cold eyes over the written words. He said nothing. "Shall I go, Armand?" she asked in tones sharp with agonized suspense.

"Yes, go."

"Do you want me to go?"

"Yes, I want you to go."

He thought Almighty God had dealt cruelly and unjustly with him; and felt, somehow, that he was paying Him back in kind when he stabbed thus into his wife's soul. Moreover he no longer loved her, because of the unconscious injury she had brought upon his home and his name.

She turned away like one stunned by a blow, and walked slowly towards the door, hoping he would call her back.

"Good-by, Armand," she moaned.

He did not answer her. That was his last blow at fate.

Désirée went in search of her child. Zandrine was pacing the sombre gallery with it. She took the little one from the nurse's arms with no word of explanation, and descending the steps, walked away, under the live-oak branches.

It was an October afternoon; the sun was just sinking. Out in the still fields the negroes were picking cotton.

Désirée had not changed the thin white garment nor the slippers which she wore. Her hair was uncovered and the sun's rays brought a golden gleam from its brown meshes. She did not take the broad, beaten road which led to the far-off plantation of Valmondé. She walked across a deserted field, where the stubble bruised her tender feet, so delicately shod, and tore her thin gown to shreds.

She disappeared among the reeds and willows that grew thick along the banks of the deep, sluggish bayou; and she did not come back again.

Some weeks later there was a curious scene enacted at L'Abri. In the centre of the smoothly swept back yard was a great bonfire. Armand Aubigny sat in the wide hallway that commanded a view of the spectacle; and it was he who dealt out to a half dozen negroes the material which kept this fire ablaze.

A graceful cradle of willow, with all its dainty furbishings, was laid upon the pyre, which had already been fed with the richness of a priceless *layette*. Then there were silk gowns, and velvet and satin ones added to these; laces, too, and embroideries; bonnets and gloves; for the *corbeille* had been of rare quality.

The last thing to go was a tiny bundle of letters; innocent little scribblings that Désirée had sent to him during the days of their espousal. There was the remnant of one back in the drawer from which he took them. But it was not Désirée's; it was part of an old letter from his mother to his father. He read it. She was thanking God for the blessing of her husband's love:—

"But, above all," she wrote, "night and day, I thank the good God for having so arranged our lives that our dear Armand will never know that his mother, who adores him, belongs to the race that is cursed with the brand of slavery."

Madame Célestin's Divorce

Madame Célestin always wore a neat and snugly fitting calico wrapper when she went out in the morning to sweep her small gallery. Lawyer Paxton thought she looked very pretty in the gray one that was made with a graceful Watteau fold at the back: and with which she invariably wore a bow of pink ribbon at the throat. She was always sweeping her gallery when lawyer Paxton passed by in the morning on his way to his office in St. Denis Street.

Sometimes he stopped and leaned over the fence to say good-morning at his ease; to criticise or admire her rosebushes; or, when he had time enough, to hear what she had to say. Madame Célestin usually had a good deal to say. She would gather up the train of her calico wrapper in one hand, and balancing the broom gracefully in the other, would go tripping down to where the lawyer leaned, as comfortably as he could, over her picket fence.

Of course she had talked to him of her troubles. Every one knew Madame Célestin's troubles.

"Really, madame," he told her once, in his deliberate, calculating, lawyer-tone, "it 's more than human nature—woman's nature—should be called upon to endure. Here you are, working your fingers off"—she glanced down at two rosy finger-tips that showed through the rents in her baggy doeskin gloves—"taking in sewing; giving music lessons; doing God knows what in the way of manual labor to support yourself and those two little ones"—Madame Célestin's pretty face beamed with satisfaction at this enumeration of her trials.

"You right, Judge. Not a picayune, not one, not one, have I lay my eyes on in the pas' fo' months that I can say Célestin give it to me or sen' it to me."

"The scoundrel!" muttered lawyer Paxton in his beard.

"An' *pourtant*," she resumed, "they say he 's making money down roun' Alexandria w'en he wants to work."

"I dare say you have n't seen him for months?" suggested the lawyer.

"It 's good six month' since I see a sight of Célestin," she admitted.

"That 's it, that 's what I say; he has practically deserted you; fails to support you. It wouldn't surprise me a bit to learn that he has ill treated you."

"Well, you know, Judge," with an evasive cough, "a man that drinks —w'at can you expec'? An' if you would know the promises he has made me! Ah, If I had as many dolla' as I had promise from Célestin, I would n' have to work, *je vous garantis*."

"And in my opinion, Madame, you would be a foolish woman to endure it longer, when the divorce court is there to offer you redress."

"You spoke about that befo', Judge; I 'm goin' think about that divo'ce. I believe you right."

Madame Célestin thought about the divorce and talked about it, too; and lawyer Paxton grew deeply interested in the theme.

"You know, about that divo'ce, Judge," Madame Célestin was waiting for him that morning, "I been talking to my family an' my frien's, an' it 's me that tells you, they all plumb agains' that divo'ce."

"Certainly, to be sure; that 's to be expected, Madame, in this community of Creoles. I warned you that you would meet with opposition, and would have to face it and brave it."

"Oh, don't fear, I 'm going to face it! Maman says it 's a disgrace like it 's neva been in the family. But it 's good for Maman to talk, her. W'at trouble she ever had? She says I mus' go by all means consult with Père Duchéron—it 's my confessor, you undastan'—Well, I 'll go, Judge, to please Maman. But all the confessor' in the worl' ent goin' make me put up with that conduc' of Célestin any longa."

A day or two later, she was there waiting for him again. "You know, Judge, about that divo'ce."

"Yes, yes," responded the lawyer, well pleased to trace a new determination in her brown eyes and in the curves of her pretty mouth. "I suppose you saw Père Duchéron and had to brave it out with him, too."

"Oh, fo' that, a perfec' sermon, I assho you. A talk of giving scandal an' bad example that I thought would neva en'! He says, fo' him, he wash' his hands; I mus' go see the bishop."

56

"You won't let the bishop dissuade you, I trust," stammered the lawyer more anxiously than he could well understand.

"You don't know me yet, Judge," laughed Madame Célestin with a turn of the head and a flirt of the broom which indicated that the interview was at an end.

"Well, Madame Célestin! And the bishop!" Lawyer Paxton was standing there holding to a couple of the shaky pickets. She had not seen him. "Oh, it 's you, Judge?" and she hastened towards him with an *empressement* that could not but have been flattering.

"Yes, I saw Monseigneur," she began. The lawyer had already gathered from her expressive countenance that she had not wavered in her determination. "Ah, he 's a eloquent man. It 's not a mo' eloquent man in Natchitoches parish. I was fo'ced to cry, the way he talked to me about my troubles; how he undastan's them, an' feels for me. It would move even you, Judge, to hear how he talk' about that step I want to take; its danga, its temptation. How it is the duty of a Catholic to stan' everything till the las' extreme. An' that life of retirement an' self-denial I would have to lead,—he tole me all that."

"But he has n't turned you from your resolve, I see," laughed the lawyer complacently.

"For that, no," she returned emphatically. "The bishop don't know w'at it is to be married to a man like Célestin, an' have to endu' that conduc' like I have to endu' it. The Pope himse'f can't make me stan' that any longer, if you say I got the right in the law to sen' Célestin sailing."

A noticeable change had come over lawyer Paxton. He discarded his work-day coat and began to wear his Sunday one to the office. He grew solicitous as to the shine of his boots, his collar, and the set of his tie. He brushed and trimmed his whiskers with a care that had not before been apparent. Then he fell into a stupid habit of dreaming as he walked the streets of the old town. It would be very good to take unto himself a wife, he dreamed. And he could dream of no other than pretty Madame Célestin filling that sweet and sacred office as she filled his thoughts, now. Old Natchitoches would not hold them comfortably, perhaps; but the world was surely wide enough to live in, outside of Natchitoches town.

His heart beat in a strangely irregular manner as he neared Madame Célestin's house one morning, and discovered her behind the rosebushes, as usual plying her broom. She had finished the gallery and steps and was sweeping the little brick walk along the edge of the violet border.

"Good-morning, Madame Célestin."

"Ah, it 's you, Judge? Good-morning." He waited. She seemed to be doing the same. Then she ventured, with some hesitancy, "You know, Judge, about that divo'ce. I been thinking,—I reckon you betta neva mine about that divo'ce." She was making deep rings in the palm of her gloved hand with the end of the broomhandle, and looking at them critically. Her face seemed to the lawyer to be unusually rosy; but maybe it was only the reflection of the pink bow at the throat. "Yes, I reckon you need n' mine. You see, Judge, Célestin came home las' night. An' he 's promise me on his word an' honor he 's going to turn ova a new leaf."

A Lady of Bayou St John

The days and the nights were very lonely for Madame Delisle. Gustave, her husband, was away yonder in Virginia somewhere, with Beauregard, and she was here in the old house on Bayou St. John, alone with her slaves.

Madame was very beautiful. So beautiful, that she found much diversion in sitting for hours before the mirror, contemplating her own loveliness; admiring the brilliancy of her golden hair, the sweet languor of her blue eyes, the graceful contours of her figure, and the peach-like bloom of her flesh. She was very young. So young that she romped with the dogs, teased the parrot, and could not fall asleep at night unless old black Manna-Loulou sat beside her bed and told her stories.

In short, she was a child, not able to realize the significance of the tragedy whose unfolding kept the civilized world in suspense. It was only the immediate effect of the awful drama that moved her: the gloom that, spreading on all sides, penetrated her own existence and deprived it of joyousness.

Sépincourt found her looking very lonely and disconsolate one day when he stopped to talk with her. She was pale, and her blue eyes were dim with unwept tears. He was a Frenchman who lived near by. He shrugged his shoulders over this strife between brothers, this quarrel which was none of his; and he resented it chiefly upon the ground that it made life uncomfortable; yet he was young enough to have had quicker and hotter blood in his veins.

When he left Madame Delisle that day, her eyes were no longer dim, and a something of the dreariness that weighted her had been lifted away. That mysterious, that treacherous bond called sympathy, had revealed them to each other.

59

He came to her very often that summer, clad always in cool, white duck, with a flower in his buttonhole. His pleasant brown eyes sought hers with warm, friendly glances that comforted her as a caress might comfort a disconsolate child. She took to watching for his slim figure, a little bent, walking lazily up the avenue between the double line of magnolias.

They would sit sometimes during whole afternoons in the vine-sheltered corner of the gallery, sipping the black coffee that Manna-Loulou brought to them at intervals; and talking, talking incessantly during the first days when they were unconsciously unfolding themselves to each other. Then a time came—it came very quickly—when they seemed to have nothing more to say to one another.

He brought her news of the war; and they talked about it listlessly, between long intervals of silence, of which neither took account. An occasional letter came by round-about ways from Gustave—guarded and saddening in its tone. They would read it and sigh over it together.

Once they stood before his portrait that hung in the drawing-room and that looked out at them with kind, indulgent eyes. Madame wiped the picture with her gossamer handkerchief and impulsively pressed a tender kiss upon the painted canvas. For months past the living image of her husband had been receding further and further into a mist which she could penetrate with no faculty or power that she possessed.

One day at sunset, when she and Sépincourt stood silently side by side, looking across the *marais*, aflame with the western light, he said to her: "*M'amie*, let us go away from this country that is so *triste*. Let us go to Paris, you and me."

She thought that he was jesting, and she laughed nervously. "Yes, Paris would surely be gayer than Bayou St. John," she answered. But he was not jesting. She saw it at once in the glance that penetrated her own; in the quiver of his sensitive lip and the quick beating of a swollen vein in his brown throat.

"Paris, or anywhere—with you—ah, *bon Dieu!*" he whispered, seizing her hands. But she withdrew from him, frightened, and hurried away into the house, leaving him alone.

That night, for the first time, Madame did not want to hear Manna-Loulou's stories, and she blew out the wax candle that till now had burned nightly in her sleeping-room, under its tall, crystal globe. She had suddenly become a woman capable of love or sacrifice. She would not hear Manna-Loulou's stories. She wanted to be alone, to tremble and to weep.

In the morning her eyes were dry, but she would not see Sépincourt when he came. Then he wrote her a letter.

"I have offended you and I would rather die!" it ran. "Do not banish me from your presence that is life to me. Let me lie at your feet, if only for a moment, in which to hear you say that you forgive me."

Men have written just such letters before, but Madame did not know it. To her it was a voice from the unknown, like music, awaking in her a delicious tumult that seized and held possession of her whole being.

When they met, he had but to look into her face to know that he need not lie at her feet craving forgiveness. She was waiting for him beneath the spreading branches of a live-oak that guarded the gate of her home like a sentinel.

For a brief moment he held her hands, which trembled. Then he folded her in his arms and kissed her many times. "You will go with me, *m'amie?* I love you—oh, I love you! Will you not go with me, *m'amie?*"

"Anywhere, anywhere," she told him in a fainting voice that he could scarcely hear.

But she did not go with him. Chance willed it otherwise. That night a courier brought her a message from Beauregard, telling her that Gustave, her husband, was dead.

When the new year was still young, Sépincourt decided that, all things considered, he might, without any appearance of indecent haste, speak again of his love to Madame Delisle. That love was quite as acute as ever; perhaps a little sharper, from the long period of silence and waiting to which he had subjected it. He found her, as he had expected, clad in deepest mourning. She greeted him precisely as she had welcomed the curé, when the kind old priest had brought to her the consolations of religion—clasping his two hands warmly, and calling him *"cher ami."* Her whole attitude and bearing brought to Sépincourt the poignant, the bewildering conviction that he held no place in her thoughts.

They sat in the drawing-room before the portrait of Gustave, which was draped with his scarf. Above the picture hung his sword, and beneath it was an embankment of flowers. Sépincourt felt an almost irresistible impulse to bend his knee before this altar, upon which he saw foreshadowed the immolation of his hopes.

There was a soft air blowing gently over the *marais*. It came to them through the open window, laden with a hundred subtle sounds and scents of the springtime. It seemed to remind Madame of something far, far away, for she gazed dreamily out into the blue firmament. It fretted Sépincourt with impulses to speech and action which he found it impossible to control.

"You must know what has brought me," he began impulsively, drawing his chair nearer to hers. "Through all these months I have never ceased to love you and to long for you. Night and day the sound of your dear voice has been with me; your eyes"—

She held out her hand deprecatingly. He took it and held it. She let it lie unresponsive in his.

"You cannot have forgotten that you loved me not long ago," he went on eagerly, "that you were ready to follow me anywhere,—anywhere; do you remember? I have come now to ask you to fulfill that promise; to ask you to be my wife, my companion, the dear treasure of my life."

She heard his warm and pleading tones as though listening to a strange language, imperfectly understood.

She withdrew her hand from his, and leaned her brow thoughtfully upon it.

"Can you not feel—can you not understand, *mon ami*," she said calmly, "that now such a thing—such a thought, is impossible to me?"

"Impossible?"

"Yes, impossible. Can you not see that now my heart, my soul, my thought—my very life, must belong to another? It could not be different."

"Would you have me believe that you can wed your young existence to the dead?" he exclaimed with something like horror. Her glance was sunk deep in the embankment of flowers before her.

"My husband has never been so living to me as he is now," she replied with a faint smile of commiseration for Sépincourt's fatuity. "Every object that surrounds me speaks to me of him. I look yonder across the *marais*, and I see him coming toward me, tired and toil-stained from the hunt. I see him again sitting in this chair or in that one. I hear his familiar voice, his footsteps upon the galleries. We walk once more together beneath the magnolias; and at night in dreams I feel that he is there, there, near me. How could it be different! Ah! I have memories, memories to crowd and fill my life, if I live a hundred years!"

Sépincourt was wondering why she did not take the sword from her altar and thrust it through his body here and there. The effect would have been infinitely more agreeable than her words, penetrating his soul like fire. He arose confused, enraged with pain.

"Then, Madame," he stammered, "there is nothing left for me but to take my leave. I bid you adieu."

"Do not be offended, *mon ami*," she said kindly, holding out her hand. "You are going to Paris, I suppose?"

"What does it matter," he exclaimed desperately, "where I go?"

"Oh, I only wanted to wish you *bon voyage*," she assured him amiably.

Many days after that Sépincourt spent in the fruitless mental effort of trying to comprehend that psychological enigma, a woman's heart.

Madame still lives on Bayou St. John. She is rather an old lady now, a very pretty old lady, against whose long years of widowhood there has never been a breath of reproach. The memory of Gustave still fills and satisfies her days. She has never failed, once a year, to have a solemn high mass said for the repose of his soul.

La Belle Zoraïde

The summer night was hot and still; not a ripple of air swept over the *marais*. Yonder, across Bayou St. John, lights twinkled here and there in the darkness, and in the dark sky above a few stars were blinking. A lugger that had come out of the lake was moving with slow, lazy motion down the bayou. A man in the boat was singing a song.

The notes of the song came faintly to the ears of old Manna-Loulou, herself as black as the night, who had gone out upon the gallery to open the shutters wide.

Something in the refrain reminded the woman of an old, half-forgotten Creole romance, and she began to sing it low to herself while she threw the shutters open:—

> "Lisett' to kité la plaine,
> Mo perdi bonhair à moué;
> Ziés à moué semblé fontaine,
> Dépi mo pa miré toué."

And then this old song, a lover's lament for the loss of his mistress, floating into her memory, brought with it the story she would tell to Madame, who lay in her sumptuous mahogany bed, waiting to be fanned and put to sleep to the sound of one of Manna-Loulou's stories. The old negress had already bathed her mistress's pretty white feet and kissed them lovingly, one, then the other. She had brushed her mistress's beautiful hair, that was as soft and shining as satin, and was the color of Madame's wedding-ring. Now, when she reëntered the room, she moved softly toward the bed, and seating herself there began gently to fan Madame Delisle.

Manna-Loulou was not always ready with her story, for Madame would hear none but those which were true. But to-night the story was all there in Manna-Loulou's head—the story of la belle Zoraïde—and she told it to her mistress in the soft Creole patois, whose music and charm no English words can convey.

"La belle Zoraïde had eyes that were so dusky, so beautiful, that any man who gazed too long into their depths was sure to lose his head, and even his heart sometimes. Her soft, smooth skin was the color of *café-au-lait*. As for her elegant manners, her *svelte* and graceful figure, they were the envy of half the ladies who visited her mistress, Madame Delarivière.

"No wonder Zoraïde was as charming and as dainty as the finest lady of la rue Royale: from a toddling thing she had been brought up at her mistress's side; her fingers had never done rougher work than sewing a fine muslin seam; and she even had her own little black servant to wait upon her. Madame, who was her godmother as well as her mistress, would often say to her:—

" 'Remember, Zoraïde, when you are ready to marry, it must be in a way to do honor to your bringing up. It will be at the Cathedral. Your wedding gown, your *corbeille*, all will be of the best; I shall see to that myself. You know, M'sieur Ambroise is ready whenever you say the word; and his master is willing to do as much for him as I shall do for you. It is a union that will please me in every way.'

"M'sieur Ambroise was then the body servant of Doctor Langlé. La belle Zoraïde detested the little mulatto, with his shining whiskers like a white man's, and his small eyes, that were cruel and false as a snake's. She would cast down her own mischievous eyes, and say:—

" 'Ah, nénaine, I am so happy, so contented here at your side just as I am. I don't want to marry now; next year, perhaps, or the next.' And Madame would smile indulgently and remind Zoraïde that a woman's charms are not everlasting.

"But the truth of the matter was, Zoraïde had seen le beau Mézor dance the Bamboula in Congo Square. That was a sight to hold one rooted to the ground. Mézor was as straight as a cypress-tree and as proud looking as a king. His body, bare to the waist, was like a column of ebony and it glistened like oil.

"Poor Zoraïde's heart grew sick in her bosom with love for le beau Mézor from the moment she saw the fierce gleam of his eye, lighted by the inspiring strains of the Bamboula, and beheld the stately movements of his splendid body swaying and quivering through the figures of the dance.

65

"But when she knew him later, and he came near her to speak with her, all the fierceness was gone out of his eyes, and she saw only kindness in them and heard only gentleness in his voice; for love had taken possession of him also, and Zoraïde was more distracted than ever. When Mézor was not dancing Bamboula in Congo Square, he was hoeing sugar-cane, barefooted and half naked, in his master's field outside of the city. Doctor Langlé was his master as well as M'sieur Ambroise's.

"One day, when Zoraïde kneeled before her mistress, drawing on Madame's silken stockings, that were of the finest, she said:

" 'Nénaine, you have spoken to me often of marrying. Now, at last, I have chosen a husband, but it is not M'sieur Ambroise; it is le beau Mézor that I want and no other.' And Zoraïde hid her face in her hands when she had said that, for she guessed, rightly enough, that her mistress would be very angry. And, indeed, Madame Delarivière was at first speechless with rage. When she finally spoke it was only to gasp out, exasperated:—

" 'That negro! that negro! Bon Dieu Seigneur, but this is too much!'

" 'Am I white, nénaine?' pleaded Zoraïde.

" 'You white! *Malheureuse!* You deserve to have the lash laid upon you like any other slave; you have proven yourself no better than the worst.'

" 'I am not white,' persisted Zoraïde, respectfully and gently. 'Doctor Langlé gives me his slave to marry, but he would not give me his son. Then, since I am not white, let me have from out of my own race the one whom my heart has chosen.'

"However, you may well believe that Madame would not hear to that. Zoraïde was forbidden to speak to Mézor, and Mézor was cautioned against seeing Zoraïde again. But you know how the negroes are, Ma'zélle Titite," added Manna-Loulou, smiling a little sadly. "There is no mistress, no master, no king nor priest who can hinder them from loving when they will. And these two found ways and means.

"When months had passed by, Zoraïde, who had grown unlike herself, —sober and preoccupied,—said again to her mistress:—

" 'Nénaine, you would not let me have Mézor for my husband; but I have disobeyed you, I have sinned. Kill me if you wish, nénaine: forgive me if you will; but when I heard le beau Mézor say to me, "Zoraïde, mo l'aime toi," I could have died, but I could not have helped loving him.'

"This time Madame Delarivière was so actually pained, so wounded at hearing Zoraïde's confession, that there was no place left in her heart for anger. She could utter only confused reproaches. But she was a woman of action rather than of words, and she acted promptly. Her first step was to induce Doctor Langlé to sell Mézor. Doctor Langlé, who was a widower, had long wanted to marry Madame Delarivière, and he would willingly have walked on all fours at noon through the Place d'Armes if she wanted him to. Naturally he lost no time in disposing of le beau Mézor, who was sold away into Georgia, or the Carolinas, or one of those distant countries far away, where he would no longer hear his Creole tongue spoken, nor dance Calinda, nor hold la belle Zoraïde in his arms.

"The poor thing was heartbroken when Mézor was sent away from her, but she took comfort and hope in the thought of her baby that she would soon be able to clasp to her breast.

"La belle Zoraïde's sorrows had now begun in earnest. Not only sorrows but sufferings, and with the anguish of maternity came the shadow of death. But there is no agony that a mother will not forget when she holds her first-born to her heart, and presses her lips upon the baby flesh that is her own, yet far more precious than her own.

"So, instinctively, when Zoraïde came out of the awful shadow she gazed questioningly about her and felt with her trembling hands upon either side of her. 'Où li, mo piti a moin? (Where is my little one?)' she asked imploringly. Madame who was there and the nurse who was there both told her in turn, 'To piti à toi, li mouri' ('Your little one is dead'), which was a wicked falsehood that must have caused the angels in heaven to weep. For the baby was living and well and strong. It had at once been removed from its mother's side, to be sent away to Madame's plantation, far up the coast. Zoraïde could only moan in reply, 'Li mouri, li mouri,' and she turned her face to the wall.

"Madame had hoped, in thus depriving Zoraïde of her child, to have her young waiting-maid again at her side free, happy, and beautiful as of old. But there was a more powerful will than Madame's at work—the will of the good God, who had already designed that Zoraïde should grieve with a sorrow that was never more to be lifted in this world. La belle Zoraïde was no more. In her stead was a sad-eyed woman who mourned night and day for her baby. 'Li mouri, li mouri,' she would sigh over and over again to those about her, and to herself when others grew weary of her complaint.

"Yet, in spite of all, M'sieur Ambroise was still in the notion to marry her. A sad wife or a merry one was all the same to him so long as that wife was Zoraïde. And she seemed to consent, or rather submit, to the approaching marriage as though nothing mattered any longer in this world.

"One day, a black servant entered a little noisily the room in which Zoraïde sat sewing. With a look of strange and vacuous happiness upon her face, Zoraïde arose hastily. 'Hush, hush,' she whispered, lifting a warning finger, 'my little one is asleep; you must not awaken her.'

"Upon the bed was a senseless bundle of rags shaped like an infant in swaddling clothes. Over this dummy the woman had drawn the mosquito bar, and she was sitting contentedly beside it. In short, from that day Zoraïde was demented. Night nor day did she lose sight of the doll that lay in her bed or in her arms.

"And now was Madame stung with sorrow and remorse at seeing this terrible affliction that had befallen her dear Zoraïde. Consulting with Doctor Langlé, they decided to bring back to the mother the real baby of flesh and blood that was now toddling about, and kicking its heels in the dust yonder upon the plantation.

"It was Madame herself who led the pretty, tiny little "griffe" girl to her mother. Zoraïde was sitting upon a stone bench in the courtyard, listening to the soft splashing of the fountain, and watching the fitful shadows of the palm leaves upon the broad, white flagging.

" 'Here,' said Madame, approaching, 'here, my poor dear Zoraïde, is your own little child. Keep her; she is yours. No one will ever take her from you again.'

"Zoraïde looked with sullen suspicion upon her mistress and the child before her. Reaching out a hand she thrust the little one mistrustfully away from her. With the other hand she clasped the rag bundle fiercely to her breast; for she suspected a plot to deprive her of it.

"Nor could she ever be induced to let her own child approach her; and finally the little one was sent back to the plantation, where she was never to know the love of mother or father.

"And now this is the end of Zoraïde's story. She was never known again as la belle Zoraïde, but ever after as Zoraïde la folle, whom no one ever wanted to marry—not even M'sieur Ambroise. She lived to be an old woman, whom some people pitied and others laughed at—always clasping her bundle of rags—her 'piti.'

"Are you asleep, Ma'zélle Titite?"

"No, I am not asleep; I was thinking. Ah, the poor little one, Man Loulou, the poor little one! better had she died!"

But this is the way Madame Delisle and Manna-Loulou really talked to each other:—

"Vou pré droumi, Ma'zélle Titite?"

"Non, pa pré droumi; mo yapré zongler. Ah, la pauv' piti, Man Loulou. La pauv' piti! Mieux li mouri!"

In Sabine

The sight of a human habitation, even if it was a rude log cabin with a mud chimney at one end, was a very gratifying one to Grégoire.

He had come out of Natchitoches parish, and had been riding a great part of the day through the big lonesome parish of Sabine. He was not following the regular Texas road, but, led by his erratic fancy, was pushing toward the Sabine River by circuitous paths through the rolling pine forests.

As he approached the cabin in the clearing, he discerned behind a palisade of pine saplings an old negro man chopping wood.

"Howdy, Uncle," called out the young fellow, reining his horse. The negro looked up in blank amazement at so unexpected an apparition, but he only answered: "How you do, suh," accompanying his speech by a series of polite nods.

"Who lives yere?"

"Hit 's Mas' Bud Aiken w'at live' heah, suh."

"Well, if Mr. Bud Aiken c'n affo'd to hire a man to chop his wood, I reckon he won't grudge me a bite o' suppa an' a couple hours' res' on his gall'ry. W'at you say, ole man?"

"I say dit Mas' Bud Aiken don't hires me to chop 'ood. Ef I don't chop dis heah, his wife got it to do. Dat w'y I chops 'ood, suh. Go right 'long in, suh; you g'ine fine Mas' Bud some'eres roun', ef he ain't drunk an' gone to bed."

Grégoire, glad to stretch his legs, dismounted, and led his horse into the small inclosure which surrounded the cabin. An unkempt, vicious-looking little Texas pony stopped nibbling the stubble there to look maliciously at him and his fine sleek horse, as they passed by. Back of the hut, and running plumb up against the pine wood, was a small, ragged specimen of a cotton-field.

Grégoire was rather undersized, with a square, well-knit figure, upon which his clothes sat well and easily. His corduroy trousers were thrust into the legs of his boots; he wore a blue flannel shirt; his coat was thrown across the saddle. In his keen black eyes had come a puzzled expression, and he tugged thoughtfully at the brown moustache that lightly shaded his upper lip.

He was trying to recall when and under what circumstances he had before heard the name of Bud Aiken. But Bud Aiken himself saved Grégoire the trouble of further speculation on the subject. He appeared suddenly in the small doorway, which his big body quite filled; and then Grégoire remembered. This was the disreputable so-called "Texan" who a year ago had run away with and married Baptiste Choupic's pretty daughter, 'Tite Reine, yonder on Bayou Pierre, in Natchitoches parish. A vivid picture of the girl as he remembered her appeared to him: her trim rounded figure; her piquant face with its saucy black coquettish eyes; her little exacting, imperious ways that had obtained for her the nick-name of 'Tite Reine, little queen. Grégoire had known her at the 'Cadian balls that he sometimes had the hardihood to attend.

These pleasing recollections of 'Tite Reine lent a warmth that might otherwise have been lacking to Grégoire's manner, when he greeted her husband.

"I hope I fine you well, Mr. Aiken," he exclaimed cordially, as he approached and extended his hand.

"You find me damn' porely, suh; but you 've got the better o' me, ef I may so say." He was a big good-looking brute, with a straw-colored "horse-shoe" moustache quite concealing his mouth, and a several days' growth of stubble on his rugged face. He was fond of reiterating that women's admiration had wrecked his life, quite forgetting to mention the early and sustained influence of "Pike's Magnolia" and other brands, and wholly ignoring certain inborn propensities capable of wrecking unaided any ordinary existence. He had been lying down, and looked frouzy and half asleep.

"Ef I may so say, you 've got the better o' me, Mr.—er"—

"Santien, Grégoire Santien. I have the pleasure o' knowin' the lady you married, suh; an' I think I met you befo',—somew'ere o' 'nother," Grégoire added vaguely.

"Oh," drawled Aiken, waking up, "one o' them Red River Sanchuns!"

and his face brightened at the prospect before him of enjoying the society of one of the Santien boys. "Mortimer!" he called in ringing chest tones worthy a commander at the head of his troop. The negro had rested his axe and appeared to be listening to their talk, though he was too far to hear what they said.

"Mortimer, come along here an' take my frien' Mr. Sanchun's hoss. Git a move thar, git a move!" Then turning toward the entrance of the cabin he called back through the open door: "Rain!" it was his way of pronouncing 'Tite Reine's name. "Rain!" he cried again peremptorily; and turning to Grégoire: "she 's 'tendin' to some or other housekeepin' truck." 'Tite Reine was back in the yard feeding the solitary pig which they owned, and which Aiken had mysteriously driven up a few days before, saying he had bought it at Many.

Grégoire could hear her calling out as she approached: "I 'm comin', Bud. Yere I come. W'at you want, Bud?" breathlessly, as she appeared in the door frame and looked out upon the narrow sloping gallery where stood the two men. She seemed to Grégoire to have changed a good deal. She was thinner, and her eyes were larger, with an alert, uneasy look in them; he fancied the startled expression came from seeing him there unexpectedly. She wore cleanly homespun garments, the same she had brought with her from Bayou Pierre; but her shoes were in shreds. She uttered only a low, smothered exclamation when she saw Grégoire.

"Well, is that all you got to say to my frien' Mr. Sanchun? That 's the way with them Cajuns," Aiken offered apologetically to his guest; "ain't got sense enough to know a white man when they see one." Grégoire took her hand.

"I 'm mighty glad to see you, 'Tite Reine," he said from his heart. She had for some reason been unable to speak; now she panted somewhat hysterically:—

"You mus' escuse me, Mista Grégoire. It 's the truth I did n' know you firs', stan'in' up there." A deep flush had supplanted the former pallor of her face, and her eyes shone with tears and ill-concealed excitement.

"I thought you all lived yonda in Grant," remarked Grégoire carelessly, making talk for the purpose of diverting Aiken's attention away from his wife's evident embarrassment, which he himself was at a loss to understand.

"Why, we did live a right smart while in Grant; but Grant ain't no parish to make a livin' in. Then I tried Winn and Caddo a spell; they was n't no better. But I tell you, suh, Sabine 's a damn' sight worse than any of 'em. Why, a man can't git a drink o' whiskey here without going out of the parish fer it, or across into Texas. I 'm fixin' to sell out an' try Vernon."

Bud Aiken's household belongings surely would not count for much in the contemplated "selling out." The one room that constituted his home was extremely bare of furnishing,—a cheap bed, a pine table, and a few chairs, that was all. On a rough shelf were some paper parcels representing the larder. The mud daubing had fallen out here and there from between the logs of the cabin; and into the largest of these apertures had been thrust pieces of ragged bagging and wisps of cotton. A tin basin outside on the gallery offered the only bathing facilities to be seen. Notwithstanding these drawbacks, Grégoire announced his intention of passing the night with Aiken.

"I 'm jus' goin' to ask the privilege o' layin' down yere on yo' gall'ry to-night, Mr. Aiken. My hoss ain't in firs'-class trim; an' a night's res' ain't goin' to hurt him o' me either." He had begun by declaring his intention of pushing on across the Sabine, but an imploring look from 'Tite Reine's eyes had stayed the words upon his lips. Never had he seen in a woman's eyes a look of such heartbroken entreaty. He resolved on the instant to know the meaning of it before setting foot on Texas soil. Grégoire had never learned to steel his heart against a woman's eyes, no matter what language they spoke.

An old patchwork quilt folded double and a moss pillow which 'Tite Reine gave him out on the gallery made a bed that was, after all, not too uncomfortable for a young fellow of rugged habits.

Grégoire slept quite soundly after he laid down upon his improvised bed at nine o'clock. He was awakened toward the middle of the night by some one gently shaking him. It was 'Tite Reine stooping over him; he could see her plainly, for the moon was shining. She had not removed the clothing she had worn during the day; but her feet were bare and looked wonderfully small and white. He arose on his elbow, wide awake at once. "W'y, 'Tite Reine! w'at the devil you mean? w'ere 's yo' husban'?"

"The house kin fall on 'im, 't en goin' wake up Bud w'en he 's sleepin'; he drink' too much." Now that she had aroused Grégoire, she stood up, and sinking her face in her bended arm like a child, began to cry softly. In an instant he was on his feet.

"My God, 'Tite Reine! w'at 's the matta? you got to tell me w'at 's the matta." He could no longer recognize the imperious 'Tite Reine, whose will had been the law in her father's household. He led her to the edge of the low gallery and there they sat down.

Grégoire loved women. He liked their nearness, their atmosphere; the tones of their voices and the things they said; their ways of moving and turning about; the brushing of their garments when they passed him by pleased him. He was fleeing now from the pain that a woman had inflicted upon him. When any overpowering sorrow came to Grégoire he felt a singular longing to cross the Sabine River and lose himself in Texas. He had done this once before when his home, the old Santien place, had gone into the hands of creditors. The sight of 'Tite Reine's distress now moved him painfully.

"W'at is it, 'Tite Reine? tell me w'at it is," he kept asking her. She was attempting to dry her eyes on her coarse sleeve. He drew a handkerchief from his back pocket and dried them for her.

"They all well, yonda?" she asked, haltingly, "my popa? my moma? the chil'en?" Grégoire knew no more of the Baptiste Choupic family than the post beside him. Nevertheless he answered: "They all right well, 'Tite Reine, but they mighty lonesome of you."

"My popa, he got a putty good crop this yea'?"

"He made right smart o' cotton fo' Bayou Pierre."

"He done haul it to the relroad?"

"No, he ain't quite finish pickin'."

"I hope they all ent sole 'Putty Girl'?" she inquired solicitously.

"Well, I should say not! Yo' pa says they ain't anotha piece o' hossflesh in the pa'ish he 'd want to swap fo' 'Putty Girl.' " She turned to him with vague but fleeting amazement,—"Putty Girl" was a cow!

The autumn night was heavy about them. The black forest seemed to have drawn nearer; its shadowy depths were filled with the gruesome noises that inhabit a southern forest at night time.

"Ain't you 'fraid sometimes yere, 'Tite Reine?" Grégoire asked, as he felt a light shiver run through him at the weirdness of the scene.

"No," she answered promptly, "I ent 'fred o' nothin' 'cep' Bud."

"Then he treats you mean? I thought so!"

"Mista Grégoire," drawing close to him and whispering in his face, "Bud 's killin' me." He clasped her arm, holding her near him, while an expression of profound pity escaped him. "Nobody don' know, 'cep' Unc' Mort'mer," she went on. "I tell you, he beats me; my back an' arms— you ought to see—it 's all blue. He would 'a' choke' me to death one day w'en he was drunk, if Unc' Mort'mer had n' make 'im lef go—with his axe ov' his head." Grégoire glanced back over his shoulder toward the room where the man lay sleeping. He was wondering if it would really be a criminal act to go then and there and shoot the top of Bud Aiken's head off. He himself would hardly have considered it a crime, but he was not sure of how others might regard the act.

"That 's w'y I wake you up, to tell you," she continued. "Then sometime' he plague me mos' crazy; he tell me 't ent no preacher, it 's a Texas drummer w'at marry him an' me; an' w'en I don' know w'at way to turn no mo', he say no, it 's a Meth'dis' archbishop, an' keep on laughin' 'bout me, an' I don' know w'at the truth!"

Then again, she told how Bud had induced her to mount the vicious little mustang "Buckeye," knowing that the little brute would n't carry a woman; and how it had amused him to witness her distress and terror when she was thrown to the ground.

"If I would know how to read an' write, an' had some pencil an' paper, it 's long 'go I would wrote to my popa. But it 's no pos'office, it 's no relroad,—nothin' in Sabine. An' you know, Mista Grégoire, Bud say he 's goin' carry me yonda to Vernon, an' fu'ther off yet,—'way yonda, an' he 's goin' turn me loose. Oh, don' leave me yere, Mista Grégoire! don' leave me behine you!" she entreated, breaking once more into sobs.

" 'Tite Reine," he answered, "do you think I 'm such a low-down scound'el as to leave you yere with that"—He finished the sentence mentally, not wishing to offend the ears of 'Tite Reine.

They talked on a good while after that. She would not return to the room where her husband lay; the nearness of a friend had already emboldened her to inward revolt. Grégoire induced her to lie down and rest upon the quilt that she had given to him for a bed. She did so, and broken down by fatigue was soon fast asleep.

He stayed seated on the edge of the gallery and began to smoke cigarettes which he rolled himself of périque tobacco. He might have gone in and shared Bud Aiken's bed, but preferred to stay there near 'Tite Reine. He watched the two horses, tramping slowly about the lot, cropping the dewy wet tufts of grass.

Grégoire smoked on. He only stopped when the moon sank down behind the pine-trees, and the long deep shadow reached out and enveloped him. Then he could no longer see and follow the filmy smoke from his cigarette, and he threw it away. Sleep was pressing heavily upon him. He stretched himself full length upon the rough bare boards of the gallery and slept until day-break.

Bud Aiken's satisfaction was very genuine when he learned that Grégoire proposed spending the day and another night with him. He had already recognized in the young creole a spirit not altogether uncongenial to his own.

'Tite Reine cooked breakfast for them. She made coffee; of course there was no milk to add to it, but there was sugar. From a meal bag that stood in the corner of the room she took a measure of meal, and with it made a pone of corn bread. She fried slices of salt pork. Then Bud sent her into the field to pick cotton with old Uncle Mortimer. The negro's cabin was the counterpart of their own, but stood quite a distance away hidden in the woods. He and Aiken worked the crop on shares.

Early in the day Bud produced a grimy pack of cards from behind a parcel of sugar on the shelf. Grégoire threw the cards into the fire and replaced them with a spic and span new "deck" that he took from his saddlebags. He also brought forth from the same receptacle a bottle of whiskey, which he presented to his host, saying that he himself had no further use for it, as he had "sworn off" since day before yesterday, when he had made a fool of himself in Cloutierville.

They sat at the pine table smoking and playing cards all the morning, only desisting when 'Tite Reine came to serve them with the gumbo-filé that she had come out of the field to cook at noon. She could afford to treat a guest to chicken gumbo, for she owned a half dozen chickens that Uncle Mortimer had presented to her at various times. There were only two spoons, and 'Tite Reine had to wait till the men had finished before eating her soup. She waited for Grégoire's spoon, though her husband was the first to get through. It was a very childish whim.

In the afternoon she picked cotton again; and the men played cards, smoked, and Bud drank.

It was a very long time since Bud Aiken had enjoyed himself so well, and since he had encountered so sympathetic and appreciative a listener to the story of his eventful career. The story of 'Tite Reine's fall from the horse he told with much spirit, mimicking quite skillfully the way in which she had complained of never being permitted "to teck a li'le pleasure," whereupon he had kindly suggested horseback riding. Grégoire enjoyed the story amazingly, which encouraged Aiken to relate many more of a similar character. As the afternoon wore on, all formality of address between the two had disappeared: they were "Bud" and

"Grégoire" to each other, and Grégoire had delighted Aiken's soul by promising to spend a week with him. 'Tite Reine was also touched by the spirit of recklessness in the air; it moved her to fry two chickens for supper. She fried them deliciously in bacon fat. After supper she again arranged Grégoire's bed out on the gallery.

The night fell calm and beautiful, with the delicious odor of the pines floating upon the air. But the three did not sit up to enjoy it. Before the stroke of nine, Aiken had already fallen upon his bed unconscious of everything about him in the heavy drunken sleep that would hold him fast through the night. It even clutched him more relentlessly than usual, thanks to Grégoire's free gift of whiskey.

The sun was high when he awoke. He lifted his voice and called imperiously for 'Tite Reine, wondering that the coffee-pot was not on the hearth, and marveling still more that he did not hear her voice in quick response with its, "I 'm comin', Bud. Yere I come." He called again and again. Then he arose and looked out through the back door to see if she were picking cotton in the field, but she was not there. He dragged himself to the front entrance. Grégoire's bed was still on the gallery, but the young fellow was nowhere to be seen.

Uncle Mortimer had come into the yard, not to cut wood this time, but to pick up the axe which was his own property, and lift it to his shoulder.

"Mortimer," called out Aiken, "whur 's my wife?" at the same time advancing toward the negro. Mortimer stood still, waiting for him. "Whur 's my wife an' that Frenchman? Speak out, I say, before I send you to h—l."

Uncle Mortimer never had feared Bud Aiken; and with the trusty axe upon his shoulder, he felt a double hardihood in the man's presence. The old fellow passed the back of his black, knotty hand unctuously over his lips, as though he relished in advance the words that were about to pass them. He spoke carefully and deliberately:

"Miss Reine," he said, "I reckon she mus' of done struck Natchitoches pa'ish sometime to'ard de middle o' de night, on dat 'ar swif' hoss o' Mr. Sanchun's."

Aiken uttered a terrific oath. "Saddle up Buckeye," he yelled, "before I count twenty, or I 'll rip the black hide off yer. Quick, thar! Thur ain't nothin' fourfooted top o' this earth that Buckeye can't run down." Uncle Mortimer scratched his head dubiously, as he answered:—

"Yas, Mas' Bud, but you see, Mr. Sanchun, he done cross de Sabine befo' sun-up on Buckeye."

A Respectable Woman

Mrs. Baroda was a little provoked to learn that her husband expected his friend, Gouvernail, up to spend a week or two on the plantation.

They had entertained a good deal during the winter; much of the time had also been passed in New Orleans in various forms of mild dissipation. She was looking forward to a period of unbroken rest, now, and undisturbed tête-à-tête with her husband, when he informed her that Gouvernail was coming up to stay a week or two.

This was a man she had heard much of but never seen. He had been her husband's college friend; was now a journalist, and in no sense a society man or "a man about town," which were, perhaps, some of the reasons she had never met him. But she had unconsciously formed an image of him in her mind. She pictured him tall, slim, cynical; with eye-glasses, and his hands in his pockets; and she did not like him. Gouvernail was slim enough, but he wasn't very tall nor very cynical; neither did he wear eye-glasses nor carry his hands in his pockets. And she rather liked him when he first presented himself.

But why she liked him she could not explain satisfactorily to herself when she partly attempted to do so. She could discover in him none of those brilliant and promising traits which Gaston, her husband, had often assured her that he possessed. On the contrary, he sat rather mute and receptive before her chatty eagerness to make him feel at home and in face of Gaston's frank and wordy hospitality. His manner was as courteous toward her as the most exacting woman could require; but he made no direct appeal to her approval or even esteem.

Once settled at the plantation he seemed to like to sit upon the wide portico in the shade of one of the big Corinthian pillars, smoking his cigar lazily and listening attentively to Gaston's experience as a sugar planter.

"This is what I call living," he would utter with deep satisfaction, as the air that swept across the sugar field caressed him with its warm and scented velvety touch. It pleased him also to get on familiar terms with the big dogs that came about him, rubbing themselves sociably against his legs. He did not care to fish, and displayed no eagerness to go out and kill grosbecs when Gaston proposed doing so.

Gouvernail's personality puzzled Mrs. Baroda, but she liked him. Indeed, he was a lovable, inoffensive fellow. After a few days, when she could understand him no better than at first, she gave over being puzzled and remained piqued. In this mood she left her husband and her guest, for the most part, alone together. Then finding that Gouvernail took no manner of exception to her action, she imposed her society upon him, accompanying him in his idle strolls to the mill and walks along the batture. She persistently sought to penetrate the reserve in which he had unconsciously enveloped himself.

"When is he going—your friend?" she one day asked her husband. "For my part, he tires me frightfully."

"Not for a week yet, dear. I can't understand; he gives you no trouble."

"No. I should like him better if he did; if he were more like others, and I had to plan somewhat for his comfort and enjoyment."

Gaston took his wife's pretty face between his hands and looked tenderly and laughingly into her troubled eyes. They were making a bit of toilet sociably together in Mrs. Baroda's dressing-room.

"You are full of surprises, ma belle," he said to her. "Even I can never count upon how you are going to act under given conditions." He kissed her and turned to fasten his cravat before the mirror.

"Here you are," he went on, "taking poor Gouvernail seriously and making a commotion over him, the last thing he would desire or expect."

"Commotion!" she hotly resented. "Nonsense! How can you say such a thing? Commotion, indeed! But, you know, you said he was clever."

"So he is. But the poor fellow is run down by overwork now. That's why I asked him here to take a rest."

"You used to say he was a man of ideas," she retorted, unconciliated. "I expected him to be interesting, at least. I'm going to the city in the morning to have my spring gowns fitted. Let me know when Mr. Gouvernail is gone; I shall be at my Aunt Octavie's."

That night she went and sat alone upon a bench that stood beneath a live oak tree at the edge of the gravel walk.

She had never known her thoughts or her intentions to be so confused. She could gather nothing from them but the feeling of a distinct necessity to quit her home in the morning.

Mrs. Baroda heard footsteps crunching the gravel; but could discern in the darkness only the approaching red point of a lighted cigar. She knew it was Gouvernail, for her husband did not smoke. She hoped to remain unnoticed, but her white gown revealed her to him. He threw away his cigar and seated himself upon the bench beside her; without a suspicion that she might object to his presence.

"Your husband told me to bring this to you, Mrs. Baroda," he said, handing her a filmy, white scarf with which she sometimes enveloped her head and shoulders. She accepted the scarf from him with a murmur of thanks, and let it lie in her lap.

He made some commonplace observation upon the baneful effect of the night air at that season. Then as his gaze reached out into the darkness, he murmured, half to himself:

> " 'Night of south winds—night of the large few stars!
> Still nodding night—' "

She made no reply to this apostrophe to the night, which indeed, was not addressed to her.

Gouvernail was in no sense a diffident man, for he was not a self-conscious one. His periods of reserve were not constitutional, but the result of moods. Sitting there beside Mrs. Baroda, his silence melted for the time.

He talked freely and intimately in a low, hesitating drawl that was not unpleasant to hear. He talked of the old college days when he and Gaston had been a good deal to each other; of the days of keen and blind ambitions and large intentions. Now there was left with him, at least, a philosophic acquiescence to the existing order—only a desire to be permitted to exist, with now and then a little whiff of genuine life, such as he was breathing now.

Her mind only vaguely grasped what he was saying. Her physical being was for the moment predominant. She was not thinking of his words, only drinking in the tones of his voice. She wanted to reach out her hand in the darkness and touch him with the sensitive tips of her fingers upon the face or the lips. She wanted to draw close to him and whisper against his cheek—she did not care what—as she might have done if she had not been a respectable woman.

The stronger the impulse grew to bring herself near him, the further, in fact, did she draw away from him. As soon as she could do so without an appearance of too great rudeness, she rose and left him there alone.

Before she reached the house, Gouvernail had lighted a fresh cigar and ended his apostrophe to the night.

Mrs. Baroda was greatly tempted that night to tell her husband—who was also her friend—of this folly that had seized her. But she did not yield to the temptation. Beside being a respectable woman she was a very sensible one; and she knew there are some battles in life which a human being must fight alone.

When Gaston arose in the morning, his wife had already departed. She had taken an early morning train to the city. She did not return till Gouvernail was gone from under her roof.

There was some talk of having him back during the summer that followed. That is, Gaston greatly desired it; but this desire yielded to his wife's strenuous opposition.

However, before the year ended, she proposed, wholly from herself, to have Gouvernail visit them again. Her husband was surprised and delighted with the suggestion coming from her.

"I am glad, chère amie, to know that you have finally overcome your dislike for him; truly he did not deserve it."

"Oh," she told him, laughingly, after pressing a long, tender kiss upon his lips, "I have overcome everything! you will see. This time I shall be very nice to him."

The Story of an Hour

Knowing that Mrs. Mallard was afflicted with a heart trouble, great care was taken to break to her as gently as possible the news of her husband's death.

It was her sister Josephine who told her, in broken sentences; veiled hints that revealed in half concealing. Her husband's friend Richards was there, too, near her. It was he who had been in the newspaper office when intelligence of the railroad disaster was received, with Brently Mallard's name leading the list of "killed." He had only taken the time to assure himself of its truth by a second telegram, and had hastened to forestall any less careful, less tender friend in bearing the sad message.

She did not hear the story as many women have heard the same, with a paralyzed inability to accept its significance. She wept at once, with sudden, wild abandonment, in her sister's arms. When the storm of grief had spent itself she went away to her room alone. She would have no one follow her.

There stood, facing the open window, a comfortable, roomy armchair. Into this she sank, pressed down by a physical exhaustion that haunted her body and seemed to reach into her soul.

She could see in the open square before her house the tops of trees that were all aquiver with the new spring life. The delicious breath of rain was in the air. In the street below a peddler was crying his wares. The notes of a distant song which some one was singing reached her faintly, and countless sparrows were twittering in the eaves.

There were patches of blue sky showing here and there through the clouds that had met and piled one above the other in the west facing her window.

She sat with her head thrown back upon the cushion of the chair, quite motionless, except when a sob came up into her throat and shook her, as a child who has cried itself to sleep continues to sob in its dreams.

She was young, with a fair, calm face, whose lines bespoke repression and even a certain strength. But now there was a dull stare in her eyes, whose gaze was fixed away off yonder on one of those patches of blue sky. It was not a glance of reflection, but rather indicated a suspension of intelligent thought.

There was something coming to her and she was waiting for it, fearfully. What was it? She did not know; it was too subtle and elusive to name. But she felt it, creeping out of the sky, reaching toward her through the sounds, the scents, the color that filled the air.

Now her bosom rose and fell tumultuously. She was beginning to recognize this thing that was approaching to possess her, and she was striving to beat it back with her will—as powerless as her two white slender hands would have been.

When she abandoned herself a little whispered word escaped her slightly parted lips. She said it over and over under her breath: "free, free, free!" The vacant stare and the look of terror that had followed it went from her eyes. They stayed keen and bright. Her pulses beat fast, and the coursing blood warmed and relaxed every inch of her body.

She did not stop to ask if it were or were not a monstrous joy that held her. A clear and exalted perception enabled her to dismiss the suggestion as trivial.

She knew that she would weep again when she saw the kind, tender hands folded in death; the face that had never looked save with love upon her, fixed and gray and dead. But she saw beyond that bitter moment a long procession of years to come that would belong to her absolutely. And she opened and spread her arms out to them in welcome.

There would be no one to live for her during those coming years; she would live for herself. There would be no powerful will bending hers in that blind persistence with which men and women believe they have a right to impose a private will upon a fellow-creature. A kind intention or a cruel intention made the act seem no less a crime as she looked upon it in that brief moment of illumination.

And yet she had loved him—sometimes. Often she had not. What did it matter! What could love, the unsolved mystery, count for in face of this possession of self-assertion which she suddenly recognized as the strongest impulse of her being!

"Free! Body and soul free!" she kept whispering.

Josephine was kneeling before the closed door with her lips to the keyhole, imploring for admission. "Louise, open the door! I beg; open the door—you will make yourself ill. What are you doing, Louise? For heaven's sake open the door."

"Go away. I am not making myself ill." No; she was drinking in a very elixir of life through that open window.

Her fancy was running riot along those days ahead of her. Spring days, and summer days, and all sorts of days that would be her own. She breathed a quick prayer that life might be long. It was only yesterday she had thought with a shudder that life might be long.

She arose at length and opened the door to her sister's importunities. There was a feverish triumph in her eyes, and she carried herself unwittingly like a goddess of Victory. She clasped her sister's waist, and together they descended the stairs. Richards stood waiting for them at the bottom.

Some one was opening the front door with a latchkey. It was Brently Mallard who entered, a little travel-stained, composedly carrying his grip-sack and umbrella. He had been far from the scene of accident, and did not even know there had been one. He stood amazed at Josephine's piercing cry; at Richards' quick motion to screen him from the view of his wife.

But Richards was too late.

When the doctors came they said she had died of heart disease—of joy that kills.

Lilacs

Mme. Adrienne Farival never announced her coming; but the good nuns knew very well when to look for her. When the scent of the lilac blossoms began to permeate the air, Sister Agathe would turn many times during the day to the window; upon her face the happy, beatific expression with which pure and simple souls watch for the coming of those they love.

But it was not Sister Agathe; it was Sister Marceline who first espied her crossing the beautiful lawn that sloped up to the convent. Her arms were filled with great bunches of lilacs which she had gathered along her path. She was clad all in brown; like one of the birds that come with the spring, the nuns used to say. Her figure was rounded and graceful, and she walked with a happy, buoyant step. The cabriolet which had conveyed her to the convent moved slowly up the gravel drive that led to the imposing entrance. Beside the driver was her modest little black trunk, with her name and address printed in white letters upon it: "Mme. A. Farival, Paris." It was the crunching of the gravel which had attracted Sister Marceline's attention. And then the commotion began.

White-capped heads appeared suddenly at the windows; she waved her parasol and her bunch of lilacs at them. Sister Marceline and Sister Marie Anne appeared, fluttered and expectant at the doorway. But Sister Agathe, more daring and impulsive than all, descended the steps and flew across the grass to meet her. What embraces, in which the lilacs were crushed between them! What ardent kisses! What pink flushes of happiness mounting the cheeks of the two women!

Once within the convent Adrienne's soft brown eyes moistened with tenderness as they dwelt caressingly upon the familiar objects about her, and noted the most trifling details. The white, bare boards of the floor had lost nothing of their luster. The stiff, wooden chairs, standing in rows against the walls of hall and parlor, seemed to have taken on an extra polish since she had seen them, last lilac time. And there was a new picture of the Sacré-Coeur hanging over the hall table. What had they done with Ste. Catherine de Sienne, who had occupied that position of honor for so many years? In the chapel—it was no use trying to deceive her—she saw at a glance that St. Joseph's mantle had been embellished with a new coat of blue, and the aureole about his head freshly gilded. And the Blessed Virgin there neglected! Still wearing her garb of last spring, which looked almost dingy by contrast. It was not just—such partiality! The Holy Mother had reason to be jealous and to complain.

But Adrienne did not delay to pay her respects to the Mother Superior, whose dignity would not permit her to so much as step outside the door of her private apartments to welcome this old pupil. Indeed, she was dignity in person; large, uncompromising, unbending. She kissed Adrienne without warmth, and discussed conventional themes learnedly and prosaically during the quarter of an hour which the young woman remained in her company.

It was then that Adrienne's latest gift was brought in for inspection. For Adrienne always brought a handsome present for the chapel in her little black trunk. Last year it was a necklace of gems for the Blessed Virgin, which the Good Mother was only permitted to wear on extra occasions, such as great feast days of obligation. The year before it had been a precious crucifix—an ivory figure of Christ suspended from an ebony cross, whose extremities were tipped with wrought silver. This time it was a linen embroidered altar cloth of such rare and delicate workmanship that the Mother Superior, who knew the value of such things, chided Adrienne for the extravagance.

"But, dear Mother, you know it is the greatest pleasure I have in life—to be with you all once a year, and to bring some such trifling token of my regard."

The Mother Superior dismissed her with the rejoinder: "Make yourself at home, my child. Sister Thérèse will see to your wants. You will occupy Sister Marceline's bed in the end room, over the chapel. You will share the room with Sister Agathe."

There was always one of the nuns detailed to keep Adrienne company during her fortnight's stay at the convent. This had become almost a fixed regulation. It was only during the hours of recreation that she found herself with them all together. Those were hours of much harmless merry-making under the trees or in the nuns' refectory.

This time it was Sister Agathe who waited for her outside of the Mother Superior's door. She was taller and slenderer than Adrienne, and perhaps ten years older. Her fair blonde face flushed and paled with every passing emotion that visited her soul. The two women linked arms and went together out into the open air.

There was so much which Sister Agathe felt that Adrienne must see. To begin with, the enlarged poultry yard, with its dozens upon dozens of new inmates. It took now all the time of one of the lay sisters to attend to them. There had been no change made in the vegetable garden, but— yes there had; Adrienne's quick eye at once detected it. Last year old Philippe had planted his cabbages in a large square to the right. This year they were set out in an oblong bed to the left. How it made Sister Agathe laugh to think Adrienne should have noticed such a trifle! And old Philippe, who was nailing a broken trellis not far off, was called forward to be told about it.

He never failed to tell Adrienne how well she looked, and how she was growing younger each year. And it was his delight to recall certain of her youthful and mischievous escapades. Never would he forget that day she disappeared; and the whole convent in a hubbub about it! And how at last it was he who discovered her perched among the tallest branches of the highest tree on the grounds, where she had climbed to see if she could get a glimpse of Paris! And her punishment afterwards!—half of the Gospel of Palm Sunday to learn by heart!

"We may laugh over it, my good Philippe, but we must remember that Madame is older and wiser now."

"I know well, Sister Agathe, that one ceases to commit follies after the first days of youth." And Adrienne seemed greatly impressed by the wisdom of Sister Agathe and old Philippe, the convent gardener.

A little later when they sat upon a rustic bench which overlooked the smiling landscape about them, Adrienne was saying to Sister Agathe, who held her hand and stroked it fondly:

"Do you remember my first visit, four years ago, Sister Agathe? and what a surprise it was to you all!"

"As if I could forget it, dear child!"

"And I! Always shall I remember that morning as I walked along the boulevard with a heaviness of heart—oh, a heaviness which I hate to recall. Suddenly there was wafted to me the sweet odor of lilac blossoms.

A young girl had passed me by, carrying a great bunch of them. Did you ever know, Sister Agathe, that there is nothing which so keenly revives a memory as a perfume—an odor?"

"I believe you are right, Adrienne. For now that you speak of it, I can feel how the odor of fresh bread—when Sister Jeanne bakes—always makes me think of the great kitchen of ma tante de Sierge, and crippled Julie, who sat always knitting at the sunny window. And I never smell the sweet scented honeysuckle without living again through the blessed day of my first communion."

"Well, that is how it was with me, Sister Agathe, when the scent of the lilacs at once changed the whole current of my thoughts and my despondency. The boulevard, its noises, its passing throng, vanished from before my senses as completely as if they had been spirited away. I was standing here with my feet sunk in the green sward as they are now. I could see the sunlight glancing from that old white stone wall, could hear the notes of birds, just as we hear them now, and the humming of insects in the air. And through all I could see and could smell the lilac blossoms, nodding invitingly to me from their thick-leaved branches. It seems to me they are richer than ever this year, Sister Agathe. And do you know, I became like an *enragée;* nothing could have kept me back. I do not remember now where I was going; but I turned and retraced my steps homeward in a perfect fever of agitation: 'Sophie! my little trunk—quick—the black one! A mere handful of clothes! I am going away. Don't ask me any questions. I shall be back in a fortnight.' And every year since then it is the same. At the very first whiff of a lilac blossom, I am gone! There is no holding me back."

"And how I wait for you, and watch those lilac bushes, Adrienne! If you should once fail to come, it would be like the spring coming without the sunshine or the song of birds.

"But do you know, dear child, I have sometimes feared that in moments of despondency such as you have just described, I fear that you do not turn as you might to our Blessed Mother in heaven, who is ever ready to comfort and solace an afflicted heart with the precious balm of her sympathy and love."

"Perhaps I do not, dear Sister Agathe. But you cannot picture the annoyances which I am constantly submitted to. That Sophie alone, with her detestable ways! I assure you she of herself is enough to drive me to St. Lazare."

"Indeed, I do understand that the trials of one living in the world must be very great, Adrienne; particularly for you, my poor child, who have to bear them alone, since Almighty God was pleased to call to himself your dear husband. But on the other hand, to live one's life along the lines which our dear Lord traces for each one of us, must bring with it resignation and even a certain comfort. You have your household duties, Adrienne, and your music, to which, you say, you continue to devote yourself. And then, there are always good works—the poor—who are always with us—to be relieved; the afflicted to be comforted."

"But, Sister Agathe! Will you listen! Is it not La Rose that I hear moving down there at the edge of the pasture? I fancy she is reproaching me with being an ingrate, not to have pressed a kiss yet on that white forehead of hers. Come, let us go."

The two women arose and walked again, hand in hand this time, over the tufted grass down the gentle decline where it sloped toward the broad, flat meadow, and the limpid stream that flowed cool and fresh from the woods. Sister Agathe walked with her composed, nunlike tread; Adrienne with a balancing motion, a bounding step, as though the earth responded to her light footfall with some subtle impulse all its own.

They lingered long upon the foot-bridge that spanned the narrow stream which divided the convent grounds from the meadow beyond. It was to Adrienne indescribably sweet to rest there in soft, low converse with this gentle-faced nun, watching the approach of evening. The gurgle of the running water beneath them; the lowing of cattle approaching in the distance, were the only sounds that broke upon the stillness, until the clear tones of the angelus bell pealed out from the convent tower. At the sound both women instinctively sank to their knees, signing themselves with the sign of the cross. And Sister Agathe repeated the customary invocation, Adrienne responding in musical tones:

"The Angel of the Lord declared unto Mary,
    And she conceived by the Holy Ghost—"
and so forth, to the end of the brief prayer, after which they arose and retraced their steps toward the convent.

It was with subtle and naïve pleasure that Adrienne prepared herself that night for bed. The room which she shared with Sister Agathe was immaculately white. The walls were a dead white, relieved only by one florid print depicting Jacob's dream at the foot of the ladder, upon which angels mounted and descended. The bare floors, a soft yellow-white, with two little patches of gray carpet beside each spotless bed. At the head of the white-draped beds were two *bénitiers* containing holy water absorbed in sponges.

Sister Agathe disrobed noiselessly behind her curtains and glided into bed without having revealed, in the faint candlelight, as much as a shadow of herself. Adrienne pattered about the room, shook and folded her garments with great care, placing them on the back of a chair as she had been taught to do when a child at the convent. It secretly pleased Sister Agathe to feel that her dear Adrienne clung to the habits acquired in her youth.

But Adrienne could not sleep. She did not greatly desire to do so. These hours seemed too precious to be cast into the oblivion of slumber.

"Are you not asleep, Adrienne?"

"No, Sister Agathe. You know it is always so the first night. The excitement of my arrival—I don't know what—keeps me awake."

"Say your 'Hail, Mary,' dear child, over and over."

"I have done so, Sister Agathe; it does not help."

"Then lie quite still on your side and think of nothing but your own respiration. I have heard that such inducement to sleep seldom fails."

"I will try. Good night, Sister Agathe."

"Good night, dear child. May the Holy Virgin guard you."

An hour later Adrienne was still lying with wide, wakeful eyes, listening to the regular breathing of Sister Agathe. The trailing of the passing wind through the treetops, the ceaseless babble of the rivulet were some of the sounds that came to her faintly through the night.

The days of the fortnight which followed were in character much like the first peaceful, uneventful day of her arrival, with the exception only that she devoutly heard mass every morning at an early hour in the convent chapel, and on Sundays sang in the choir in her agreeable, cultivated voice, which was heard with delight and the warmest appreciation.

When the day of her departure came, Sister Agathe was not satisfied to say good-by at the portal as the others did. She walked down the drive beside the creeping old cabriolet, chattering her pleasant last words. And then she stood—it was as far as she might go—at the edge of the road, waving good-by in response to the fluttering of Adrienne's handkerchief. Four hours later Sister Agathe, who was instructing a class of little girls for their first communion, looked up at the classroom clock and murmured: "Adrienne is at home now."

Yes, Adrienne was at home. Paris had engulfed her.

At the very hour when Sister Agathe looked up at the clock, Adrienne, clad in a charming negligé, was reclining indolently in the depths of a luxurious armchair. The bright room was in its accustomed state of picturesque disorder. Musical scores were scattered upon the open piano. Thrown carelessly over the backs of chairs were puzzling and astonishing-looking garments.

In a large gilded cage near the window perched a clumsy green parrot. He blinked stupidly at a young girl in street dress who was exerting herself to make him talk.

In the centre of the room stood Sophie, that thorn in her mistress's side. With hands plunged in the deep pockets of her apron, her white starched cap quivering with each emphatic motion of her grizzled head, she was holding forth, to the evident ennui of the two young women. She was saying:

"Heaven knows I have stood enough in the six years I have been with Mademoiselle; but never such indignities as I have had to endure in the past two weeks at the hands of that man who calls himself a manager! The very first day—and I, good enough to notify him at once of Mademoiselle's flight—he arrives like a lion; I tell you, like a lion. He insists upon knowing Mademoiselle's whereabouts. How can I tell him any more than the statue out there in the square? He calls me a liar! Me, me—a liar! He declares he is ruined. The public will not stand La Petite Gilberta in the role which Mademoiselle has made so famous—La Petite Gilberta, who dances like a jointed wooden figure and sings like a *traînée* of a *café chantant*. If I were to tell La Gilberta that, as I easily might, I guarantee it would not be well for the few straggling hairs which he has left on that miserable head of his!

"What could he do? He was obliged to inform the public that Mademoiselle was ill; and then began my real torment! Answering this one and that one with their cards, their flowers, their dainties in covered dishes! which, I must admit, saved Florine and me much cooking. And all the while having to tell them that the physician had advised for Mademoiselle a rest of two weeks at some watering-place, the name of which I had forgotten!"

Adrienne had been contemplating old Sophie with quizzical, half-closed eyes, and pelting her with hot-house roses which lay in her lap, and which she nipped off short from their graceful stems for that purpose. Each rose struck Sophie full in the face; but they did not disconcert her or once stem the torrent of her talk.

"Oh, Adrienne!" entreated the young girl at the parrot's cage. "Make her hush; please do something. How can you ever expect Zozo to talk? A dozen times he has been on the point of saying something! I tell you, she stupefies him with her chatter."

"My good Sophie," remarked Adrienne, not changing her attitude, "you see the roses are all used up. But I assure you, anything at hand goes," carelessly picking up a book from the table beside her. "What is this? Mons. Zola! Now I warn you, Sophie, the weightiness, the heaviness of Mons. Zola are such that they cannot fail to prostrate you; thankful you may be if they leave you with energy to regain your feet."

"Mademoiselle's pleasantries are all very well; but if I am to be shown the door for it—if I am to be crippled for it—I shall say that I think Mademoiselle is a woman without conscience and without heart. To torture a man as she does! A man? No, an angel!

"Each day he has come with sad visage and drooping mien. 'No news, Sophie?'

" 'None, Monsieur Henri.' 'Have you no idea where she has gone?' 'Not any more than the statue in the square, Monsieur.' 'Is it perhaps possible that she may not return at all?' with his face blanching like that curtain.

"I assure him you will be back at the end of the fortnight. I entreat him to have patience. He drags himself, *désolé*, about the room, picking up Mademoiselle's fan, her gloves, her music, and turning them over and over in his hands. Mademoiselle's slipper, which she took off to throw at me in the impatience of her departure, and which I purposely left lying where it fell on the chiffonier—he kissed it—I saw him do it—and thrust it into his pocket, thinking himself unobserved.

"The same song each day. I beg him to eat a little good soup which I have prepared. 'I cannot eat, my dear Sophie.' The other night he came and stood long gazing out of the window at the stars. When he turned he was wiping his eyes; they were red. He said he had been riding in the dust, which had inflamed them. But I knew better; he had been crying.

"*Ma foi!* in his place I would snap my finger at such cruelty. I would go out and amuse myself. What is the use of being young!"

Adrienne arose with a laugh. She went and seizing old Sophie by the shoulders shook her till the white cap wobbled on her head.

"What is the use of all this litany, my good Sophie? Year after year the same! Have you forgotten that I have come a long, dusty journey by rail, and that I am perishing of hunger and thirst? Bring us a bottle of Château Yquem and a biscuit and my box of cigarettes." Sophie had freed herself, and was retreating toward the door. "And, Sophie! If Monsieur Henri is still waiting, tell him to come up."

It was precisely a year later. The spring had come again, and Paris was intoxicated.

Old Sophie sat in her kitchen discoursing to a neighbor who had come in to borrow some trifling kitchen utensil from the old *bonne*.

"You know, Rosalie, I begin to believe it is an attack of lunacy which seizes her once a year. I wouldn't say it to everyone, but with you I know it will go no further. She ought to be treated for it; a physician should be consulted; it is not well to neglect such things and let them run on.

"It came this morning like a thunder clap. As I am sitting here, there had been no thought or mention of a journey. The baker had come into the kitchen—you know what a gallant he is—with always a girl in his eye. He laid the bread down upon the table and beside it a bunch of lilacs. I didn't know they had bloomed yet. 'For Mam'selle Florine, with my regards,' he said with his foolish simper.

"Now, you know I was not going to call Florine from her work in order to present her the baker's flowers. All the same, it would not do to let them wither. I went with them in my hand into the dining room to get a majolica pitcher which I had put away in the closet there, on an upper shelf, because the handle was broken. Mademoiselle, who rises early, had just come from her bath, and was crossing the hall that opens into the dining room. Just as she was, in her white *peignoir*, she thrust her head into the dining room, snuffling the air and exclaiming, 'What do I smell?'

"She espied the flowers in my hand and pounced upon them like a cat upon a mouse. She held them up to her, burying her face in them for the longest time, only uttering a long 'Ah!'

"Sophie, I am going away. Get out the little black trunk; a few of the plainest garments I have; my brown dress that I have not yet worn."

" 'But, Mademoiselle,' I protested, 'you forget that you have ordered a breakfast of a hundred francs for tomorrow.'

" 'Shut up!' she cried, stamping her foot.

" 'You forget how the manager will rave,' I persisted, 'and vilify me. And you will go like that without a word of adieu to Monsieur Paul, who is an angel if ever one trod the earth.'

"I tell you, Rosalie, her eyes flamed.

" 'Do as I tell you this instant,' she exclaimed, 'or I will strangle you—with your Monsieur Paul and your manager and your hundred francs!' "

"Yes," affirmed Rosalie, "it is insanity. I had a cousin seized in the same way one morning, when she smelled calf's liver frying with onions. Before night it took two men to hold her."

"I could well see it was insanity, my dear Rosalie, and I uttered not another word as I feared for my life. I simply obeyed her every command in silence. And now—whiff, she is gone! God knows where. But between us, Rosalie—I wouldn't say it to Florine—but I believe it is for no good. I, in Monsieur Paul's place, should have her watched. I would put a detective upon her track.

"Now I am going to close up; barricade the entire establishment. Monsieur Paul, the manager, visitors, all—all may ring and knock and shout themselves hoarse. I am tired of it all. To be vilified and called a liar—at my age, Rosalie!"

Adrienne left her trunk at the small railway station, as the old cabriolet was not at the moment available; and she gladly walked the mile or two of pleasant roadway which led to the convent. How infinitely calm, peaceful, penetrating was the charm of the verdant, undulating country spreading out on all sides of her! She walked along the clear smooth road, twirling her parasol; humming a gay tune; nipping here and there a bud or a waxlike leaf from the hedges along the way; and all the while drinking deep draughts of complacency and content.

She stopped, as she had always done, to pluck lilacs in her path.

As she approached the convent she fancied that a whitecapped face had glanced fleetingly from a window; but she must have been mistaken. Evidently she had not been seen, and this time would take them by surprise. She smiled to think how Sister Agathe would utter a little joyous cry of amazement, and in fancy she already felt the warmth and tenderness of the nun's embrace. And how Sister Marceline and the others would laugh, and make game of her puffed sleeves! For puffed sleeves had come into fashion since last year; and the vagaries of fashion always afforded infinite merriment to the nuns. No, they surely had not seen her.

She ascended lightly the stone steps and rang the bell. She could hear the sharp metallic sound reverberate through the halls. Before its last note had died away the door was opened very slightly, very cautiously by a lay sister who stood there with downcast eyes and flaming cheeks. Through the narrow opening she thrust forward toward Adrienne a package and a letter, saying, in confused tones: "By order of our Mother Superior." After which she closed the door hastily and turned the heavy key in the great lock.

Adrienne remained stunned. She could not gather her faculties to grasp the meaning of this singular reception. The lilacs fell from her arms to the stone portico on which she was standing. She turned the note and the parcel stupidly over in her hands, instinctively dreading what their contents might disclose.

The outlines of the crucifix were plainly to be felt through the wrapper of the bundle, and she guessed, without having courage to assure herself, that the jeweled necklace and the altar cloth accompanied it.

Leaning against the heavy oaken door for support, Adrienne opened the letter. She did not seem to read the few bitter reproachful lines word by word—the lines that banished her forever from this haven of peace, where her soul was wont to come and refresh itself. They imprinted themselves as a whole upon her brain, in all their seeming cruelty—she did not dare to say injustice.

There was no anger in her heart; that would doubtless possess her later, when her nimble intelligence would begin to seek out the origin of this treacherous turn. Now, there was only room for tears. She leaned her forehead against the heavy oaken panel of the door and wept with the abandonment of a little child.

She descended the steps with a nerveless and dragging tread. Once as she was walking away, she turned to look back at the imposing façade of the convent, hoping to see a familiar face, or a hand, even, giving a faint token that she was still cherished by some one faithful heart. But she saw only the polished windows looking down at her like so many cold and glittering and reproachful eyes.

In the little white room above the chapel, a woman knelt beside the bed on which Adrienne had slept. Her face was pressed deep in the pillow in her efforts to smother the sobs that convulsed her frame. It was Sister Agathe.

After a short while, a lay sister came out of the door with a broom, and swept away the lilac blossoms which Adrienne had let fall upon the portico.

Regret

Mamzelle Aurélie possessed a good strong figure, ruddy cheeks, hair that was changing from brown to gray, and a determined eye. She wore a man's hat about the farm, and an old blue army overcoat when it was cold, and sometimes topboots.

Mamzelle Aurélie had never thought of marrying. She had never been in love. At the age of twenty she had received a proposal, which she had promptly declined, and at the age of fifty she had not yet lived to regret it.

So she was quite alone in the world, except for her dog Ponto, and the negroes who lived in her cabins and worked her crops, and the fowls, a few cows, a couple of mules, her gun (with which she shot chicken-hawks), and her religion.

One morning Mamzelle Aurélie stood upon her gallery, contemplating, with arms akimbo, a small band of very small children who, to all intents and purposes, might have fallen from the clouds, so unexpected and bewildering was their coming, and so unwelcome. They were the children of her nearest neighbor, Odile, who was not such a near neighbor, after all.

The young woman had appeared but five minutes before, accompanied by these four children. In her arms she carried little Elodie; she dragged Ti Nomme by an unwilling hand; while Marcéline and Marcélette followed with irresolute steps.

Her face was red and disfigured from tears and excitement. She had been summoned to a neighboring parish by the dangerous illness of her mother; her husband was away in Texas—it seemed to her a million miles away; and Valsin was waiting with the mule-cart to drive her to the station.

"It's no question, Mamzelle Aurélie; you jus' got to keep those young-sters fo' me tell I come back. Dieu sait, I would n' botha you with 'em if it was any otha way to do! Make 'em mine you, Mamzelle Aurélie; don' spare 'em. Me, there, I'm half crazy between the chil'ren, an' Léon not home, an' maybe not even to fine po' maman alive encore!"—a harrowing possibility which drove Odile to take a final hasty and con-vulsive leave of her disconsolate family.

She left them crowded into the narrow strip of shade on the porch of the long, low house; the white sunlight was beating in on the white old boards; some chickens were scratching in the grass at the foot of the steps, and one had boldly mounted, and was stepping heavily, solemnly, and aimlessly across the gallery. There was a pleasant odor of pinks in the air, and the sound of negroes' laughter was coming across the flowering cotton-field.

Mamzelle Aurélie stood contemplating the children. She looked with a critical eye upon Marcéline, who had been left staggering beneath the weight of the chubby Elodie. She surveyed with the same calculating air Marcélette mingling her silent tears with the audible grief and rebellion of Ti Nomme. During those few contemplative moments she was collecting herself, determining upon a line of action which should be identical with a line of duty. She began by feeding them.

If Mamzelle Aurélie's responsibilities might have begun and ended there, they could easily have been dismissed; for her larder was amply provided against an emergency of this nature. But little children are not little pigs; they require and demand attentions which were wholly un-expected by Mamzelle Aurélie, and which she was ill prepared to give.

She was, indeed, very inapt in her management of Odile's children during the first few days. How could she know that Marcélette always wept when spoken to in a loud and commanding tone of voice? It was a peculiarity of Marcélette's. She became acquainted with Ti Nomme's passion for flowers only when he had plucked all the choicest gardenias and pinks for the apparent purpose of critically studying their botanical construction.

" 'Tain't enough to tell 'im, Mamzelle Aurélie," Marcéline instructed her; "you got to tie 'im in a chair. It's w'at maman all time do w'en he's bad: she tie 'im in a chair." The chair in which Mamzelle Aurélie tied Ti Nomme was roomy and comfortable, and he seized the opportunity to take a nap in it, the afternoon being warm.

At night, when she ordered them one and all to bed as she would have shooed the chickens into the hen-house, they stayed uncomprehending before her. What about the little white nightgowns that had to be taken from the pillow-slip in which they were brought over, and shaken by some strong hand till they snapped like ox-whips? What about the tub of water which had to be brought and set in the middle of the floor, in which the little tired, dusty, sunbrowned feet had every one to be washed sweet and clean? And it made Marcéline and Marcélette laugh merrily —the idea that Mamzelle Aurélie should for a moment have believed that Ti Nomme could fall asleep without being told the story of *Croquemitaine* or *Loup-garou*, or both; or that Elodie could fall asleep at all without being rocked and sung to.

"I tell you, Aunt Ruby," Mamzelle Aurélie informed her cook in confidence; "me, I'd rather manage a dozen plantation' than fo' chil'ren. It's terrassent! Bonté! Don't talk to me about chil'ren!"

" 'Tain' ispected sich as you would know airy thing 'bout 'em, Mamzelle Aurélie. I see dat plainly yistiddy w'en I spy dat li'le chile playin' wid yo' baskit o' keys. You don' know dat makes chillun grow up hardheaded, to play wid keys? Des like it make 'em teeth hard to look in a lookin'-glass. Them's the things you got to know in the raisin' an' manigement o' chillun."

Mamzelle Aurélie certainly did not pretend or aspire to such subtle and far-reaching knowledge on the subject as Aunt Ruby possessed, who had "raised five an' bared (buried) six" in her day. She was glad enough to learn a few little mother-tricks to serve the moment's need.

Ti Nomme's sticky fingers compelled her to unearth white aprons that she had not worn for years, and she had to accustom herself to his moist kisses—the expressions of an affectionate and exuberant nature. She got down her sewing-basket, which she seldom used, from the top shelf of the armoire, and placed it within the ready and easy reach which torn slips and buttonless waists demanded. It took her some days to become accustomed to the laughing, the crying, the chattering that echoed through the house and around it all day long. And it was not the first or the second night that she could sleep comfortably with little Elodie's hot, plump body pressed close against her, and the little one's warm breath beating her cheek like the fanning of a bird's wing.

But at the end of two weeks Mamzelle Aurélie had grown quite used to these things, and she no longer complained.

It was also at the end of two weeks that Mamzelle Aurélie, one evening, looking away toward the crib where the cattle were being fed, saw Valsin's blue cart turning the bend of the road. Odile sat beside the mulatto, upright and alert. As they drew near, the young woman's beaming face indicated that her homecoming was a happy one.

But this coming, unannounced and unexpected, threw Mamzelle Aurélie into a flutter that was almost agitation. The children had to be gathered. Where was Ti Nomme? Yonder in the shed, putting an edge on his knife at the grindstone. And Marcéline and Marcélette? Cutting and fashioning doll-rags in the corner of the gallery. As for Elodie, she was safe enough in Mamzelle Aurélie's arms; and she had screamed with delight at sight of the familiar blue cart which was bringing her mother back to her.

The excitement was all over, and they were gone. How still it was when they were gone! Mamzelle Aurélie stood upon the gallery, looking and listening. She could no longer see the cart; the red sunset and the blue-gray twilight had together flung a purple mist across the fields and road that hid it from her view. She could no longer hear the wheezing and creaking of its wheels. But she could still faintly hear the shrill, glad voices of the children.

She turned into the house. There was much work awaiting her, for the children had left a sad disorder behind them; but she did not at once set about the task of righting it. Mamzelle Aurélie seated herself beside the table. She gave one slow glance through the room, into which the evening shadows were creeping and deepening around her solitary figure. She let her head fall down upon her bended arm, and began to cry. Oh, but she cried! Not softly, as women often do. She cried like a man, with sobs that seemed to tear her very soul. She did not notice Ponto licking her hand.

The Kiss

It was still quite light out of doors, but inside with the curtains drawn and the smouldering fire sending out a dim, uncertain glow, the room was full of deep shadows.

Brantain sat in one of these shadows; it had overtaken him and he did not mind. The obscurity lent him courage to keep his eyes fastened as ardently as he liked upon the girl who sat in the firelight.

She was very handsome, with a certain fine, rich coloring that belongs to the healthy brune type. She was quite composed, as she idly stroked the satiny coat of the cat that lay curled in her lap, and she occasionally sent a slow glance into the shadow where her companion sat. They were talking low, of indifferent things which plainly were not the things that occupied their thoughts. She knew that he loved her—a frank, blustering fellow without guile enough to conceal his feelings, and no desire to do so. For two weeks past he had sought her society eagerly and persistently. She was confidently waiting for him to declare himself and she meant to accept him. The rather insignificant and unattractive Brantain was enormously rich; and she liked and required the entourage which wealth could give her.

During one of the pauses between their talk of the last tea and the next reception the door opened and a young man entered whom Brantain knew quite well. The girl turned her face toward him. A stride or two brought him to her side, and bending over her chair—before she could suspect his intention, for she did not realize that he had not seen her visitor—he pressed an ardent, lingering kiss upon her lips.

Brantain slowly arose; so did the girl arise, but quickly, and the newcomer stood between them, a little amusement and some defiance struggling with the confusion in his face.

"I believe," stammered Brantain, "I see that I have stayed too long. I—I had no idea—that is, I must wish you good-by." He was clutching his hat with both hands, and probably did not perceive that she was extending her hand to him, her presence of mind had not completely deserted her; but she could not have trusted herself to speak.

"Hang me if I saw him sitting there, Nattie! I know it's deuced awkward for you. But I hope you'll forgive me this once—this very first break. Why, what's the matter?"

"Don't touch me; don't come near me," she returned angrily. "What do you mean by entering the house without ringing?"

"I came in with your brother, as I often do," he answered coldly, in self-justification. "We came in the side way. He went upstairs and I came in here hoping to find you. The explanation is simple enough and ought to satisfy you that the misadventure was unavoidable. But do say that you forgive me, Nathalie," he entreated, softening.

"Forgive you! You don't know what you are talking about. Let me pass. It depends upon—a good deal whether I ever forgive you."

At that next reception which she and Brantain had been talking about she approached the young man with a delicious frankness of manner when she saw him there.

"Will you let me speak to you a moment or two, Mr. Brantain?" she asked with an engaging but perturbed smile. He seemed extremely unhappy; but when she took his arm and walked away with him, seeking a retired corner, a ray of hope mingled with the almost comical misery of his expression. She was apparently very outspoken.

"Perhaps I should not have sought this interview, Mr. Brantain; but —but, oh, I have been very uncomfortable, almost miserable since that little encounter the other afternoon. When I thought how you might have misinterpreted it, and believed things"—hope was plainly gaining the ascendancy over misery in Brantain's round, guileless face—"of course, I know it is nothing to you, but for my own sake I do want you to understand that Mr. Harvy is an intimate friend of long standing. Why, we have always been like cousins—like brother and sister, I may say. He is my brother's most intimate associate and often fancies that he is entitled to the same privileges as the family. Oh, I know it is absurd, uncalled for, to tell you this; undignified even," she was almost weeping, "but it makes so much difference to me what you think of—of me." Her voice had grown very low and agitated. The misery had all disappeared from Brantain's face.

"Then you do really care what I think, Miss Nathalie? May I call you Miss Nathalie?" They turned into a long, dim corridor that was lined on either side with tall, graceful plants. They walked slowly to the very end of it. When they turned to retrace their steps Brantain's face was radiant and hers was triumphant.

Harvy was among the guests at the wedding; and he sought her out in a rare moment when she stood alone.

"Your husband," he said, smiling, "has sent me over to kiss you."

A quick blush suffused her face and round polished throat. "I suppose it's natural for a man to feel and act generously on an occasion of this kind. He tells me he doesn't want his marriage to interrupt wholly that pleasant intimacy which has existed between you and me. I don't know what you've been telling him," with an insolent smile, "but he has sent me here to kiss you."

She felt like a chess player who, by the clever handling of his pieces, sees the game taking the course intended. Her eyes were bright and tender with a smile as they glanced up into his; and her lips looked hungry for the kiss which they invited.

"But, you know," he went on quietly, "I didn't tell him so, it would have seemed ungrateful, but I can tell you. I've stopped kissing women; it's dangerous."

Well, she had Brantain and his million left. A person can't have everything in this world; and it was a little unreasonable of her to expect it.

Athénaïse

I

Athénaïse went away in the morning to make a visit to her parents, ten miles back on rigolet de Bon Dieu. She did not return in the evening, and Cazeau, her husband, fretted not a little. He did not worry much about Athénaïse, who, he suspected, was resting only too content in the bosom of her family; his chief solicitude was manifestly for the pony she had ridden. He felt sure those "lazy pigs," her brothers, were capable of neglecting it seriously. This misgiving Cazeau communicated to his servant, old Félicité, who waited upon him at supper.

His voice was low pitched, and even softer than Félicité's. He was tall, sinewy, swarthy, and altogether severe looking. His thick black hair waved, and it gleamed like the breast of a crow. The sweep of his mustache, which was not so black, outlined the broad contour of the mouth. Beneath the under lip grew a small tuft which he was much given to twisting, and which he permitted to grow, apparently for no other purpose. Cazeau's eyes were dark blue, narrow and overshadowed. His hands were coarse and stiff from close acquaintance with farming tools and implements, and he handled his fork and knife clumsily. But he was distinguished looking, and succeeded in commanding a good deal of respect, and even fear sometimes.

He ate his supper alone, by the light of a single coal-oil lamp that but faintly illuminated the big room, with its bare floor and huge rafters, and its heavy pieces of furniture that loomed dimly in the gloom of the apartment. Félicité, ministering to his wants, hovered about the table like a little, bent, restless shadow.

She served him with a dish of sunfish fried crisp and brown. There was nothing else set before him beside the bread and butter and the bottle of red wine which she locked carefully in the buffet after he had poured his second glass. She was occupied with her mistress's absence, and kept reverting to it after he had expressed his solicitude about the pony.

"Dat beat me! on'y marry two mont', an' got de head turn' a'ready to go 'broad. C'est pas Chrétien, tenez!"

Cazeau shrugged his shoulders for answer, after he had drained his glass and pushed aside his plate. Félicité's opinion of the unchristianlike behavior of his wife in leaving him thus alone after two months of marriage weighed little with him. He was used to solitude, and did not mind a day or a night or two of it. He had lived alone ten years, since his first wife died, and Félicité might have known better than to suppose that he cared. He told her she was a fool. It sounded like a compliment in his modulated, caressing voice. She grumbled to herself as she set about clearing the table, and Cazeau arose and walked outside on the gallery; his spur, which he had not removed upon entering the house, jangled at every step.

The night was beginning to deepen, and to gather black about the clusters of trees and shrubs that were grouped in the yard. In the beam of light from the open kitchen door a black boy stood feeding a brace of snarling, hungry dogs; further away, on the steps of a cabin, some one was playing the accordion; and in still another direction a little negro baby was crying lustily. Cazeau walked around to the front of the house, which was square, squat and one-story.

A belated wagon was driving in at the gate, and the impatient driver was swearing hoarsely at his jaded oxen. Félicité stepped out on the gallery, glass and polishing towel in hand, to investigate, and to wonder, too, who could be singing out on the river. It was a party of young people paddling around, waiting for the moon to rise, and they were singing Juanita, their voices coming tempered and melodious through the distance and the night.

Cazeau's horse was waiting, saddled, ready to be mounted, for Cazeau had many things to attend to before bed-time; so many things that there was not left to him a moment in which to think of Athénaïse. He felt her absence, though, like a dull, insistent pain.

However, before he slept that night he was visited by the thought of her, and by a vision of her fair young face with its drooping lips and sullen and averted eyes. The marriage had been a blunder; he had only to look into her eyes to feel that, to discover her growing aversion. But it was a thing not by any possibility to be undone. He was quite prepared to make the best of it, and expected no less than a like effort on her part. The less she revisited the rigolet, the better. He would find means to keep her at home hereafter.

These unpleasant reflections kept Cazeau awake far into the night, notwithstanding the craving of his whole body for rest and sleep. The moon was shining, and its pale effulgence reached dimly into the room, and with it a touch of the cool breath of the spring night. There was an unusual stillness abroad; no sound to be heard save the distant, tireless, plaintive notes of the accordion.

II

Athénaïse did not return the following day, even though her husband sent her word to do so by her brother, Montéclin, who passed on his way to the village early in the morning.

On the third day Cazeau saddled his horse and went himself in search of her. She had sent no word, no message, explaining her absence, and he felt that he had good cause to be offended. It was rather awkward to have to leave his work, even though late in the afternoon,—Cazeau had always so much to do; but among the many urgent calls upon him, the task of bringing his wife back to a sense of her duty seemed to him for the moment paramount.

The Michés, Athénaïse's parents, lived on the old Gotrain place. It did not belong to them; they were "running" it for a merchant in Alexandria. The house was far too big for their use. One of the lower rooms served for the storing of wood and tools; the person "occupying" the place before Miché having pulled up the flooring in despair of being able to patch it. Upstairs, the rooms were so large, so bare, that they offered a constant temptation to lovers of the dance, whose importunities Madame Miché was accustomed to meet with amiable indulgence. A dance at Miché's and a plate of Madame Miché's gumbo filé at midnight were pleasures not to be neglected or despised, unless by such serious souls as Cazeau.

Long before Cazeau reached the house his approach had been observed, for there was nothing to obstruct the view of the outer road; vegetation was not yet abundantly advanced, and there was but a patchy, straggling stand of cotton and corn in Miché's field.

Madame Miché, who had been seated on the gallery in a rocking-chair, stood up to greet him as he drew near. She was short and fat, and wore a black skirt and loose muslin sack fastened at the throat with a hair brooch. Her own hair, brown and glossy, showed but a few threads of silver. Her round pink face was cheery, and her eyes were bright and good humored. But she was plainly perturbed and ill at ease as Cazeau advanced.

Montéclin, who was there too, was not ill at ease, and made no attempt to disguise the dislike with which his brother-in-law inspired him. He was a slim, wiry fellow of twenty-five, short of stature like his mother, and resembling her in feature. He was in shirt-sleeves, half leaning, half sitting, on the insecure railing of the gallery, and fanning himself with his broad-rimmed felt hat.

"Cochon!" he muttered under his breath as Cazeau mounted the stairs,—"sacré cochon!"

"Cochon" had sufficiently characterized the man who had once on a time declined to lend Montéclin money. But when this same man had had the presumption to propose marriage to his well-beloved sister, Athénaïse, and the honor to be accepted by her, Montéclin felt that a qualifying epithet was needed fully to express his estimate of Cazeau.

Miché and his oldest son were absent. They both esteemed Cazeau highly, and talked much of his qualities of head and heart, and thought much of his excellent standing with city merchants.

Athénaïse had shut herself up in her room. Cazeau had seen her rise and enter the house at perceiving him. He was a good deal mystified, but no one could have guessed it when he shook hands with Madame Miché. He had only nodded to Montéclin, with a muttered "Comment ça va?"

"Tiens! something tole me you were coming to-day!" exclaimed Madame Miché, with a little blustering appearance of being cordial and at ease, as she offered Cazeau a chair.

He ventured a short laugh as he seated himself.

"You know, nothing would do," she went on, with much gesture of her small, plump hands, "nothing would do but Athénaïse mus' stay las' night fo' a li'le dance. The boys wouldn' year to their sister leaving."

Cazeau shrugged his shoulders significantly, telling as plainly as words that he knew nothing about it.

"Comment! Montéclin didn' tell you we were going to keep Athénaïse?" Montéclin had evidently told nothing.

"An' how about the night befo'," questioned Cazeau, "an' las' night? It isn't possible you dance every night out yere on the Bon Dieu!"

Madame Miché laughed, with amiable appreciation of the sarcasm; and turning to her son, "Montéclin, my boy, go tell yo' sister that Monsieur Cazeau is yere."

Montéclin did not stir except to shift his position and settle himself more securely on the railing.

"Did you year me, Montéclin?"

"Oh yes, I yeard you plain enough," responded her son, "but you know as well as me it's no use to tell 'Thénaïse anything. You been talkin' to her yo'se'f since Monday; an' pa's preached himse'f hoa'se on the subject; an' you even had uncle Achille down yere yesterday to reason with her. W'en 'Thénaïse said she wasn' goin' to set her foot back in Cazeau's house, she meant it."

This speech, which Montéclin delivered with thorough unconcern, threw his mother into a condition of painful but dumb embarrassment. It brought two fiery red spots to Cazeau's cheeks, and for the space of a moment he looked wicked.

What Montéclin had spoken was quite true, though his taste in the manner and choice of time and place in saying it were not of the best. Athénaïse, upon the first day of her arrival, had announced that she came to stay, having no intention of returning under Cazeau's roof. The announcement had scattered consternation, as she knew it would. She had been implored, scolded, entreated, stormed at, until she felt herself like a dragging sail that all the winds of heaven had beaten upon. Why in the name of God had she married Cazeau? Her father had lashed her with the question a dozen times. Why indeed? It was difficult now for her to understand why, unless because she supposed it was customary for girls to marry when the right opportunity came. Cazeau, she knew, would make life more comfortable for her; and again, she had liked him, and had even been rather flustered when he pressed her hands and kissed them, and kissed her lips and cheeks and eyes, when she accepted him.

Montéclin himself had taken her aside to talk the thing over. The turn of affairs was delighting him.

"Come, now, 'Thénaïse, you mus' explain to me all about it, so we can settle on a good cause, an' secu' a separation fo' you. Has he been mistreating an' abusing you, the sacré cochon?" They were alone together in her room, whither she had taken refuge from the angry domestic elements.

107

"You please to reserve yo' disgusting expressions, Montéclin. No, he has not abused me in any way that I can think."

"Does he drink? Come 'Thénaïse, think well over it. Does he ever get drunk?"

"Drunk! Oh, mercy, no,—Cazeau never gets drunk."

"I see; it's jus' simply you feel like me; you hate him."

"No, I don't hate him," she returned reflectively; adding with a sudden impulse, "It's jus' being married that I detes' an' despise. I hate being Mrs. Cazeau, an' would want to be Athénaïse Miché again. I can't stan' to live with a man; to have him always there; his coats an' pantaloons hanging in my room; his ugly bare feet—washing them in my tub, befo' my very eyes, ugh!" She shuddered with recollections, and resumed, with a sigh that was almost a sob: "Mon Dieu, mon Dieu! Sister Marie Angélique knew w'at she was saying; she knew me better than myse'f w'en she said God had sent me a vocation an' I was turning deaf ears. W'en I think of a blessed life in the convent, at peace! Oh, w'at was I dreaming of!" and then the tears came.

Montéclin felt disconcerted and greatly disappointed at having obtained evidence that would carry no weight with a court of justice. The day had not come when a young woman might ask the court's permission to return to her mamma on the sweeping ground of a constitutional disinclination for marriage. But if there was no way of untying this Gordian knot of marriage, there was surely a way of cutting it.

"Well, 'Thénaïse, I'm mighty durn sorry you got no better groun's 'an w'at you say. But you can count on me to stan' by you w'atever you do. God knows I don' blame you fo' not wantin' to live with Cazeau."

And now there was Cazeau himself, with the red spots flaming in his swarthy cheeks, looking and feeling as if he wanted to thrash Montéclin into some semblance of decency. He arose abruptly, and approaching the room which he had seen his wife enter, thrust open the door after a hasty preliminary knock. Athénaïse, who was standing erect at a far window, turned at his entrance.

She appeared neither angry nor frightened, but thoroughly unhappy, with an appeal in her soft dark eyes and a tremor on her lips that seemed to him expressions of unjust reproach, that wounded and maddened him at once. But whatever he might feel, Cazeau knew only one way to act toward a woman.

"Athénaïse, you are not ready?" he asked in his quiet tones. "It's getting late; we havn' any time to lose."

She knew that Montéclin had spoken out, and she had hoped for a wordy interview, a stormy scene, in which she might have held her own as she had held it for the past three days against her family, with Montéclin's aid. But she had no weapon with which to combat subtlety. Her husband's looks, his tones, his mere presence, brought to her a sudden sense of hopelessness, an instinctive realization of the futility of rebellion against a social and sacred institution.

Cazeau said nothing further, but stood waiting in the doorway. Madame Miché had walked to the far end of the gallery, and pretended to be occupied with having a chicken driven from her parterre. Montéclin stood by, exasperated, fuming, ready to burst out.

Athénaïse went and reached for her riding skirt that hung against the wall. She was rather tall, with a figure which, though not robust, seemed perfect in its fine proportions. "La fille de son père," she was often called, which was a great compliment to Miché. Her brown hair was brushed all fluffily back from her temples and low forehead, and about her features and expression lurked a softness, a prettiness, a dewiness, that were perhaps too childlike, that savored of immaturity.

She slipped the riding-skirt, which was of black alpaca, over her head, and with impatient fingers hooked it at the waist over her pink linen-lawn. Then she fastened on her white sunbonnet and reached for her gloves on the mantelpiece.

"If you don' wan' to go, you know w'at you got to do, 'Thénaïse," fumed Montéclin. "You don' set yo' feet back on Cane River, by God, unless you want to,—not w'ile I'm alive."

Cazeau looked at him as if he were a monkey whose antics fell short of being amusing.

Athénaïse still made no reply, said not a word. She walked rapidly past her husband, past her brother; bidding good-bye to no one, not even to her mother. She descended the stairs, and without assistance from any one mounted the pony, which Cazeau had ordered to be saddled upon his arrival. In this way she obtained a fair start of her husband, whose departure was far more leisurely, and for the greater part of the way she managed to keep an appreciable gap between them. She rode almost madly at first, with the wind inflating her skirt balloon-like about her knees, and her sunbonnet falling back between her shoulders.

At no time did Cazeau make an effort to overtake her until traversing an old fallow meadow that was level and hard as a table. The sight of a great solitary oak-tree, with its seemingly immutable outlines, that had been a landmark for ages—or was it the odor of elderberry stealing up from the gully to the south? or what was it that brought vividly back to Cazeau, by some association of ideas, a scene of many years ago? He had passed that old live-oak hundreds of times, but it was only now that the memory of one day came back to him. He was a very small boy that day, seated before his father on horse-back. They were proceeding slowly, and Black Gabe was moving on before them at a little dog-trot. Black Gabe had run away, and had been discovered back in the Gotrain swamp. They had halted beneath this big oak to enable the negro to take breath; for Cazeau's father was a kind and considerate master, and every one had agreed at the time that Black Gabe was a fool, a great idiot indeed, for wanting to run away from him.

The whole impression was for some reason hideous, and to dispel it Cazeau spurred his horse to a swift gallop. Overtaking his wife, he rode the remainder of the way at her side in silence.

It was late when they reached home. Félicité was standing on the grassy edge of the road, in the moonlight, waiting for them.

Cazeau once more ate his supper alone; for Athénaïse went to her room, and there she was crying again.

III

Athénaïse was not one to accept the inevitable with patient resignation, a talent born in the souls of many women; neither was she the one to accept it with philosophical resignation, like her husband. Her sensibilities were alive and keen and responsive. She met the pleasurable things of life with frank, open appreciation, and against distasteful conditions she rebelled. Dissimulation was as foreign to her nature as guile to the breast of a babe, and her rebellious outbreaks, by no means rare, had hitherto been quite open and aboveboard. People often said that Athénaïse would know her own mind some day, which was equivalent to saying that she was at present unacquainted with it. If she ever came to such knowledge, it would be by no intellectual research, by no subtle analyses or tracing the motives of actions to their source. It would come to her as the song to the bird, the perfume and color to the flower.

Her parents had hoped—not without reason and justice—that marriage would bring the poise, the desirable pose, so glaringly lacking in Athénaïse's character. Marriage they knew to be a wonderful and powerful agent in the development and formation of a woman's character; they had seen its effect too often to doubt it.

"And if this marriage does nothing else," exclaimed Miché in an outburst of sudden exasperaton, "it will rid us of Athénaïse; for I am at the end of my patience with her! You have never had the firmness to manage her,"—he was speaking to his wife,—"I have not had the time, the leisure, to devote to her training; and what good we might have accomplished, that maudit Montéclin—Well, Cazeau is the one! It takes just such a steady hand to guide a disposition like Athénaïse's, a master hand, a strong will that compels obedience."

And now, when they had hoped for so much, here was Athénaïse, with gathered and fierce vehemence, beside which her former outbursts appeared mild, declaring that she would not, and she would not, and she would not continue to enact the role of wife to Cazeau. If she had had a reason! as Madame Miché lamented; but it could not be discovered that she had any sane one. He had never scolded, or called names, or deprived her of comforts, or been guilty of any of the many reprehensible acts commonly attributed to objectionable husbands. He did not slight nor neglect her. Indeed, Cazeau's chief offense seemed to be that he loved her, and Athénaïse was not the woman to be loved against her will. She called marriage a trap set for the feet of unwary and unsuspecting girls, and in round, unmeasured terms reproached her mother with treachery and deceit.

"I told you Cazeau was the man," chuckled Miché, when his wife had related the scene that had accompanied and influenced Athénaïse's departure.

Athénaïse again hoped, in the morning, that Cazeau would scold or make some sort of a scene, but he apparently did not dream of it. It was exasperating that he should take her acquiescence so for granted. It is true he had been up and over the fields and across the river and back long before she was out of bed, and he may have been thinking of something else, which was no excuse, which was even in some sense an aggravation. But he did say to her at breakfast, "That brother of yo's, that Montéclin, is unbearable."

"Montéclin? Par exemple!"

Athénaïse, seated opposite to her husband, was attired in a white morning wrapper. She wore a somewhat abused, long face, it is true,— an expression of countenance familiar to some husbands,—but the expression was not sufficiently pronounced to mar the charm of her youthful freshness. She had little heart to eat, only playing with the food before her, and she felt a pang of resentment at her husband's healthy appetite.

"Yes, Montéclin," he reasserted. "He's developed into a firs'-class nuisance; an' you better tell him, Athénaïse,—unless you want me to tell him,—to confine his energies after this to matters that concern him. I have no use fo' him or fo' his interference in w'at regards you an' me alone."

This was said with unusual asperity. It was the little breach that Athenaïse had been watching for, and she charged rapidly: "It's strange, if you detes' Montéclin so heartily, that you would desire to marry his sister." She knew it was a silly thing to say, and was not surprised when he told her so. It gave her a little foothold for further attack, however. "I don't see, anyhow, w'at reason you had to marry me, w'en there were so many others," she complained, as if accusing him of persecution and injury. "There was Marianne running after you fo' the las' five years till it was disgraceful; an' any one of the Dortrand girls would have been glad to marry you. But no, nothing would do; you mus' come out on the rigolet fo' me." Her complaint was pathetic, and at the same time so amusing that Cazeau was forced to smile.

"I can't see w'at the Dortrand girls or Marianne have to do with it," he rejoined; adding, with no trace of amusement, "I married you because I loved you; because you were the woman I wanted to marry, an' the only one. I reckon I tole you that befo'. I thought—of co'se I was a fool fo' taking things fo' granted—but I did think that I might make you happy in making things easier an' mo' comfortable fo' you. I expected—I was even that big a fool—I believed that yo' coming yere to me would be like the sun shining out of the clouds, an' that our days would be like w'at the story-books promise after the wedding. I was mistaken. But I can't imagine w'at induced you to marry me. W'atever it was, I reckon you foun' out you made a mistake, too. I don' see anything to do but make the best of a bad bargain, an' shake han's over it." He had arisen from the table, and, approaching, held out his hand to her. What he had said was commonplace enough, but it was significant, coming from Cazeau, who was not often so unreserved in expressing himself.

Athénaïse ignored the hand held out to her. She was resting her chin in her palm, and kept her eyes fixed moodily upon the table. He rested his hand, that she would not touch, upon her head for an instant, and walked away out of the room.

She heard him giving orders to workmen who had been waiting for him out on the gallery, and she heard him mount his horse and ride away. A hundred things would distract him and engage his attention during the day. She felt that he had perhaps put her and her grievance from his thoughts when he crossed the threshold; whilst she—

Old Félicité was standing there holding a shining tin pail, asking for flour and lard and eggs from the storeroom, and meal for the chicks.

Athénaïse seized the bunch of keys which hung from her belt and flung them at Félicité's feet.

"Tiens! tu vas les garder comme tu as jadis fait. Je ne veux plus de ce train là, moi!"

The old woman stooped and picked up the keys from the floor. It was really all one to her that her mistress returned them to her keeping, and refused to take further account of the ménage.

IV

It seemed now to Athénaïse that Montéclin was the only friend left to her in the world. Her father and mother had turned from her in what appeared to be her hour of need. Her friends laughed at her, and refused to take seriously the hints which she threw out,—feeling her way to discover if marriage were as distasteful to other women as to herself. Montéclin alone understood her. He alone had always been ready to act for her and with her, to comfort and solace her with his sympathy and his support. Her only hope for rescue from her hateful surroundings lay in Montéclin. Of herself she felt powerless to plan, to act, even to conceive a way out of this pitfall into which the whole world seemed to have conspired to thrust her.

She had a great desire to see her brother, and wrote asking him to come to her. But it better suited Montéclin's spirit of adventure to appoint a meeting-place at the turn of the lane, where Athénaïse might appear to be walking leisurely for health and recreation, and where he might seem to be riding along, bent on some errand of business or pleasure.

There had been a shower, a sudden downpour, short as it was sudden, that had laid the dust in the road. It had freshened the pointed leaves of the live-oaks, and brightened up the big fields of cotton on either side of the lane till they seemed carpeted with green, glittering gems.

Athénaïse walked along the grassy edge of the road, lifting her crisp skirts with one hand, and with the other twirling a gay sunshade over her bare head. The scent of the fields after the rain was delicious. She inhaled long breaths of their freshness and perfume, that soothed and quieted her for the moment. There were birds splashing and spluttering in the pools, pluming themselves on the fence-rails, and sending out little sharp cries, twitters, and shrill rhapsodies of delight.

She saw Montéclin approaching from a great distance,—almost as far away as the turn of the woods. But she could not feel sure it was he; it appeared too tall for Montéclin, but that was because he was riding a large horse. She waved her parasol to him; she was so glad to see him. She had never been so glad to see Montéclin before; not even the day when he had taken her out of the convent, against her parents' wishes, because she had expressed a desire to remain there no longer. He seemed to her, as he drew near, the embodiment of kindness, of bravery, of chivalry, even of wisdom; for she had never known Montéclin at a loss to extricate himself from a disagreeable situation.

He dismounted, and, leading his horse by the bridle, started to walk beside her, after he had kissed her affectionately and asked her what she was crying about. She protested that she was not crying, for she was laughing, though drying her eyes at the same time on her handkerchief, rolled in a soft mop for the purpose.

She took Montéclin's arm, and they strolled slowly down the lane; they could not seat themselves for a comfortable chat, as they would have liked, with the grass all sparkling and bristling wet.

Yes, she was quite as wretched as ever, she told him. The week which had gone by since she saw him had in no wise lightened the burden of her discontent. There had even been some additional provocations laid upon her, and she told Montéclin all about them,—about the keys, for instance, which in a fit of temper she had returned to Félicité's keeping; and she told how Cazeau had brought them back to her as if they were something she had accidentally lost, and he had recovered; and how he had said, in that aggravating tone of his, that it was not the custom on Cane river for the negro servants to carry the keys, when there was a mistress at the head of the household.

But Athénaïse could not tell Montéclin anything to increase the disrespect which he already entertained for his brother-in-law; and it was then he unfolded to her a plan which he had conceived and worked out for her deliverance from this galling matrimonial yoke.

It was not a plan which met with instant favor, which she was at once ready to accept, for it involved secrecy and dissimulation, hateful alternatives, both of them. But she was filled with admiration for Montéclin's resources and wonderful talent for contrivance. She accepted the plan; not with the immediate determination to act upon it, rather with the intention to sleep and to dream upon it.

Three days later she wrote to Montéclin that she had abandoned herself to his counsel. Displeasing as it might be to her sense of honesty, it would yet be less trying than to live on with a soul full of bitterness and revolt, as she had done for the past two months.

V

When Cazeau awoke, one morning at his usual very early hour, it was to find the place at his side vacant. This did not surprise him until he discovered that Athénaïse was not in the adjoining room, where he had often found her sleeping in the morning on the lounge. She had perhaps gone out for an early stroll, he reflected, for her jacket and hat were not on the rack where she had hung them the night before. But there were other things absent,—a gown or two from the armoire; and there was a great gap in the piles of lingerie on the shelf; and her traveling-bag was missing, and so were her bits of jewelry from the toilet tray—and Athénaïse was gone!

But the absurdity of going during the night, as if she had been a prisoner, and he the keeper of a dungeon! So much secrecy and mystery, to go sojourning out on the Bon Dieu! Well, the Michés might keep their daughter after this. For the companionship of no woman on earth would he again undergo the humiliating sensation of baseness that had overtaken him in passing the old oak-tree in the fallow meadow.

But a terrible sense of loss overwhelmed Cazeau. It was not new or sudden; he had felt it for weeks growing upon him, and it seemed to culminate with Athénaïse's flight from home. He knew that he could again compel her return as he had done once before,— compel her to return to the shelter of his roof, compel her cold and unwilling submission to his love and passionate transports; but the loss of self-respect seemed to him too dear a price to pay for a wife.

He could not comprehend why she had seemed to prefer him above others; why she had attracted him with eyes, with voice, with a hundred womanly ways, and finally distracted him with love which she seemed, in her timid, maidenly fashion, to return. The great sense of loss came from the realization of having missed a chance for happiness,—a chance that would come his way again only through a miracle. He could not think of himself loving any other woman, and could not think of Athénaïse ever—even at some remote date—caring for him.

He wrote her a letter, in which he disclaimed any further intention of forcing his commands upon her. He did not desire her presence ever again in his home unless she came of her free will, uninfluenced by family or friends; unless she could be the companion he had hoped for in marrying her, and in some measure return affection and respect for the love which he continued and would always continue to feel for her. This letter he sent out to the rigolet by a messenger early in the day. But she was not out on the rigolet, and had not been there.

The family turned instinctively to Montéclin, and almost literally fell upon him for an explanation; he had been absent from home all night. There was much mystification in his answers, and a plain desire to mislead in his assurances of ignorance and innocence.

But with Cazeau there was no doubt or speculation when he accosted the young fellow. "Montéclin, w'at have you done with Athénaïse?" he questioned bluntly. They had met in the open road on horseback, just as Cazeau ascended the river bank before his house.

"W'at have you done to Athénaïse?" returned Montéclin for answer.

"I don't reckon you've considered yo' conduct by any light of decency an' propriety in encouraging yo' sister to such an action, but let me tell you"—

"Voyons! you can let me alone with yo' decency an' morality an' fiddlesticks. I know you mus' 'a' done Athénaïse pretty mean that she can't live with you; an' fo' my part, I'm mighty durn glad she had the spirit to quit you."

"I ain't in the humor to take any notice of yo' impertinence, Montéclin; but let me remine you that Athénaïse is nothing but a chile in character; besides that, she's my wife, an' I hole you responsible fo' her safety an' welfare. If any harm of any description happens to her, I'll strangle you, by God, like a rat, and fling you in Cane river, if I have to hang fo' it!" He had not lifted his voice. The only sign of anger was a savage gleam in his eyes.

"I reckon you better keep yo' big talk fo' the women, Cazeau," replied Montéclin, riding away.

But he went doubly armed after that, and intimated that the precaution was not needless, in view of the threats and menaces that were abroad touching his personal safety.

VI

Athénaïse reached her destination sound of skin and limb, but a good deal flustered, a little frightened, and altogether excited and interested by her unusual experiences.

Her destination was the house of Sylvie, on Dauphine Street, in New Orleans,—a three-story gray brick, standing directly on the banquette, with three broad stone steps leading to the deep front entrance. From the second-story balcony swung a small sign, conveying to passers-by the intelligence that within were "*chambres garnies*."

It was one morning in the last week of April that Athénaïse presented herself at the Dauphine Street house. Sylvie was expecting her, and introduced her at once to her apartment, which was in the second story of the back ell, and accessible by an open, outside gallery. There was a yard below, paved with broad stone flagging; many fragrant flowering shrubs and plants grew in a bed along the side of the opposite wall, and others were distributed about in tubs and green boxes.

It was a plain but large enough room into which Athénaïse was ushered, with matting on the floor, green shades and Nottingham-lace curtains at the windows that looked out on the gallery, and furnished with a cheap walnut suit. But everything looked exquisitely clean, and the whole place smelled of cleanliness.

Athénaïse at once fell into the rocking-chair, with the air of exhaustion and intense relief of one who has come to the end of her troubles. Sylvie, entering behind her, laid the big traveling-bag on the floor and deposited the jacket on the bed.

She was a portly quadroon of fifty or there-about, clad in an ample *volante* of the old-fashioned purple calico so much affected by her class. She wore large golden hoop-earrings, and her hair was combed plainly, with every appearance of effort to smooth out the kinks. She had broad, coarse features, with a nose that turned up, exposing the wide nostrils, and that seemed to emphasize the loftiness and command of her bearing, —a dignity that in the presence of white people assumed a character of respectfulness, but never of obsequiousness. Sylvie believed firmly in maintaining the color line, and would not suffer a white person, even a child, to call her "Madame Sylvie,"—a title which she exacted religiously, however, from those of her own race.

"I hope you be please' wid yo' room, madame," she observed amiably. "Dat's de same room w'at yo' brother, M'sieur Miché, all time like w'en he come to New Orlean'. He well, M'sieur Miché? I receive' his letter las' week, an' dat same day a gent'man want I give 'im dat room. I say, 'No, dat room already ingage'.' Ev-body like dat room on 'count it so quite (quiet). M'sieur Gouvernail, dere in nax' room, you can't pay 'im! He been stay t'ree year' in dat room; but all fix' up fine wid his own furn'ture an' books, 'tel you can't see! I say to 'im plenty time', 'M'sieur Gouvernail, w'y you don't take dat t'ree-story front, now, long it's empty?' He tells me, 'Leave me 'lone, Sylvie; I know a good room w'en I fine it, me.' "

She had been moving slowly and majestically about the apartment, straightening and smoothing down bed and pillows, peering into ewer and basin, evidently casting an eye around to make sure that everything was as it should be.

"I sen' you some fresh water, madame," she offered upon retiring from the room. "An' w'en you want an't'ing, you jus' go out on de gall'ry an' call Pousette: she year you plain,—she right down dere in de kitchen."

Athénaïse was really not so exhausted as she had every reason to be after that interminable and circuitous way by which Montéclin had seen fit to have her conveyed to the city.

Would she ever forget that dark and truly dangerous midnight ride along the "coast" to the mouth of Cane river! There Montéclin had parted with her, after seeing her aboard the St. Louis and Shreveport packet which he knew would pass there before dawn. She had received instructions to disembark at the mouth of Red river, and there transfer to the first south-bound steamer for New Orleans; all of which instructions she had followed implicitly, even to making her way at once to Sylvie's upon her arrival in the city. Montéclin had enjoined secrecy and much caution; the clandestine nature of the affair gave it a savor of adventure which was highly pleasing to him. Eloping with his sister was only a little less engaging than eloping with some one else's sister.

But Montéclin did not do the *grand seigneur* by halves. He had paid Sylvie a whole month in advance for Athénaïse's board and lodging. Part of the sum he had been forced to borrow, it is true, but he was not niggardly.

Athénaïse was to take her meals in the house, which none of the other lodgers did; the one exception being that Mr. Gouvernail was served with breakfast on Sunday mornings.

Sylvie's clientèle came chiefly from the southern parishes; for the most part, people spending but a few days in the city. She prided herself upon the quality and highly respectable character of her patrons, who came and went unobtrusively.

The large parlor opening upon the front balcony was seldom used. Her guests were permitted to entertain in this sanctuary of elegance,— but they never did. She often rented it for the night to parties of respectable and discreet gentlemen desiring to enjoy a quiet game of cards outside the bosom of their families. The second-story hall also led by a long window out on the balcony. And Sylvie advised Athénaïse, when she grew weary of her back room, to go and sit on the front balcony, which was shady in the afternoon, and where she might find diversion in the sounds and sights of the street below.

Athénaïse refreshed herself with a bath, and was soon unpacking her few belongings, which she ranged neatly away in the bureau drawers and the armoire.

She had revolved certain plans in her mind during the past hour or so. Her present intention was to live on indefinitely in this big, cool, clean back room on Dauphine street. She had thought seriously, for moments, of the convent, with all readiness to embrace the vows of poverty and chastity; but what about obedience? Later, she intended, in some roundabout way, to give her parents and her husband the assurance of her safety and welfare; reserving the right to remain unmolested and lost to them. To live on at the expense of Montéclin's generosity was wholly out of the question, and Athénaïse meant to look about for some suitable and agreeable employment.

The imperative thing to be done at present, however, was to go out in search of material for an inexpensive gown or two; for she found herself in the painful predicament of a young woman having almost literally nothing to wear. She decided upon pure white for one, and some sort of a sprigged muslin for the other.

VII

On Sunday morning, two days after Athénaïse's arrival in the city, she went in to breakfast somewhat later than usual, to find two covers laid

119

at table instead of the one to which she was accustomed. She had been to mass, and did not remove her hat, but put her fan, parasol, and prayer-book aside. The dining-room was situated just beneath her own apartment, and, like all rooms of the house, was large and airy; the floor was covered with a glistening oil-cloth.

The small, round table, immaculately set, was drawn near the open window. There were some tall plants in boxes on the gallery outside; and Pousette, a little, old, intensely black woman, was splashing and dashing buckets of water on the flagging, and talking loud in her Creole patois to no one in particular.

A dish piled with delicate river-shrimps and crushed ice was on the table; a caraffe of crystal-clear water, a few *hors d'œuvres*, beside a small golden-brown crusty loaf of French bread at each plate. A half-bottle of wine and the morning paper were set at the place opposite Athénaïse.

She had almost completed her breakfast when Gouvernail came in and seated himself at table. He felt annoyed at finding his cherished privacy invaded. Sylvie was removing the remains of a mutton-chop from before Athénaïse, and serving her with a cup of café au lait.

"M'sieur Gouvernail," offered Sylvie in her most insinuating and impressive manner, "you please leave me make you acquaint' wid Madame Cazeau. Dat's M'sieur Miché's sister; you meet 'im two t'ree time', you rec'lec', an' been one day to de race wid 'im. Madame Cazeau, you please leave me make you acquaint' wid M'sieur Gouvernail."

Gouvernail expressed himself greatly pleased to meet the sister of Monsieur Miché, of whom he had not the slightest recollection. He inquired after Monsieur Miché's health, and politely offered Athénaïse a part of his newspaper,—the part which contained the Woman's Page and the social gossip.

Athénaïse faintly remembered that Sylvie had spoken of a Monsieur Gouvernail occupying the room adjoining hers, living amid luxurious surroundings and a multitude of books. She had not thought of him further than to picture him a stout, middle-aged gentleman, with a bushy beard turning gray, wearing large gold-rimmed spectacles, and stooping somewhat from much bending over books and writing material. She had confused him in her mind with the likeness of some literary celebrity that she had run across in the advertising pages of a magazine.

Gouvernail's appearance was, in truth, in no sense striking. He looked older than thirty and younger than forty, was of medium height and weight, with a quiet, unobtrusive manner which seemed to ask that he be let alone. His hair was light brown, brushed carefully and parted in the middle. His mustache was brown, and so were his eyes, which had a mild, penetrating quality. He was neatly dressed in the fashion of the day; and his hands seemed to Athénaïse remarkably white and soft for a man's.

He had been buried in the contents of his newspaper, when he suddenly realized that some further little attention might be due to Miché's sister. He started to offer her a glass of wine, when he was surprised and relieved to find that she had quietly slipped away while he was absorbed in his own editorial on Corrupt Legislation.

Gouvernail finished his paper and smoked his cigar out on the gallery. He lounged about, gathered a rose for his buttonhole, and had his regular Sunday-morning confab with Pousette, to whom he paid a weekly stipend for brushing his shoes and clothing. He made a great pretense of haggling over the transaction, only to enjoy her uneasiness and garrulous excitement.

He worked or read in his room for a few hours, and when he quitted the house, at three in the afternoon, it was to return no more till late at night. It was his almost invariable custom to spend Sunday evenings out in the American quarter, among a congenial set of men and women,— *des esprits forts*, all of them, whose lives were irreproachable, yet whose opinions would startle even the traditional "sapeur," for whom "nothing is sacred." But for all his "advanced" opinions, Gouvernail was a liberal-minded fellow; a man or woman lost nothing of his respect by being married.

When he left the house in the afternoon, Athénaïse had already ensconced herself on the front balcony. He could see her through the jalousies when he passed on his way to the front entrance. She had not yet grown lonesome or homesick; the newness of her surroundings made them sufficiently entertaining. She found it diverting to sit there on the front balcony watching people pass by, even though there was no one to talk to. And then the comforting, comfortable sense of not being married!

She watched Gouvernail walk down the street, and could find no fault with his bearing. He could hear the sound of her rockers for some little distance. He wondered what the "poor little thing" was doing in the city, and meant to ask Sylvie about her when he should happen to think of it.

VIII

The following morning, towards noon, when Gouvernail quitted his room, he was confronted by Athénaïse, exhibiting some confusion and trepidation at being forced to request a favor of him at so early a stage of their acquaintance. She stood in her doorway, and had evidently been sewing, as the thimble on her finger testified, as well as a long-threaded needle thrust in the bosom of her gown. She held a stamped but unaddressed letter in her hand.

And would Mr. Gouvernail be so kind as to address the letter to her brother, Mr. Montéclin Miché? She would hate to detain him with explanations this morning,—another time, perhaps,—but now she begged that he would give himself the trouble.

He assured her that it made no difference, that it was no trouble whatever; and he drew a fountain pen from his pocket and addressed the letter at her dictation, resting it on the inverted rim of his straw hat. She wondered a little at a man of his supposed erudition stumbling over the spelling of "Montéclin" and "Miché."

She demurred at overwhelming him with the additional trouble of posting it, but he succeeded in convincing her that so simple a task as the posting of a letter would not add an iota to the burden of the day. Moreover, he promised to carry it in his hand, and thus avoid any possible risk of forgetting it in his pocket.

After that, and after a second repetition of the favor, when she had told him that she had had a letter from Montéclin, and looked as if she wanted to tell him more, he felt that he knew her better. He felt that he knew her well enough to join her out on the balcony, one night, when he found her sitting there alone. He was not one who deliberately sought the society of women, but he was not wholly a bear. A little commiseration for Athénaïse's aloneness, perhaps some curiosity to know further what manner of woman she was, and the natural influence of her feminine charm were equal unconfessed factors in turning his steps towards the balcony when he discovered the shimmer of her white gown through the open hall window.

It was already quite late, but the day had been intensely hot, and neighboring balconies and doorways were occupied by chattering groups of humanity, loath to abandon the grateful freshness of the outer air. The voices about her served to reveal to Athénaïse the feeling of loneliness that was gradually coming over her. Notwithstanding certain dormant impulses, she craved human sympathy and companionship.

She shook hands impulsively with Gouvernail, and told him how glad she was to see him. He was not prepared for such an admission, but it pleased him immensely, detecting as he did that the expression was as sincere as it was outspoken. He drew a chair up within comfortable conversational distance of Athénaïse, though he had no intention of talking more than was barely necessary to encourage Madame—He had actually forgotten her name!

He leaned an elbow on the balcony rail, and would have offered an opening remark about the oppressive heat of the day, but Athénaïse did not give him the opportunity. How glad she was to talk to some one, and how she talked!

An hour later she had gone to her room, and Gouvernail stayed smoking on the balcony. He knew her quite well after that hour's talk. It was not so much what she had said as what her half saying had revealed to his quick intelligence. He knew that she adored Montéclin, and he suspected that she adored Cazeau without being herself aware of it. He had gathered that she was self-willed, impulsive, innocent, ignorant, unsatisfied, dissatisfied; for had she not complained that things seemed all wrongly arranged in this world, and no one was permitted to be happy in his own way? And he told her he was sorry she had discovered that primordial fact of existence so early in life.

He commiserated her loneliness, and scanned his bookshelves next morning for something to lend her to read, rejecting everything that offered itself to his view. Philosophy was out of the question, and so was poetry; that is, such poetry as he possessed. He had not sounded her literary tastes, and strongly suspected she had none; that she would have rejected The Duchess as readily as Mrs. Humphry Ward. He compromised on a magazine.

It had entertained her passably, she admitted, upon returning it. A New England story had puzzled her, it was true, and a Creole tale had offended her, but the pictures had pleased her greatly, especially one which had reminded her so strongly of Montéclin after a hard day's ride that she was loath to give it up. It was one of Remington's Cowboys, and Gouvernail insisted upon her keeping it,—keeping the magazine.

He spoke to her daily after that, and was always eager to render her some service or to do something towards her entertainment.

One afternoon he took her out to the lake end. She had been there once, some years before, but in winter, so the trip was comparatively new and strange to her. The large expanse of water studded with pleasure-boats, the sight of children playing merrily along the grassy palisades, the music, all enchanted her. Gouvernail thought her the most beautiful woman he had ever seen. Even her gown—the sprigged muslin—appeared to him the most charming one imaginable. Nor could anything be more becoming than the arrangement of her brown hair under the white sailor hat, all rolled back in a soft puff from her radiant face. And she carried her parasol and lifted her skirts and used her fan in ways that seemed quite unique and peculiar to herself, and which he considered almost worthy of study and imitation.

They did not dine out there at the water's edge, as they might have done, but returned early to the city to avoid the crowd. Athénaïse wanted to go home, for she said Sylvie would have dinner prepared and would be expecting her. But it was not difficult to persuade her to dine instead in the quiet little restaurant that he knew and liked, with its sanded floor, its secluded atmosphere, its delicious menu, and its obsequious waiter wanting to know what he might have the honor of serving to "monsieur et madame." No wonder he made the mistake, with Gouvernail assuming such an air of proprietorship! But Athénaïse was very tired after it all; the sparkle went out of her face, and she hung draggingly on his arm in walking home.

He was reluctant to part from her when she bade him good-night at her door and thanked him for the agreeable evening. He had hoped she would sit outside until it was time for him to regain the newspaper office. He knew that she would undress and get into her peignoir and lie upon her bed; and what he wanted to do, what he would have given much to do, was to go and sit beside her, read to her something restful, soothe her, do her bidding, whatever it might be. Of course there was no use in thinking of that. But he was surprised at his growing desire to be serving her. She gave him an opportunity sooner than he looked for.

"Mr. Gouvernail," she called from her room, "will you be so kine as to call Pousette an' tell her she fo'got to bring my ice-water?"

He was indignant at Pousette's negligence, and called severely to her over the banisters. He was sitting before his own door, smoking. He knew that Athénaïse had gone to bed, for her room was dark, and she had opened the slats of the door and windows. Her bed was near a window.

Pousette came flopping up with the ice-water, and with a hundred excuses: "Mo pa oua vou à tab c'te lanuite, mo cri vou pé gagni déja

124

là-bas; parole! Vou pas cri conté ça Madame Sylvie?" She had not seen Athénaïse at table, and thought she was gone. She swore to this, and hoped Madame Sylvie would not be informed of her remissness.

A little later Athénaïse lifted her voice again: "Mr. Gouvernail, did you remark that young man sitting on the opposite side from us, coming in, with a gray coat an' a blue ban' aroun' his hat?"

Of course Gouvernail had not noticed any such individual, but he assured Athénaïse that he had observed the young fellow particularly.

"Don't you think he looked something,—not very much, of co'se,— but don't you think he had a little faux-air of Montéclin?"

"I think he looked strikingly like Montéclin," asserted Gouvernail, with the one idea of prolonging the conversation. "I meant to call your attention to the resemblance, and something drove it out of my head."

"The same with me," returned Athénaïse. "Ah, my dear Montéclin! I wonder w'at he is doing now?"

"Did you receive any news, any letter from him to-day?" asked Gouvernail, determined that if the conversation ceased it should not be through lack of effort on his part to sustain it.

"Not to-day, but yesterday. He tells me that maman was so distracted with uneasiness that finally, to pacify her, he was fo'ced to confess that he knew w'ere I was, but that he was boun' by a vow of secrecy not to reveal it. But Cazeau has not noticed him or spoken to him since he threaten' to throw po' Montéclin in Cane river. You know Cazeau wrote me a letter the morning I lef', thinking I had gone to the rigolet. An' maman opened it, an' said it was full of the mos' noble sentiments, an' she wanted Montéclin to sen' it to me; but Montéclin refuse' poin' blank, so he wrote to me."

Gouvernail preferred to talk of Montéclin. He pictured Cazeau as unbearable, and did not like to think of him.

A little later Athénaïse called out, "Good-night, Mr. Gouvernail."

"Good-night," he returned reluctantly. And when he thought that she was sleeping, he got up and went away to the midnight pandemonium of his newspaper office.

IX

Athénaïse could not have held out through the month had it not been for Gouvernail. With the need of caution and secrecy always uppermost in her mind, she made no new acquaintances, and she did not seek out persons already known to her; however, she knew so few, it required little effort to keep out of their way. As for Sylvie, almost every moment of her time was occupied in looking after her house; and, moreover, her deferential attitude towards her lodgers forbade anything like the gossipy chats in which Athénaïse might have condescended sometimes to indulge with her land-lady. The transient lodgers, who came and went, she never had occasion to meet. Hence she was entirely dependent upon Gouvernail for company.

He appreciated the situation fully; and every moment that he could spare from his work he devoted to her entertainment. She liked to be out of doors, and they strolled together in the summer twilight through the mazes of the old French quarter. They went again to the lake end, and stayed for hours on the water; returning so late that the streets through which they passed were silent and deserted. On Sunday morning he arose at an unconscionable hour to take her to the French market, knowing that the sights and sounds there would interest her. And he did not join the intellectual coterie in the afternoon, as he usually did, but placed himself all day at the disposition and service of Athénaïse.

Notwithstanding all, his manner toward her was tactful, and evinced intelligence and a deep knowledge of her character, surprising upon so brief an acquaintance. For the time he was everything to her that she would have him; he replaced home and friends. Sometimes she wondered if he had ever loved a woman. She could not fancy him loving any one passionately, rudely, offensively, as Cazeau loved her. Once she was so naïve as to ask him outright if he had ever been in love, and he assured her promptly that he had not. She thought it an admirable trait in his character, and esteemed him greatly therefor.

He found her crying one night, not openly or violently. She was leaning over the gallery rail, watching the toads that hopped about in the moonlight, down on the damp flagstones of the courtyard. There was an oppressively sweet odor rising from the cape jessamine. Pousette was down there, mumbling and quarreling with some one, and seeming to be having it all her own way,—as well she might, when her companion was only a black cat that had come in from a neighboring yard to keep her company.

Athénaïse did admit feeling heart-sick, body-sick, when he questioned her; she supposed it was nothing but homesick. A letter from Montéclin had stirred her all up. She longed for her mother, for Montéclin; she was sick for a sight of the cotton-fields, the scent of the ploughed earth, for the dim, mysterious charm of the woods, and the old tumble-down home on the Bon Dieu.

As Gouvernail listened to her, a wave of pity and tenderness swept through him. He took her hands and pressed them against him. He wondered what would happen if he were to put his arms around her.

He was hardly prepared for what happened, but he stood it courageously. She twined her arms around his neck and wept outright on his shoulder; the hot tears scalding his cheek and neck, and her whole body shaken in his arms. The impulse was powerful to strain her to him; the temptation was fierce to seek her lips; but he did neither.

He understood a thousand times better than she herself understood it that he was acting as substitute for Montéclin. Bitter as the conviction was, he accepted it. He was patient; he could wait. He hoped some day to hold her with a lover's arms. That she was married made no particle of difference to Gouvernail. He could not conceive or dream of it making a difference. When the time came that she wanted him,—as he hoped and believed it would come,—he felt he would have a right to her. So long as she did not want him, he had no right to her,—no more than her husband had. It was very hard to feel her warm breath and tears upon his cheek, and her struggling bosom pressed against him and her soft arms clinging to him and his whole body and soul aching for her, and yet to make no sign.

He tried to think what Montéclin would have said and done, and to act accordingly. He stroked her hair, and held her in a gentle embrace, until the tears dried and the sobs ended. Before releasing herself she kissed him against the neck; she had to love somebody in her own way! Even that he endured like a stoic. But it was well he left her, to plunge into the thick of rapid, breathless, exacting work till nearly dawn.

Athénaïse was greatly soothed, and slept well. The touch of friendly hands and caressing arms had been very grateful. Henceforward she would not be lonely and unhappy, with Gouvernail there to comfort her.

X

The fourth week of Athénaïse's stay in the city was drawing to a close. Keeping in view the intention which she had of finding some suitable and agreeable employment, she had made a few tentatives in that direction. But with the exception of two little girls who had promised to take piano lessons at a price that would be embarrassing to mention, these attempts had been fruitless. Moreover, the homesickness kept coming back, and Gouvernail was not always there to drive it away.

She spent much of her time weeding and pottering among the flowers down in the courtyard. She tried to take an interest in the black cat, and a mockingbird that hung in a cage outside the kitchen door, and a disreputable parrot that belonged to the cook next door, and swore hoarsely all day long in bad French.

Beside, she was not well; she was not herself, as she told Sylvie. The climate of New Orleans did not agree with her. Sylvie was distressed to learn this, as she felt in some measure responsible for the health and well-being of Monsieur Miché's sister; and she made it her duty to inquire closely into the nature and character of Athénaïse's malaise.

Sylvie was very wise, and Athénaïse was very ignorant. The extent of her ignorance and the depth of her subsequent enlightenment were bewildering. She stayed a long, long time quite still, quite stunned, after her interview with Sylvie, except for the short, uneven breathing that ruffled her bosom. Her whole being was steeped in a wave of ecstasy. When she finally arose from the chair in which she had been seated, and looked at herself in the mirror, a face met hers which she seemed to see for the first time, so transfigured was it with wonder and rapture.

One mood quickly followed another, in this new turmoil of her senses, and the need of action became uppermost. Her mother must know at once, and her mother must tell Montéclin. And Cazeau must know. As she thought of him, the first purely sensuous tremor of her life swept over her. She half whispered his name, and the sound of it brought red blotches into her cheeks. She spoke it over and over, as if it were some new, sweet sound born out of darkness and confusion, and reaching her for the first time. She was impatient to be with him. Her whole passionate nature was aroused as if by a miracle.

She seated herself to write to her husband. The letter he would get in the morning, and she would be with him at night. What would he say? How would he act? She knew that he would forgive her, for had he not written a letter?—and a pang of resentment toward Montéclin shot through her. What did he mean by withholding that letter? How dared he not have sent it?

Athénaïse attired herself for the street, and went out to post the letter which she had penned with a single thought, a spontaneous impulse. It would have seemed incoherent to most people, but Cazeau would understand.

She walked along the street as if she had fallen heir to some magnificent inheritance. On her face was a look of pride and satisfaction that passersby noticed and admired. She wanted to talk to some one, to tell some person; and she stopped at the corner and told the oyster-woman, who was Irish, and who God-blessed her, and wished prosperity to the race of Cazeaus for generations to come. She held the oyster-woman's fat, dirty little baby in her arms and scanned it curiously and observingly, as if a baby were a phenomenon that she encountered for the first time in life. She even kissed it!

Then what a relief it was to Athénaïse to walk the streets without dread of being seen and recognized by some chance acquaintance from Red river! No one could have said now that she did not know her own mind.

She went directly from the oyster-woman's to the office of Harding & Offdean, her husband's merchants; and it was with such an air of partnership, almost proprietorship, that she demanded a sum of money on her husband's account, they gave it to her as unhesitatingly as they would have handed it over to Cazeau himself. When Mr. Harding, who knew her, asked politely after her health, she turned so rosy and looked so conscious, he thought it a great pity for so pretty a woman to be such a little goose.

Athénaïse entered a dry-goods store and bought all manner of things, —little presents for nearly everybody she knew. She bought whole bolts of sheerest, softest, downiest white stuff; and when the clerk, in trying to meet her wishes, asked if she intended it for infant's use, she could have sunk through the floor, and wondered how he might have suspected it.

As it was Montéclin who had taken her away from her husband, she wanted it to be Montéclin who should take her back to him. So she wrote him a very curt note,—in fact it was a postal card,—asking that he meet her at the train on the evening following. She felt convinced that after what had gone before, Cazeau would await her at their own home; and she preferred it so.

Then there was the agreeable excitement of getting ready to leave, of packing up her things. Pousette kept coming and going, coming and going; and each time that she quitted the room it was with something that Athénaïse had given her,—a handkerchief, a petticoat, a pair of stockings with two tiny holes at the toes, some broken prayer-beads, and finally a silver dollar.

Next it was Sylvie who came along bearing a gift of what she called "a set of pattern'," —things of complicated design which never could have been obtained in any new-fangled bazaar or pattern-store, that Sylvie had acquired of a foreign lady of distinction whom she had nursed years before at the St. Charles hotel. Athénaïse accepted and handled them with reverence, fully sensible of the great compliment and favor, and laid them religiously away in the trunk which she had lately acquired.

She was greatly fatigued after the day of unusual exertion, and went early to bed and to sleep. All day long she had not once thought of Gouvernail, and only did think of him when aroused for a brief instant by the sound of his foot-falls on the gallery, as he passed in going to his room. He had hoped to find her up, waiting for him.

But the next morning he knew. Some one must have told him. There was no subject known to her which Sylvie hesitated to discuss in detail with any man of suitable years and discretion.

Athénaïse found Gouvernail waiting with a carriage to convey her to the railway station. A momentary pang visited her for having forgotten him so completely, when he said to her, "Sylvie tells me you are going away this morning."

He was kind, attentive, and amiable, as usual, but respected to the utmost the new dignity and reserve that her manner had developed since yesterday. She kept looking from the carriage window, silent, and embarrassed as Eve after losing her ignorance. He talked of the muddy streets and the murky morning, and of Montéclin. He hoped she would find everything comfortable and pleasant in the country, and trusted she would inform him whenever she came to visit the city again. He talked as if afraid or mistrustful of silence and himself.

At the station she handed him her purse, and he bought her ticket, secured for her a comfortable section, checked her trunk, and got all the bundles and things safely aboard the train. She felt very grateful. He pressed her hand warmly, lifted his hat, and left her. He was a man of intelligence, and took defeat gracefully; that was all. But as he made his way back to the carriage, he was thinking, "By heaven, it hurts, it hurts!"

XI

Athénaïse spent a day of supreme happiness and expectancy. The fair sight of the country unfolding itself before her was balm to her vision and to her soul. She was charmed with the rather unfamiliar, broad, clean sweep of the sugar plantations, with their monster sugar-houses, their rows of neat cabins like little villages of a single street, and their impressive homes standing apart amid clusters of trees. There were sudden glimpses of a bayou curling between sunny, grassy banks, or creeping sluggishly out from a tangled growth of wood, and brush, and fern, and poison-vines, and palmettos. And passing through the long stretches of monotonous woodlands, she would close her eyes and taste in anticipation the moment of her meeting with Cazeau. She could think of nothing but him.

It was night when she reached her station. There was Montéclin, as she had expected, waiting for her with a two-seated buggy, to which he had hitched his own swift-footed, spirited pony. It was good, he felt, to have her back on any terms; and he had no fault to find since she came of her own choice. He more than suspected the cause of her coming; her eyes and her voice and her foolish little manner went far in revealing the secret that was brimming over in her heart. But after he had deposited her at her own gate, and as he continued his way toward the rigolet, he could not help feeling that the affair had taken a very disappointing, an ordinary, a most commonplace turn, after all. He left her in Cazeau's keeping.

Her husband lifted her out of the buggy, and neither said a word until they stood together within the shelter of the gallery. Even then they did not speak at first. But Athénaïse turned to him with an appealing gesture. As he clasped her in his arms, he felt the yielding of her whole body against him. He felt her lips for the first time respond to the passion of his own.

The country night was dark and warm and still, save for the distant notes of an accordion which some one was playing in a cabin away off. A little negro baby was crying somewhere. As Athénaïse withdrew from her husband's embrace, the sound arrested her.

"Listen, Cazeau! How Juliette's baby is crying! Pauvre ti chou, I wonder w'at is the matter with it?"

Two Summers and Two Souls

I

He was a fine, honest-looking fellow; young, impetuous, candid; and he was bidding her good-bye.

It was in the country, where she lived, and where her soul and senses were slowly unfolding, like the languid petals of some white and fragrant blossom.

Five weeks—only five weeks he had known her. They seemed to him a flash, an eternity, a rapturous breath, an existence—a re-creation of light and life, and soul and senses. He tried to tell her something of this when the hour of parting came. But he could only say that he loved her; nothing else that he wanted to say seemed to mean so much as this. She was glad, and doubtful, and afraid, and kept reiterating:

"Only five weeks! so short! and love and life are so long."

"Then you don't love me!"

"I don't know. I want to be with you—near you."

"Then you do love me!"

"I don't know. I thought love meant something different—powerful, overwhelming. No. I am afraid to say."

He talked like a mad man then, and troubled and bewildered her with his incoherence. He begged for love as a mendicant might beg for alms, without reserve and without shame, and the passion within him gave an unnatural ring to his voice and a new, strange look to his eyes that chilled her unawakened senses and sent her shivering within herself.

"No, no, no!" was all she could say to him.

He willed not to believe it; he had felt so sure of her. And she was not one to play fast and loose, with those honest eyes whose depths had convinced while they ensnared him.

"Don't send me away like this," he pleaded, "without a crumb of hope to feed on and keep me living."

She dismissed him with a promise that it might not be final. "Who knows! I will think; but leave me alone. Don't trouble me; and I will see—Good-bye."

He did not once look back after leaving her, but walked straight on with a step that was quick and firm from habit. But he was almost blind and senseless from pain.

She stayed watching him cross the lawn and the long stretch of meadow beyond. She watched him till the deepening shadows of the coming night crept between them. She stayed troubled, uncertain; tearful because she did not know!

II

"I remember quite well the words I told you a year ago when we parted," she wrote to him. "I told you I did not know, I wanted to think, I even wanted to pray, but I believe I did not tell you that. And now, will you believe me when I say that I have not been able to think— hardly to pray. I have only been able to feel. When you went away that day you seemed to leave me in an empty world. I kept saying to myself, 'to-morrow or next day it will be different; it will be with me as it was before he came.' Then your letters coming—three of them, one upon the other—gave voice to the empty places. You were everywhere after that. And still I doubted, and I was cautious; for it has seemed to me that the love which is to hold two beings together through life must be love indeed.

"But what is the use of saying more than that I love you. I would not care to live without you; I think I could not. Come back to me."

III

When this letter reached him he was in preparation for a journey with a party of friends. It came with a batch of business letters, and in the midst of the city's rush and din which he had meant in another day to leave behind him.

He was all unprepared for its coming and unable at once to master the shock of it, that bewildered and unnerved him.

Then came back to him the recollection of pain—a remembrance always faint and unreal; but there was complete inability to revive the conditions that had engendered it.

How he had loved her and how he had suffered! especially during those first days, and even months, when he slept and waked dreaming of her; when his letters remained unanswered, and when existence was but a name for bitter endurance.

How long had it lasted? Could he tell? The end began when he could wake in the morning without the oppression, and free from the haunting pain. The end was that day, that hour or second, when he thought of her without emotion and without regret; as he thought of her now, with unstirred pulses. There was even with him now the touch of something keener than indifference—something engendered by revolt.

It was as if one loved, and dead and forgotten had returned to life; with the strange illusion that the rush of existence had halted while she lay in her grave; and with the still more singular delusion that love is eternal.

He did not hesitate as though confronted by a problem. He did not think of leaving the letter unnoticed. He did not think of telling her the truth. If he thought of these expedients, it was only to dismiss them.

He simply went to her. As he would have gone unflinchingly to meet the business obligation that he knew would leave him bankrupt.

Two Portraits

I

Alberta having looked not very long into life, had not looked very far. She put out her hands to touch things that pleased her and her lips to kiss them. Her eyes were deep brown wells that were drinking, drinking impressions and treasuring them in her soul. They were mysterious eyes and love looked out of them.

Alberta was very fond of her mama who was really not her mama; and the beatings which alternated with the most amiable and generous indulgence, were soon forgotten by the little one, always hoping that there would never be another, as she dried her eyes.

She liked the ladies who petted her and praised her beauty, and the artists who painted it naked, and the student who held her upon his knee and fondled and kissed her while he taught her to read and spell.

There was a cruel beating about that one day, when her mama happened to be in the mood to think her too old for fondling. And the student had called her mama some very vile names in his wrath, and had asked the woman what else she expected.

There was nothing very fixed or stable about her expectations—whatever they were—as she had forgotten them the following day, and Alberta, consoled with a fantastic bracelet for her plump little arm and a shower of bonbons, installed herself again upon the student's knee. She liked nothing better, and in time was willing to take the beating if she might hold his attentions and her place in his affections and upon his knee.

Alberta cried very bitterly when he went away. The people about her seemed to be always coming and going. She had hardly the time to fix her affections upon the men and the women who came into her life before they were gone again.

Her mama died one day—very suddenly; a self-inflicted death, she heard the people say. Alberta grieved sorely, for she forgot the beatings and remembered only the outbursts of a torrid affection. But she really did not belong anywhere then, nor to anybody. And when a lady and gentleman took her to live with them, she went willingly as she would have gone anywhere, with any one. With them she met with more kindness and indulgence than she had ever known before in her life.

There were no more beatings; Alberta's body was too beautiful to be beaten—it was made for love. She knew that herself; she had heard it since she had heard anything. But now she heard many things and learned many more. She did not lack for instruction in the wiles—the ways of stirring a man's desire and holding it. Yet she did not need instruction—the secret was in her blood and looked out of her passionate, wanton eyes and showed in every motion of her seductive body.

At seventeen she was woman enough, so she had a lover. But as for that, there did not seem to be much difference. Except that she had gold now—plenty of it with which to make herself appear more beautiful, and enough to fling with both hands into the laps of those who came whining and begging to her.

Alberta is a most beautiful woman, and she takes great care of her body, for she knows that it brings her love to squander and gold to squander.

Some one has whispered in her ear:

"Be cautious, Alberta. Save, save your gold. The years are passing. The days are coming when youth slips away, when you will stretch out your hands for money and for love in vain. And what will be left for you but—"

Alberta shrunk in horror before the pictured depths of hideous degradation that would be left for her. But she consoles herself with the thought that such need never be—with death and oblivion always within her reach.

Alberta is capricious. She gives her love only when and where she chooses. One or two men have died because of her withholding it. There is a smooth-faced boy now who teases her with his resistance; for Alberta does not know shame or reserve.

One day he seems to half-relent and another time he plays indifference, and she frets and she fumes and rages.

But he had best have a care; for since Alberta has added much wine to her wantonness she is apt to be vixenish; and she carries a knife.

II

Alberta having looked not very long into life, had not looked very far. She put out her hands to touch things that pleased her, and her lips to kiss them. Her eyes were deep brown wells that were drinking, drinking impressions and treasuring them in her soul. They were mysterious eyes and love looked out of them.

It was a very holy woman who first took Alberta by the hand. The thought of God alone dwelt in her mind, and his name and none other was on her lips.

When she showed Alberta the creeping insects, the blades of grass, the flowers and trees; the rain-drops falling from the clouds; the sky and the stars and the men and women moving on the earth, she taught her that it was God who had created all; that God was great, was good, was the Supreme Love.

And when Alberta would have put out her hands and her lips to touch the great and all-loving God, it was then the holy woman taught her that it is not with the hands and lips and eyes that we reach God, but with the soul; that the soul must be made perfect and the flesh subdued. And what is the soul but the inward thought? And this the child was taught to keep spotless—pure, and fit as far as a human soul can be, to hold intercourse with the all-wise and all-seeing God.

Her existence became a prayer. Evil things approached her not. The inherited sin of the blood must have been washed away at the baptismal font; for all the things of this world that she encountered—the pleasures, the trials and even temptations, but turned her gaze within, through her soul up to the fountain of all love and every beatitude.

When Alberta had reached the age when with other women the languor of love creeps into the veins and dreams begin, at such a period an overpowering impulse toward the purely spiritual possessed itself of her. She could no longer abide the sights, the sounds, the accidental happenings of life surrounding her, that tended but to disturb her contemplation of the heavenly existence.

It was then she went into the convent—the white convent on the hill that overlooks the river; the big convent whose long, dim corridors echo with the soft tread of a multitude of holy women; whose atmosphere of chastity, poverty and obedience penetrates to the soul through benumbed senses.

But of all the holy women in the white convent, there is none so saintly as Alberta. Any one will tell you that who knows them. Even her pious guide and counsellor does not equal her in sanctity. Because Alberta is endowed with the powerful gift of a great love that lifts her above common mortals, close to the invisible throne. Her ears seem to hear sounds that reach no other ears; and what her eyes see, only God and herself know. When the others are plunged in meditation, Alberta is steeped in an oblivious ecstasy. She kneels before the Blessed Sacrament with stiffened, tireless limbs; with absorbing eyes that drink in the holy mystery till it is a mystery no longer, but a real flood of celestial love deluging her soul. She does not hear the sound of bells nor the soft stir of disbanding numbers. She must be touched upon the shoulder; roused, awakened.

Alberta does not know that she is beautiful. If you were to tell her so she would not blush and utter gentle protest and reproof as might the others. She would only smile, as though beauty were a thing that concerned her not. But she is beautiful, with the glow of a holy passion in her dark eyes. Her face is thin and white, but illumined from within by a light which seems not of this world.

She does not walk upright; she could not, overpowered by the Divine Presence and the realization of her own nothingness. Her hands, slender and blue-veined, and her delicate fingers seem to have been fashioned by God to be clasped and uplifted in prayer.

It is said—not broadcast, it is only whispered—that Alberta sees visions. Oh, the beautiful visions! The first of them came to her when she was rapped in suffering, in quivering contemplation of the bleeding and agonizing Christ. Oh, the dear God! Who loved her beyond the power of man to describe, to conceive. The God-Man, the Man-God, suffering, bleeding, dying for her, Alberta, a worm upon the earth; dying that she might be saved from sin and transplanted among the heavenly delights. Oh, if she might die for him in return! But she could only abandon herself to his mercy and his love. "Into thy hands, Oh Lord! Into thy hands!"

She pressed her lips upon the bleeding wounds and the Divine Blood transfigured her. The Virgin Mary enfolded her in her mantle. She could not describe in words the ecstasy; that taste of the Divine love which only the souls of the transplanted could endure in its awful and complete intensity. She, Alberta, had received this sign of Divine favor; this foretaste of heavenly bliss. For an hour she had swooned in rapture; she had lived in Christ. Oh, the beautiful visions!

The visions come often to Alberta now, refreshing and strengthening her soul; it is being talked about a little in whispers.

And it is said that certain afflicted persons have been helped by her prayers. And others having abounding faith, have been cured of bodily ailments by the touch of her beautiful hands.

Fedora

Fedora had determined upon driving over to the station herself for Miss Malthers.

Though one or two of them looked disappointed—notably her brother —no one opposed her. She said the brute was restive, and shouldn't be trusted to the handling of the young people.

To be sure Fedora was old enough, from the standpoint of her sister Camilla and the rest of them. Yet no one would ever have thought of it but for her own persistent affectation and idiotic assumption of superior years and wisdom. She was thirty.

Fedora had too early in life formed an ideal and treasured it. By this ideal she had measured such male beings as had hitherto challenged her attention, and needless to say she had found them wanting. The young people—her brothers' and sisters' guests, who were constantly coming and going that summer—occupied her to a great extent, but failed to interest her. She concerned herself with their comforts—in the absence of her mother—looked after their health and well-being; contrived for their amusements, in which she never joined. And, as Fedora was tall and slim, and carried her head loftily, and wore eye-glasses and a severe expression, some of them—the silliest—felt as if she were a hundred years old. Young Malthers thought she was about forty.

One day when he stopped before her out in the gravel walk to ask her some question pertaining to the afternoon's sport, Fedora, who was tall, had to look up into his face to answer him. She had known him eight years, since he was a lad of fifteen, and to her he had never been other than the lad of fifteen.

But that afternoon, looking up into his face, the sudden realization came home to her that he was a man—in voice, in attitude, in bearing, in every sense—a man.

In an absorbing glance, and with unaccountable intention, she gathered in every detail of his countenance as though it were a strange, new thing to her, presenting itself to her vision for the first time. The eyes were blue, earnest, and at the moment a little troubled over some trivial affair that he was relating to her. The face was brown from the sun, smooth, with no suggestion of ruddiness, except in the lips, that were strong, firm and clean. She kept thinking of his face, and every trick of it after he passed on.

From that moment he began to exist for her. She looked at him when he was near by, she listened for his voice, and took notice and account of what he said. She sought him out; she selected him when occasion permitted. She wanted him by her, though his nearness troubled her. There was uneasiness, restlessness, expectation when he was not there within sight or sound. There was redoubled uneasiness when he was by —there was inward revolt, astonishment, rapture, self-contumely; a swift, fierce encounter betwixt thought and feeling.

Fedora could hardly explain to her own satisfaction why she wanted to go herself to the station for young Malthers' sister. She felt a desire to see the girl, to be near her; as unaccountable, when she tried to analyze it, as the impulse which drove her, and to which she often yielded, to touch his hat, hanging with others upon the hall pegs, when she passed it by. Once a coat which he had discarded hung there too. She handled it under pretense of putting it in order. There was no one near, and, obeying a sudden impulse, she buried her face for an instant in the rough folds of the coat.

Fedora reached the station a little before train time. It was in a pretty nook, green and fragrant, set down at the foot of a wooded hill. Off in a clearing there was a field of yellow grain, upon which the sinking sunlight fell in slanting, broken beams. Far down the track there were some men at work, and the even ring of their hammers was the only sound that broke upon the stillness. Fedora loved it all—sky and woods and sunlight; sounds and smells. But her bearing—elegant, composed, reserved—betrayed nothing emotional as she tramped the narrow platform, whip in hand, and occasionally offered a condescending word to the mail man or the sleepy agent.

Malthers' sister was the only soul to disembark from the train. Fedora had never seen her before; but if there had been a hundred, she would have known the girl. She was a small thing; but aside from that, there was the coloring; there were the blue, earnest eyes; there, above all, was the firm, full curve of the lips; the same setting of the white, even teeth. There was the subtle play of feature, the elusive trick of expression, which she had thought peculiar and individual in the one, presenting themselves as family traits.

The suggestive resemblance of the girl to her brother was vivid, poignant even to Fedora, realizing, as she did with a pang, that familiarity and custom would soon blur the image.

Miss Malthers was a quiet, reserved creature, with little to say. She had been to college with Camilla, and spoke somewhat of their friendship and former intimacy. She sat lower in the cart than Fedora, who drove, handling whip and rein with accomplished skill.

"You know, dear child," said Fedora, in her usual elderly fashion, "I want you to feel completely at home with us." They were driving through a long, quiet, leafy road, into which the twilight was just beginning to creep. "Come to me freely and without reserve—with all your wants; with any complaints. I feel that I shall be quite fond of you."

She had gathered the reins into one hand, and with the other free arm she encircled Miss Malthers' shoulders.

When the girl looked up into her face, with murmured thanks, Fedora bent down and pressed a long, penetrating kiss upon her mouth.

Malthers' sister appeared astonished, and not too well pleased. Fedora, with seemingly unruffled composure, gathered the reins, and for the rest of the way stared steadily ahead of her between the horses' ears.

A Pair of Silk Stockings

Little Mrs. Sommers one day found herself the unexpected possessor of fifteen dollars. It seemed to her a very large amount of money, and the way in which it stuffed and bulged her worn old *porte-monnaie* gave her a feeling of importance such as she had not enjoyed for years.

The question of investment was one that occupied her greatly. For a day or two she walked about apparently in a dreamy state, but really absorbed in speculation and calculation. She did not wish to act hastily, to do anything she might afterward regret. But it was during the still hours of the night when she lay awake revolving plans in her mind that she seemed to see her way clearly toward a proper and judicious use of the money.

A dollar or two should be added to the price usually paid for Janie's shoes, which would insure their lasting an appreciable time longer than they usually did. She would buy so and so many yards of percale for new shirt waists for the boys and Janie and Mag. She had intended to make the old ones do by skilful patching. Mag should have another gown. She had seen some beautiful patterns, veritable bargains in the shop windows. And still there would be left enough for new stockings—two pairs apiece —and what darning that would save for a while! She would get caps for the boys and sailor-hats for the girls. The vision of her little brood looking fresh and dainty and new for once in their lives excited her and made her restless and wakeful with anticipation.

The neighbors sometimes talked of certain "better days" that little Mrs. Sommers had known before she had ever thought of being Mrs. Sommers. She herself indulged in no such morbid retrospection. She had no time—no second of time to devote to the past. The needs of the present absorbed her every faculty. A vision of the future like some dim, gaunt monster sometimes appalled her, but luckily to-morrow never comes.

Mrs. Sommers was one who knew the value of bargains; who could stand for hours making her way inch by inch toward the desired object that was selling below cost. She could elbow her way if need be; she had learned to clutch a piece of goods and hold it and stick to it with persistence and determination till her turn came to be served, no matter when it came.

But that day she was a little faint and tired. She had swallowed a light luncheon—no! when she came to think of it, between getting the children fed and the place righted, and preparing herself for the shopping bout, she had actually forgotten to eat any luncheon at all!

She sat herself upon a revolving stool before a counter that was comparatively deserted, trying to gather strength and courage to charge through an eager multitude that was besieging breast-works of shirting and figured lawn. An all-gone limp feeling had come over her and she rested her hand aimlessly upon the counter. She wore no gloves. By degrees she grew aware that her hand had encountered something very soothing, very pleasant to touch. She looked down to see that her hand lay upon a pile of silk stockings. A placard near by announced that they had been reduced in price from two dollars and fifty cents to one dollar and ninety-eight cents; and a young girl who stood behind the counter asked her if she wished to examine their line of silk hosiery. She smiled, just as if she had been asked to inspect a tiara of diamonds with the ultimate view of purchasing it. But she went on feeling the soft, sheeny luxurious things—with both hands now, holding them up to see them glisten, and to feel them glide serpent-like through her fingers.

Two hectic blotches came suddenly into her pale cheeks. She looked up at the girl.

"Do you think there are any eights-and-a-half among these?"

There were any number of eights-and-a-half. In fact, there were more of that size than any other. Here was a light-blue pair; there were some lavender, some all black and various shades of tan and gray. Mrs. Sommers selected a black pair and looked at them very long and closely. She pretended to be examining their texture, which the clerk assured her was excellent.

"A dollar and ninety-eight cents," she mused aloud. "Well, I'll take this pair." She handed the girl a five-dollar bill and waited for her change and for her parcel. What a very small parcel it was! It seemed lost in the depths of her shabby old shopping-bag.

Mrs. Sommers after that did not move in the direction of the bargain counter. She took the elevator, which carried her to an upper floor into the region of the ladies' waiting-rooms. Here, in a retired corner, she exchanged her cotton stockings for the new silk ones which she had just bought. She was not going through any acute mental process or reasoning with herself, nor was she striving to explain to her satisfaction the motive of her action. She was not thinking at all. She seemed for the time to be taking a rest from that laborious and fatiguing function and to have abandoned herself to some mechanical impulse that directed her actions and freed her of responsibility.

How good was the touch of the raw silk to her flesh! She felt like lying back in the cushioned chair and reveling for a while in the luxury of it. She did for a little while. Then she replaced her shoes, rolled the cotton stockings together and thrust them into her bag. After doing this she crossed straight over to the shoe department and took her seat to be fitted.

She was fastidious. The clerk could not make her out; he could not reconcile her shoes with her stockings, and she was not too easily pleased. She held back her skirts and turned her feet one way and her head another way as she glanced down at the polished, pointed-tipped boots. Her foot and ankle looked very pretty. She could not realize that they belonged to her and were a part of herself. She wanted an excellent and stylish fit, she told the young fellow who served her, and she did not mind the difference of a dollar or two more in the price so long as she got what she desired.

It was a long time since Mrs. Sommers had been fitted with gloves. On rare occasions when she had bought a pair they were always "bargains," so cheap that it would have been preposterous and unreasonable to have expected them to be fitted to the hand.

Now she rested her elbow on the cushion of the glove counter, and a pretty, pleasant young creature, delicate and deft of touch, drew a long-wristed "kid" over Mrs. Sommer's hand. She smoothed it down over the wrist and buttoned it neatly, and both lost themselves for a second or two in admiring contemplation of the little symmetrical gloved hand. But there were other places where money might be spent.

There were books and magazines piled up in the window of a stall a few paces down the street. Mrs. Sommers bought two high-priced magazines such as she had been accustomed to read in the days when she had been accustomed to other pleasant things. She carried them without wrapping. As well as she could she lifted her skirts at the crossings. Her stockings and boots and well fitting gloves had worked marvels in her bearing—had given her a feeling of assurance, a sense of belonging to the well-dressed multitude.

She was very hungry. Another time she would have stilled the cravings for food until reaching her own home, where she would have brewed herself a cup of tea and taken a snack of anything that was available. But the impulse that was guiding her would not suffer her to entertain any such thought.

There was a restaurant at the corner. She had never entered its doors; from the outside she had sometimes caught glimpses of spotless damask and shining crystal, and soft-stepping waiters serving people of fashion.

When she entered her appearance created no surprise, no consternation, as she had half feared it might. She seated herself at a small table alone, and an attentive waiter at once approached to take her order. She did not want a profusion; she craved a nice and tasty bite—a half dozen blue-points, a plump chop with cress, a something sweet—a crème-frappée, for instance; a glass of Rhine wine, and after all a small cup of black coffee.

While waiting to be served she removed her gloves very leisurely and laid them beside her. Then she picked up a magazine and glanced through it, cutting the pages with a blunt edge of her knife. It was all very agreeable. The damask was even more spotless than it had seemed through the window, and the crystal more sparkling. There were quiet ladies and gentlemen, who did not notice her, lunching at the small tables like her own. A soft, pleasing strain of music could be heard, and a gentle breeze was blowing through the window. She tasted a bite, and she read a word or two, and she sipped the amber wine and wiggled her toes in the silk stockings. The price of it made no difference. She counted the money out to the waiter and left an extra coin on his tray, whereupon he bowed before her as before a princess of royal blood.

There was still money in her purse, and her next temptation presented itself in the shape of a matinée poster.

It was a little later when she entered the theatre, the play had begun and the house seemed to her to be packed. But there were vacant seats here and there, and into one of them she was ushered, between brilliantly dressed women who had gone there to kill time and eat candy and display their gaudy attire. There were many others who were there solely for the play and acting. It is safe to say there was no one present who bore quite the attitude which Mrs. Sommers did to her surroundings. She gathered in the whole—stage and players and people in one wide impression, and absorbed it and enjoyed it. She laughed at the comedy and wept—she and the gaudy woman next to her wept over the tragedy. And they talked a little together over it. And the gaudy woman wiped her eyes and sniffled on a tiny square of filmy, perfumed lace and passed little Mrs. Sommers her box of candy.

The play was over, the music ceased, the crowd filed out. It was like a dream ended. People scattered in all directions. Mrs. Sommers went to the corner and waited for the cable car.

A man with keen eyes, who sat opposite to her, seemed to like the study of her small, pale face. It puzzled him to decipher what he saw there. In truth, he saw nothing—unless he were wizard enough to detect a poignant wish, a powerful longing that the cable car would never stop anywhere, but go on and on with her forever.

Aunt Lympy's Interference

The day was warm, and Melitte, cleaning her room, strayed often to the south window that looked out toward the Annibelles' place. She was a slender young body of eighteen with skirts that escaped the ground and a pink-sprigged shirt-waist. She had the beauty that belongs to youth—the freshness, the dewiness—with healthy brown hair that gleamed and honest brown eyes that could be earnest as well as merry.

Looking toward the Annibelles' place, Melitte could see but a speck of the imposing white house through the trees. Men were at work in the field, head and shoulders above the cotton. She could occasionally hear them laugh or shout. The air came in little broken waves from the south, bringing the hot, sweet scent of flowers and sometimes the good smell of the plowed earth.

Melitte always cleaned her room thoroughly on Saturday, because it was her only free day; of late she had been conducting a small school which stood down the road at the far end of the Annibelle place.

Almost every morning, as she trudged to school, she saw Victor Annibelle mending the fence; always mending it, but why so much nailing and bracing were required, no one but himself knew. The spectacle of the young man so persistently at work was one to distress Melitte in the goodness of her soul.

"My! but you have trouble with yo' fence, Victor," she called out to him in passing.

His good-looking face changed from a healthy brown to the color of one of his own cotton blooms; and never a phrase could his wits find till she was out of ear-shot; for Melitte never stopped to talk. She would but fling him a pleasant word, turning her face to him framed, buried, in a fluted pink sunbonnet.

He had not always been so diffident—when they were youngsters, for instance, and he lent her his pony, or came over to thrash the pecan-tree for her. Now it was different. Since he had been long away from home and had returned at twenty-two, she gave herself the airs and graces of a young lady.

He did not dare to call her "Melitte," he was ashamed to call her "Miss," so he called her nothing, and hardly spoke to her.

Sometimes Victor went over to visit in the evenings, when he would be amiably entertained by Melitte, her brother, her brother's wife, her two little nieces and one little nephew. On Saturdays the young man was apparently less concerned about the condition of his fences, and passed frequently up and down the road on his white horse.

Melitte thought it was perhaps he, calling upon some pretext, when the little tot of a nephew wabbled in to say that some one wanted to see her on the front gallery. She gave a flurried glance at the mirror and divested her head of the dust-cloth.

"It's Aunt Lympy!" exclaimed the two small nieces, who had followed in the wake of the toddling infant.

"She won't say w'at she wants, *ti tante*," pursued one of them. "She don't look pleased, an' she sittin' down proud as a queen in the big chair."

There, in fact, Melitte found Aunt Lympy, proud and unbending in all the glory of a flowered "challie" and a black grenadine shawl edged with a purple satin quilling; she was light-colored. Two heavy bands of jet-black hair showed beneath her bandanna and covered her ears down to the gold hoop earrings.

"W'y, Aunt Lympy!" cried the girl, cordially, extending both hands. "Didn't I hear you were in Alexandria?"

"Tha's true, ma' Melitte." Aunt Lympy spoke slowly and with emphasis. "I ben in Alexandria nussin' Judge Morse's wife. She well now, an' I ben sence Chuseday in town. Look like Severin git 'long well 'idout me, an' I ant hurry to go home." Her dusky eyes glowed far from cheerfully.

"I yeard some'in' yonda in town," the woman went on, "w'at I don' wan' to b'lieve. An' I say to myse'f, 'Olympe, you don' listen to no sich tale tell you go axen ma' Melitte.' "

149

"Something you heard about me, Aunt Lympy?" Melitte's eyes were wide.

"I don' wan' to spick about befo' de chillun," said Aunt Lympy.

"I yeard yonda in town, ma' Melitte," she went on after the children had gone, "I yeard you was turn school-titcher! Dat ant true?"

The question in her eyes was almost pathetic.

"Oh!" exclaimed Melitte; an utterance that expressed relief, surprise, amusement, commiseration, affirmation.

"Den it's true," Aunt Lympy almost whispered; "a De Broussard turn school-titcher!" The shame of it crushed her into silence.

Melitte felt the inutility of trying to dislodge the old family servant's deep-rooted prejudices. All her effort was directed toward convincing Aunt Lympy of her complete self-satisfaction in this new undertaking.

But Aunt Lympy did not listen. She had money in her reticule, if that would do any good. Melitte gently thrust it away. She changed the subject, and kindly offered the woman a bit of refreshment. But Aunt Lympy would not eat, drink, unbend, nor lend herself to the subterfuge of small talk. She said good-by, with solemnity, as we part from those in sore affliction. When she had mounted into her ramshackle open buggy the old vehicle looked someway like a throne.

Scarcely a week after Aunt Lympy's visit Melitte was amazed by receiving a letter from her uncle, Gervais Leplain, of New Orleans. The tone of the letter was sad, self-condemnatory, reminiscent. A flood of tender recollection of his dead sister seemed to have suddenly overflowed his heart and glided from the point of his pen.

He was asking Melitte to come to them there in New Orleans and be as one of his own daughters, who were quite as eager to call her "sister" as he was desirous of subscribing himself always henceforward, her father. He sent her a sum of money to supply her immediate wants, and informed her that he and one of his daughters would come for her in person at an early date.

Never a word was said of a certain missive dictated and sent to him by Aunt Lympy, every line of which was either a stinging rebuke or an appeal to the memory of his dead sister, whose child was tasting the bitter dregs of poverty. Melitte would never have recognized the overdrawn picture of herself.

From the very first there seemed to be no question about her accepting the offer of her uncle. She had literally not time to lift her voice in protest, before relatives, friends, acquaintances throughout the country raised a very clamor of congratulation. What luck! What a chance! To form one of the Gervais Leplain household!

Perhaps Melitte did not know that they lived in the most sumptuous style in la rue Esplanade, with a cottage across the lake; and they travelled—they spent summers at the North! Melitte would see the great, the big, the beautiful world! They already pictured little Melitte gowned *en Parisienne;* they saw her name figuring in the society columns of the Sunday papers! as attending balls, dinners, luncheons and card parties.

The whole proceeding had apparently stunned Melitte. She sat with folded hands; except that she put the money carefully aside to return to her uncle. She would in no way get it confounded with her own small hoard; that was something precious and apart, not to be contaminated by gift-money.

"Have you written to yo' uncle to thank him, Melitte?" asked the sister-in-law.

Melitte shook her head. "No; not yet."

"But, Melitte!"

"Yes; I know."

"Do you want yo' brother to write?"

"No! Oh, no!"

"Then don't put it off a day longer, Melitte. Such rudeness! W'at will yo' Uncle Gervais an' yo' cousins think!"

Even the babies that loved her were bitten with this feverish ambition for Melitte's worldly advancement. " 'Taint you, *ti tante,* that's goin' to wear a sunbonnet any mo', or calico dresses, or an apron, or feed the chickens!"

"Then you want *ti tante* to go away an' leave you all?"

They were not ready to answer, but hung their heads in meditative silence, which lasted until the full meaning of *ti tante's* question had penetrated the inner consciousness of the little man, whereupon he began to howl, loud and deep and long.

Even the curé, happy to see the end of a family estrangement, took Melitte's acceptance wholly for granted. He visited her and discoursed at length and with vivid imagination upon the perils and fascinations of "the city's" life, presenting impartially, however, its advantages, which he hoped she would use to the betterment of her moral and intellectual faculties. He recommended to her a confessor at the cathedral who had travelled with him from France so many years ago.

"It's time you were dismissing an' closing up that school of yo's,

Melitte," advised her sister-in-law, puzzled and disturbed, as Melitte was preparing to leave for the schoolhouse.

She did not answer. She seemed to have been growing sullen and ill-humored since her great piece of good luck; but perhaps she did not hear, with the pink sunbonnet covering her pink ears.

Melitte was sensible of a strong attachment for the things about her—the dear, familiar things. She did not fully realize that her surroundings were poor and pinched. The thought of entering upon a different existence troubled her.

Why was every one, with single voice, telling her to "go"? Was it that no one cared? She did not believe this, but chose to nourish the fancy. It furnished her a pretext for tears.

Why should she not go, and live in ease, free from responsibility and care? Why should she stay where no soul had said, "I can't bear to have you go, Melitte?"

If they had only said, "I shall miss you, Melitte," it would have been something—but no! Even Aunt Lympy, who had nursed her as a baby, and in whose affection she had always trusted—even she had made her appearance and spent a whole day upon the scene, radiant, dispensing compliments, self-satisfied, as one who feels that all things are going well in her royal possessions.

"Oh, I'll go! I will go!" Melitte was saying a little hysterically to herself as she walked. The familiar road was a brown and green blur, for the tears in her eyes.

Victor Annibelle was not mending his fence that morning; but there he was, leaning over it as Melitte came along. He had hardly expected she would come, and at that hour he should have been back in the swamp with the men who were hired to cut timber; but the timber could wait, and the men could wait, and so could the work. It did not matter. There would be days enough to work when Melitte was gone.

She did not look at him; her head was down and she walked steadily on, carrying her bag of books. In a moment he was over the fence; he did not take the time to walk around to the gate; and with a few long strides he had joined her.

"Good morning, Melitte." She gave a little start, for she had not heard him approaching.

"Oh—good morning. How is it you are not at work this morning?"

"I'm going a little later. An' how is it you are at work, Melitte? I didn't expect to see you passing by again."

"Then you were going to let me leave without coming to say good-by?" she returned with an attempt at sprightliness.

And he, after a long moment's hesitation, "Yes, I believe I was. W'en do you go?"

"When do you go! When do you go!" There it was again! Even he was urging her. It was the last straw.

"Who said I was going?" She spoke with quick exasperation. It was warm, and he would have lingered beneath the trees that here and there flung a pleasant shade, but she led him a pace through the sun.

"Who said?" he repeated after her. "W'y, I don't know—everybody. You are going, of co'se?"

"Yes."

She walked slowly and then fast in her agitation, wondering why he did not leave her instead of remaining there at her side in silence.

"Oh, I can't bear to have you go, Melitte!"

They were so near the school it seemed perfectly natural that she should hurry forward to join the little group that was there waiting for her under a tree. He made no effort to follow her. He expected no reply; the expression that had escaped him was so much a part of his unspoken thought, he was hardly conscious of having uttered it.

But the few spoken words, trifling as they seemed, possessed a power to warm and brighten greater than that of the sun and the moon. What mattered now to Melitte if the hours were heavy and languid; if the children were slow and dull! Even when they asked, "W'en are you going, Miss Melitte?" she only laughed and said there was plenty of time to think of it. And were they so anxious to be rid of her? she wanted to know. She some way felt that it would not be so very hard to go now. In the afternoon, when she had dismissed the scholars, she lingered a while in the schoolroom. When she went to close the window, Victor Annibelle came up and stood outside with his elbows on the sill.

"Oh!" she said, with a start, "why are you not working this hour of the day?" She was conscious of reiteration and a sad lack of imagination or invention to shape her utterances. But the question suited his intention well enough.

"I haven't worked all day," he told her. "I haven't gone twenty paces from this schoolhouse since you came into it this morning." Every particle of diffidence that had hampered his intercourse with her during the past few months had vanished.

"I'm a selfish brute," he blurted, "but I reckon it's instinct fo' a man to fight fo' his happiness just as he would fight fo' his life."

"I mus' be going, Victor. Please move yo' arms an' let me close the window."

"No, I won't move my arms till I say w'at I came here to say." And seeing that she was about to withdraw, he seized her hand and held it. "If you go away, Melitte—if you go I—oh! I don't want you to go. Since morning—I don't know w'y—something you said—or some way, I have felt that maybe you cared a little; that you might stay if I begged you. Would you, Melitte—would you?"

"I believe I would, Victor. Oh—never mind my hand; don't you see I must shut the window?"

So after all Melitte did not go to the city to become a *grande dame*. Why? Simply because Victor Annibelle asked her not to. The old people when they heard it shrugged their shoulders and tried to remember that they, too, had been young once; which is, sometimes, a very hard thing for old people to remember. Some of the younger ones thought she was right, and many of them believed she was wrong to sacrifice so brilliant an opportunity to shine and become a woman of fashion.

Aunt Lympy was not altogether dissatisfied; she felt that her interference had not been wholly in vain.

A Family Affair

The moment that the wagon rattled out of the yard away to the station, Madame Solisainte settled herself into a state of nervous expectancy.

She was superabundantly fat; and her body accommodated itself to the huge chair in which she sat, filling up curves and crevices like water poured into a mould. She was clad in an ample muslin *peignoir* sprigged with brown. Her cheeks were flabby, her mouth thin-lipped and decisive. Her eyes were small, watchful, and at the same time timid. Her brown hair, streaked with gray, was arranged in a bygone fashion, a narrow mesh being drawn back from the centre of the forehead to conceal a bald spot, and the sides plastered down smooth over her small, close ears.

The room in which she sat was large and uncarpeted. There were handsome and massive pieces of furniture decorating the apartment, and a magnificent brass clock stood on the mantelpiece.

Madame Solisainte sat at a back window which overlooked the yard, the brick kitchen—a little removed from the house—and the field road which led down to the negro quarters. She was unable to leave her chair. It was an affair of importance to get her out of bed in the morning, and an equally arduous task to put her back there at night.

It was a sore affliction to the old woman to be thus incapacitated during her latter years, and rendered unable to watch and control her household affairs. She was sure that she was being robbed continuously and on all sides. This conviction was nourished and kept alive by her confidential servant, Dimple, a very black girl of sixteen, who trod softly about on her bare feet and had thereby made herself unpopular in the kitchen and down at the quarters.

The notion had entered Madame Solisainte's head to have one of her nieces come up from New Orleans and stay with her. She thought it would be doing the niece and her family a great kindness, and would furthermore be an incalculable saving to herself in many ways, and far cheaper than hiring a housekeeper.

There were four nieces, not too well off, with whom she was indifferently acquainted. In selecting one of these to make her home on the plantation she exercised no choice, leaving that matter to her sister and the girls, to be settled among them.

It was Bosey who consented to go to her aunt. Her mother spelled her name Bosé. She herself spelled it Bosey. But as often as not she was called plain Bose. It was she who was sent, because, as her mother wrote to Madame Solisainte, Bosé was a splendid manager, a most excellent housekeeper, and moreover possessed a temperament of such rare amiability that none could help being cheered and enlivened by her presence.

What she did not write was that none of the other girls would entertain the notion for an instant of making even a temporary abiding place with their *Tante* Félicie. And Bosey's consent was only wrung from her with the understanding that the undertaking was purely experimental, and that she bound herself by no cast-iron obligations.

Madame Solisainte had sent the wagon to the station for her niece, and was impatiently awaiting its return.

"It's no sign of the wagon yet, Dimple? You don't see it? You don't year it coming?"

"No'um; 'tain't no sign. De train des 'bout lef' de station. I yeard it w'istle." Dimple stood on the back porch beside her mistress' open window. She wore a calico dress so skimp and inadequate that her growing figure was bursting through the rents and apertures. She was constantly pinning it at the back of the waist with a bent safety-pin which was forever giving way. The task of pinning her dress and biting the old brass safety-pin into shape occupied a great deal of her time.

"It's true," Madame said. "I recommend to Daniel to drive those mule' very slow in this hot weather. They are not strong, those mule'."

"He drive 'em slow 'nough long 's he's in the fiel' road!" exclaimed Dimple. "Time he git roun' in de big road whar you kain't see 'im—uh! uh! he make' dem mule' fa'r' lope!"

Madame tightened her lips and blinked her eyes. She rarely replied otherwise to these disclosures of Dimple, but they sank into her soul and festered there.

The cook—in reality a big-boned field hand—came in with pans and pails to get out the things for supper. Madame kept her provisions right there under her nose in a large closet, or cupboard, which she had had built in the side of the room. A small supply of butter was in a jar that stood on the hearth, and the eggs were kept in a basket that hung on a peg near by.

Dimple came in and unlocked the cupboard, taking the keys from her mistress' bag. She gave out a little flour, a little meal, a cupful of coffee, some sugar and a piece of bacon. Four eggs were wanted for a pudding, but Madame thought that two would be enough, finally compromising, however, upon three.

Miss Bosey Brantonniere arrived at her aunt's house with three trunks, a large, circular, tin bathtub, a bundle of umbrellas and sunshades, and a small dog. She was a pretty, energetic-looking girl, with her chin in the air, tastefully dressed in the latest fashion, and dispersing an atmosphere of bustle and importance about her. Daniel had driven her up the field road, depositing her at the back entrance, where Madame, from her window, commanded a complete view of her arrival.

"I thought you would have sent the carriage for me, *Tante* Félicie, but Daniel tells me you have no carriage," said the girl after the first greetings were over. She had had her trunks taken to her room, the tub slipped under the bed, and now she sat fondling the dog and talking to *Tante* Félicie.

The old lady shook her head dismally and her lips curled into a disparaging smile.

"Oh! no, no! The ol' carriage 'as been sol' ages ago to Zéphire Lablatte. It was falling to piece' in the shed. Me—I never stir f'um w'ere you see me; it is good two year' since I 'ave been inside the church, let alone to go *en promenade.*"

"Well, I'm going to take all care and bother off your shoulders, *Tante* Félicie," uttered the girl cheerfully. "I'm going to brighten things up for you, and we'll see how quickly you'll improve. Why, in less than two months I'll have you on your feet, going about as spry as anybody."

Madame was far less hopeful. "My ol' mother was the same," she replied with dejected resignation. "Nothing could 'elp her. She lived many year' like you see me; your mamma mus' 'ave often tol' you."

Mrs. Brantonniere had never related to the girls anything disparaging concerning their Aunt Félicie, but other members of the family had been less considerate, and Bosey had often been told of her aunt's avarice and grasping ways. How she had laid her clutch upon her mother's belongings, taking undisputed possession by the force of audacity alone. The girl could not help thinking it must have been while her grandmother sat so helpless in her huge chair that *Tante* Félicie had made herself mistress of the situation. But she was not one to harbor malice. She felt very sorry for *Tante* Félicie, so afflicted in her childless old age.

Madame lay long awake that night troubled someway over the advent of this niece from New Orleans, who was not precisely what she had expected. She did not like the excess of trunks, the bathtub and the dog, all of which savored of extravagance. Nor did she like the chin in the air, which indicated determination and promised trouble.

Dimple was warned next morning to say nothing to her mistress concerning a surprise which Miss Bosey had in store for her. This surprise was that, instead of being deposited in her accustomed place at the back window, where she could keep an eye upon her people, Madame was installed at the front-room window that looked out toward the live oaks and along a leafy, sleepy road that was seldom used.

"*Jamais! Jamais!* it will never do! *Pas possible!*" cried out the old lady with helpless excitement when she perceived what was about to be done to her.

"You'll do just as I say, *Tante* Félicie," said Bosey, with sprightly determination. "I'm here to take care of you and make you comfortable, and I'm going to do it. Now, instead of looking out on that hideous back yard, full of dirty little darkies, and pigs and chickens wallowing round, here you have this sweet, peaceful view whenever you look out of the window. Now, here comes Dimple with the magazines and things. Bring them right here, Dimple, and lay them on the table beside Ma'me Félicie. I brought these up from the city expressly for you, *Tante*, and I have a whole trunkful more when you are through with them."

Dimple was entering, staggering with arms full of books and periodicals of all sizes, shapes and colors. The strain of carrying the weight of literature had caused the safety-pin to give way, and Dimple greatly feared it might have fallen and been lost.

"So, *Tante* Félicie, you'll have nothing to do but read and enjoy yourself. Here are some French books mamma sent you, something by Daudet, something by Maupassant and a lot more. Here, let me brighten up your spectacles." She brightened the old lady's glasses with a piece of thin tissue paper which fell from one of the books.

"And now, Madame Solisainte, you give me all the keys! Turn them right over, and I'll go out and make myself thoroughly acquainted with everything." Madame spasmodically clutched the bag that swung to the arm of her chair.

"Oh! a whole bagful!" exclaimed the girl, gently but firmly disengaging it from her aunt's claw-like fingers. "My, what an undertaking I have before me! Dimple had better show me round this morning until I get thoroughly acquainted. You can knock on the floor with your stick when you want her. Come along, Dimple. Fasten your dress." The girl was scanning the floor for the safety-pin, which she found out in the hall.

During all of Madame Solisainte's days no one had ever spoken to her with the authority which this young woman assumed. She did not know what to make of it. She felt that she should have revolted at once against being thus banished to the front room. She should have spoken out and maintained possession of her keys when demanded, with the spirit of a highway robber, to give them up. She pounded her stick on the floor with loud and sudden energy. Dimple appeared with inquisitive eyes.

"Dimple," said Madame, "tell Miss Bosé to please 'ave the kin'ness an sen' me back my bag of key'."

Dimple vanished and returned almost on the instant.

"Miss Bosey 'low don't you bodda. Des you go on lookin' at de picters. She ain' gwine let nuttin' happen to de keys."

After an uneasy interval Madame recalled the girl.

"Dimple, if you could look in the bag an' bring me my armoire key— you know it—the brass one. Do not let on as though I would want that key in partic'lar."

"De bag hangin' on her arm. She got de string twis' roun' her wris'," reported Dimple presently. Madame Félicie inwardly fumed with impotent rage.

"W'at is she doing, Dimple?" she asked uneasily.

"She got de cubbud do's fling wide open. She standin' on a cha'r lookin' in de corners an' behin' eve'ything."

"Dimple!" called out Bosey from the far room. And away flew Dimple, who had not been so pleasingly agitated since the previous Christmas.

After a little while, of her own accord she stole noiselessly back into the room where Madame Félicie sat in speechless wrath beside the table of books. She closed the door behind her, rolled her eyes, and spoke in a hoarse whisper:

"She done fling 'way de barrel o' meal; 'low it all fill up wid weevils."

"Weevil'!" cried out her mistress.

"Yas'um, weevils; 'low it plumb sp'ilt. 'Low it on'y fitten fo' de chickens an' hogs; 'tain't fitten fo' folks. She done make Dan'el roll it out on de gal'ry."

"Weevil'!" reiterated Madame Félicie, tremulous with suppressed excitement. "Bring me some of that meal in a saucer, Dimple. Don't let on anything."

She and Dimple bent over the cup of meal which the girl brought concealed under her skirt.

"Do you see any weevil', you, Dimple?"

"No'um." Dimple smelled it, and Madame felt the sample of meal and rolled a pinch or two between her fingers. It was lumpy, musty and old.

"She got Susan out dah helpin' her," insinuated Dimple, "an' Sam an' Dan'el; all helpin' her."

"*Bon Dieu!* it won't be a grain of sugar left, a bar of soap—nothing! nothing! Go watch, Dimple. Don't stan' there like a stick."

"She 'low she gwine sen' Susan back to wuk in de fiel'," went on Dimple, heedless of her mistress' admonition. "She 'low Susan don' know how to cook. Susan say she willin' to go back, her. An' Miss Bosey, she ax Dan'el ef he know a fus'-class cook, w'at kin brile chicken an' steak an' make good soup, an' waffles, an' rolls, an' fricassée, an' dessert, an' custud, an sich."

She passed her tongue over a slobbering lip. "Dan'el say his wife Mandy done cook fo' de pa'tic'lest people in town, but she don' wuk cheap 'nough fo' Ma'me Félicie. An' Miss Bosey, she 'low it don' make no odd' 'bout de price, 'long she git hole o' somebody w'at know how to cook."

Madame's fingers worked nervously at the illuminated cover of a magazine. She said nothing. Only tightened her lips and blinked her small eyes.

When Bosey thrust her head in at the door to inquire how "*Tantine*" was getting on, the old lady fumbled at the books with a pretense of having been occupied with looking at them.

"That's right, *Tante* Félicie! You look as comfortable as can be. I wanted to make you a nice glass of lemonade, but Susan tells me there isn't a lemon on the place. I told Fannie's boy to bring up half a box of lemons from Lablatte's store in the handcart. There's nothing healthier than lemonade in summer. And he's going to bring a chunk of ice, too. We'll have to order ice from town after this." She had on a white apron over her gingham dress, and her sleeves were rolled to the elbows.

"I detes' lemonade; it is bad for *mon estomac*," interposed Madame vehemently. "We 'ave no use in the worl' for lemon', an' there is no place vere to keep ice. Tell Fannie's boy never min' about lemon' an' ice."

160

"Oh, he's gone long ago! And as for the ice, why, Daniel says he can make me a box lined with sawdust—he made one for Doctor Godfrey. We can keep it under the back porch." And away she went, the embodiment of the thoroughgoing, bustling little housewife. Somewhat past noon, Dimple came in with an air of importance, removed the books, and spread a white damask cloth upon the table. It was like spreading a red cloth before a sullen bull. Madame's eyes glared at the cloth.

"W'ere did you get that?" she asked as if she would have annihilated Dimple on the spot.

"Miss Bosey, she tuck it out de big press; tuck some mo' out; 'low she kain't eat on dat meal-sack w'at we alls calls de table-clot'e." The damask cloth bore the initials of Madame's mother, embroidered in a corner.

"She done kilt two dem young pullets in de *basse-cour*," went on Dimple, like a croaking raven. "Mandy come lopin' up f'om de quarters time Dan'el told 'er. She yonder, rarin' roun' in de kitchen. Dey done sent fo' some sto' lard an' bakin' powders down to Lablatte's. Fannie's boy, he ben totin' all mornin'. De cubbud done look lak a sto'."

"Dimple!" called Bosey in the distance.

When she returned it was with a pompous air, her head uplifted, and stepping carefully like a fat chicken. She bore a tray weighted with a repast such as she had never before in her life served to Madame Solisainte.

Mandy had outdone herself. She had broiled the breast of a pullet to a turn. She had fried the potatoes after a New Orleans receipt, and had made a pudding of richest ingredients of her own invention which had given her a name in the parish. There were two milky-looking poached eggs, and the biscuits were as light as snowflakes and the color of gold. The forks and spoons were of massive silver, also bearing the initials of Madame's mother. They had been reclaimed from the press with the table linen.

Under this new, strange influence Madame Solisainte seemed to have been deprived of the power of asserting her will. There was an occasional outburst like the flare of a smouldering fire, but she was outwardly timid and submissive. Only when she was alone with her young handmaid did she speak her mind.

Bosey took special care in arranging her aunt's toilet one morning not long after her arrival. She fastened a sheer white 'kerchief (which she found in the press) about the old lady's neck. She powdered her face from her own box of *duvet de cygne* ; and she gave her a fine linen handkerchief (which she also found in the press), sprinkling it from the bottle of cologne water which she had brought from New Orleans. She filled the vase upon the table with fresh flowers, and dusted and rearranged the books there.

Madame had been moving forward the bookmark in the novel to pretend that she was reading it.

These unusual preparations were explained an hour or two later, when Bosey introduced into Madame Solisainte's presence their neighbor, Doctor Godfrey. He was a youngish, good-looking man, with a loud, cheery voice and a superabundance of animal spirits. He seemed to carry about with him the very atmosphere of health and to dispense it broadcast in invisible waves.

"Do you see, *Tante* Félicie, how I think of everything? When I saw, last night, the suffering you endured at being put to bed, I decided that you ought to be under a physician's treatment. So the first thing I did this morning was to send a messenger for Doctor Godfrey, and here he is!"

Madame glared at him as he drew up a chair on the opposite side of the table and began to talk about how long it was since he had seen her.

"I do not need a physician!" she cried in tones of exasperation, looking from one to the other. "All the physician' in the worl' cannot 'elp me. My mother was the same; she try all the physician' of the parish. She went to the 'ot spring', to *la Nouvelle Orleans*, an' she die' at las' in this chair. Nothing will 'elp me."

"That is for me to say, Madame Solisainte," said the Doctor, with cheerful assurance. "It is a good idea of your niece's that you should place yourself under a physician's care. I don't say mine, understand—there are many excellent physicians in the parish—but some one ought to look after you, if it is only to keep you in comfortable condition."

Madame blinked at him under lowered brows. She was thinking of his bill for this visit, and determined that he should not make a second one. She saw ruin staring her in the face, and felt as if she were being borne along on a raging torrent of extravagance to meet it.

Bosey had already explained Madame's symptoms to the Doctor, and he said he would send or bring over a preparation which Madame Solisainte must take night and morning till he saw fit to alter or discontinue it. Then he glanced at the magazines, while he and the girl engaged in a lively conversation across Madame's chair. His eyes sparkled with animation as he looked at Bosey, as fresh and sweet in her pink dimity gown as one of the flowers there on the table.

He came very often, and Madame grew sick with apprehension and uncertainty, unable to distinguish between his professional and social visits. At first she refused to take his medicine until Bosey stood over her one evening with a spoonful, gently but firmly expressing a determination to stand there till morning, if necessary, and Madame consented to swallow the mixture. The Doctor took Bosey out driving in his new buggy behind two fast trotters. The first time, after she had driven away, Madame Félicie charged Dimple to go into Miss Bosey's room and search everywhere for the bag of keys. But they were not to be found.

"She mus' kiard 'em wid 'er. She all time got 'em twis' roun' 'er arm. I believe she sleep wid 'em twis' roun' 'er arm," offered Dimple in explanation of her failure.

Unable to find the keys, she turned to examining the young girl's dainty belongings—such as were not under lock. She crept back into Madame Félicie's room, carrying a lace-frilled parasol which she silently held out for Madame's inspection. The lace was simple and inexpensive, but the old woman shuddered at sight of it as if it had been the rarest d'Alençon.

Perceiving the impression created by the gay sunshade, Dimple next brought in a pair of slippers with spangled toes, a fine pair of stockings that hung on the back of a chair, an embroidered petticoat, and finally a silk waist. She brought the articles one by one, with a certain solemnity rendered doubly impressive by her silence.

Dimple was wearing her best dress—a red calico with ruffles and puffed sleeves (Miss Bosey had compelled her to discard the other). As a consequence of this holiday attire Dimple gave herself Sunday airs, and passed her time hanging to the gallery post or doubling her body across the bannister rail.

Bosey grew more and more prolific in devices for her Aunt Félicie's comfort and entertainment. She invited Madame's old friends to visit her, singly and in groups; to spend the day—in some instances several days.

She began to have company herself. The young gentlemen and girls of the parish came from miles around to pay their respects. She was of a hospitable turn, and dispensed iced lemonade on such occasions, and sangaree—Lablatte having ordered a case of red wine from the city. There was constant baking of cakes going on in the kitchen, Daniel's wife surpassing all her former efforts in that direction.

Bosey gave lawn parties, with the Chinese lanterns all festooned among the oaks, with three musicians from the quarters playing the fiddle, the guitar and accordion on the gallery, right under Madame Solisainte's nose. She gave a ball and dressed *Tante* Félicie up for the occasion in a silk *peignoir* which she had had made in the city as a surprise.

The Doctor took Bosey driving or horseback riding every other day. He all but lived at Madame Solisainte's, and was in danger of losing all his practice, till Bosey, in mercy, promised to marry him.

She kept her engagement a secret from *Tante* Félicie, pursuing her avocation of the ministering angel up to the very day of her departure for the city to make preparations for her approaching marriage.

A beatitude, a beneficent joy settled upon Madame when Bosey announced her engagement to the Doctor and her intention to leave the plantation that afternoon.

"Oh! You can't imagine, *Tante* Félicie, how I regret to leave you—just as I was getting things so comfortably and pleasantly settled about you, too. If you want, perhaps Fifine or sister Adèle would come——"

"No! no!" cried Madame in shrill protest. "Nothing of the kin'! I insist, let them stay w'ere they are. I am ole; I am use' to my ways. It is not 'ard for me to be alone. I will not year of it!"

Madame could have sung for very joy as she listened all morning to the bustle of her niece's packing. She even petted doggie in her exuberance, for she had aimed many a blow at him with her stick when he had had the temerity to trust himself alone with her.

The trunks and the bathtub were sent away at noon. The clatter accompanying their departure sounded like sweet music in Madame Solisainte's ears. It was with almost a feeling of affection that she embraced her niece when the girl came and kissed her good-by. The Doctor was going to drive his *fiancée* to the station in his buggy.

He told Madame Félicie that he felt like an archangel. In reality, he looked demented with happiness and excitement. She was as suave as honey to him. She was thinking that in the character of a nephew he would not have the indelicacy to present a bill for professional services.

The Doctor hurried out to turn the horses and to get ready the lap-robe to spread over the knees of his divinity. Bosey looked as dainty as the day she had made her appearance, in the same brown linen gown and jaunty traveling hat. There was a fathomless look in her blue eyes.

"And now, *Tante* Félicie," she said finally, "here is your bag of keys. You will find everything in perfect order, and I hope you will be satisfied. All the purchases have been entered in the book—you will find Lablatte's bills and everything correct. But, by the way, *Tante* Félicie, I want to tell you—I have made an equal division of grandmother's silver and table linen and jewels which I found in the strong box, and sent them to mamma. You know yourself it was only just; mamma had as much right to them as you. So, good-by, *Tante* Félicie. You are quite sure you wouldn't like to have sister Adèle?"

"*Voleuse! voleuse! voleuse!*" she heard her aunt's voice lifted after her in a shrill scream. It followed her as far as the leafy road beyond the live oaks.

Madame Solisainte trembled with excitement and agitation. She looked into the bag and counted the keys. They were all there.

"*Voleuse!*" she kept muttering. She was convinced that Bosey had robbed her of everything she possessed. The jewels were gone, she was sure of it—all gone. Her mother's watch and chain; bracelets, rings, ear-rings, everything gone. All the silver; the table, the bed linen, her mother's clothes—ah! that was why she had brought those three trunks!

Madame Solisainte clutched the brass key and glared at it with eyes wild with apprehension. She pounded her stick upon the floor till the rafters rang. But at that time of the afternoon—the hours between dinner and supper—the yard was deserted. And Dimple, still under the delusion created by the red ruffles and puffed sleeves, was strolling leisurely toward the station to see Miss Bosey off.

Madame pounded and called. In her wrath she overturned the table and sent the books and magazines flying in all directions. She sat a while a prey to the most violent agitation, the most turbulent misgivings, that made the pulses throb in her head and the blood course through her body as though the devil himself were at the valve.

"Robbed! Robbed! Robbed!" she repeated. "My gold; the rings; the necklace! I might have known! Oh! fool! Ah! *cher maître! pas possible!*"

Her head quivered as with a palsy upon its fat bulk. She clutched the arm of her chair and attempted to rise; her effort was fruitless. A second attempt, and she drew herself a few inches out of the chair and fell back again. A third effort, in which her whole big body shook and swayed like a vessel which has sprung a leak, and Madame Solisainte stood upon her feet.

She grasped the cane there at hand and stood helpless, screaming for Dimple. Then she began to walk—or rather drag her feet along the floor, slowly and with painful effort, shaking and leaning heavily upon her stick.

Madame did not think it strange or miraculous that she should be moving thus upon her tottering limbs, which for two years had refused to do their office. Her whole attention was bent upon reaching the press in her bedroom across the hall. She clutched the brass key; she had let all the other keys go, and she said nothing now but "*Volé, volé, volé!*"

Madame Solisainte managed to reach the room without other assistance than the chairs in her way afforded her, and the walls along which she propped her body as she sidled along. Her first thought upon unlocking the press was for her gold. Yes, there it was, all of it, in little piles as she had so often arranged it. But half the silver was gone; half the jewels and table linen.

When the servants began to congregate in the yard, they discovered Madame Félicie standing upon the gallery waiting for them. They uttered exclamations of wonder and consternation. Dimple became hysterical, and began to cry and scream out.

"Go an' fin' Richmond," said Madame to Daniel, and without comment or question he hurried off in search of the overseer.

"I will 'ave the law! Ah! *par exemple! pas possible!* to be rob' in that way! I will 'ave the law. Tell Lablatte I will not pay the bills. Mandy, go back to the quarters, an' sen' Susan to the kitchen. Dimple! Go an' carry all those book' an' magazine' up in the attic, an' put on you' other dress. Do not let me fin' you array in those flounce' again! *Pas possible! volé comme ça!* I will 'ave the law!"

At the 'Cadian Ball

Bobinôt, that big, brown, good-natured Bobinôt, had no intention of going to the ball, even though he knew Calixta would be there. For what came of those balls but heartache, and a sickening disinclination for work the whole week through, till Saturday night came again and his tortures began afresh? Why could he not love Ozéina, who would marry him to-morrow; or Fronie, or any one of a dozen others, rather than that little Spanish vixen? Calixta's slender foot had never touched Cuban soil; but her mother's had, and the Spanish was in her blood all the same. For that reason the prairie people forgave her much that they would not have overlooked in their own daughters or sisters.

Her eyes,—Bobinôt thought of her eyes, and weakened,—the bluest, the drowsiest, most tantalizing that ever looked into a man's; he thought of her flaxen hair that kinked worse than a mulatto's close to her head; that broad, smiling mouth and tiptilted nose, that full figure; that voice like a rich contralto song, with cadences in it that must have been taught by Satan, for there was no one else to teach her tricks on that 'Cadian prairie. Bobinôt thought of them all as he plowed his rows of cane.

There had even been a breath of scandal whispered about her a year ago, when she went to Assumption,—but why talk of it? No one did now. "C'est Espagnol, ça," most of them said with lenient shoulder-shrugs. "Bon chien tient de race," the old men mumbled over their pipes, stirred by recollections. Nothing was made of it, except that Fronie threw it up to Calixta when the two quarreled and fought on the church steps after mass one Sunday, about a lover. Calixta swore roundly in fine 'Cadian French and with true Spanish spirit, and slapped Fronie's face. Fronie had slapped her back; "Tiens, cocotte, va!" "Espèce de lionèse; prends ça, et ça!'' till the curé himself was obliged to hasten and make peace between them. Bobinôt thought of it all, and would not go to the ball.

But in the afternoon, over at Friedheimer's store, where he was buying a trace-chain, he heard some one say that Alcée Laballière would be there. Then wild horses could not have kept him away. He knew how it would be—or rather he did not know how it would be—if the handsome young planter came over to the ball as he sometimes did. If Alcée happened to be in a serious mood, he might only go to the card-room and play a round or two; or he might stand out on the galleries talking crops and politics with the old people. But there was no telling. A drink or two could put the devil in his head,—that was what Bobinôt said to himself, as he wiped the sweat from his brow with his red bandanna; a gleam from Calixta's eyes, a flash of her ankle, a twirl of her skirts could do the same. Yes, Bobinôt would go to the ball.

That was the year Alcée Laballière put nine hundred acres in rice. It was putting a good deal of money into the ground, but the returns promised to be glorious. Old Madame Laballière, sailing about the spacious galleries in her white *volante*, figured it all out in her head. Clarisse, her goddaughter, helped her a little, and together they built more air-castles than enough. Alcée worked like a mule that time; and if he did not kill himself, it was because his constitution was an iron one. It was an every-day affair for him to come in from the field well-nigh exhausted, and wet to the waist. He did not mind if there were visitors; he left them to his mother and Clarisse. There were often guests: young men and women who came up from the city, which was but a few hours away, to visit his beautiful kinswoman. She was worth going a good deal farther than that to see. Dainty as a lily; hardy as a sunflower; slim, tall, graceful, like one of the reeds that grew in the marsh. Cold and kind and cruel by turn, and everything that was aggravating to Alcée.

He would have liked to sweep the place of those visitors, often. Of the men, above all, with their ways and their manners; their swaying of fans like women, and dandling about hammocks. He could have pitched them over the levee into the river, if it had n't meant murder. That was Alcée. But he must have been crazy the day he came in from the rice-field, and, toil-stained as he was, clasped Clarisse by the arms and panted a volley of hot, blistering love-words into her face. No man had ever spoken love to her like that.

"Monsieur!" she exclaimed, looking him full in the eyes, without a quiver. Alcée's hands dropped and his glance wavered before the chill of her calm, clear eyes.

"*Par exemple!*" she muttered disdainfully, as she turned from him, deftly adjusting the careful toilet that he had so brutally disarranged.

That happened a day or two before the cyclone came that cut into the rice like fine steel. It was an awful thing, coming so swiftly, without a moment's warning in which to light a holy candle or set a piece of blessed palm burning. Old madame wept openly and said her beads, just as her son Didier, the New Orleans one, would have done. If such a thing had happened to Alphonse, the Laballière planting cotton up in Natchitoches, he would have raved and stormed like a second cyclone, and made his surroundings unbearable for a day or two. But Alcée took the misfortune differently. He looked ill and gray after it, and said nothing. His speechlessness was frightful. Clarisse's heart melted with tenderness; but when she offered her soft, purring words of condolence, he accepted them with mute indifference. Then she and her nénaine wept afresh in each other's arms.

A night or two later, when Clarisse went to her window to kneel there in the moonlight and say her prayers before retiring, she saw that Bruce, Alcée's negro servant, had led his master's saddle-horse noiselessly along the edge of the sward that bordered the gravel-path, and stood holding him near by. Presently, she heard Alcée quit his room, which was beneath her own, and traverse the lower portico. As he emerged from the shadow and crossed the strip of moonlight, she perceived that he carried a pair of well-filled saddle-bags which he at once flung across the animal's back. He then lost no time in mounting, and after a brief exchange of words with Bruce, went cantering away, taking no precaution to avoid the noisy gravel as the negro had done.

Clarisse had never suspected that it might be Alcée's custom to sally forth from the plantation secretly, and at such an hour; for it was nearly midnight. And had it not been for the telltale saddle-bags, she would only have crept to bed, to wonder, to fret and dream unpleasant dreams. But her impatience and anxiety would not be held in check. Hastily unbolting the shutters of her door that opened upon the gallery, she stepped outside and called softly to the old negro.

"Gre't Peter! Miss Clarisse. I was n' sho it was a ghos' o' w'at, stan'in' up dah, plumb in de night, dataway."

He mounted halfway up the long, broad flight of stairs. She was standing at the top.

"Bruce, w'ere has Monsieur Alcée gone?" she asked.

"W'y, he gone 'bout he business, I reckin," replied Bruce, striving to be non-committal at the outset.

"W'ere has Monsieur Alcée gone?" she reiterated, stamping her bare foot. "I won't stan' any nonsense or any lies; mine, Bruce."

"I don' ric'lic ez I eva tole you lie *yit*, Miss Clarisse. Mista Alcée, he all broke up, sho."

"W'ere—has—he gone? Ah, Sainte Vierge! faut de la patience! butor, va!"

"W'en I was in he room, a-breshin' off he clo'es to-day," the darkey began, settling himself against the stair-rail, "he look dat speechless an' down, I say, 'You 'pear to me like some pussun w'at gwine have a spell o' sickness, Mista Alcée.' He say, 'You reckin?' 'I dat he git up, go look hisse'f stiddy in de glass. Den he go to de chimbly an' jerk up de quinine bottle an' po' a gre't hoss-dose on to he han'. An' he swalla dat mess in a wink, an' wash hit down wid a big dram o' w'iskey w'at he keep in he room, aginst he come all soppin' wet outen de fiel'.

"He 'lows, 'No, I ain' gwine be sick, Bruce.' Den he square off. He say, 'I kin mak out to stan' up an' gi' an' take wid any man I knows, lessen hit 's John L. Sulvun. But w'en God A'mighty an' a 'oman jines fo'ces agin me, dat 's one too many fur me.' I tell 'im, 'Jis so,' whils' I 'se makin' out to bresh a spot off w'at ain' dah, on he coat colla. I tell 'im, 'You wants li'le res', suh.' He say, 'No, I wants li'le fling; dat w'at I wants; an' I gwine git it. Pitch me a fis'ful o' clo'es in dem 'ar saddle-bags.' Dat w'at he say. Don't you bodda, missy. He jis' gone a-caperin' yonda to de Cajun ball. Uh—uh—de skeeters is fair' a-swarmin' like bees roun' yo' foots!"

The mosquitoes were indeed attacking Clarisse's white feet savagely. She had unconsciously been alternately rubbing one foot over the other during the darkey's recital.

"The 'Cadian ball," she repeated contemptuously. "Humph! *Par exemple!* Nice conduc' for a Laballière. An' he needs a saddle-bag, fill' with clothes, to go to the 'Cadian ball!"

"Oh, Miss Clarisse; you go on to bed, chile; git yo' soun' sleep. He 'low he come back in couple weeks o' so. I kiarn be repeatin' lot o' truck w'at young mans say, out heah face o' young gal."

Clarisse said no more, but turned and abruptly reëntered the house.

"You done talk too much wid yo' mouf a'ready, you ole fool nigga, you," muttered Bruce to himself as he walked away.

170

Alcée reached the ball very late, of course—too late for the chicken gumbo which had been served at midnight.

The big, low-ceiled room—they called it a hall—was packed with men and women dancing to the music of three fiddles. There were broad galleries all around it. There was a room at one side where sober-faced men were playing cards. Another, in which babies were sleeping, was called *le parc aux petits*. Any one who is white may go to a 'Cadian ball, but he must pay for his lemonade, his coffee and chicken gumbo. And he must behave himself like a 'Cadian. Grosbœuf was giving this ball. He had been giving them since he was a young man, and he was a middle-aged one, now. In that time he could recall but one disturbance, and that was caused by American railroaders, who were not in touch with their surroundings and had no business there. "Ces maudits gens du raiderode," Grosbœuf called them.

Alcée Laballière's presence at the ball caused a flutter even among the men, who could not but admire his "nerve" after such misfortune befalling him. To be sure, they knew the Laballières were rich—that there were resources East, and more again in the city. But they felt it took a *brave homme* to stand a blow like that philosophically. One old gentleman, who was in the habit of reading a Paris newspaper and knew things, chuckled gleefully to everybody that Alcée's conduct was altogether *chic*, *mais chic*. That he had more *panache* than Boulanger. Well, perhaps he had.

But what he did not show outwardly was that he was in a mood for ugly things to-night. Poor Bobinôt alone felt it vaguely. He discerned a gleam of it in Alcée's handsome eyes, as the young planter stood in the doorway, looking with rather feverish glance upon the assembly, while he laughed and talked with a 'Cadian farmer who was beside him.

Bobinôt himself was dull-looking and clumsy. Most of the men were. But the young women were very beautiful. The eyes that glanced into Alcée's as they passed him were big, dark, soft as those of the young heifers standing out in the cool prairie grass.

But the belle was Calixta. Her white dress was not nearly so handsome or well made as Fronie's (she and Fronie had quite forgotten the battle on the church steps, and were friends again), nor were her slippers so stylish as those of Ozéina; and she fanned herself with a handkerchief, since she had broken her red fan at the last ball, and her aunts and uncles were not willing to give her another. But all the men agreed she was at her best to-night. Such animation! and abandon! such flashes of wit!

"Hé, Bobinôt! *Mais* w'at 's the matta? W'at you standin' *planté là* like ole Ma'ame Tina's cow in the bog, you?"

That was good. That was an excellent thrust at Bobinôt, who had forgotten the figure of the dance with his mind bent on other things, and it started a clamor of laughter at his expense. He joined good-naturedly. It was better to receive even such notice as that from Calixta than none at all. But Madame Suzonne, sitting in a corner, whispered to her neighbor that if Ozéina were to conduct herself in a like manner, she should immediately be taken out to the mule-cart and driven home. The women did not always approve of Calixta.

Now and then were short lulls in the dance, when couples flocked out upon the galleries for a brief respite and fresh air. The moon had gone down pale in the west, and in the east was yet no promise of day. After such an interval, when the dancers again assembled to resume the interrupted quadrille, Calixta was not among them.

She was sitting upon a bench out in the shadow, with Alcée beside her. They were acting like fools. He had attempted to take a little gold ring from her finger; just for the fun of it, for there was nothing he could have done with the ring but replace it again. But she clinched her hand tight. He pretended that it was a very difficult matter to open it. Then he kept the hand in his. They seemed to forget about it. He played with her earring, a thin crescent of gold hanging from her small brown ear. He caught a wisp of the kinky hair that had escaped its fastening, and rubbed the ends of it against his shaven cheek.

"You know, last year in Assumption, Calixta?" They belonged to the younger generation, so preferred to speak English.

"Don't come say Assumption to me, M'sieur Alcée. I done yeard Assumption till I 'm plumb sick."

"Yes, I know. The idiots! Because you were in Assumption, and I happened to go to Assumption, they must have it that we went together. But it was nice—*hein*, Calixta?—in Assumption?"

They saw Bobinôt emerge from the hall and stand a moment outside the lighted doorway, peering uneasily and searchingly into the darkness. He did not see them, and went slowly back.

"There is Bobinôt looking for you. You are going to set poor Bobinôt crazy. You 'll marry him some day; *hein*, Calixta?"

"I don't say no, me," she replied, striving to withdraw her hand, which he held more firmly for the attempt.

"But come, Calixta; you know you said you would go back to Assumption, just to spite them."

"No, I neva said that, me. You mus' dreamt that."

"Oh, I thought you did. You know I 'm going down to the city."

"W'en?"

"To-night."

"Betta make has'e, then; it 's mos' day."

"Well, to-morrow 'll do."

"W'at you goin' do, yonda?"

"I don't know. Drown myself in the lake, maybe; unless you go down there to visit your uncle."

Calixta's senses were reeling; and they well-nigh left her when she felt Alcée's lips brush her ear like the touch of a rose.

"Mista Alcée! Is dat Mista Alcée?" the thick voice of a negro was asking; he stood on the ground, holding to the banister-rails near which the couple sat.

"W'at do you want now?" cried Alcée impatiently. "Can't I have a moment of peace?"

"I ben huntin' you high an' low, suh," answered the man. "Dey—dey some one in de road, onda de mulbare-tree, want see you a minute."

"I would n't go out to the road to see the Angel Gabriel. And if you come back here with any more talk, I 'll have to break your neck." The negro turned mumbling away.

Alcée and Calixta laughed softly about it. Her boisterousness was all gone. They talked low, and laughed softly, as lovers do.

"Alcée! Alcée Laballière!"

It was not the negro's voice this time; but one that went through Alcée's body like an electric shock, bringing him to his feet.

Clarisse was standing there in her riding-habit, where the negro had stood. For an instant confusion reigned in Alcée's thoughts, as with one who awakes suddenly from a dream. But he felt that something of serious import had brought his cousin to the ball in the dead of night.

"W'at does this mean, Clarisse?" he asked.

"It means something has happen' at home. You mus' come."

"Happened to maman?" he questioned, in alarm.

"No; nénaine is well, and asleep. It is something else. Not to frighten you. But you mus' come. Come with me, Alcée."

There was no need for the imploring note. He would have followed the voice anywhere.

She had now recognized the girl sitting back on the bench.

"Ah, c'est vous, Calixta? Comment ça va, mon enfant?"

"Tcha va b'en; et vous, mam'zélle?"

Alcée swung himself over the low rail and started to follow Clarisse, without a word, without a glance back at the girl. He had forgotten he was leaving her there. But Clarisse whispered something to him, and he turned back to say "Good-night, Calixta," and offer his hand to press through the railing. She pretended not to see it.

"How come that? You settin' yere by yo'se'f, Calixta?" It was Bobinôt who had found her there alone. The dancers had not yet come out. She looked ghastly in the faint, gray light struggling out of the east.

"Yes, that's me. Go yonda in the *parc aux petits* an' ask Aunt Olisse fu' my hat. She knows w'ere 't is. I want to go home, me."

"How you came?"

"I come afoot, with the Cateaus. But I 'm goin' now. I ent goin' wait fu' 'em. I 'm plumb wo' out, me."

"Kin I go with you, Calixta?"

"I don' care."

They went together across the open prairie and along the edge of the fields, stumbling in the uncertain light. He told her to lift her dress that was getting wet and bedraggled; for she was pulling at the weeds and grasses with her hands.

"I don' care; it 's got to go in the tub, anyway. You been sayin' all along you want to marry me, Bobinôt. Well, if you want, yet, I don' care, me."

The glow of a sudden and overwhelming happiness shone out in the brown, rugged face of the young Acadian. He could not speak, for very joy. It choked him.

"Oh well, if you don' want," snapped Calixta, flippantly, pretending to be piqued at his silence.

"*Bon Dieu!* You know that makes me crazy, w'at you sayin'. You mean that, Calixta? You ent goin' turn roun' agin?"

"I neva tole you that much *yet*, Bobinôt. I mean that. *Tiens*," and she held out her hand in the business-like manner of a man who clinches a bargain with a hand-clasp. Bobinôt grew bold with happiness and asked Calixta to kiss him. She turned her face, that was almost ugly after the night's dissipation, and looked steadily into his.

"I don' want to kiss you, Bobinôt," she said, turning away again, "not to-day. Some other time. *Bonté divine!* ent you satisfy, *yet!*"

"Oh, I 'm satisfy, Calixta," he said.

Riding through a patch of wood, Clarisse's saddle became ungirted, and she and Alcée dismounted to readjust it.

For the twentieth time he asked her what had happened at home.

"But, Clarisse, w'at is it? Is it a misfortune?"

"Ah Dieu sait! It 's only something that happen' to me."

"To you!"

"I saw you go away las' night, Alcée, with those saddle-bags," she said, haltingly, striving to arrange something about the saddle, "an' I made Bruce tell me. He said you had gone to the ball, an' wouldn' be home for weeks an' weeks. I thought, Alcée—maybe you were going to—to Assumption. I got wild. An' then I knew if you did n't come back, *now*, to-night, I could n't stan' it,—again."

She had her face hidden in her arm that she was resting against the saddle when she said that.

He began to wonder if this meant love. But she had to tell him so, before he believed it. And when she told him, he thought the face of the Universe was changed—just like Bobinôt. Was it last week the cyclone had well-nigh ruined him? The cyclone seemed a huge joke, now. It was he, then, who, an hour ago was kissing little Calixta's ear and whispering nonsense into it. Calixta was like a myth, now. The one, only, great reality in the world was Clarisse standing before him, telling him that she loved him.

In the distance they heard the rapid discharge of pistol-shots; but it did not disturb them. They knew it was only the negro musicians who had gone into the yard to fire their pistols into the air, as the custom is, and to announce "*le bal est fini.*"

The Storm

A Sequel to "At the 'Cadian Ball"

I

The leaves were so still that even Bibi thought it was going to rain. Bobinôt, who was accustomed to converse on terms of perfect equality with his little son, called the child's attention to certain sombre clouds that were rolling with sinister intention from the west, accompanied by a sullen, threatening roar. They were at Friedheimer's store and decided to remain there till the storm had passed. They sat within the door on two empty kegs. Bibi was four years old and looked very wise.

"Mama'll be 'fraid, yes," he suggested with blinking eyes.

"She'll shut the house. Maybe she got Sylvie helpin' her this evenin'," Bobinôt responded reassuringly.

"No; she ent got Sylvie. Sylvie was helpin' her yistiday," piped Bibi.

Bobinôt arose and going across to the counter purchased a can of shrimps, of which Calixta was very fond. Then he returned to his perch on the keg and sat stolidly holding the can of shrimps while the storm burst. It shook the wooden store and seemed to be ripping great furrows in the distant field. Bibi laid his little hand on his father's knee and was not afraid.

II

Calixta, at home, felt no uneasiness for their safety. She sat at a side window sewing furiously on a sewing machine. She was greatly occupied and did not notice the approaching storm. But she felt very warm and often stopped to mop her face on which the perspiration gathered in beads. She unfastened her white sacque at the throat. It began to grow dark, and suddenly realizing the situation she got up hurriedly and went about closing windows and doors.

Out on the small front gallery she had hung Bobinôt's Sunday clothes to air and she hastened out to gather them before the rain fell. As she stepped outside, Alcée Laballière rode in at the gate. She had not seen him very often since her marriage, and never alone. She stood there with Bobinôt's coat in her hands, and the big rain drops began to fall. Alcée rode his horse under the shelter of a side projection where the chickens had huddled and there were plows and a harrow piled up in the corner.

"May I come and wait on your gallery till the storm is over, Calixta?" he asked.

"Come 'long in, M'sieur Alcée."

His voice and her own startled her as if from a trance, and she seized Bobinôt's vest. Alcée, mounting to the porch, grabbed the trousers and snatched Bibi's braided jacket that was about to be carried away by a sudden gust of wind. He expressed an intention to remain outside, but it was soon apparent that he might as well have been out in the open: the water beat in upon the boards in driving sheets, and he went inside, closing the door after him. It was even necessary to put something beneath the door to keep the water out.

"My! what a rain! It's good two years sence it rain' like that," exclaimed Calixta as she rolled up a piece of bagging and Alcée helped her to thrust it beneath the crack.

She was a little fuller of figure than five years before when she married; but she had lost nothing of her vivacity. Her blue eyes still retained their melting quality; and her yellow hair, dishevelled by the wind and rain, kinked more stubbornly than ever about her ears and temples.

The rain beat upon the low, shingled roof with a force and clatter that threatened to break an entrance and deluge them there. They were in the dining room—the sitting room—the general utility room. Adjoining was her bed room, with Bibi's couch along side her own. The door stood open, and the room with its white, monumental bed, its closed shutters, looked dim and mysterious.

Alcée flung himself into a rocker and Calixta nervously began to gather up from the floor the lengths of a cotton sheet which she had been sewing.

"If this keeps up, *Dieu sait* if the levees goin' to stan' it!" she exclaimed.

"What have you got to do with the levees?"

"I got enough to do! An' there's Bobinôt with Bibi out in that storm—if he only didn' left Friedheimer's!"

"Let us hope, Calixta, that Bobinôt's got sense enough to come in out of a cyclone."

She went and stood at the window with a greatly disturbed look on her face. She wiped the frame that was clouded with moisture. It was stiflingly hot. Alcée got up and joined her at the window, looking over her shoulder. The rain was coming down in sheets obscuring the view of far-off cabins and enveloping the distant wood in a gray mist. The playing of the lightning was incessant. A bolt struck a tall chinaberry tree at the edge of the field. It filled all visible space with a blinding glare and the crash seemed to invade the very boards they stood upon.

Calixta put her hands to her eyes, and with a cry, staggered backward. Alcée's arm encircled her, and for an instant he drew her close and spasmodically to him.

"*Bonté!*" she cried, releasing herself from his encircling arm and retreating from the window, "the house'll go next! If I only knew w'ere Bibi was!" She would not compose herself; she would not be seated. Alcée clasped her shoulders and looked into her face. The contact of her warm, palpitating body when he had unthinkingly drawn her into his arms, had aroused all the old-time infatuation and desire for her flesh.

"Calixta," he said, "don't be frightened. Nothing can happen. The house is too low to be struck, with so many tall trees standing about. There! aren't you going to be quiet? say, aren't you?" He pushed her hair back from her face that was warm and steaming. Her lips were as red and moist as pomegranate seed. Her white neck and a glimpse of her full, firm bosom disturbed him powerfully. As she glanced up at him the fear in her liquid blue eyes had given place to a drowsy gleam that unconsciously betrayed a sensuous desire. He looked down into her eyes and there was nothing for him to do but to gather her lips in a kiss. It reminded him of Assumption.

"Do you remember—in Assumption, Calixta?" he asked in a low voice broken by passion. Oh! she remembered; for in Assumption he had kissed her and kissed and kissed her; until his senses would well nigh fail, and to save her he would resort to a desperate flight. If she was not an immaculate dove in those days, she was still inviolate; a passionate creature whose very defenselessness had made her defense, against which his honor forbade him to prevail. Now—well, now—her lips seemed in a manner free to be tasted, as well as her round, white throat and her whiter breasts.

They did not heed the crashing torrents, and the roar of the elements made her laugh as she lay in his arms. She was a revelation in that dim, mysterious chamber; as white as the couch she lay upon. Her firm, elastic flesh that was knowing for the first time its birthright, was like a creamy lily that the sun invites to contribute its breath and perfume to the undying life of the world.

The generous abundance of her passion, without guile or trickery, was like a white flame which penetrated and found response in depths of his own sensuous nature that had never yet been reached.

When he touched her breasts they gave themselves up in quivering ecstasy, inviting his lips. Her mouth was a fountain of delight. And when he possessed her, they seemed to swoon together at the very borderland of life's mystery.

He stayed cushioned upon her, breathless, dazed, enervated, with his heart beating like a hammer upon her. With one hand she clasped his head, her lips lightly touching his forehead. The other hand stroked with a soothing rhythm his muscular shoulders.

The growl of the thunder was distant and passing away. The rain beat softly upon the shingles, inviting them to drowsiness and sleep. But they dared not yield.

The rain was over; and the sun was turning the glistening green world into a palace of gems. Calixta, on the gallery, watched Alcée ride away. He turned and smiled at her with a beaming face; and she lifted her pretty chin in the air and laughed aloud.

III

Bobinôt and Bibi, trudging home, stopped without at the cistern to make themselves presentable.

"My! Bibi, w'at will yo' mama say! You ought to be ashame'. You oughtn' put on those good pants. Look at 'em! An' that mud on yo' collar! How you got that mud on yo' collar, Bibi? I never saw such a boy!" Bibi was the picture of pathetic resignation. Bobinôt was the embodiment of serious solicitude as he strove to remove from his own person and his son's the signs of their tramp over heavy roads and through wet fields. He scraped the mud off Bibi's bare legs and feet with a stick and carefully removed all traces from his heavy brogans. Then, prepared for the worst—the meeting with an over-scrupulous housewife, they entered cautiously at the back door.

Calixta was preparing supper. She had set the table and was dripping coffee at the hearth. She sprang up as they came in.

"Oh, Bobinôt! You back! My! but I was uneasy. W'ere you been during the rain? An' Bibi? he ain't wet? he ain't hurt?" She had clasped Bibi and was kissing him effusively. Bobinôt's explanations and apologies which he had been composing all along the way, died on his lips as Calixta felt him to see if he were dry, and seemed to express nothing but satisfaction at their safe return.

"I brought you some shrimps, Calixta," offered Bobinôt, hauling the can from his ample side pocket and laying it on the table.

"Shrimps! Oh, Bobinôt! you too good fo' anything! and she gave him a smacking kiss on the cheek that resounded. "*J'vous réponds*, we'll have a feas' to night! umph-umph!"

Bobinôt and Bibi began to relax and enjoy themselves, and when the three seated themselves at table they laughed much and so loud that anyone might have heard them as far away as Laballière's.

IV

Alcée Laballière wrote to his wife, Clarisse, that night. It was a loving letter, full of tender solicitude. He told her not to hurry back, but if she and the babies liked it at Biloxi, to stay a month longer. He was getting on nicely; and though he missed them, he was willing to bear the separation a while longer—realizing that their health and pleasure were the first things to be considered.

V

As for Clarisse, she was charmed upon receiving her husband's letter. She and the babies were doing well. The society was agreeable; many of her old friends and acquaintances were at the bay. And the first free breath since her marriage seemed to restore the pleasant liberty of her maiden days. Devoted as she was to her husband, their intimate conjugal life was something which she was more than willing to forego for a while.

So the storm passed and every one was happy.

Charlie

Six of Mr. Laborde's charming daughters had been assembled for the past half hour in the study room. The seventh, Charlotte, or Charlie as she was commonly called, had not yet made her appearance. The study was a very large corner room with openings leading out upon the broad upper gallery.

Hundreds of birds were singing out in the autumn foliage. A little stern-wheeler was puffing and sputtering, making more commotion than a man-o'-war as she rounded the bend. The river was almost under the window—just on the other side of the high green levee.

At one of the windows, seated before a low table covered with kindergarten paraphernalia were the twins, nearing six, Paula and Pauline, who were but a few weeks old when their mother died. They were round-faced youngsters with white pinafores and chubby hands. They peeped out at the little snorting stern-wheeler and whispered to each other about it. The eldest sister, Julia, a slender girl of nineteen, rapped upon her desk. She was diligently reading her English Literature. Her hands were as white as lilies and she wore a blue ring and a soft white gown. The other sisters were Charlotte, the absentee, just past her seventeenth birthday, Amanda, Irene and Fidelia; girls of sixteen, fourteen and ten who looked neat and trim in their ginghams; with shining hair plaited on either side and tied with large bows of ribbon.

Each girl occupied a separate desk. There was a broad table at one end of the room before which Miss Melvern the governess seated herself when she entered. She was tall, with a refined though determined expression. The "Grandfather's Clock" pointed to a quarter of nine as she came in. Her pupils continued to work in silence while she busied herself in arranging the contents of the table.

The little stern-wheeler had passed out of sight though not out of hearing. But again the attention of the twins was engaged with something outside and again their curly heads met across the table.

"Paula," called Miss Melvern, "I don't think it is quite nice to whisper in that way and interrupt your sisters at their work. What are you two looking at out of the window?"

"Looking at Charlie," spoke Paula quite bravely while Pauline glanced down timidly and picked her fingers. At the mention of Charlie, Miss Melvern's face assumed a severe expression and she cautioned the little girls to confine their attention to the task before them.

The sight of Charlie galloping along the green levee summit on a big black horse, as if pursued by demons, was surely enough to distract the attention of any one from any thing.

Presently there was a clatter of hoofs upon the ground below, the voice of a girl pitched rather high was heard and the apologetic, complaining whine of a young negro.

"I didn' have no time, Miss Charlie. It's hones', I never had no time. I tole Marse Laborde you gwine git mad an' fuss. You c'n ax Aleck."

"Get mad and fuss! Didn't have time! Look at that horse's back—look at it. I'll give you time and something else in the bargain. Just let me catch Tim's back looking like that again, sir."

The twins were plainly agitated, and kept looking alternately at Miss Melvern's imperturbable face and at the door through which they expected their sister to enter.

A quick footstep sounded along the corridor, the door was thrown hurriedly open, and in came Charlie. She looked right up at the clock, uttered an exclamation of disgust, jerked off her little cloth cap and started toward her desk. She was robust and pretty well grown for her age. Her hair was cut short and was so damp with perspiration that it clung to her head and looked almost black. Her face was red and overheated at the moment. She wore a costume of her own devising, something between bloomers and a divided skirt which she called her "trouserlets." Canvas leggings, dusty boots and a single spur completed her costume.

"Charlotte!" called Miss Melvern arresting the girl. Charlie stood still and faced the governess. She felt in both side pockets of her trouserlets

182

for a handkerchief which she finally abstracted from a hip pocket. It was not a very white or fresh looking handkerchief; nevertheless she wiped her face with it.

"If you remember," said Miss Melvern, "the last time you came in late to study—which was only the day before yesterday—I told you that if it occurred again I should have to speak to your father. It's getting to be an almost every day affair, and I cannot consent to have your sisters repeatedly interrupted in this way. Take your books and go elsewhere to study until I can see your father." Charlie was gazing dejectedly at the polished floor and continuing to mop her face with the soiled handkerchief. She started to blurt out an apology, checked herself and crossing over to her desk provided herself with a few books and some scraps of paper.

"I'd rather you wouldn't speak to father this once," she appealed, but Miss Melvern only motioned with her head toward the door and the girl went out; not sullenly, but lugubriously. The twins looked at each other with serious eyes while Irene frowned savagely behind the pages of her geography.

It was not many moments before a young black girl came and thrust her head in at the door, rolling two great eyes which she had under very poor control.

"Miss Charlie 'low, please sen' her pencil w'at she lef' behine; an' if Miss Julia wants to give her some dem smove sheets o' paper; an' she be obleege if Miss Irene len' her de fountain pen, des dis once."

Irene darted forward, but subsided at a glance from Miss Melvern. That lady handed the black emissary a pencil and tablet from the table.

Before very long she was back again interrupting the exercises to lay a bulky wad before the governess. It was an elaborate description of the unavoidable adventures which had retarded Charlie's appearance in the study room.

"That will do, Blossom," said Miss Melvern severely, motioning the girl to be gone.

"She wants me to wait fo' an' answer," responded Blossom settling herself comfortably against the door jamb.

"That will do, Blossom," with distinct emphasis, whereupon Blossom reluctantly took her leave. But before long she was back again, nothing daunted and solemnly placed in Miss Melvern's unwilling hand a single folded sheet. Whereupon she retired with a slow dignity which convinced the twins that a telling and important strike had been accomplished by the absent Charlie. This time it was a poem—an original poem, and it began:

"Relentless Fate, and thou, relentless Friend!"

Its composition had cost Charlie much laborious breathing and some hard wrung drops from her perspiring brow. Charlie had a way, when strongly moved, of expressing herself in verse. She was greatly celebrated for two notable achievements in her life. One was the writing of a lengthy ode upon the occasion of her Grandmother's seventieth birthday; but she was perhaps more distinguished for having once saved the levee during a time of perilous overflow when her father was away. It was a story in which an unloaded revolver played a part, demoralized negroes and earth-filled gunny sacks. It got into the papers and made a heroine of her for a week or two.

On the other hand, it would be difficult to enumerate Charlie's shortcomings. She never seemed to do anything that anyone except her father approved of. Yet she was popularly described as not having a mean bone in her body.

Charlie was seated in a tilted chair, her heels on the rung, and in the intervals of composition her attention was greatly distracted by her surroundings. She sat outside on the brick or "false gallery" that formed a sort of long corridor at the back of the house. There was always a good deal going on out there. The kitchen was a little removed from the house. There was a huge live oak under whose spreading branches a few negro children were always playing—a few clucking chickens always scratching in the dust. People who rode in from the field always fastened their horses there. A young negro was under the tree, sharpening his axe at the grindstone while the big fat cook stood in the kitchen door abusing him in unmeasured terms. He was her own child, so she enjoyed the privilege of dealing with him as harshly as the law allowed.

"W'at you did wid dat gode (gourd) you, Demins! You kiar water to de grine stone wid it! I tell you, boy, dey be kiarrin' water in yo' skull time I git tho' wid you. Fetch dat gode back heah whar it b'longs. I gwine break eve'y bone in yo' body, an' I gwine tu'n you over to yo' pa: he make jelly outen yo' hide an taller."

The fat woman's vituperations were interrupted by the shock of a well-aimed missile squarely striking her broad body.

"If there are going to be any bones broken around here, I'll take a hand in it and I'll begin with you, Aunt Maryllis. What do you mean by making such a racket when you see me studying out here?"

"I gwine tell yo' pa, Miss Charlie. Dis time I gwine tell 'im sho'. Marse Laborde ain' gwine let you keep on cripplin' his han's scand'lous like you does. You, Demins! run 'long to de cabin, honey, an' fetch yo' mammy de spirits o' camphire." She turned back in the kitchen bent almost double, holding her hand sprawled over her ponderous side.

It was indeed very trying to Charlie to be thus interrupted in her second stanza as she was vainly striving after a suitable rhyme for "persecution." And again there was Aurendele, the 'Cadian girl, stalking across the yard with a brace of chickens to sell. She had them tied together at the legs with a strip of cotton cloth and they hung from her hand head downward motionless.

"He! what do you want? Aurendele!" Charlie called out. The girl piped shrilly back from the depths of a gingham sunbonnet.

"I lookin' fo' Ma'me Philomel, see if she want buy couple fine pullets. They fine, yes," she reiterated holding them out for Charlie's inspection. "We raise 'em from that Plymouth Rock. They ain't no Creole chicken, them, they good breed, you c'n see fo' yo'se'f."

"Plymouth fiddlesticks! You'd better hold on to them and try to sell them to the circus as curiosities: 'The feathered skeletons.' Here, Demins! turn these martyrs loose. Give them water and corn and rub some oil on their legs . . .

"No, Aurendele, I was only joking. I don't know how you can part with those Plymouth Rocks; you'll feel the separation and it'll go hard with your mother and the children. What do you want for them?"

Aurendele only wanted a little coffee and flour, a piece of fine soap, some blue ribbon such as her sister Odélia had bought at the store and a yard of "cross-bars" for a sunbonnet for Nannouche.

Charlie directed the girl to Ma'me Philomel. "And you ought to know better," she added, "than to stand here talking when you see I'm busy with my lessons."

"You please escuse me, Miss Charlie, I didn' know you was busy. W'ere you say I c'n fine Ma'me Philomel?"

And Charlie went back to the closing stanza which was something of an exhortation: "Let me not look again upon thy face While frowning mood, of joy usurps the place."

The poem being finished, signed and duly delivered by Blossom, the sister of Demins, Charlie felt that she had brought her intellectual labors to a fitting close.

A moment before, a negro had wheeled into the yard on a hand-cart

Charlie's new bicycle. It had been deposited at the landing by the little stern-wheeler earlier in the morning, and to witness and superintend its debarkation had been the cause of Charlie's tardiness in the class room. Now, with the assistance of Demins and Blossom the wheel was unpacked and adjusted under the live oak. It was a beauty, of very latest construction. Charlie had traded her old wheel with Uncle Ruben for an afflicted pony which she had great hope of saving and training for speed. The discarded bicycle was intended as a gift for Uncle Ruben's bride. Since its presentation the bride had not been seen in public.

Charlie mounted and gave an exhibition of her skill to a delighted audience of negroes, chickens and a few dogs. Then she decided that she would ride out in search of her father. It was not on her own account that she had entreated Miss Melvern's silence, it was on his. She realized that she was a difficult and perhaps annoying problem for him, and did not relish the idea of adding to his perplexity.

As Charlie wheeled past the kitchen she peeped furtively in at the window. Aunt Maryllis was kneading a lump of dough with one hand while the other was still clapped to her side. Charlie felt remorseful and wondered whether Aunt Maryllis would rather have fifty cents or a new bandana! But the gate was open, and away she went, down the long inviting level road that led to the sugar mill.

II

Miss Melvern in a moment of exasperation had once asked Charlie if she were wholly devoid of a moral sense. The expression was rather cruelly forceful, but the provocation had been unusually trying. And Charlie was so far devoid of the sense in question as not to be stung by the implication. She really felt that nothing made much difference so long as her father was happy. Her actions were reprehensible in her own eyes only so far as they interfered with his peace of mind. Therefore a great part of her time was employed in apologetic atonement and the framing of vast and unattainable resolutions.

An easy solution would have been to send Charlie away to boarding school. But upon the point of separation from any of his daughters, Mr. Laborde had set his heart with stubborn determination. He had once vaguely entertained the expedient of a second marriage, but was quite willing to abandon the idea on the strength of a touching petition framed by Charlie and signed by the seven sisters—the twins setting down their marks with heavy emphasis. And then Charlie could ride and shoot and fish; she was untiring and fearless. In many ways she filled the place of that ideal son he had always hoped for and that had never come.

He was standing at the mill holding the bridle of his horse and watching Charlie's approach with complicated interest. He was preposterously young looking—slender, with a clean shaved face and deep set blue eyes like Charlie's, and dark brown hair. The gray hairs on his temples might have been counted and often were, by the twins, perched on either arm of his chair.

"Well, Dad, how do you like it? Isn't it a beaut!" Charlie exclaimed as she flung herself off her wheel and wiped her steaming face with her bended arm. Mr. Laborde took a fresh linen handkerchief from his pocket and passed it over her face as if she had been a little child.

"If I hadn't been down at the landing this morning, goodness knows what they would have done with it. What do you suppose? That idiot of a Lulin swore it wasn't aboard. If I hadn't gone aboard myself and found it—well—that's why I happened to be late again. Miss Melvern is going to speak to you." A grieved and troubled look swept into his face, and was more stinging than if he had upbraided her. This way there was no excuse—no denial that she could make.

"And what are you doing out here now? Why aren't you in with the others at work?" he questioned.

"She sent me away—she's getting tired." Charlie's face was a picture of impotent regret as she looked down and uprooted a clump of grass with the toe of her clumsy boot. "I worked some, though, and then I just *had* to see about the wheel. I couldn't have trusted Demins."

It was one of the occasions when she regretted that her father was not a more talkative man. His silences gave her no opportunity to defend herself. When he rode away and left her there she noticed that he did not hold his chin in the air with his glance directed across the fields as usual, but looked meditatively between his horse's ears. Then she knew that he was perplexed again.

Charlie just wished that Miss Melvern with her rules and regulations was back in Pennsylvania where she came from. What was the use of learning tasks one week only to forget them the next? What was the use of hammering a lot of dates and figures into her head beclouding her intelligence and imagination? Wasn't it enough to have six well educated daughters!

But troubled thoughts, doubts, misgivings found no refuge in Charlie's bosom and they glanced away from her as lightly as winged messengers. Her father was plainly hurt and had not invited her to join him as he sometimes did. Miss Melvern had declined to entertain her apologies and, she knew, would not admit her into the class room. Anyway she felt that God must have intended people to be out of doors on a day like that, or why should he have given it to them? Like many older and more intelligent than herself, Charlie sometimes aspired to a knowledge of God's ways.

Far down the lane on the edge of a field was the Bichous' cabin—the parents of Aurendele, from whom Charlie had that morning purchased the chickens. Youngsters were swarming to their noontide meal and the odor within of frying bacon made Charlie sensible of the fact that she was hungry. She rode into the enclosure with an air of proprietorship which no one ever dreamed of resenting, and informed the Bichou family that she had come to dine with them.

"I thought you was *so* busy, Miss Charlie," remarked Aurendele with fine sarcasm.

"You mustn't think so hard, Aurendele. That's what Tinette's baby died of last week."

Aurendele had obtained the yard of "cross-bar" and was cutting out the sun bonnet for Nannouche who happened to have a good complexion which her relatives thought it expedient to preserve.

"Tinette's baby died o' the measles!" screamed Nannouche who knew everything.

"That's what I said. If she had only thought she didn't have the measles instead of thinking so hard that she did, she wouldn't have died. That's a new religion; but you haven't got sense enough to understand it. You haven't an idea above corn bread and molasses."

Charlie seemed not to have many ideas above corn bread and molasses herself when she sat down to dine with the Bichous. She shared the children's *couche couche* in the homely little yellow bowl like the rest of them—and did not disdain to partake of a goodly share of salt pork and greens with which Father Bichou regaled himself. His wife stood up at the head of the table serving every one with her long bare arms that had a tremendous reach.

Charlie made herself exceedingly entertaining by furnishing a condensed chronicle of the news in the great world, colored by her own lively imagination. They had a way of believing everything she said—which was a powerful temptation that many a sterner spirit would have found difficult to resist.

She was on the most intimate and friendly terms with the children and it was Xenophore who procured a fine hickory stick for her when, after dinner she expressed a desire to have one. She trimmed it down to her liking, seated on the porch rail.

"There are lots of bears where I'm going; maybe tigers," she threw off indifferently as she whittled away.

"W'ere you goin'?" demanded Xenophore with round eyed credulity.

"Yonder in the woods."

"I never yeared they any tigers in the wood. Bears, yes. Mr. Gail killed one w'en I been a baby."

"When you 'been a baby,' what do you call yourself now? But tigers or bears, it's all the same to me. I haven't killed quite as many tigers; but tigers die harder. And then if the stick goes back on me, why, I have my diamond ring."

"Yo' diamon' ring!" echoed Xenophore fixing his eyes solemnly on a shining cluster that adorned Charlie's middle finger.

"You see if I find myself in a tight place all I have to do is to turn the ring three times, repeat a Latin verse, and presto! I disappear like smoke. A tiger wouldn't know me from a hickory sapling."

She got down off the rail, brandished the stick around to test its quality, buckled her belt a bit tighter and announced that she would be off. She asked the Bichous to look after her wheel.

"And don't you attempt to ride it, Aurendele," she cautioned. "You might break your head and you'd be sure to break the wheel."

"I got plenty to do, me, let alone ridin' yo' bicyc'," retorted the girl with lofty indifference.

"It wouldn't matter so much about the head—there are plenty to spare around here—but there isn't another wheel like that in America; and I reckon you heard about Ruben's bride."

"W'at about Ruben's bride?"

"Well, never mind about what, but you keep off that wheel."

Charlie started off down the lane with a brisk step.

"W'ere she goin'?" demanded Mother Bichou looking after her. "My! my! she's a piece, that Charlie! W'ere she goin'?"

"She goin' yonder in the wood," replied Xenophore from the abundance of his knowledge. Ma'me Bichou still gazed after the retreating figure of the girl.

189

"You better go 'long behine her, you, Xenophore."

Xenophore did not wait to be told twice. In three seconds he was off, after Charlie; his little blue-jeaned legs and brown feet moving rapidly beneath the shade thrown by the circle of his enormous straw hat.

The strip of wood toward which Charlie was directing her steps was by no means of the wild and gloomy character of other woods further away. It was hardly more than a breathing spot, a solemn, shady grove inviting dreams and repose. Along its edge there was a road which led to the station. Charlie had reached the wood before she perceived that Xenophore was at her heels. She turned and seized the youngster by the shoulder giving him a vigorous shake.

"What do you mean by following me? If I was 'anxious for your company I would have invited you, or I could have stayed at the cabin and enjoyed your society. Speak up, why are you tagging along after me like this?"

"Maman sen' me, it's her sen' me behine you."

"Oh, I see; for an escort, a protector. But tell the truth, Xenophore, you came to see me kill the tigers and bears; own up. And just to punish you I'm not going to disturb them. I'm not even going in the direction where they stay."

Xenophore's face clouded, but he continued to follow, confident that despite her disappointing resolutions in regard to the wild beasts, Charlie would furnish diversion of some sort or other. They walked on for a while in silence and when they came to a fallen tree, Charlie sat herself down and Xenophore flopped himself beside her, his brown little hands folded over the blue jeans, and peeping up at her from under the brim of his enormous hat.

"I tell you what it is Xenophore, usually, when I come in the woods, after slaying a panther or so, I sit down and write a poem or two. That's why I came out here to day—to write a poem. There are lots of things troubling me, and nothing comforts me like that. But Tennyson himself couldn't write poetry with a little impish 'Cadian staring at him like this. I tell you what let's do, Xenophore," and she pulled a pad of paper from some depths of her trouserlets. "I think I'll practise my shooting; I'm getting a little rusty; only hit nine alligators out of ten last week in bayou Bonfils."

"It's pretty good, nine out o' ten," proclaimed Xenophore with an appreciative bob.

"Do you think so?" in amazement, "why I never think about the nine, only about the one I missed," and she proceeded to tear into little squares portions of the tablet Miss Melvern had sent her by Blossom in the morning. Handing a slip to Xenophore:

"Go stick this to that big tree yonder, as high as you can reach, and come back here." The youngster obeyed with alacrity. Charlie, taking from her back pocket a small pistol which no one on earth knew she possessed except her sister Irene, began to shoot at the mark, keeping Xenophore trotting back and forth to report results. Some of the shots were wide of the mark, and it was with the utmost reluctance that Xenophore admitted these failures.

There was a sudden loud, peremptory cry uttered near at hand.

"Stop that shooting, you idiots!" A young man came stalking through the bushes as if he had popped out of the ground.

"You young scamp! I'll thrash the life out of you," he exclaimed, mistaking Charlie for a boy at first. "Oh! I beg pardon. This is great sport for a girl, I must say. Don't you know you might have killed me? That last ball passed so near that—that—"

"That it hit you!" cried Charlie perceiving with her quick and practised glance a red blotch on the sleeve of his white shirt, above the elbow. He had been walking briskly and carried his coat across his arm. At her exclamation he looked down, turned pale, and then foolishly laughed at the idea of being wounded and not knowing it, or else in appreciation of his deliverance from an untimely death.

"It's no laughing matter," she said with a proffered motion to be of some assistance.

"It might have been worse," he cheerfully admitted, reaching for his handkerchief. With Charlie's help he bound the ugly gash, for the ball had plowed pretty deep into the flesh.

The girl was conscience stricken and too embarrassed to say much. But she invited the victim of her folly to accompany her to Les Palmiers.

That was precisely his original destination, he was pleased to tell her. He was on a business mission from a New Orleans firm. The beauty of the day had tempted him to take a short cut through the woods.

His name was Walton—Firman Walton, which information, together with his business card he conveyed to Charlie as they walked along. Xenophore kept well abreast, his little heart fluttering with excitement over the stirring adventure.

Charlie glanced absently at the card, as though it had nothing to do with the situation, and proceeded to roll it into a narrow cylinder while a troubled look spread over her face.

"I'm dreadfully sorry," she said. "I'm always getting into trouble, no matter what I do. I don't know what father'll say this time—about the gun, and hitting you and all that. He won't forgive me this time!" Her expression was one of abject wretchedness. He glanced down at her with amused astonishment.

"The hurt wasn't anything," he said. "I shall say nothing about it—absolutely nothing; and we'll give this young man a quarter to hold his tongue." She shook her head hopelessly.

"It'll have to be dressed and looked after."

"Please don't think of it," he entreated, "and say nothing more about it."

At half past one the family assembled at dinner. It was always Julia who presided at table. She looked very womanly with her long braid of light-brown hair wound round and round till it formed a coil as large as a dessert plate. Her father sat at the opposite end of the table and the children, the governess and Madame Philomel were dispersed on either side. There were always a few extra places set for unexpected guests. Uncle Ruben, in a white linen apron served the soup and carved the meats at a side table while the plates and dishes were passed around by Demins and a young mulatto girl.

The dining room was on the ground floor and opened upon the false gallery where Charlie had spent a portion of her morning in composition. The absence of that young person from her accustomed place at table was immediately observed and commented upon by her father.

"Where's Charlie" he asked, of everybody—of nobody in particular.

Julia looked a little helpless, the others nonplussed, while Pauline picked her fingers in painful embarrassment. Madame Philomel, who was fat and old fashioned, thought that the new bicycle would easily account for her absence.

"If Charlotte appears befo' sundown, it will be a subjec' of astonishment," she said with an air of conviction and irresponsibility. Every one assumed an air of irresponsibility in regard to Charlie which was annoying to Mr. Laborde as it implied that the whole burden of responsibility lay upon his own shoulders, and he was conscious of not bearing it gracefully. He had spent the half hour before dinner in consultation with Miss Melvern, who prided herself upon her firmness—as if firmness were heaven's first law. Mr. Laborde was in a position to convey to her

Charlie's latest resolutions, in which Miss Melvern placed but a small degree of faith. Mr. Laborde himself believed firmly in the ultimate integrity of his daughter's intentions. Miss Melvern's strongest point of objection was the pernicious example which Charlie furnished to her well-meaning sisters, and the interruptions occasioned by her misdirected impulses. Her tardiness of the morning, though not a great fault in itself, was the culmination of a long line of offenses. It might in fact be said that it was the last straw *but one*. Miss Melvern was inclined to think it *was* the last straw. But as hers was not the back which bore the brunt of the burden, she was not wholly qualified to judge. Mr. Laborde began to perceive that there might be a last straw.

Blossom, who assumed the role of a privileged character—the velvet footed Blossom stepped softly into the dining room and spoke, while her glance revolved and fixed itself upon the ceiling.

"Yonder Miss Charlie comin' 'long de fiel' road wid a young gent'man. Nary one ain't ridin' de bicycle—des steppin' out slow a-shovin' it 'long. 'Tain't Mr. Gus an' 'tain't Mr. Joe Slocum. 'Tain't nobody we all knows." Whereupon Blossom withdrew, being less anxious to witness the effect of her announcement than to assist at the arrival of Charlie, the gentleman and the bicycle.

Though accustomed to face situations, this young gentleman exhibited some natural trepidation at being ushered unexpectedly into the bosom of a dining family. He was good looking, intelligent looking. His appearance in itself was a guarantee of his respectability.

"This is Mr. Walton, dad," announced Charlie without preliminary, "he was coming to see you anyhow. He took a short cut through the woods and—and I shot him by mistake in the arm. Better have some antiseptic and stuff on it before he sits down. I had my dinner with the Bichous."

III

There seemed to be a universal, tacit understanding that Charlie was in disgrace, that she herself had deposited the last straw and that there would be results. The silence and outward calm with which her father had met this latest offense were ominous. She was made to stand and deliver her firearm together with her ammunition.

"Take care, father, it's loaded," she cautioned as she placed it upon his writing table.

She was informed that she would not be expected to join the others in the class room and was instructed to go and get her wardrobe in order and to discard her trouserlets as soon as possible.

Mr. Walton was not taken into the family confidence, but he realized that his coming was in the nature of a catastrophe. Having dispatched the business which brought him he would have continued on his way, but the scratch on his arm was rather painful, and that night he had some fever. Mr. Laborde insisted upon his remaining a few days. He knew the young man's people in New Orleans and did business with the firm which he represented.

To young Walton the place seemed charming—like a young ladies' Seminary. And well it might. Madame Philomel taught the girls music and drawing; accomplishments which she had herself acquired at the Ursulines in her youth. During the afternoon hour there was nearly always to be heard the sound of the piano: exercises and scales, interspersed with variations upon the Operas.

"Who is playing the piano?" asked Walton. He leaned against a pillar of the portico, his arm in a sling, and caressing a big dog with the other hand. Charlie sat dejectedly on the step. She still wore the trouserlets, having been unable to procure at so short notice anything that she considered suitable.

"The piano?" she echoed, looking up. "Fidelia, I suppose. It all sounds alike to me except that Fidelia plays the loudest. She's so clumsy and heavy-handed."

Fidelia in fact was thickwaisted and breathed hard. She was given over to afflictions of the throat and made to take exercise which, being lazy, she did not like to do.

"What a lot of you there are," said the young fellow. "Your eldest sister is beautiful, isn't she! It seems to me she's the most beautiful girl I almost ever saw."

"She has a right to be beautiful. She looks like dad and has a character like Aunt Clementine. Aunt Clementine is a perfect angel. If ever there was a saint on earth—Hi, Pitts! catch 'im! catch 'im Pitts!" The dog bounded away after a pig that had mysteriously escaped from its pen and made its way around to the front, prospecting.

Julia, with Amanda and Irene had driven away a while before in the ample barouche. Nothing could have been daintier than Julia in a soft blue "jaconette" that brightened her color and brought out the blue of her eyes.

"Why didn't you go along driving?" asked Walton when the dog had darted away and he seated himself beside Charlie on the step.

"They're going over to Colimarts to take a dancing lesson."

"Don't you like to dance?"

"I haven't time. Maybe if I liked to, I'd find time. Madame Philomel made a row about me not taking dancing and music and all that, and Dad said I might do as I liked about it. So Ma'me Philo stopped interfering. 'I 'ave nothing to say!' that's her attitude now towards poor me."

"I'm awfully sorry," said the young man earnestly.

"Sorry! about the dancing? pshaw! what difference—"

"No—no, sorry about the accident of the other day. I'm afraid, perhaps it's going to get you into trouble."

"It'll get me into trouble all right; I see it coming."

"I hope you'll forgive me," he asked persistently, as though he had been the offender.

"It wasn't your fault," she said with condescension. "If it hadn't been that it would have been something else. I don't know what's going to happen; boarding school I'm afraid."

A small figure came gliding around the corner of the house. It was Xenophore, blue jeans, legs, hat and all. He came quietly and seated himself on a step at some little distance.

"What do you want?" she asked in French.

"Nothing."

They both laughed at the youngster. Far from being offended he smiled and peered slyly up from under his hat.

"Mr. Gus sen' word howdy," piped Xenophore a little later apropos of nothing, breaking right into the conversation.

"W'ere you saw Mr. Gus?" asked Charlie, falling into the 'Cadian speech as she sometimes did when talking to the Bichous.

"He pass yonder by de house on 'is ho'se. He say 'How you come on, Xenophore; w'en you see Miss Charlie?' I say, 'I see Miss Charlie to s'mornin',' an' he say 'Tell Miss Charlie howdy fo' me.' "

Then Xenophore arose and turning mechanically, glided noiselessly around the corner of the house.

It was dusk and the moon was already shining in the river and breaking with a pale glow through the magnolia leaves when the girls came home from their dancing lesson. It was nearing the supper hour so they did not linger, and Charlie went with them into the house, bent upon making a bit of toilet for the evening. She was secretly in hopes that Amanda would lend her a dress. Julia's gowns were quite too young-ladified; they touched the ground, often with a graceful sweep. One of Amanda's would have done nicely. But Amanda looked sidewise from her long, narrow, dark eyes when Charlie approached her with the request and blankly refused. Irene grew excited and indignant.

"Don't ask her, Charlie; why do you ask her? She thinks her clothes are made of diamonds and pearls, too good for Queen Victoria! What about my pink gingham if I ripped out the tucks?"

"Oh! it's no use," wailed Charlie. "There isn't time to rip anything and I could never get into it."

They were in Amanda's room, Irene and Charlie seated on a box lounge and Amanda decorating herself before the mirror. She had laid her own evening toilet on the bed and carefully locked closet, wardrobe and bureau drawers. She always kept things locked and had an ostentatious way of carrying her highly polished keys that were on a ring. Charlie gazed at her sister's reflected image with a sort of despair but with no trace of malice.

"If there's a thing I hate, it's to have people sit and stare when I'm dressing," remarked Amanda. The two girls got up and went out and Amanda locked the door behind them.

"Why not wear your Sunday dress, Charlie?" offered Irene as they walked down the long hall, arm in arm.

"You know what Julia said about its being so short and the sleeves so old fashioned and she wouldn't be seen at church with me if I wore it again. So I gave it to Aurendele the other day."

But it was Julia who came to the rescue. She fastened and pinned and tucked up one of her own gowns on Charlie and the effect, if not completely happy, could not have been called a distinct failure.

No one remarked upon the metamorphosis when she appeared thus arrayed at table. Miss Melvern and Madame Philomel were far too polite to seem to notice. The twins only beamed their approval and astonishment. Fidelia gasped and stared, closed her lips tight and sought Miss Melvern's glance for direction. Blossom alone expressed herself in a smothered explosion in the door way, and went outside and clung to a post for support.

To Mr. Laborde there was something poignant in the sight of his beloved daughter in this unfamiliar garb. It seemed a dismal part of the unhappy situation which had given him such heartache to solve—for he had solved it. He avoided looking at Charlie and wore an expression which reminded them all of the time he heard of his brother's death in Old Mexico.

Mr. Laborde had that evening reached a conclusion which was communicated to Charlie directly after supper when the others strolled out upon the veranda and she went with him to his study. She was to go to New Orleans and enter a private school noted for its excellent discipline. Two weeks at Aunt Clementine's would enable her to be fitted out as became her age, sex and condition in life. Julia was to go to the city with her, to see that she was properly equipped and later her father would join her and accompany her to the Young Ladies' Seminary.

She fingered the lace ruffle on Julia's sleeve as she looked down and listened to her father's admonitions.

"I'm sorry to give you all this worry, dad," she said, "but I'm not going to make any more promises; it's a farce, the way I've persistently broken them. I hope I shan't give you any more trouble." He took her in his arms, and kissed her fervently. Charlie was exceedingly astonished to discover that the arrangement planned by her father was not so distasteful as it would have seemed a while ago. It was not at all distasteful and she secretly marvelled.

When she and her father rejoined the others on the veranda they found that a visitor had arrived, Mr. Gus Bradley, the son of a neighboring planter and an intimate friend of the family. He had been painfully disconcerted at finding a stranger when he had expected to meet only familiar faces and the effect was not happy. Mr. Gus was so shy that it had never yet been discovered whom his visits at Les Palmiers were intended for. It was, however, generally believed that he favored Charlie on account of the messages which he so often sent her through Xenophore and others. He had given her a fine dog and a riding whip. But he had also made the twins a present of a gentle Shetland pony, and he had sent Amanda his photograph! He was a big fellow and awkward only from shyness and when in company, for in the saddle or out in the road or the fields he had a fine, free carriage. His hair was light and fine and his face smooth and looked as if it belonged to a far earlier period of society and had no connection with the fevered and modern present day.

The moon sent a great flood of light in upon the group—the only shadows were cast by the big round pillars and the fantastic quivering vines. Amanda sat by herself, tip toeing in a hammock and picking a tune on the mandolin. Madame Philomel was telling the twins a marvelous story in French about *Croque Mitaine*. Fidelia was drinking in words of wisdom at Miss Melvern's feet. It was Irene who was entertaining Mr. Gus and endeavoring to account to him in veiled whispers for young Walton's presence on the scene. She might have spoken as loud as she liked for the young gentleman in question was entirely absorbed in Julia's conversation and had ears for nothing else.

"I'm not going to stay," said Mr. Gus, almost apologetically. "I only rode over for a minute. I wanted to see your sister Charlie. I had something important to tell her."

"She'll be out pretty soon; she's inside talking to father."

When Charlie came out she went and seated herself beside Irene on the long bench that stood by the railing. Mr. Gus was near by in a camp chair. He was so flustered at seeing Charlie in frills and furbelows that he could scarcely articulate.

"I didn't know you," he blurted.

"Oh, well, I have to begin some time."

Irene got up and left them alone, remembering Mr. Gus's admission of an important communication for Charlie's ears alone.

"I haven't long to stay," he began. "I heard about Tim's shoulder and brought you a recipe for gall. It's the finest thing ever was. You'll find all the ingredients in your father's workshop, and you'd better mix it yourself; don't trust any one else. If you'd like, I'll put it up myself and bring it around tomorrow."

Irene off in the distance was positively agitated. She firmly believed Charlie was receiving her first proposal.

"Thank you, Mr. Gus, but it's no use," said Charlie. "Some one else is going to look after Tim from now on; I'm going away."

"Going away!"

"Yes, going to the Seminary in the city. Dad thinks it's best; I suppose it is."

He found absolutely nothing to say, but his mobile face took on a crestfallen look that the moonlight made pathetic; and Irene from her corner of observation, concluded that he had been rejected as she knew he would.

"I'll send dear old Pitts back. You keep him for me. I reckon they wouldn't let me have him in the Seminary."

"I'll come for him tomorrow," responded Mr. Gus with dreary eagerness. "When do you go?"

"In a day or two. The sooner the better as long as there's no getting out of it."

Two days later Charlie left the plantation accompanied by her sister Julia, young Walton and Madame Philomel. They boarded the little sputtering stern-wheeler about nine in the morning. It seemed as if the whole plantation, blacks and whites, had turned out to bid her *bon voyage*. The sisters were in tears. Even Amanda seemed moved and Irene was frankly hysterical. Miss Melvern was under a big sunshade with Fidelia, and the twins held their father's hands. All the Bichous had come; Aurendele in Charlie's "Sunday dress," Xenophore, round eyed, serious, unable to cry, unable to laugh, apprehending calamity. Mr. Gus galloped up with a huge bouquet of flowers, striving to appear as if it were wholly by accident.

Charlie was completely overcome. She would not go up to the cabin but stayed dejectedly seated on a cotton bale, alternately wiping her eyes and waving her handkerhcief until it was too limp to flutter.

IV

The change, or rather the revolution in Charlie's character at this period was so violent and pronounced that for a while it rendered Julia helpless. The trouble which Julia had anticipated was entirely of an opposite nature from the one which confronted her and it took her some time to realize the situation and ajust herself to it. As it happened, the combined efforts of both Aunt Clementine and Julia were insufficient to keep Charlie within bounds; to give her a proper appreciation of values after the feminine instinct had been aroused in her.

The diamond ring she had always with her. It was her mother's engagement ring. Hitherto she had worn it for the tender associations which made her love the bauble. Now she began to look upon it as an adornment. She possessed a round gold locket containing her mother's and father's pictures. This she suspended from her neck by a long thin gold chain. Such family jewels as had by inheritance descended to her, seemed to the young thing insufficient to proclaim the gentle quality of sex. She would have cajoled her father into extravagances. She wanted lace and embroideries upon her garments; and she longed to bedeck herself with ribbons and *passementeries* which the shops displayed in such tempting array.

Her short cropped hair was a sore grievance to Charlie when she viewed herself in the mirror and she resorted to the disfiguring curling irons with results which were, to say the least, appalling to Julia who came in one afternoon and discovered her entertaining young Walton with her head looking like a prize chrysanthemum.

"I can't understand her, Aunt," Julia confided to her Aunt Clementine with tears in her blue eyes. "It's bad enough as it is, but just imagine what a spectacle she would make of herself if we permitted it. I'm afraid she's a little out of her senses. I'd almost rather think that than to believe she could develop such vulgar instincts."

Aunt Clementine would do no more than shrug her shoulders and look placidly and blamelessly perplexed. She was quite sure that Charlie did not take after any member of her side of the family; so the blame of heredity, if any, had naturally to be traced to other sides of the family.

Through mild and firm coercion Charlie was brought to understand that such excessive ornamentation as she favored would not for a moment be tolerated by the disciplinarians at the Seminary. When finally that young person was admitted to the refined precincts—save for the diamond ring and the locket, in the matter of which she had taken a stubborn stand—no fault could have been found with her appearance which was in every way consistent with that of the well mannered girl of seventeen.

She had spent a delightful fortnight. Aunt Clementine who was at once a lady of fashion and a person of gentle refinement had provided entertainment such as Charlie had not yet encountered outside of novels of high life: her Aunt Clementine's *ménage* having not before been to her liking.

They drove, they visited and received calls, dined and went to the opera. There was much shopping, perambulating and trying on of gowns and hats. There was a perpetual flutter, and indescribable excitement awaiting her at every turn. Young Walton was persistent in his attentions to the sisters, but as there were other and many claims upon Julia it was oftener Charlie who entertained him, walked abroad with him and even accompanied him on one occasion to Church.

The first moment that Charlie found herself alone in the privacy of her own room at the Seminary, she devoted that moment to unburdening her soul. She sat beside the window and looked out a while. There was not much inspiration to be gathered from the big red brick building opposite. But her inspiration was not dependent upon anything extraneous; it was bubbling up inside of her and generating an energy that found a vent in its natural channel.

Equipped with a very fine pen point and the filmiest sheet of filmy writing paper, Charlie wrote some lines of poetry in the smallest possible cramped hand. She did not hesitate or bite her pen or frown, seeking for words and rhymes. She had made it all up beforehand and its rhythm kept time with the beating of her heart. Poor little thing! Let her alone. It would be cruel to tell the whole story. When the lines were written she folded the sheet over and over and over, making it as flat and thin as possible. Then with her hat pin she picked out the little glass frame that contained her mother's picture in the locket, and laying the scrap of poetry in the cover, replaced the picture.

As the young girls at the Seminary were all of gentle breeding they gave no pronounced exhibition of their astonishment at Charlie's lack of accomplishments. She herself felt her shortcomings keenly and read their guarded wonder. With dogged determination she had made up her mind to transform herself from a hoyden to a fascinating young lady, if persistence and hard work could do it.

As for hard work, there was enough of it! Hoeing, or chopping cane seemed child's play compared with the excruciating intricacies which the piano offered her. She began to have some respect for Fidelia's ponderous talent and even wondered at the twins. After some lessons in drawing, the instructor disinterestedly advised her to save her money. He was gloomy about it. The spirit of commercialism, he said, had not touched him to the crass extent of countenancing robbery. With some sinking of heart, Charlie let the drawing go, but when it came to dancing, she would yield not an inch. She practised the steps in the narrow confines of her room, and when opportunity favored her, she waltzed and two-stepped up and down the long corridors. Some of the girls took pity and gave her private instructions, for which she offered tempting inducements to their cupidity in the shape of chocolate bon-bons and stick-pins.

She was immensely liked, though they had small respect for her abilities until one day it fell upon them with the startling bewilderment of lightning from a clear sky that Charlie was a poet. It happened in this wise: The fête of the foundress of the Seminary was to be celebrated and the young ladies were desired to write addresses in her honor, the worthiest of these addresses to be selected and delivered in the venerable lady's presence upon the date in question.

It was so much easier for Charlie to write twenty or fifty lines of verse than pages and pages of prose.

When the announcement of the award was made in a most flattering little speech to the assembled classes by the lady directress, the girls were stupefied, and Charlie herself almost as well pleased as if she had been able to play a minuet upon the piano or go through the figures of a dance without blundering.

"Did you ever!" "Well, I knew there was something in her!"

"I told you she wasn't as stupid as she looks!"

"Why didn't she say so!" were a few of the comments passed upon Charlie's suddenly unearthed talent.

A group besieged her in her room that afternoon.

"Out with them!" cried the spokesman, armed with a box of chocolate creams, "every last of them. Where do you keep them? Hand over the key of that desk. You're a barefaced impostor, if you want to know it."

They seated themselves on chairs, stools, the lounge, the floor and the bed—as many as could crowd in a row, and awaited with the pleased expectancy of girls ready to extract entertainment from any situation that presents itself.

Charlie had no thought of reluctance. She brought forth the mass of manuscript and delivered it over to the chocolate bearer who had a sonorous voice and a reputation as an elocutionist.

One by one the poems were read, with fictitious fire, with melting pathos as the occasion called for, while silently the chocolates were passed around and around.

Charlie rocked violently and tried to look indifferent. Her hair was long enough to tie back now with a bow of ribbon. On her forehead she wore a few little curls made with the curling irons, and as she glanced in the mirror while she rocked she wondered if her face would ever get beautiful and silky white. Charlie took no part in the athletic sports such as tennis and basket ball, though urged to do so. She was given over to putting some kind of greasy stuff on her hands at night and slept in a pair of her father's old gloves.

"Well," commented the reader, laying down the leaves.

"Moonlight on the Mississippi."

"This is the finest thing I ever read. I wish you'd give me this, I'd like to send it to mother. And all I've got to say for you is that you are a large sized goose. The idea of keeping such poetry as that cooped up here! Why don't you go to work and publish those things in the Magazines, I'd like to know. I tell you, they'd jump at the—well! I like this! Empty! where are all those chocolates gone? The next time I go halves in a box of chocolates you people'll know it!"

It need not be supposed that Charlie saw nothing of her home folks during her stay at the Seminary. They came in squads and detachments. Julia must have been spending much time with her Aunt Clementine, for the two not infrequently drove around in Aunt Clementine's victoria upon which occasions Charlie was very proud of her sister's beauty and air of distinctintion which the other girls did not fail to observe and rave over.

Amanda and Irene came down from the plantation with their father expressly to see her. The girls who caught a glimpse of them did not hesitate to pronounce Mr. Laborde the handsomest man they had ever set eyes upon; Amanda a most striking and fascinating personality. But of Irene they held their estimate in reserve, as the poor girl had seemed demented, laughing in the midst of tears, weeping to an accompaniment of laughter.

Once Miss Melvern made her appearance with Fidelia. It was a great pleasure to introduce the governess to the faculty and the methods, while Fidelia trod heavily and seriously at her side, crimson under the scrutiny of so many strange eyes.

Last came Madame Philomel one morning with the twins and whom beside but Aurendele and Xenophore! She wore a beautiful new bonnet, a sprigged challie dress with a black mantilla and kid gloves. The young ladies who were growing more and more interested in Charlie's family with every fresh installment, to quote them literally, lost their minds over the twins who were like two chubby rosy-cheeked angels in spotless white.

"It's positively paralyzing!"

"How do you tell them apart?"

"I must have a sketch of them."

"How do they know themselves, which is which?"

"Oh! *we* know them of course," said Charlie with laudable pride, "but strangers can tell by their difference of manner: Pauline is timid and Paula dreadfully mischievous. Would you believe it? She fooled dad one day by hanging her head and picking her fingers when he asked her an embarrassing question. There was no trouble at this juncture in discovering which was which."

Aurendele, still wearing Charlie's "Sunday dress" which was getting sadly small for her and a sailor hat of Irene's, was alert, but overawed and unable to remember the multitude of things she had stored up in her brain to communicate to Charlie. And as for Xenophore, he felt there had been a convulsion of nature and he was powerless to place the responsibility. To be sitting there in "store clothes," brogans, twirling in his hands a little felt hat no bigger than a plate, Miss Charlie in hair ribbons and dressed like a girl! He was speechless. It was only toward the close of the visit that he uttered his first word.

"Mr. Gus sen' word 'howdy.' "

"W'en you saw Mr. Gus?" asked Charlie laughing.

"He pass by the house an' he say, 'How you come on, Xenophore! w'at you all year f'om Miss Charlie?' I tell 'im I'm goin' to the city to see you an' he say, 'Tell Miss Charlie howdy fo' me.' "

But when her father came alone one morning quite early—he had remained over night in the city that he might be early—and carried her off with him for the day, her delight knew no bounds. He did not tell her in so many words how hungry he was for her, but he showed it in a hundred ways. He was like a school boy on a holiday; it was like a conspiracy; there was a flavor of secrecy about it too. They did not go near Aunt Clementine's. They saw no one they knew except Young Walton who was busy over accounts in the commission office where Mr. Laborde stopped to supply himself with money enough to pay his way. The young fellow turned crimson with unexpected pleasure when he saw them. He was eager to know if any other members of the family were in the city. He showed a disposition to be excused from the office and to join them, a suggestion which Mr. Laborde did not favor, which rather alarmed him and hurried his departure. Moreover he could see that Charlie did not like the young man, and he could not blame her for that, all things considered! She gave her whole attention to her gloves and the clasp of her parasol while there.

It was well they provided themselves with money. Charlie needed every thing she could think of and what she forgot her father remembered. He carried her jacket and assisted her over the crossings like an experienced cavalier. He helped her to select a new sailor hat and saw that she put it on straight. Not approving of her hat pin he bought her another, besides handkerchiefs, a fan, stick pins, presents for the girls and the favorite teachers, books of poetry, and the latest novels. The maid at the Seminary was kept busy all afternoon carrying in bundles.

They went to the lake to eat breakfast; a second breakfast to be sure, but such exceedingly young persons could not be expected to restrict themselves to the conventional order in the matter of refreshment. It was a great delight to be abroad: the air was soft and moist and the warm sun of early March brought out the scent of the earth and of distant gardens and the weedy smell from the still pools.

They were almost alone at the lake end save for the habitual fishermen and sportsmen, the *restaurateurs* and lazy looking *garçons*. Their small table was out where the capricious breeze beat about them, and they sat looking across the glistening water, watching the slow sails and feeling like a couple of bees in clover.

Charlie drew off a glove, looked at her hand and silently held it out for her father's inspection, right under his eyes.

"What do you think of that, dad?" she asked finally. He gazed at the hand and rubbed his cheek, meditatively, as he would have pulled his moustache if he had had one.

"Just take a good look at it. Notice anything?" He took her hand, scrutinizing the ring.

"No stones missing, are there?"

"I don't mean the ring, but the hand," turning her palm uppermost. "Feel that. You know what it used to be. Ever feel anything softer than that?"

He held the hand fondly in both of his, but she withdrew it, holding it at arm's length.

"Now, dad, I want your candid opinion; don't say anything you don't believe; but do you think it's as white as—Julia's, for instance?"

He narrowed his eyes, surveying the little hand that gleamed in the sun, like a connoisseur sizing up a picture.

"I don't want to be hasty," he said quizzically. "I'm not too sure that I remember, and I shouldn't like to do Julia's hand an injustice, but my opinion is that yours is whiter."

She threw an arm around his neck and hugged him, to the astonishment of a lame oysterman and a little Brazilian monkey that squealed in his cage with amusement.

"It's all right, Charlie dear, but you know you mustn't think too much about the hands and all that. Take care of the head, too, and the temper."

"Don't fret, dad," tapping her forehead under the rim of the 'sailor,' "the head's coming right up to the front: history, literature, ologies, everything but dates and figures; getting right in here; consumed with ambition. And the girls didn't think I'd ever learn to dance until I gave them a double shuffle and a Coonpine! Now I'm giving lessons. Never mind! some of these days they'll be asking your permission to make me queen of the Carnival. And as for temper! Why, it's ridiculous, dad. I'm beginning to—to bleat!"

Well, it was a day full to the brim. In the afternoon they heard a wonderful pianist play. It gave Charlie a feeling of exaltation, a new insight; the music somehow filled her soul with its power.

It was nearly dark when she embraced her father and bade him good bye. For weeks the memory of that day lasted.

It was in the full flush of April that a telegram came summoning Charlie home at once. Terror seized her like some tangible thing. She feared some one was dead.

Her father had been injured, they told her. Not fatally, but he wanted her.

V

It was one of those terrible catastrophes which seem so impossible, so uncalled for when they come home to us, that stupefy with grief and regret; an accident at the sugar mill; a bit of perilous repairing in which he chose to assume the risk rather than expose others to danger. It was hard to say what had happened to him. He was alive; that was all, but torn, maimed and unconscious. The surgeon, who was coming as fast as steam and the iron wheels could bring him, would tell them more of it. The surgeon was on the train with Charlie and so was the professional nurse. They seemed to her like monsters; because he read a newspaper and conversed with the conductor about crops and the weather; and the other, demure in her grey dress and close bonnet, displayed an interest in a group of children who were traveling with their mother.

Charlie could not speak. Her brain was confused with horror and her thoughts were beyond control. Every thing had lost significance but her grief and nothing was real but her despair. Emotion stupefied her when she thought that he would not be there at the station waiting for her with outstretched arms and beaming visage; that she would perhaps never see him again as he had been that day at the lake, robust and beautiful, clasping her with loving arms when he said good bye in the soft twilight. She became keenly conscious of the rhythm of the iron wheels that seemed to mock her and keep time to the throbbing in her head and bosom.

There was a hush upon the whole plantation. Silent embraces; serious faces and tearful eyes greeted her. It seemed inexpressibly hard that she should be kept from him while the surgeon and the nurse were hurried to his side. A physician was already there, and so was Mr. Gus.

During the hour or more that followed, Charlie sat alone on the upper gallery. Madame Philomel with Julia and Amanda were indoors praying upon their knees. The others were speechless with anxiety. Charlie alone was quiet and dull. It had rained and there was a delicious freshness in the air, the birds were mad with joy among the dripping leaves that glistened with the filtering rays of the setting sun. She sat and stared at the water still pouring from a tin spout.

The twins came and leaned their heads against her. She took Pauline into her lap and fastened the child's shoestring that had come untied. She stared at them both with absent-minded eyes. Then Irene came and led them away. The water had stopped flowing from the spout and Charlie fixed her eyes upon the peacock that moved with low trailing plumage over the wet grass.

There was a sweet, sickening odor stealing from the house, more penetrating than the scent of the rain-washed flowers. She groaned as the fumes of the anesthetic reached her. She leaned her elbows upon the rail and with her head clasped in her hands, stared down at the gravel before the steps.

Someone came out upon the porch and stood beside her; it was Mr. Gus, all his shyness submerged for the moment in quick sympathy.

"Poor old Charlie," he said softly and took her hand.

"Is he dead, Mr. Gus? have they killed him?" she asked dully.

"He isn't dead. He won't die if he can help it."

"What have they done to him?"

"Never mind now, Charlie; just thank God that he is left to us."

A deep prayer of thankfulness went up from every heart. The crushing pressure was lifted, and they rejoiced that it was to be life rather than death—life at any price.

With the changed conditions that so soon make themselves familiar, a new character was stamped upon the family life at Les Palmiers. There was a quiet and unconscious readjustment. The center of responsibility shifted and sought as it were to find lodgment for a time in every individual breast. The family took turns in watching at the bedside after the quiet woman in grey had gone. Then it was that even Demins showed fine mettle in those days. Money might have paid his services, it could never balance his devotion.

Charlie forgot that she was young and that the sun was shining out of doors and the voices of the woods and fields awaited her. But between sick-watches she took again to the task of beautifying her outward and inward being. She sought after becoming arrangements of her hair; over the kitchen fire she mixed ointments for the whitening of her skin; and while committing to memory tasks that filled her sisters with admiration, she polished her pointed nails till they rivalled the pearly rose of the conch-shells which Mme. Philomel kept upon either side of her hearth.

It was getting pretty warm and systematic work in the class room had been abandoned. Miss Melvern went away on her annual home visit and Aunt Clementine came up to the plantation to condole and to read the riot-act.

Her brother was sufficiently recovered to be scolded, to listen to the truth as Aunt Clementine defined her plain talk. It was high time he gave over thinking he might keep his daughters always like a bouquet of flowers, in a bunch, as it were, on the family hearth. He was not quite equal to the task of disagreeing with her. She had plans for separating these blossoms so that they might disseminate their sweetness even across the seas. Julia and Amanda should accompany her abroad in the Autumn. A winter in Paris and Rome, not to mention Florence, would accomplish more for them than years in the class room. Aunt Clementine saw great possibilities of a fine lady in Amanda. The girl presented more crude, promising material than Julia even. A year at the Seminary for Irene, and Charlie—

"Please leave me out of your calculations, Aunt," said Charlie with a flash of her old rebellious nature. "Dad'll have something to say when he's able to bother about it, and in the meantime I propose to take care of myself and the youngsters and of Dad, and this meeting's got to end right here. When he is strong enough to talk back, Aunt Clementine, you may come and have it out with him." Aunt Clementine had always considered the girl coarse and she surveyed the girl with compassion.

"Charlie, remember to whom you are speaking," said Julia with gentle rebuke. But they all filed out of the sick room, Amanda with a calm exultation in her face—and left Charlie to smoothe the pillow and quiet the nerves of the convalescent.

Julia seemed to be always more than ready to accept an invitation from her aunt. Life in the country began apparently to weary her, and, without too much urging she accompanied Aunt Clementine back to the city.

Young Walton had been up to Les Palmiers on a visit of sympathy and had had a conversation alone with Mr. Laborde which had been to the last degree satisfactory. Charlie wore her pink organdie and her grandmother's pearls during his visit and puffed her hair.

It was a week or so after Julia's departure for the city that the remaining sisters were all assembled on the false gallery one forenoon awaiting the return of Demins with the mail. Twice a day it was Demins' duty to fetch and carry the family mail from and to the station. Amanda's familiarity with keys seemed to entitle her to the office of locking and unlocking the canvas bag and it was she who distributed the mail.

There was a letter from Julia for each one of the sisters, under separate cover; even the twins got one between them. A proceeding so unfamiliar on the part of the undemonstrative Julia caused more than a flutter of wonder and comment. Envelopes were torn open, exclamations followed: rejoicing, dismay, elation, consternation! Engaged! Julia engaged! and the sky still in its place overhead and not crumbling about their ears!

Charlie alone said nothing at first, then in a voice hideous with anger:

"She's a deceitful hypocrite, she's no sister of mine, I hate her!" She turned and went into the house leaving Julia's letter lying upon the bricks. Pauline began to utter little choking sobs at once. Fidelia grew red with indecision and dismay.

"She can't bear him," said Irene with shame-faced apology.

"Charlie's a goose," remarked Amanda picking up the letter and folding it back into its envelope, "let's go and hear what father has to say."

A little later Charlie in her trouserlets, boots and leggings, mounted black Tim and galloped madly away, no one knew where.

"Look like ol' Nick took hol' o' Miss Charlie again," commented Aunt Maryllis leaning from the kitchen window.

"She mad 'cause Miss Julia g'in git ma'rid to de young man w'at she shot," said Blossom. "I yeard 'em. Miss Irene 'low Miss Charlie f'or hate dat man like pizen."

At the sound of Tim's pounding hoofs upon the road, Xenophore darted from the cabin door. And at sight of Charlie rushing past in the old familiar guise of a whirlwind, the youngster threw himself flat down and rolled in the dust with glee, even though he knew his mother would whip the dust from his jeans without the trouble of removing them from his small person.

No one ever knew where Charlie ate her dinner that day. She did not quite kill Tim but it took days of care to set him on his accustomed legs again. She did not join the family at the evening meal and remained apart in her own room, refusing admittance to those who sought to reach her.

In her mad ride Charlie had thrown off the savage impulse which had betrayed itself in such bitter denunciation of her sister. Shame and regret had followed and now she was steeped in humiliation such as she had never felt before. She did not feel worthy to approach her father or her sisters. The girlish infatuation which had blinded her was swept away in the torrents of a deeper emotion, and left her a woman.

It was trivial, perhaps, for her to take the little poem from the back of her mother's miniature and holding it on the point of a hat pin, consume it in the flame of a match.

During the stillness of the night when she could not sleep, she crept out of bed and lit her lamp, shading it so that its glimmer could not be detected from without.

Removing the precious diamond ring from her finger she began to polish and brighten it till the glittering stones were scintillant in their dazzling whiteness. The task over, she put the ring in a little blue velvet cover which she took from her bureau drawer and laid it upon the pin cushion. Then Charlie went back to bed and slept till the sun was high in the heavens.

She had little to say at breakfast the next morning and there was no one who felt privileged to question her. With the others she gathered on the false gallery to wait for the mail as she had done the day before. When her letters were handed to her she also took her father's mail and turned to go with it.

"Girls," she said bravely, half turning. "I want to tell you I am ashamed of what I said yesterday. I hope you'll forget it. I mean to try to make you forget it." That was all. She went on up to her father.

He was stretched upon a cot near the window, like a pale shadow of himself.

"Where have you been all this time, Charlie?" he asked, with reproachful eyes. She stood over his cot couch for a moment silent.

"I've been climbing a high mountain, dad." He was used to her flights of speech when they were alone.

"And what did you see from the top, little girl?" he questioned with a smile.

"I saw the new moon. But here are your letters, dad." She drew a low chair and sat close, close to his bed.

"Isn't Gus coming up?" he asked. Mr. Gus came each morning to offer his services in reading or answering letters.

"I'm jealous of Mr. Gus," she said. "I know as much as he, more perhaps when it comes to writing letters. I know as much about the plantation as you do, dad; you know I do. And from now on I'm going to be—to be your right hand—your poor right hand," she almost sobbed sinking her face in the pillow. The arm that was left to him he folded around her and pressed his lips to her brow.

"Look, Dad," she exclaimed, cheerfully recovering herself and plunging her hand in her pocket. "What do you think of this for a wedding present for Julia?" She held the open blue velvet case before his eyes.

"You rave! nonsense. I thought you prized it more than any of your possessions; more than Tim even."

"I do. That's why I give it. There'd be no value in giving a thing I didn't prize," she said inconsequentially.

While she was writing out the card of presentation at the table, Mr. Gus came in and Charlie joined him at the bed side.

"This little woman has an idea she can run the plantation, Gus, till I get on my feet," said Mr. Laborde more cheerfully than he had spoken since his accident. "What do you think about it?"

Mr. Gus turned a fine pink under his burned skin.

"If she says so, I don't doubt it," he agreed, "and I'm always ready to lend a hand; you know that. I'm going towards the mill now, and if Charlie cares—I see her horse saddled out there," peering from the window as if the sight of the horse saddled, awaiting its rider, was something he had not perceived before.

"Here are your letters, dad. One of the girls will come up and get them ready for you and when I come back I'll answer them. I'll save Mr. Gus that much."

From his window Mr. Laborde watched the two mount their horses under the live oak tree.

Aunt Maryllis was standing in the kitchen door holding a small tin cup.

"Miss Charlie," she called out, "heah dis heah grease you mix' up fo' yo' han's; w'at I gwine do wid it?"

"Throw it away, Aunt Maryllis," cried Charlie over her shoulder.

The old woman sniffed at the cup. It smelled good. She thrust the tip of a knotty black finger into the creamy white mixture and rubbed it on her hand. Then she deliberately hid the tin in a piece of newspaper and set it away on the chimney shelf.

There is no telling what would have become of Les Palmiers that summer if it had not been for Charlie and Mr. Gus. It was precisely a year since Charlie had been hustled away to the boarding school in a state of semi-disgrace. Now, with all the dignity and grace which the term implied, she was mistress of Les Palmiers.

Julia was married and away on her wedding journey prior to making her home in the city. Amanda was qualifying in Paris under the tutelage of Aunt Clementine to enter the lists as a fine lady of fashion. The others were back in the class room with Miss Melvern in her old place. Mr. Laborde had recuperated slowly from the terrible shock to his nervous system six months before; and though he was getting about, he spent much time reclining in the long lounge in the upper hall.

It was a moonlight night and very quiet. He could sometimes faintly hear the lap of the great river, and he caught the low hum of voices below. It was Mr. Gus and Charlie conversing in the lower veranda. Mr. Gus was stripping a long, thin branch of its thorns and leaves and tangling his speech into incoherence.

"There's no hurry. I just mentioned it, Charlie, because I—couldn't help it."

"No, there's no hurry," agreed Charlie leaning back against a pillar and gazing up at the sky. "I couldn't dream of leaving Dad without a right arm."

"Of course not; I couldn't expect it. But then couldn't he have two right arms!"

"And then the twins. I've come to be a sort of mother to them rather than a sister; and you see I'd have to wait till they grew up."

"Yes, I suppose so. About how old are the twins now?"

"Nearly seven. But we'll talk of all that some other time. Didn't you hear Dad cough? That's a sly way he has of attracting my attention. He doesn't like to call me outright." Mr. Gus was beating the switch upon the gravel.

"There's something I wanted to ask you."

"I know. You want to ask me not to call you 'Mr.' Gus any more."

"How did you know?"

"I am a clairvoyant. And besides you want to ask me if I like you pretty well."

"You *are* a clairvoyant!"

"It seems to me I've always liked you better than any one, and that I'll keep on liking you more and more. So there! Good night." She ran lightly away into the house and left him in an ecstasy in the moonlight.

"Is that you, Charlie?" asked her father at the sound of her light footfall. She came and took his hand, leaning fondly over him as he lay in the soft, dim light.

"Did you want anything, Dad?"

"I only wanted to know if you were there."

The Women's Press aims to publish lively, intelligent books by women chiefly in the areas of fiction, literary and art history, physical and mental health and politics.

We are a small group of women responsible for our publishing and our future. Please help us to survive and progress by buying our books, by bringing them to the attention of bookshops, educational institutes and libraries and by sharing with us your comments and suggestions.

A complete list of our titles is available. Please send return postage with all enquiries.

The Women's Press Limited, 124 Shoreditch High Street, London E1 6JE.

VIRGINIA WOOLF
Women and Writing
INTRODUCED BY MICHELE BARRETT

Since her death Virginia Woolf's reputation has rested chiefly on
her novels and her position as *doyenne* of 'Bloomsbury'. In her lifetime, however, she was regarded as a major essayist and critic, with
a special interest in women's writing and contemporary literature.
The *Times Literary Supplement* called her 'The most brilliant pam-
phleteer in England' and fifty years after the publication of *A Room
of One's Own* it is time to reconsider Woolf's arguments about
women and writing and her critical assessment of individual authors
from the Duchess of Newcastle, born in 1624, to Dorothy Richard-
son who died in 1957.

In her introduction to the essays she selected, Michele Barrett
draws out the multiple threads of Woolf's theory of literature and
her work on the female literary tradition. *Women and Writing* can
and should be read alongside Woolf's full-length political works:
A Room of One's Own and *Three Guineas*.

Literary Criticism   £2.50

COLETTE
Duo & Le Toutounier

Two short linked novels in which Colette sharply and ironically depicts the conflicts and contradictions inherent in relationships between men and women. *Duo* concentrates on Alice and Michel, torn apart after the chance discovery of a half-forgotten infidelity by Alice. *Le Toutounier* shows Alice back in the womb-like home of her two sisters, continuing her search for unquestioning love but pulled too by her powerful need for autonomy.

'Drenched with her talent at its best'   *Sunday Times*

Fiction   £1.50

Break of Day

'Love, one of the great commonplaces of existence, is slowly leaving mine.' Colette wrote this line for her seemingly autobiographical novel, *Break of Day*, in which a woman called Colette passes a summer in Provence, contemplating her past and laying plans for a future which may not include sexual love.

'Easily Colette's most original novel'
                                        Robert Phelps, *Belles Saisons*

Fiction   £1.50